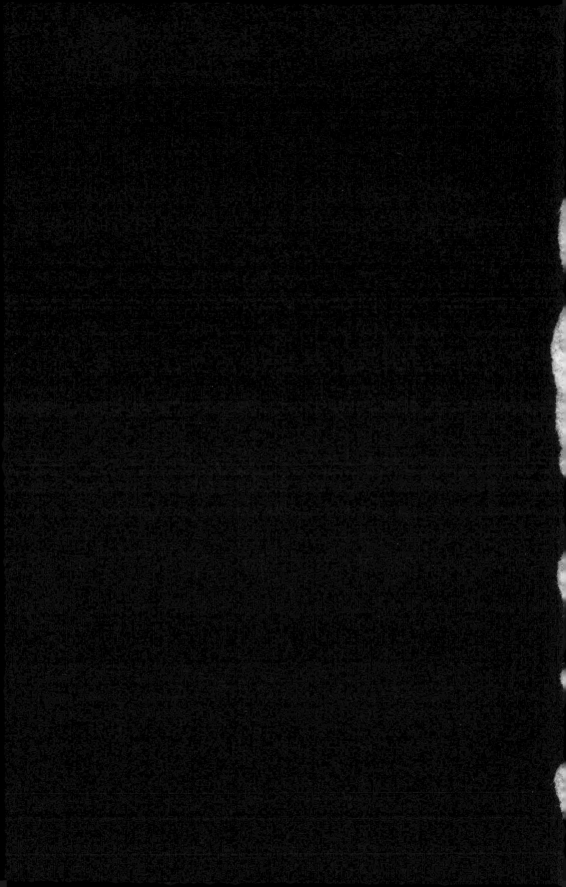

Tales of
Burning Love

Tales of
Burning Love

§

Louise Erdrich

HarperCollins*Publishers*

All the characters in this book are products of the author's imagination. Any resemblance they bear to persons living or dead is pure coincidence.

The author would like to thank the editors of the following magazines, in which sections of this book previously appeared in slightly different form: *Harper's*, "First Draw," originally titled "Mauser and Mauser"; also, "The Leap." *The New Yorker*, "Caryl Moon" (in Part 1), originally titled "Mauser." *Vogue*, "Best Western." *Granta*, "Night Prayer." *American Fiction*, "The Red Slip," originally titled "The Hat." *Cosmopolitan*, "The Levels."

HarperCollins books may be purchased for educational, business, or sales promotional use. For information please write: Special Markets Department, HarperCollins Publishers, Inc., 10 East 53rd Street, New York, NY 10022.

FIRST EDITION

Designed by C. Linda Dingler

Library of Congress Cataloging-in-Publication Data

Erdrich, Louise.
   Tales of burning love/Louise Erdrich. — 1st ed.
     p.   cm.
   ISBN 0–06–017605–9
   1. Divorced Women — North Dakota — Fiction.   2. Blizzards — North Dakota — Fiction.   3. Funerals — North Dakota — Fiction.   I. Title.
PS3555.R42T3   1996
813'.54 — dc20   95-53315

---

96 97 98 99 00 ❖/HC 10 9 8 7 6 5 4 3 2 1

To Michael
♥Q, ♥J

Acknowledgments

I would like to thank Diane Reverand for her thoughtful work as editor, and Susan Moldow, who brought this book to its publisher. Eileen Cowin for her photographs that provoke and console. Gail Hand, thanks for playing blackjack with me in West Fargo on a stormy night. To the crew at Northern Improvement, my foreman Hadji, friends in Wahpeton, and another Jack who told me all about lien waivers on the Empire Builder across Montana. Mr. Ralph Erdrich, dear father, for pertinent clippings. Sandi Campbell, you made it possible in countless ways, every day. Trent Duffy, genius of details, many thanks. Michael, so close to these pages, so essential and so much the story, thank you always for your tough and generous attention.

PART ONE

Jack of Sunflowers

§

Easter Snow

1981

Williston, North Dakota

*H*oly Saturday in an oil boomtown with no insurance. Toothache. From his rent-by-the-week motel unit, Jack Mauser called six numbers. His jawbone throbbed, silver-fine needles sank and disappeared. A handful of aspirin was no help. A rock, maybe better—something to bang his head against. He tried, he tried, but he could not get numb. The stray cat he had allowed to sleep in the bathtub eased against his pants legs. He kept on dialing and redialing until at last a number was answered by a chipper voice. Uncalled for, his thought was, wrong. Perky traits in a dental office receptionist. He craved compassion, lavish pity. He described his situation, answered questions, begged for an appointment although he had no real stake in the town—he was no more than tempo-rary, a mud engineer due for a transfer. Today! Please? He heard pages rustle, gum snap. The cat stretched, tapped his knee with a sheathed paw, and fixed its eyes on Jack's lap where it had been petted. Jack cuffed at the stray. The orange-striped tom batted him back, playful.

"Mr. Mauser?"

The voice was sly, as though asking him a trick question. Air would hit the tooth, still he opened his mouth to plead and stood up, dizzy from too much aspirin. Just then, the cat, determined, launched itself straight upward to climb Jack like a tree. It sank thick razor claws a half inch deep into Jack's thigh. Hung there.

Jack screamed into the telephone. The claws clenched in panic, and Jack, whirling in an awful dance, ripped the cat from his legs and threw the creature with such force that it bounced off a wall, but twisted over and came up strolling. No loss of dignity.

There was silence on the other end of the connection, and then the voice, less chipper.

"Are you experiencing discomfort?"

Jack whimpered as a muffled consultation took place, her hand presumably clapped over the receiver.

"The doctor will make room for you in his schedule." The voice was solemn. "About an hour from now?"

On his way to an unknown dentist, holes punched in his thigh, his jaw a throbbing lump he wanted to saw off his face, Jack sought temporary anesthesia. He was tall, in his early thirties, and the pain gave him an air of concentration. Otherwise, he didn't stand out much except for his eyes, a deeper slanting brown than most, or his hands, very rough but still attentive to the things they touched. His grim self-sorry mouth. From inside the Rigger Bar, he watched the street. A woman passing by outside briefly struck a light inside of him — her hips, full-not-too-full, bare cold hands, taut legs. He hit the window with his knuckles, caught her attention, saluted. As she walked in, he wasn't sure about her. But then, there she was, slim in a white leatherette jacket, hair a dark teased mass, delicate Chippewa face scarred by drink.

She watched him peel an Easter egg, blue, her eyes sad in

harsh makeup, then her face relaxed. She sat down beside him and shifted her legs, lightly crossed one thigh over the other to make that V shape.

"What's wrong with you?" she asked.

"Toothache."

"Too bad." She put a finger on the pack of cigarettes he laid down between them, arched her eyebrows, plucked one cigarette out, and held it poised for him to light. He nodded. She grinned awkwardly and bummed another for her purse. The flare of his cardboard match warmed the smooth rounds of her cheekbones, lit the slight crinkle of laugh lines around her moody eyes. She had a pretty smile—one tooth, a little crooked, overlapped. He put his hand out as though to touch it, one finger.

She drew back.

"Does it hurt much?"

"This'll help."

He drank from the unhurt side of his mouth and then he ordered a beer for her.

"Better yet," she turned from him. "This old Ojibwa remedy? You take a clove in your mouth."

"I hate cloves."

"Well, you gotta suffer then," she laughed.

Besides, he felt better halfway through the second drink. "Cloves, aren't they from Europe or something?"

"Okay, maybe. Horseweed. You pinch it up like this"—she rolled imaginary lint between her fingers—"stuff it all around that tooth. Deadens it."

She took an egg, dyed blue like the one he'd been peeling when she walked in the door. She shucked and ate it quickly, he noticed, while the bartender had his back turned. Right off, he knew that she was from his mother's home reservation, just by little things she did and said.

"All right!" He stood up. He felt so much better he could not believe it.

"That doesn't work," she started on another egg, "you take a hammer . . ."

"Oh, Christ, don't tell me." But he was unaffected, feeling the pain but not caring anymore. There was just a buoyant ease he'd have to monitor, control so it did not shoot him skyward too quickly. So it did not send him whirling, like the cat.

"I have a cat."

"What's its name?"

"Doesn't have a name."

"If you had a cat, it would have a name."

She took a long drink, held the liquor in her mouth, swallowed.

"I have a son," she said, after a few moments.

Jack didn't want to touch that.

"We'll go back to my motel. The cat's lonely there. I've got a whole, ah, suite—we'll visit him. He clawed my leg this morning." Jack pointed.

"Where?" She laughed suddenly, a little painfully, too hard. Stopped when Jack stared overlong at her.

"Come on, let's go check the cat."

"No way." She looked serious, put down her drink. "I've got a bus to catch."

"Where you going?"

Her gaze flickered up to his and then held steady.

"Home."

It was later, much later, the dental appointment missed. She refused again to visit the cat but went along with him as he made his rounds. One bar, the next. By then she maybe knew who he was although he lied and said that he did not know his mother's maiden name, or his grandmother's. His family would say too much to the woman, make her wary of him. So he pretended that he was adopted, taken out of the tribe too young to remember.

"Raised white?" She frowned.

"Don't I look it?"

"You act it. How's your tooth?"

It came to life, a flare of anguish.

"I need another drink. A double. I drink like an Indian though, huh?"

Mistake. She didn't think that was funny, didn't laugh. After a bit, she asked somebody next to her the time and frowned gently, troubled.

"I missed my bus, Andy."

"My fault." He had given her a fake name. "Here, you need a refill too."

Her hair was long, fine, slightly wavy, caught up in a cheap clip. He reached around and undid the barrette. At once, electric, her hair billowed around her face in a dark cloud. Storm's rising. He closed his eyes, imagined it falling in blowing scarves around his own face as her mouth lowered to meet his. Her hidden mouth. He kept wanting to press his finger on her tooth, line it up with the others. It would require an ever so slight tap. Her mouth was even prettier than when she first smiled—as she relaxed a deep curve formed in her lower lip. Very sad, though, her eyes watching him so close sometimes. He put away his money.

"Hey," she mumbled, once. "You got to be."

He did not want to ask her what, but he did, tightening his arm around her. She would have told him anyway.

"You got to be different," she breathed.

He pretended not to hear.

"I know you," she said, louder. "You're the one. You're him."

He shrugged off her words. The afternoon darkened and the beer lamps went on—bright colors, wagons and horses, fake Tiffany. Still, they kept drinking. They kept drinking and then they met up with some people. They got hungry, or needed something to do, anyway. They went out to eat. Steak, baked potato, salad with French dressing. She ordered these things in a shy voice, polite, saying thank you when the waitress set them down before her. As she put the first taste of meat in her mouth, she sighed, tried not to gulp it too quickly, put her fork down every second bite. She was hardly drinking anything by then. He caught her gaze once. His face was falling toward hers. Falling. Her face was still, a waiting pool, regarding him with kindness. The hard lines around her eyes had smudged into a softer mystery. Eyes half closed, she smiled over at him, and, suddenly, he realized she was the most precious, the most beautiful, the most extraordinary treasure of a woman he had ever known.

"Jack." A buddy of his, a roommate sometimes, nudged him. "Your squaw called you Andy."

"Shut up. You're an asshole."

Laughter. Laughter.

"We're leaving."

"Aw, c'mon."

"No hard feelings."

"Just a joke."

"We're getting married." He spoke into his buddy's face, put his arm around the woman's shoulders, very carefully, underneath her hair. He felt her thin shoulder blades, stroked her slim arm. Her hand went up to his immediately, clasped his fingers in what seemed to him a very sweet, a childlike way, as if he were somehow going to protect her. "Is there a reverend in the house?" Jack bawled, crossing over to the bar. "Ship's captain? Priest?"

Immediately beside him, a man sitting on a padded stool answered in a soothing voice, half sloshed yet genteel.

"I'm available. Would you like to see my card?"

Card produced. Certified reverend. Be double damned.

"Yo. Best man? Where are you?"

A false power surged up in Jack. He tossed back another drink, bought one for his bride, too, a double. Yet another. Then they both were laughing and the people they'd met up with were engaged as witnesses. Jack held a twenty in the fork of his fingers for the reverend. They were put into formation, weaving, vision tunneling into dark space so they could hardly fit their fingers into their beer-can pop-top wedding rings. The certified reverend adjusted his glasses and rumpled his hair and said the words, made them answer, said the words again. Slurred and solemn, but legal to a certain degree. Hold up in court! he promised more than once. Jack lurched. Andy, he regave the fake name. Hers, what? May? June? Some month. The matchbook preacher's smile twitched as he pronounced them man and wife.

They rode out of town for miles on the highway, then turned, aimless, bounced out farther, slowly on the old road, gravel. She sat right next to him, her hand on his thigh. The cat claw marks stung. He knew that he would make love with her, knew it—well, they were married, right? Honeymoon time. She was so quiet. She seemed smaller next to him, light as a girl. For several hours she'd been drinking slower. She'd nursed her last one along until he gulped it for her. She was older than him, by more than he thought at first. But those years, her overlapped tooth, her sad eyes made him ache for her, painfully, with more than the usual. More. Different. She was right.

She'd take him in like a stray, he vaguely felt, protect him the way she thought he was protecting her. Once he entered her he would be safe. He would be whole. He would be easy with who he was, and it would all turn out. His life. By climbing into her body, he would exist. So when they stopped and when he turned to her he was roaring inside, loud as the heater, his blood burning, hands heavy. Hands slow moving. He pushed up her knitted top and her breast curved warm at his mouth. Then a white screen showed, blank.

With sinking embarrassment, he realized that he was not hard. Then worse. Tears were sliding down his face.

His skin, painfully tender all of a sudden, registered each hot trail. The tears itched and stung. He put his head down, stopped moving, breathed slow. She shook him, but he did not dare move. She called him Andy. All was silent. Then the heater stammered on and breathed hoarse dry air upon them both. He felt her sit up beside him, adjusting, straightening herself. She fluffed up her hair and latched her purse as though getting ready to go to church. She hit the door handle and jumped out. He heard her land, lightly, in the gravel. And then her footsteps crunched twice. He lay there for a moment longer and then sat up in the blast of the heater, turned it low, drew the door shut and put the truck in gear, switching on the headlights. He was going to drive after her, but about a half mile on the headlights caught off the road, disappearing on the other side of the fence.

She was walking over a slight rise, alert, her jacket glowing whiter than the snow. Her step was firm, deerlike, as though she was eager to get where she was going. She kept her footing, moved quickly, never looked back to see whether he followed. He flicked the lights once, then shut them off. She didn't turn or stop. He jumped out of the cab and stood on the margin of the road.

Outside, the dark was rushing, raw, the air was watery with unshed snow. Bright clouds scudded fast in the fresh wind and drove shadows across the moon. Low clouds sheltered her retreating figure. He was going to call her name, but then his throat closed. He'd never made sure and now he could not remember. He turned away, and still the shadows rode across the icy crust of open ranch land, the pastures, pure and roadless, the fields, the open spaces.

The snow fell all night and all the next day, deeper. Holed up in his room, Jack knew what he had done but kept telling himself that he was not the one. He was not the one. Still, he saw her constantly, wherever he looked, in his mind's eye. He threw the pop top in the trash basket, where it haunted him until he folded it small and tried to feed it to the cat. Cat resisted. Jack swallowed the ring. Hating the taste of metal, the tooth swelled and bit him. Pain exploded every time Jack lowered his head to the pillow. Drunk, he watched the tooth on a screen in his head. The root was black hooks. The nerve a thin blue buzzing light. Tears leaked from the corners of his eyes and then the pith throbbed slowly dead. Eventually, he felt nothing, but her face was there, watching. The direct pity in her look made him repeat his denial and with the cat purring on his chest, he said it out loud again. Not the one. Still the ceiling dragged lower, and with each swallow, lower, so that he was nearly crushed by the time he emptied the bottle and called the local police.

State police, too. The storm had blown in and over with the speed of all spring lapses. The men in sober uniforms fanned forward in mild sunshine. Jack followed her then and so he was one of the ones who found her miles out in the grazing land. She'd gotten tired of walking in those thin shoes, and sat down against a fence post. To wait for the bus, he thought. She was looking to the east, her hair loaded with melting stars. No one had touched her yet. Her face was complex in its expectations. A fist of air punched Jack to earth and he knelt before her with his hands outstretched. But then the officer reached past him, thumbed her eyelids down, took her purse from her lap, knocked off her blanket of snow.

§

Hot June Morning

1994

Argus, North Dakota

*W*hen they tore down the Argus railroad depot with a
wrecking ball and a thousand blows of hammers, the gap
where it once stood let through a view of the horizon from the
main street, a relief of light and space interrupted only by a
distant clump of trees and a slanted sheet of roof that glowered
in the sun. The stone-walled and shingled convent of Our
Lady of the Wheat, a mile away to the south, floated on a
watery mirage of unsettled dust. The murk was raised by road
equipment. For at the same time the depot was demolished, an
interstate highway access was constructed, a connecting artery
that would save the town's economy.

Trains still flowed through east to west but the schedules
were erratic. Every year there was a cutback, one stop less, a
change in schedule, so that now, although the freights hauled
cargo, there was nothing aboard vital to the town. The trains
carried people, but no one who mattered to anyone in Argus—
no relatives, no farm implement dealers, no grain inspectors,

seed salesmen, and certainly no tourists. The train's passing was a backyard music in the night and no one noticed if it was an hour, even two hours, late. The feeder road was now the town's lifeline. Everything important to Argus came rolling in on highways, on the piggyback trailers of eighteen-wheel semis that hissed and sank, air brakes groaning, at the first stoplight.

Aboard one such powerful truck, on a still morning in the early drought of spring, Jack Mauser, older by thirteen years since that Holy Saturday when June froze, married three times since, by justices in civil ceremonies, and now married yet again to a woman with red-brown hair, arrived in town. He didn't touch booze, not anymore, but only since very recently. Two months ago. His features were lucid, strained with a deep and withheld purpose, sober. Only a few dark capillaries showed his long, steady, offhand pollution. His body was no longer rebar, a whip of metal, but he was still hard-muscled and tough. As for the marriages, here was the truth he knew: he couldn't hold on to a woman ever since he let the first one walk from his arms into Easter snow.

The company truck stopped. *Mauser and Mauser* was painted on the door. Jack swung down. In his pocket there was an expensive ring, a blue diamond caught in a claw of white gold and held on a band of the same thick metal. The last ring he would give, he promised. He vowed. He had no luggage. The ring was unpaid for, and would one day be repossessed, but at the time Jack Mauser still owned the truck and employed the man who drove it, pulling away with a small nod.

Jack, fatherless and motherless, had moved around a lot. One year of high school he had spent in Argus—his best year, he always thought. He still had connections there. Football buddies. Business associates. His former wife, Eleanor, too.

She termed herself a professional Catholic, a dilettante, a Dysfunctional Diva, Queen of Ambivalence—she had a lot of names she called herself. She was a difficult person. Although she had subdued her worst habits over the years, she was still her own *Reader's Digest* Most Remarkable Character, Jack thought, though she would have scoffed at his pedestrian reading tastes if he had ever told her that. He wondered whether he would run into her, and was disturbed at and tamped back the leap in his heart. That was over. She was arresting, dramatic in looks and spirit, unpredictable. Her enthusiasms were momentous, but often short-lived. She was doing some sort of research with local nuns, but Jack wasn't sure where she was staying.

And he wouldn't bother to find out. Absolutely not, he told himself.

For Jack had come full circle, at last. His latest and final wife had also grown up in Argus. Dot Adare Nanapush had refused to sleep with him unless he married her. She hadn't thought he would call her bluff, but he had proposed immediately and then driven to the county courthouse, trapping her. Direct, practical, and fierce, Dot had first caught his eye with her headlong progress across the construction yard. She never strolled or even walked. Dot charged, a purpose in her every move. Even on a calm day she seemed headed into the wind. Dot's energy was much like Jack's and she was sexy in a capable way—she took care of him with firm dispatch. Then, too, she had saved his business with her accounting skills. He liked her square body and thick, tousled hair. Sometimes she was beautiful, sometimes bull-solid, blocky. It was hard to form a picture of someone so formidably restless. She could be bone-tough, but then again so soft. At times, her brown eyes sparked his own. Still, he hadn't gone crazy over Dot the way he had with the others, but that was good. He was through with that form of special madness, he hoped. He wanted someone who could add, subtract, multiply, divide, and take pity on him. He wanted someone who would stick by him in his ruin. Dot was tough. Someone with strict principles. She wouldn't sleep with him. Impressive. He'd had enough of his own fuzzy morals, oh, he'd wallowed! He'd had enough of rationalizing—the past thirteen years of his life had been nothing but excuses and disasters, and the last two were the worst.

During those years he'd borrowed and lost a million dollars, run away from his debts, sung to forget in motel lounges, built a dream house he could not pay off. He had divorced the only woman who'd ever borne him a child, and married another whom he'd only known for one month. But he still believed that he was starting over, starting once again with Dot.

In order to give his new wife an hour with her mother, he'd decided to take the long way, to walk. Apparently Dot needed to set the stage. Let off on the sizzling main street sidewalk, Jack immediately sighted through the depot gap and headed south. He moved as though he were invisible to others and greeted no one in his path. The streets were longer, the houses newer and newer as he walked until they were only unfinished model units. Argus had grown evenly since his time, outward from its center, except for the eastern side bounded by the river. Jack paused, wiped sweat from his face, turned entirely around as though to consult the horizon. Through the outskirts, and on, through a minor new development of pastel ranch styles, toward the convent and the surrounding land. Old farmsteads with swayback barns and browning grass. Tiny-windowed homes hunkered square underneath the towering cottonwood and box elder, windbreaks planted when the century turned. He was not interested in these. He was looking for a garden-green house in a blast of lilacs, a place Dot had described to him during their one whirlwind distracting weekend. His new wife also had a gaze of dire intensity. The thought of her stare drew him through the hot air, through the dust.

§

A Wedge of Shade

JUNE 1994

Dot

*E*very place that I could name you, in the whole world around us, has better things about it than Argus. I just happened to grow up here and the soil got to be part of me, the air has something in it that I breathed. Argus water, pumped from deep aquifer, always tasted stale, of ancient minerals. Add to that now leaching fertilizer. Still, the first thing I do, walking back into my mother's house, is stand at the kitchen sink and toss down glass after glass.

"Are you filled up?" My mother stands behind me. "Sit down if you are."

She's tall and board-square, with long arms and big knuckles. Her face is rawboned, fierce and almost masculine in its edges and planes. Several months ago, a beauty operator convinced her that she should feminize her look with curls. Now the permanent, grown out in grizzled streaks, bristles like the coat of a terrier. I don't look like her. Not just the hair, since hers is salt-and-pepper, mine is a reddish brown, but my build.

I'm strong-built, shorter, boxy, more like my Aunt Mary, although there's not much about me that corresponds even to her—except it's true that I can't seem to shake this town. I keep coming back here. Aunt Mary and Mom keep hoping I will stay.

"There's jobs at the beet plant."

This rumor, probably false as so many people are in a slump that no one gives up a job anymore, drops into the dim close air of the kitchen. We have the shades drawn because it's a hot June, over a hundred degrees, and we're trying to stay cool. Outside, the water has been sucked from everything. The veins in the leaves are hollow, the ditch-grass is crackling. The sky has absorbed every drop. It's a thin whitish blue veil stretched from end to end over us, a flat gauze tarp.

We're sweating like we're in an oven, a big messy one. For a week, it's been too hot to move much or even clean, and the crops are stunted, failing. The farmer next to us just sold his field for a subdivision, but the workers aren't doing much. They're wearing wet rags on their heads, sitting near the house sites in a white-hot noon. The studs of wood stand uselessly upright, over them. Nothing casts a shadow. The sun has dried them up too.

"The beet plant," my mother says again.

"Maybe so," I allow.

I've left my daughter in Fargo so that my mother and I can have a personal conversation. I've got something on my mind to tell. I'm a grown woman. I have coached myself. Still everything I say sounds juvenile and I am nervous.

"Maybe I'll go out there and apply," I tell her, stalling.

"Oh?" She's intrigued now, wonders if I've quit my Fargo job. Or lost it. She takes in my green skirt and T-shirt, too casual to have come from work. My flip-flop sandals. Frowns.

"You all right? Where's Shawn?" Her look is penetrating.

"God, this is terrible!" I grab the glass of water and tip some on my head. I don't feel cooler though, I just feel the steam rising off me.

"The fan broke down," she states. "Both of them are kaput

now. The motors or something. If Mary would get the damn tax refund we'd run out to Pamida, buy a couple more, set up a breeze."

"Your garden must be dead," I lift the edge of the pull-shade.

"It's sick, but I watered. And I won't mulch, that draws the damn slugs."

"Nothing could live out there, no bug." My eyes smart from even looking at the yard, cleared on the north, almost incandescent.

"You'd be surprised."

I wish I could blurt it out, just tell her. Even now, the words swell in my mouth, the one sentence, but I'm scared and with good reason. There is this thing about my mother. It is awful to see her angry. Her lips press together and she stiffens herself within, growing wooden. Her features become fixed and remote, she will not speak. It takes a long time, and until her words drop into the vacuum you are held in suspense. Nothing that she says, in the end, is as bad as that feeling of dread. So I wait, half-believing that she'll figure out my secret for herself, or drag it out of me, not that she ever tries. She's not like Aunt Mary, who forces me to say more than I know is on my mind.

My mother sighs. "It's too hot to bake. It's too hot to cook. But it's too hot to eat, anyway." She's talking to herself, which makes me reckless. Perhaps she is so preoccupied by the heat that I can slip my announcement past her. I should just say it, but I lose nerve, make an introduction that alerts her.

"I have something to tell you."

I've cast my lot, there's no going back unless I think quickly. My thoughts hum.

But she waits, forgetting the heat for a moment.

"Ice," I say. "We have to have ice." I speak intensely, leaning toward her, almost glaring, but she is not fooled.

"Don't make me laugh," she says. "There's not a cube in town. The refrigerators can't keep cold enough."

She eyes me as if I'm an animal about to pop from its den and run.

"Okay," I break down. "I really do have something." I stand, turn my back. In this lightless warmth I'm dizzy, almost sick. Now I've gotten to her and she's frightened to hear, breathless.

"Tell me," she urges. "Go on, get it over with."

And so I say it.

"I got married again."

There is a surge of relief, as if a wind blows through the room, but then it's gone. The curtain flaps and we're caught once more, stunned in an even denser heat. It's now my turn to wait, and I whirl around and sit right across from her. But I can't bear the picture she makes, the surprise that parts her lips, the stunned hurt in her eyes that I should go and get married on her, twice, without giving her notice.

"When did you . . ." She's faltering, but she grasps hold of the situation. "When did you and Gerry divorce?"

Gerry is my first husband, in prison serving two life sentences. I cannot answer my mother, although my mouth opens dutifully. I don't know how to say this: I wasn't, am not, capable of divorcing my first husband, even though I've married a second one. My silence says this for me and my mother nods in awakening comprehension.

"Isn't that Mormonism?" she asks, too calm.

"Mormons do the opposite. More wives than husbands."

She is sure nonetheless that I am breaking a commandment, at least a church doctrine, though I don't go to church. She keeps racking her mind, pulling remarks from her hat.

"It's impossible. They wouldn't have given you a license, even in South Dakota."

"We got married in Minneapolis," I say to her.

"Minneapolis!" She looks aghast, as though I've said Pluto.

In a moment, though, because she is my mother, she goes from disbelief and refusal and shock into justification. There must be a loophole, she thinks, somewhere.

"Maybe your license with Gerry was only valid in one state . . . Maybe once he crossed state lines . . . Maybe there's some fee he forgot to pay. Some glitch. The old Chippewas could do this, in the old days, I'm sure," she says, concentrating as she sits hard in her chair. "Besides, there's right of occupancy. Some kind of statute of limitations on marriage with a man in prison. The Laws of Consummation, can they be invoked? I've heard of those, I think. Automatic annulment, too, after so many years. You have been so good to each other," she says softly. "I'm sure Gerry will understand."

"I don't plan on telling him," I say, so that she won't. "It might take away his will to go on."

She understands. She worries.

"But what about this man? What does he think? And it's so sudden! Are you . . ."

Involuntarily, her look assesses me. But I'm no more than the same solid ten pounds over my perfect weight that I always have been — no different. No softness.

Not pregnant, she decides, but goes back to the timing problem.

"Sudden!" she says again.

"You hate weddings!" I answer. "Just think, just picture it. Me, white net. Or off-white, I guess. On a day like this. You, stuffed in your summer wool, and Aunt Mary, God knows . . . and the tux, the rental, the groom . . ."

Her head has lowered as my words fell on her, but now her forehead tips up and her eyes come into view, already hardening. My tongue flies back into my mouth.

She mimics, making it a question, "The groom . . . ?"

I'm caught, my lips half open, a stuttering noise in my throat. How to begin? I have rehearsed this but my lines melt away, my opening, my casual introductions. I can think of nothing that would, even in a small way, convey any part of who he is. There is no picture adequate, no representation that captures him. So I just put my hand across the table, and I touch her hand

"Mother," I say, like we're in a staged drama. "He'll arrive here shortly."

There is something forming in her, some reaction. I am afraid to let it take complete shape.

"Let's go out and wait on the steps, Mom. Then you'll see him."

"I do not understand," she says in a frighteningly neutral voice. This is what I mean. Everything is forced, unnatural, as though we're reading lines.

"He'll approach from a distance." I can't help speaking like a bad actor. "I told him to give me an hour. He'll wait, then he'll come walking down the road."

We rise and unstick our shirts from our stomachs, our skirts from the backs of our legs. Then we walk out front in single file, me behind, and settle ourselves on the middle step. A scrubby box elder tree on one side casts a light shade, and the dusty lilacs seem to catch a little breeze on the other. It's not so bad out here, still hot, but not so dim, contained. It is worse past the trees. The heat shimmers in a band, rising off the fields, out of the spars and bones of houses that will wreck our view. The horizon and the edge of town show through the spacing now, and as we sit we watch the workers move, slowly, almost in a practiced recital, back and forth. Cooling, water-soaked head rags hang to their shoulders. Their hard hats are dabs of yellow, and their white T-shirts blend into the fierce air and sky. They don't seem to be doing anything, although we hear faint thuds from their hammers. Otherwise, except for the whistles of a few birds, there is silence. We certainly don't speak.

It is a longer wait than I anticipated, maybe because he wants to give me time. At last the shadows creep out, hard, hot, charred, and the heat begins to lengthen and settle. We are going into the worst of the afternoon when a dot begins to form at the end of the road.

Mom and I are both watching. We have not moved our eyes around much, and we blink and squint to focus. The dot doesn't change, not for a long while. And then it suddenly springs clear in relief, a silhouette, lost a moment in the shimmer, reappearing. In that shining expanse he is a little wedge of moving shade. He continues, growing imperceptibly, until there are variations in the outline, and it can be seen that he is a tall man, powerfully built. As he passes the construction workers, they turn and stop, all alike in their hats, stock-still.

Growing larger yet as if he has absorbed their stares, he nears us. Now we can see the details. He is older, the first thing. I have not told my mother. His arms are thick, his chest is wide, and the features of his face are stark and brooding. He carries nothing in his hands. He wears a white shirt, sleeves rolled, and boots like the construction workers. He's a boss, my boss to be exact. His jeans are held under his hard stomach by a belt with a brass eagle on the buckle. His hair is thick brown with no gray yet, cut short. I am the wrong woman for him. I am paler, shorter, unmagnificent. But I stand up. Mom joins me, and when she asks, "His name?," I answer proudly.

"Jack."

We descend one step, and stop again. It is here we will receive him. Our hands are folded at our waists. We're balanced, composed. He continues to stroll toward us, his white smile widening, his eyes filling with the sight of me as mine are filling with him. At the end of the road, behind him, another dot has appeared. It is fast moving and the sun flares off it twice, a vehicle. Now there are two figures. One approaching in a spume of dust from the rear, and Jack, unmindful, not slackening or quickening his pace, continuing on. It is like a choreography design. They move in complementary speeds, in front of our eyes. At the same moment, at the end of our yard, as if we have concluded a performance now, both of them halt.

Jack stands, looking toward us, his thumbs in his belt. He nods respectfully to Mom, looks calmly at me, and half-smiles. He raises his brows, and we're suspended. Officer Lovchik emerges from the police car, stooped and tired. He walks up behind Jack Mauser and says a few words. Jack shrugs and puts his hands behind his back. I hear the snap of handcuffs, then I jump. I'm stopped by Jack's gaze though, as he backs away from me, still smiling tenderly. I am paralyzed halfway down the walk. He kisses the air while Lovchik cautiously prods at him, fitting his prize into the car. And then the doors slam, the engine roars and they back out, turn around. As they

move away there is no siren. I think I've heard Lovchik mention questioning. I'm sure it is lots of fuss for nothing, a mistake, but it cannot be denied, this is terrible timing.

I shake my shoulders, smooth my skirt, and turn to Mom
with a look of outrage.

"How do you like that?" I try.

She's astounded, too. Her voice is impressed, relieved.

"They sure work quick. But then, everybody is computer-
ized. What will they do, revoke your wedding license?"

"Oh, it's not that," I tell her. "It's a bankruptcy proceeding,
among a few other things." My voice fades, thinking of the
book of checks I told Jack were rubber now, the account
defunct. Has he carefully snaked them from my bottom file
drawer? "Failed payment, subcontractors, misunderstand-
ings." I recover. "But all white-collar stuff. Crime. Basically."

She's got her purse in one hand, all of a sudden, her car
keys out.

"Let's go," she says. "That's about as much as I can take."

"Okay," I answer, marching behind her toward the car.
"Fine. Where?"

"Aunt Mary's."

"I'd rather go and bail him out, Mom."

"Bail," she says. "*Bail?*"

She gives me such a look of cold and furious surprise that I
sink immediately into the front seat, lean back against the
vinyl. I almost welcome the sting of the heated plastic on my
back, thighs, shoulders.

Aunt Mary's dogs are rugs in the dirt, flattened by the heat of
the day. Not one of them barks at us to warn her. We step over
them and get no more reaction than a whine, the slow beat of a
tail. Inside, we get no answer either, although we call Aunt
Mary up and down the hall. We enter the kitchen and sit at the
table, with its grouping of health salts and vitamin bottle. By
the sink, in a tin box, are cigarettes. My mother takes one and
carefully puts the match to it, frowning.

"I know what," she says. "Go check the lockers."

There are two, a big freezer full of labeled meats and rental space, and another, smaller one that is just a side cooler. I notice, walking past the display counter, that the red beacon beside the outside switch of the cooler is glowing. That tells you when the light is on inside.

I pull the long metal handle toward me and the thick door swishes open. I step into the cool, spicy air. She is there. Too proud ever to register a hint of surprise, Aunt Mary simply nods and looks away, as if I've just gone out for a minute although we've not seen one another in two months or more. She is relaxing, reading a scientific magazine article. I sit down on a barrel of alum labeled Zanzibar and drop my bomb with no warning. "I'm married again." It doesn't matter how I tell it to Aunt Mary, because she won't be, refuses to be, surprised.

"What's he do?" she simply asks, still holding the sheaf of paper. I thought that her first reaction would be to scold me for fooling my mother. But it's odd. For two women who have lived through boring times and disasters, how rarely one comes to the other's defense, and how often they are willing to take advantage of the other's absence. But I'm benefiting here. It seems that Aunt Mary is truly interested in Jack. So I'm honest.

"He's a contractor, a builder. He's into developments. There's been trouble though, problems of a financial nature."

She gives me a long, shrewd stare.

"Is he your boss?"

I nod. She knows I do the taxes.

"Did he marry you so you can't testify against him?"

"No." I'm too struck with the thought to respond with sharp anger. "He didn't," I whisper to myself. "Of course not."

Her skin is too tough to wrinkle, but she doesn't look young. All around us hang loops of sausages, every kind you can imagine, every color from the purple black of blutwurst to the pale whitish links that my mother likes best. Blocks of butter and headcheese, a can of raw milk, wrapped parcels, and cured bacons are stuffed onto the shelves around us. My heart has gone still and cool inside of me.

"Why did he marry you then?"

I pause, smoothing down my shirt. "Love."

"Enlarge on that?"

"Love," I repeat, more insistent.

She stares, her eyes narrow.

The door swings open and Mom comes in with us, takes a load off, sits down on a can of dried milk. She sighs at the delicious feeling of the air, absorbing from the silence the fact Aunt Mary and I have talked.

"So you're hitched." Aunt Mary tries to snap her fingers nonchalantly, but they're greased from the tubs of sausage. "Like that."

"I know it's sudden, but who likes weddings? I hate them, all that mess with the bridesmaids' gowns, getting material to match. I don't have girlfriends, I mean, how embarrassing, right? Who would sing 'Oh Perfect Love'? Carry the ring?"

She isn't really listening.

"So he's in trouble."

"That's right."

"Money problems."

I nod. She lets the pages fall now, cocks her head to the side, and stares at me without blinking her cold yellow eyes. She has the look of a hawk, of a person who can see into the future but won't tell you about it. She's lost business for staring too long at customers, but she doesn't care.

"Why didn't you come to me first? I'm good at fixing things!"

She jumps to her feet, stands over me, a stocky woman with terse features and short, thin points of gray hair. Her earrings tremble and flash, small fiery opals. Her brown plastic glasses hang crooked on a cord around her neck. I have never seen her become quite so instantaneously furious, so disturbed.

"You marry a man in trouble, and you've got a kid," she says.

The cooler instantly feels smaller, the sausages knock at my shoulder, and the harsh light makes me blink. I am as stubborn as Aunt Mary, however, and she knows that I can go head-to-head with her.

"We're married and that's final. Shawn likes him." I manage to stamp my foot.

Aunt Mary throws an arm back, blows air through her cheeks, and vigorously waves away my statement.

"Plus, can he support you?"

I frown at my lap, trace the threads in my blue cotton skirt, and tell her that he's solvent, more or less. Plus, money is irrelevant.

"Big words," she says sarcastically.

"Bottom line!" I say. "So what . . . I mean, haven't you ever been in love, hasn't someone ever gotten you *right here*?" I smash my fist on my chest. We lock our eyes, but she doesn't waste a second in feeling hurt, and she knows that my first love is Gerry, anyway. I seem destined for men in trouble.

"Sure, sure I've been in love," my aunt raves. "You think I haven't? I know what it feels like, you smart-ass. You'd be surprised. But he was no criminal, losing everything. Now listen . . . ." She stops, draws breath, and I let her. "Here's what I mean by 'fix.' If he should lose his shirt, I'll teach the sausage-making trade to him, you too, and the grocery business. I've about had it anyway, and so's your mother. We'll do the same as my aunt and uncle—leave the shop to you and move to Arizona. Florida. Somewhere cooler than North Dakota in the summer. I like this place." She looks up at the burning safety bulb, down to me again. Her face drags in the light. "But what the hell. I always wanted to travel."

I'm kind of stunned, flattened out, and I'm ashamed of myself for arguing with such pure motives.

"You hate going anywhere," I say, which is true.

For a long while we sit there, then, deflated. As the coolness sinks in, my mother's eyes fall shut. Aunt Mary too. I can't help it either. My eyelids drop although my brain is alert and conscious. From the darkness, I can see us in the brilliance. The light rains down on us. We sit the way we have been sitting, on our cans of milk and flour, upright and still.

Our hands are curled loosely in our laps. Our faces are blank as the gods. We could be statues in a tomb sunk into the side of a mountain. We could be dreaming the world up in our brains.

It is later and the weather has no mercy. We are drained of everything but simple thoughts. It's too hot for feelings. Driving home, we see how field after field of beets has gone into shock, and even some of the soybeans. The plants splay, limp, burned into the ground. Only the sunflowers continue to struggle upright, bristling but small.

What drew me in the first place to my first husband, Gerry, was the unexpected. I went to hear him talk just after I enrolled at the U of M and then I demonstrated when they came and got him off the stage. He always went so willingly, accommodating everyone, sort of the way Jack went along with Lovchik earlier. Polite. I began to visit him. I sold lunar calendars and posters to support his cause and eventually free him. One thing led to another and one night we found ourselves alone in a Howard Johnson's in Grand Forks where they put him up when his speech was finished. There were beautiful women after him, he could have had his pick of Swedes or Yankton Sioux girls, who are the best-looking of all. But I was different, he says. He liked my slant on life. And then there was no going back once it started, no turning, as though it were meant. We had no choice.

I still do have a choice with Jack, I think.

I have this intuition he will be there as we near the house, in the fateful quality of light, as in the turn of the day the heat continues to press and the blackness, into which the warmth usually lifts, lowers steadily. We must come to the end of something. There must be a close to this day.

As we turn into the yard we see that Jack is sitting on the stairs. Now it is our turn to be received. I throw open the car door and stumble out before the motor even cuts. I run to him and hold him, as my mother, pursuing the order of events, parks carefully. Then she walks over too, carrying her purse by the strap. She stands before him and says no word but simply looks into his face, staring as if he's cardboard, a man behind glass who cannot see her. I think she's rude, but then I realize that he is staring back, that they are the same height. Their eyes are level. He puts his hand out.

"My name's Jack."

"Jack what?"

"Mauser."

"What's your mother's name?"

He frowns uneasily at her, opens his mouth, but his voice catches and the word comes out in such a low whisper I can't hear.

She nods, shifts her weight. "You're from that line, the old strain, the ones . . ." She does not finish.

"Kashpaws," she changes direction, "are my branch of course. We're probably related."

They do not move. They are like two opponents from the same divided country, staring across the makeshift border. They do not shift or blink and I see that they are more alike than I am like either one of them, so tall, solid, dark haired. I hadn't known he had any connection to my mother's reservation. But then, I've really only known him one month, total, except for I remember him from the year he lived in Argus. He never told me about the rest of his background. I never asked. It is a sudden thing—this marriage. Now he seems all placed and inventoried. Still, there is so much that we don't know about each other.

"Well, I guess you should come in," Mom offers. "You are a distant relative, after all." She looks at me. "Distant enough."

Whole swarms of mosquitoes are whining down, discovering us. There is no question of staying where we are. And so we walk into the house, much hotter than outside with the gathered heat. Instantly the sweat springs from our skin and I can think of nothing else but cooling off. I try to force the windows higher in their sashes, but there's no breeze anyway, nothing stirs, no air.

"Are you sure," I gasp, "about those fans?"

"Oh, they're *very* broke," my mother assures me. I rarely hear this distress in her voice. She switches on the lights, which makes the room seem hotter, and we lower ourselves into the easy chairs. Our words echo, as though the walls have baked and dried hollow.

"Show me those fans," says Jack.

My mother points toward the kitchen. "They're sitting on the table. I tinkered with them too much, maybe. See what you can do."

And so he does. After a while Mom hoists herself and walks out back with him. Their voices close together now, absorbed, and their tools clank frantically as if they are fighting a duel. But it is a race with the bell of darkness and their waning energy. I think of ice. I get ice on the brain.

"Be right back," I call out, taking the keys from my mother's purse. "Do you need anything?"

There is no answer from the kitchen except a furious sputter of metal, the clatter of nuts and bolts spilling to the floor.

I drive out to the Super Pumper, a big new gas station complex on the edge of town where my mother most likely has never been. She doesn't know about convenience stores, has no credit cards for groceries, gas, pays only with small bills and change. She never has used an ice machine. It would grate on her that a bag of frozen water costs ninety cents, but it doesn't bother me. I take the Styrofoam cooler and I fill it for a few dollars. I buy two six-packs of Shasta sodas and I plunge them into the uniform coins of ice. I drink two myself, on the way home, and I lift the whole heavy cooler out of the trunk, lug it to the door.

The fans are whirring, thrashing the air.

I hear them going in the living room the minute I come in. The only light shines from the kitchen. Jack and my mother have thrown the pillows from the couch onto the living room floor, and they are sitting in the rippling currents of air. I bring in the cooler and put it near us. I have chosen all dark flavors—black cherry, grape, black raspberry, so as we drink it almost seems the darkness swirls inside us with the night air, sweet and sharp, driven by small motors.

I drag down more pillows upstairs. There is no question of attempting the bedrooms, the stifling beds. And so, in the dark, I hold hands with Jack. He slides a ring onto my finger and I say out loud, *no fair*, but he is talking to my mother. While I hold my finger up to my face, wondering what kind of ring he has surprised me with, he settles down between the two of us. I still have a choice, I think, pulling the loose ring on, off, on. How can he afford it? I have to wonder. The stone feels big, and I hope it's real and hope it isn't all at once. Still have a choice. Shawn doesn't really know him yet as a stepfather. I could still call this off. I haven't divorced Gerry, after all. How real is this marriage, anyway? I turn over, I turn away, I turn back. I lean toward my mother. But she is suddenly so far away and he is huge as a hill between the two of us, solid in the beating wind.

§

White Musk

OCTOBER 1993

Eleanor

A raw fall night at a trendy restaurant in Minneapolis. Eleanor Mauser, second ex-wife to Jack, prayed gloatingly with her fork poised over a plate of smoked salmon. After every third bite of melting peach-pink flesh, she nipped a bit of crisp scallion. When she had eaten the onion down to the shank, she threw the stiff green shoots at her companion and smiled when he plucked the leaves awkwardly from his lap. He was thin, curly haired, with striking, butterfly-lashed blue eyes, and an air of puppy shyness. She could not remember his name. Kim, Tim, Vim, or something like that.

"Im," she said softly. He looked up at her and grinned very shyly. It was heartbreaking, how young he was, his skin blooming. Flushed.

She was wearing a new red velvet, a dress shaped to her body. Her hair was short and thick, and she wore a silver cross in one ear and an ankh in the other. Her stockings were a shadowy maroon and on her feet she'd stuck bloodred expensive shoes with four-inch heels. Credit card shoes. She'd racked up huge bills, but her grant would surely come through and anyway, she was proud of her feet. They were a nice medium size, arched, very flexible, buffed to an extreme smoothness, toenails polished. That instead of sentences, paragraphs, chapters! During writing blocks she groomed herself. Now she was so immaculate it hurt to even think about her precious feet. She kicked off a heel and put her foot into the boy's lap. There was no tablecloth and hardly any elbow room. The boy's face went stark with unhappiness as the waiter set Eleanor's plate of salmon to one side and brought dessert. She never ate entrées. Eleanor watched her own face gleaming in the mirrored wall behind the boy. She tipped her chin back, stroked the curve of her throat. Her features were strong, stagy, the twin of her mother's at this age.

The waiter set another plate before Eleanor, a smooth base of custardy cream swirled with raspberry, a small cake in the center.

"Rorschach food." Eleanor stared with absent thought at the design, removing sprigs of mint.

The boy peered over at her plate.

"You know"—she turned the plate slowly—"the shrink's test where you name what you see in those splotchy patterns."

"Oh, yeah. The inkblots."

"What do you see?" she asked him, her voice too sweet.

The boy squinted.

"Mouse ears?"

Eleanor murmured, turned the plate, stroked the surface of the sauce with the tine of her fork. "I see people, two people together." Something wicked and cool came up in her heart. "And she's sitting in a rocking chair, naked. Her legs are spread apart. The man . . . I don't know."

The boy's mouth opened, hung. Eleanor put her fork down and lifted her spoon.

"He's kneeling before her with his face between her legs," she said softly. With a tender scooping gesture she took the crème fraîche into her mouth and held the rich taste on her tongue looking seriously at her companion, who started and then dropped his gaze to his hand, fumbled a forkful of food into his mouth.

"Do you know what I wish?" she swallowed, smiled, talking past him.

He nodded, his mouth full, his eyes staring.

"I wish," said Eleanor, meditating aloud, "for old lovers. I've left behind a string of bad feelings, after all, cut ties. *Unhappiness.*" She looked at him skeptically and licked the spoon clean of raspberry sauce. "Do you know what that is?"

He gave her an eager, uncertain nod.

"Of course you don't. I wish, oh god, how I wish, I could go back to every one of my dear lovers and treat them with the kindness they deserve."

She kept on speaking, gestured with her fork.

"I'm serious! It makes me angry to think that I will probably die without letting them know, one man in particular that he gratified me utterly in spite of my cruelties to him, and another, that I never stopped thinking of him and regretting the stupid note I sent. I hate myself for the pompous and self-important ways I conducted my love affairs, even my marriage, how everything had to be centered on *me, me, me.* I'd go back and do it over. I wouldn't torture. I'd be more understanding, take no pleasure in their longing, unless of course I meant to satisfy it. No!" Eleanor now thoroughly mixed the sauce into a scarlet blur and ate it lingeringly, with a few bites of cake. "I'd be a better woman. I'd have higher feelings and awarenesses. I'd be someone else entirely if I could go back. If I could only go back. How I'd love to spend one night with each of them again!"

"And how long would that take?" the boy asked. Marvelously, Eleanor thought at first and then, with disappointment, she understood that he'd asked the question with no sense of irony at all.

"Weeks, months, days do you mean?"

He went slowly red in the ears at that.

"Months," Eleanor decided. "It would take months, two of

them, forty or fifty days and nights, to be absolutely conscientious about the project. I am not interested in new men, you see, not in the least. I want the old ones back, the ones to whom I was everything, even if just for a short while, so I can see what has happened to them, so I can at last say *here I am* and meet them on a human and mature level."

"Are they all still alive?" the boy asked.

Eleanor's features dulled. She pulled a cigarette from her purse, though she rarely smoked anymore.

It was a mistake to talk so long. The boy managed another forkful of slippery pasta, ducked his head to the plate. She drank deeply, finishing her wine, and lapsed into a thoughtful silence, breathing out light smoke in a tremulous cloud. Suddenly she jammed her foot, forgotten in the boy's lap, hard.

"Some are married," said Eleanor. "Of course, I would make it clear to their wives that I wanted nothing of their husbands, not a phone call or a letter, nothing more beyond that one night!"

The boy's mouth was frozen in a speechless O. Feeling triumphantly savage, Eleanor plunged the butt of her cigarette sizzling into the ruins of her expensive fish. A very seventies gesture, she thought with satisfaction, ugly. Not in vogue anymore, anywhere. The boy looked positively sick.

As she made love to him, later, on the complex pattern of an antique Caucasian rug in her apartment, Eleanor watched her own face again in her mind's eye. Her self-destructive greed both bored and excited her. The more she touched the boy, the emptier her hands felt. She stroked him hard, strength flowed through her right arm. She slapped his face and tears of surprise came into his eyes.

"You're just a baby," she said, her voice both disdaining and indulgent.

The less she felt, the more she acted, crying out, whimpering fake pleasure that was more like pain. She tried to shake some passion out of him but at last he froze, tense, wilted, and sweat a sharp, adolescent odor.

"Jesus," Eleanor swore. "Calm down. You're like a nervous mutt." Then, more kindly, she whispered, "You're being marvelous, A plus."

But he was trembling, his breath so quick and cold he seemed about to faint, and after a while his terror annoyed Eleanor, and shamed her too. She pulled a lamb's wool blanket off the couch, wrapped him in it tightly, and flicked on the television by remote. A gurgling laugh track filled the room. She lighted a cigarette and from down below her hips the student waved away the smoke. Pouting. Unless she got away quickly she'd kick him. It was hard staying open to experience when some experiences turned out to be this abysmally stupid.

"Let yourself out when Dave's over," she said, touching the glossy, sullen tangle of his forelock. She breathed out. Averted disaster. He didn't look at her, but she knew he'd be in class tomorrow, carrying his effete little hardbound artist's notebook, copying down each word she said, and hoping for another kind of A. His collar would be turned up, his tie dangling. *I'll address a question to him, let a girl answer it.* Eleanor made another mental list. *I will also pretend for my own self-respect that this never happened.*

She walked into her bathroom, locked the door, and ran scalding water into the tub. She dumped in several capfuls of lavender scent, then white musk, then jasmine. The conversation over dinner, her wishful thinking, stirred too many memories. She missed Jack Mauser, missed him down through the core of herself. They rarely spoke for long, only during some crisis or another. She was restless with him, but she never would have hurt him, not now anyway. He struck a tender nerve in her and she resented those feelings, but they were always there anyway, reliable and largely useless. Of all the men she'd known, he was the only one she'd ever married and the only one she ever dreamed about. Transparent dreams. Embarrassing. She never had to analyze them. Evidently, she told herself, Jack matched some hidden paradigm for the way a man should be, the way a man should touch, walk, laugh, throw a baseball, crouch, wipe his hands with dirt. She couldn't push him around. He did things that drove her crazy with impatience, with desire.

Stop! Her brain hummed with weariness. She'd been driven, falling apart all month and now she decided, as she had every other day, that right here and now in *this* moment of clarity she would change. Never mind all former moments of realization that came and went. This one, now, counted for the rest of all time. She would stop thinking futile thoughts of Jack and she would discipline herself, continue writing on her newest project regarding saintly hungers, those of one particular aged nun named Leopolda. *I study saints because I'm so far from being one myself. At last*, the knowledge hit her, a satisfaction bloomed—here it was. She grabbed her notebook from the tub-side shelf.

I've scraped bottom, she wrote, rejoicing. *This is it. I've seduced an undergraduate! A minor! Probably now he'll become a priest, having been screwed up by me, and he isn't even an interesting boy! He doesn't have a thing to say for himself, no cogent thought at all, no ideas but vague moony jottings in his pathetic notebooks—raw pretension. Hopeless!*

B minus, Eleanor finished. *Maybe C minus. D. As for me, this is a deeply necessary turning point.*

She moaned out loud, in pleasure now, and squeezed her eyes shut, sinking into the tingling heat. Eleanor had told herself for many years that she lived according to certain principles. Even when she violated her codes, they were her codes. Her commandments. Now she seemed to operate in a space beyond morality where loss drove her, need drove her, anxiety and sorrow. *My life is intolerable*, she thought, at peace.

It was about to get worse.

When she graded him B minus, the boy brought charges of sexual harassment against her to the college ethics committee. He told his parents all the details of the seduction—the foot in his lap, the rug, her slap, her promised grade of A plus, the works. The outraged mother slammed into the office of the college president and two hours later that same woman emerged, exhausted in a wrinkled linen suit, but carrying Eleanor's letter of resignation, signed. A group of students splintered off from Eleanor's seminar on The New Celibacy and claimed they had been brainwashed. A personals ad attributed to Eleanor was tacked onto her office door, and a reporter called.

"Would you characterize your resignation," he inquired, "as asked to leave, or kicked out?"

"Set free," decided Eleanor, after a beat of silence.

All of her life, Eleanor had suffered from a happy childhood. Every time things went wrong she retreated into the safety of her past. An only child, she received her parents' total attention and secret hopes—up until the catastrophe of her parents' separation, that is, when everything had changed. While very young, there had been a garden. A window seat. A doll her own size, and shelves and shelves of books. Her mother rocked her in a wide cinnamon brown chair and wept with her over the prospect of inoculations and the shock of scraped knees. Her father toughened his hands, raised blisters, hammered his fingernails making a playhouse for Eleanor. Nothing matched her early childhood perfection—no worries, sweet care. She was even rescued the time their house caught fire! Eleanor was not prepared for life to go the way it usually went for her as an adult. Unmet desire. Dissatisfaction. Intellectual hunger. An acute mind but lazy work habits. Self-doubt. A frail serenity pierced time and again by arrows. Arrows of light. Wanting. Thirst. Sexual need. Years piling onto years. An eagerness for freedom and a boredom with isolation. Oh, and lack of money too!

Deciding to sublet her apartment helped. But she hated small economies, and hated leaving her nest, a plush lair with an antique fireplace and tall, sexy, vine-covered windows. Late one night, curled in old velvet pillows in golden lamplight, all of her red wine gone and sleep elusive, Eleanor hit upon the perfect solution. Her idea sprang fully formed into the room and she decided immediately to act. She would visit the subject of her work: Leopolda herself. Interview the old nun. Work with her. Gain her confidence while living near, even within, the religious community. Loneliness solved. The Mother Superior would allow her the use of a convent room. She'd pay a token fee. Money problem solved. Gather information, do research, live as the other women lived. Celibate. One other added bonus—no men around. Just priests. Not that she hadn't been tempted even there. She wouldn't, though, get in trouble. Not this time and not ever, ever again. *No sex is worth the anguish*, she decided blearily, sinking back into the sandalwood hush. The candles on her bedside table guttered, burning low in blue votive glasses. *Then again*. Her thoughts wandered down the years, other moments, certain nights. *Maybe it was worth it. Sometimes. Those times.*

§

Trust in the Known

JUNE 1994

Argus, North Dakota

*D*eep in the close heat of the night, in the warm and churning air, Jack's eyes open and he's already at the end of a thought. He doesn't mean to, surely he doesn't, but he can't help picturing Eleanor. He has found out for sure that she is at the retreat house run by the convent in Argus. He sees her meditating in a tight leotard, unable to keep from fidgeting. Or doing research, pen clenched between her teeth, round old-fashioned silver glasses that she puts on, takes off. He twists, his bones aching on his new mother-in-law's hard floor, and he remembers Eleanor's bed—firm, wide, comfortable, and loaded with books and pens. Trays of tea, apple cores, goldfish crackers. Extra condoms in foil coins that he'd mistaken for chocolates. She's always been into her own brainy, steamy, little world, given to quotes and speeches. Boring. Pedantic. So touching. He had loved her painfully. And of course, she eventually left him, like they all did, like this one would too.

Not that he would give Dot a chance! She breathed comfortably beside him, exhausted with the heat. Here he was, once again, caught between a mother and a daughter. That was just one of several themes in his life. This would be different. He was eager to tell Eleanor about his sudden sobriety—at last, a new scenario! She'd laugh at him, but she'd approve. Perhaps he'd spent his passion, killed it off. He wasn't exactly in love, but that was a relief all in itself. He and Dot were more business associates, with all their work in common, always talking the same language, his language. It was new for him to feel so comfortable and connected with someone. Dot. Dot Adare. Previously married to a Nanapush, of course. Didn't surprise him he and she were from the same background; in fact, that was probably part of the ease he felt in the relationship. And her daughter, Shawn—tough, big, pretty—he liked having her around. He would be careful not to give Dot any reason to go, but she scared him with her fierce threats, her independence, her sudden gusts of temper. Too much like his own.

Even so, the old need for confession plagued him. His firm was working on the overpass near the convent where Eleanor was staying. He always found out her whereabouts, it was just something he did as second nature. It was important to him to know where she was—he kept her filed. She was in his desk at home, her casual postcards filling up two rolltop slots. Since their divorce, long ago, they had maintained a loose intimacy of talk. He could go for stretches without needing it, and then he'd hit a low, get desperate. Each new relationship was frightening for its lack of history, for the raw newness, for the false instantaneous greed of sex, for the illusions in which he knew he'd founder. For him, Eleanor was all history, all knowledge.

Married, unmarried, he and Eleanor still loved and fought. She would see him, he was sure of it, even in that Dark Ages place she'd landed—a convent, typical! He thought of her thin fingers and heavy, short, manlike hair. Sometimes her voice grated on his nerves like a high-speed drill, but then he'd feel the crackle, the band tone of her intelligence turned on him, and he'd surrender to the gossipy speculation she loved, and he did, too, the endlessly fascinating game of self-examination. Oh, and her forehead, the sea-blue vein that beat at her temple, the tiny pulse, almost as if you could see her mind at work. He used to kiss it, knew just where to touch her arms and wrists. That, of course, was finished. They'd agreed.

§

Night Prayer

JUNE 1994

Eleanor, Leopolda, and Jack

*I*t was hot and windy in the garden of Our Lady of the Wheat, but inside the convent it was worse. The walls were stifling, the cells infernos, and Eleanor had tossed for hours, unable to find a slim thread of forgetfulness. She was thinking, madly thinking. Ideas turned in her brain. She roused herself, jotted down a few notes into a tiny spiral-bound she kept on her bedside table. *Actual effect of prayer upon material objects—test! Freudian analysis of reception in convent of bushels of pickling cucumbers. Question of happiness—actual or immaterial? Leopolda's diet at one time included moss or lichens, her "thirty days in the wilderness." First mixed-blood saint?*

When Eleanor finally gave up on sleep, it was almost time for night prayer anyway and so she put on her cotton shift, a flowing brown habit she'd begged, even a novice's cloak. The heat was brewing a storm, but she swiped the cloak for its potential romantic concealment. There, in the convent, she missed her own dramatic clothes. She slipped outside. Though by night the garden was usually forbidden, this had been such a dry and unforgiving spring that no word of reproach was spoken if a sister was found at the feet of the Blessed Virgin's shrine asking for Her intercession, begging that She save the local farmers by reviving their crops, seeded into dust, the new shoots wilting in the flat alluvial fields.

Just beyond the walls of the convent, the pounding of machinery working on the new interstate had stopped and started all the past month. First there was the long hauling and grading of base materials, then the loads of rebar to tie, the concrete to pour. Eventually, tons of steaming asphalt would be dumped and rolled flat. The construction seemed to be taking forever. Feeling that her house deserved a favor, the Mother Superior had prevailed upon the foreman of the crew to remove a cracked wooden statue of the Blessed Virgin from her pedestal. A new statue, quite an artwork, was due to arrive from Italy and the Mother Superior wanted to make certain that the pedestal in the center of the garden was ready.

Just recently, Eleanor had watched the operation from the small, square window of her upstairs room. The lineman lowered the gawky arm of the crane over the wall. One of the men who worked for Jack got out, and three others helped push, pull, and wrestle the stone virgin into the bucket. The statue ascended through the narrow sheaves of willows and paused, swaying, directly across from Eleanor. At that moment, Eleanor thought, the carved expression on one half of the face palpably lifted. *A trick of leafy shadows? Perhaps the Virgin is tired of being worshiped.* Eleanor was about to pursue the idea in writing when her attention was drawn by the men below. Jack's crew. *Mauser and Mauser.* Eleanor watched the men and mentally groaned at the new company logo, a blue and yellow truck and the words *Mauser and Mauser.* Stamped on the hats, the logo blared out to advertise his failing construction firm.

For years she'd been hearing of his financial troubles. It was no surprise to her—he always acted like a boy playing trucks. And crude. Even the lettering he used on the hats was crude, from a child's stencil set. Either he wasn't professional enough to make it in this world, or his consciousness, Eleanor thought, was still divided. He might have gone back to college after engineering school, become an academic or an architect. But no, he had chosen to leave school and enter the building trade, to work his way up only to slip back down once he became his own boss.

Eleanor had turned away from the window, back into her own immediate concerns. What began as the research project was lengthening, just as Eleanor had hoped, to week after week of quiet living. No papers. No publications. No manuscript. No dissertation. No students. She simply jotted notes and as discreetly as possible followed Leopolda through the day. No deadlines. No overseers. Sheer inspiration! Eleanor's ideas flowed like water, too fast to catch. Sometimes she temporarily dammed the flow, attempted to organize. She imagined her notebooks published—scraps and jottings and observations, a collage of brilliant unlinked thought having to do with sainthood, yes, but also other topics. For instance, the spaces between words.

Who has investigated the spaces between words? Any link to the messenger chemicals, connections in the brain?

Worth thinking about. While at the convent, her mind had befriended itself, her days had fused into a state of constant fascination. Leopolda was magnetic. The old woman despised her! Perfect! She hadn't dared to tell Leopolda, yet, that she was writing a book. She feared it would completely alienate the surly, saintly old woman. Eleanor was in her early thirties, had two M.A.s and an arrest record as a scofflaw and now, very nearly, as a cradle robber, too. Thank god these nuns did not read newspapers. Her continued presence at the convent was something of an annoyance to the sisters, but in addition to their vow of hospitality they were also curious about Eleanor's explorations and proud to think that they harbored a subject worthy of her study. Besides, Leopolda was exhausting. One more pair of hands helped. They let her stay.

There is a Minnesota vineyard that boasts, on its wine

label, of the suffering of its grapes. Midwestern intellectuals are like those grapes, Eleanor decided—the insecurity, the cold, the loneliness, produce a peculiar resonance. Eleanor stayed on and on to test her will, to ascertain the possibilities. Often, she ended up changing bed linen. Fetching water for the old nun. Cold water. Hot. Lukewarm. The woman had fixated on the temperature and not the contents of her simple cup. Each time Eleanor swept the cubicle floor or picked up a dropped missal or baked an apple to tempt Leopolda or rubbed her bent, numb feet, she gathered hope. Though Leopolda remained steadfast, and had not opened her life to Eleanor's pen, she had not refused to do so, either. The situation seemed to have a reason beyond reason, to demand an irrational trust. Just recently, Eleanor had begun to attain a hint of the peace of mind she sought, and she expected the gradual pursuit of Leopolda to yield fruit.

There was, specifically, an old report written by a reservation priest. He had documented Leopolda's presence at a case in which a reservation girl's hands opened, bleeding in the exact wounds of Christ. Stigmata. Minor cures. Mysterious anecdotes. Eleanor didn't want to undo difficult progress. She bent over her journal, plotting and speculating. Tried to concentrate. But the news of Jack and then the sight of the clumsily painted construction hats had intruded, disturbing her mental repose.

Two days ago, Eleanor had also found a memo in her message niche: *Meet me in the garden at midnight.* Every few hours, she checked the box for more, for the note hadn't specified which night. She knew Jack's handwriting—the firm, half-schooled, draftsman's print. Through the long, dark hours of the first evening, she had argued feebly with the stronger part of herself, the part perpetually curious about Jack. By the time the black heat lowered in her bedroom, there was no question she would meet him.

Now the night garden was lush and blowing. Scents of earth wafted—rain, hot fragrance, crushed geranium. Behind the walls there resonated a beat of stillness, then air funneled swiftly through. Entering, Eleanor closed her eyes and attempted to restore some continuity to her thoughts. The odor of spent honeysuckle swirled around her shoulders and grit blew from the path, stinging her cheek.

The wind died down. She was suddenly alert. From beyond the high wall—she was sure of it—Eleanor heard the drum of a large diesel motor. Tires crunched on the gravel road, and air brakes hissed with a sinking croak.

Heart tapping, she gripped her hands tightly together, and stepped away from the statue's base. Edging into the shadows of the bean vines, Eleanor waited.

The motor caught again. She heard the thick whine of the truck's hydraulic lifter, and looked quickly at the residence to see if any lights went on. The windows glittered, black, sending off reflections of silver-bellied storm clouds. Gibbous, football-shaped, the moon eased out for a moment and suddenly there was enough clear light to see the reach-all arm and bucket crest smoothly over the wall.

The machine paused, swaying, and Jack Mauser righted himself, standing high in his metal roost. He scanned the garden below, passed over Eleanor once, then his eyes returned as he marked her out from the pattern of shadows and leaves. He nodded, pulled a billed hat lower, then pressed the controls and brought himself to earth. Just at the height of the grass, Mauser stopped the machine and unlatched a small door on the side of the bucket. He had the muscular and easy-moving grace of a former high school all-star. He swiveled sideways, posed a moment near the machine, raised his eyebrows, and sauntered loose-limbed over to Eleanor. Her silence and solemnity seemed to crack his confidence, however, and as he neared her he stuffed his hands into the pockets of a light denim jacket, hesitated. A cloud flapped across the moon and the wind rushed overhead.

"I had to see you," he explained.

Her eyes were full of him. She hadn't been this close to a man for months and he smelled, elusively, of earthly things like paint and wool and fresh-cut lumber. She stepped nearer.

He cleared his throat and spoke roughly. "What the hell are you doing here, stuck away like this?"

She didn't want to tell the stupid story of her dismissal. Tears started, blazed up suddenly behind her eyes, and she felt a startling jab of shame. Just seeing him smashed an invisible glass inside of her. She'd been unharmed on the outside by the absurd sexual episode and scandal, but deep down, bubble-wrapped, a pearly vase had been ready to shatter.

She wanted to say how easy it was, how frighteningly cool she'd felt, how little she recognized the person who seduced boys and hit them and manipulated students and made insinuating comments to priests. A powerful wave of confusion knocked her, though, and more tears surged up behind her eyes. Tears were damaging. They bit like acid.

"I'm married again," Jack used Eleanor's silence.

Eleanor got hold of herself. What could she be thinking? She had been caught sideways, off-guard, by a wave of old feelings. Her reactions were too close to the surface. She tried to summon the words, to wish him well, at least to inquire, but she couldn't force out the required sentence and instead made a dry sound of contempt.

"Nobody you would know."

Jack's voice immediately went cold. He had always been able to lower the mask, to make his eyes, his whole demeanor, remote and robotic at will. He'd learned how to stare down others. But what to do when the other, the looker, regarded you from within? The distancing ruse still worked with Eleanor—only he was now aware of drawing the shell over himself and he felt puppetlike, desperate, unnatural.

"Please," he whispered, his voice low.

"No," said Eleanor.

She leaned forward, but drew back from the warmth of his breath on her fingers. Behind the walls, she heard the sisters moving in the dark. They owned nothing, not one possession. They rose at this hour to pray for the sins that the rest of the world was busy committing. It was unthinkable that they find

Mauser here, but Eleanor's throat closed when she tried to tell him he should go. Married again! The idiot. She wanted him to stay. She couldn't think fast enough, needed time.

The convent door thudded shut. There was a rattling cough, a low mutter from the path. Someone was coming. Questions shone and diminished on Mauser's face. He turned to go, turned back to stay. Held up his hands. Eleanor decided. To disguise him, she quickly wrapped the cloak she carried around his shoulders. As she fastened the catch underneath his chin, her fingertips brushed the lobe of one ear. He reached toward her, but she ducked away, walked over to the lift, and selected a glowing button marked on the control panel. She pushed the button firmly. Up floated the empty bucket, disappearing into the night.

Blown dirt flew through the air, and Eleanor turned to Mauser in its force, took his work-scarred hand, and pulled him to the pedestal of the statue that had been removed. She shoved him into the niche formed by the pruned boughs of yew and mock orange. Clumsily, wild with apprehension, she stripped branches off the flowering bushes and smacked them into his arms.

"Get up there and stand still. Hold these. Keep your hood down."

The air turned blacker, the shadows thickened, the sky rolled in so fast that all the garden trembled. Lightning, caught up in the baskets of the clouds, clenched and unclenched without striking. From the back entry of the convent, now, a tiny stumplike figure tottered, pulling itself along the garden path behind a shining aluminum walker. It was Sister Leopolda, 108 years old, so light and ancient that her bones could barely support the garments of her habit. Though absentminded and crippled, she still roamed the garden at any hour. Eleanor had heard she was beatified, or nearly, after all. It was rumored that she had caused a replication of the marvel of the loaves and the fishes during one lean winter, when a great bowl of custard kept in the convent refrigerator was filled and refilled over the course of many nights. Leopolda's dreams predicted events, and her advice was often sought though the meaning of her words had become somewhat obscure. Still, she was venerated, and suffered to make her own rules. Tonight, as she did on many nights, she steered herself to the statue of the Virgin to recite her solitary devotions. As she drew into the alcove, she saw the edge of Eleanor's robe, and stopped.

Eleanor did the only thing that she could think of—she knelt at Mauser's feet as if in prayer. Immediately, as had happened during their marriage when she was compelled into a subordinate position to him, a fork of black rage stabbed. In a childish burst of irritation, she crossed her fingers as she crossed herself. He had no power over her, not anymore, and yet she moaned at the foolishness of her situation. Catching herself, she tried to turn the sound into the mumble of a litany.

Leopolda's voice joined hers. Reedy, thin, its tone was clear as a flute, honed by her decades of contemplative silence.

"Dear child." The aged nun's fingers flailed and reached.

"Take my hand," said Eleanor.

"Oh." The nun peered close and then reared back in irritation. "It's you again."

"I'm sorry." Eleanor attempted to keep her voice humble.

The wind blew Leopolda's garment out with a crack, reversed, and buckled it tight around her body. Eleanor steadied and composed the hunched woman, helped her kneel. Taking each brittle leg in her hands, she bent with all her strength, as though the ancient nun were a large doll. Gradually and with great exertion the nun was eased onto the wooden kneeler. The storm had moved closer, up to the walls of the garden, and now the eye of it appeared to center just above the low stone convent. The black leaves trembled on their stems, yet the air was still.

"Leave me," the nun commanded, dismissing Eleanor. "Go in peace." But, of course, Eleanor could not. Instead, she sank onto the edge of an apron of watered lawn that surrounded the shrine and asked, in a low and respectful tone, if she could join her sister in her prayers.

"I pray alone!" Leopolda's voice was emphatic. Eleanor would have to strategize. Though Leopolda's eyes were clouded, her body weak, her strength easily exhausted, there was the danger that in a moment of clarity she might look closely at the statue or remember that the real one had been removed. Who knew how long it had been since she had seen an unordained man? Although Leopolda was in the habit of absently eating bits of paper or whatever else she found in her fingers when she was hungry, although she gazed for hours at the single rose or zinnia placed next to her bed each morning, although at times she seemed to dwell halfway in another world, she was also keen-minded and known for her sudden penetrations of understanding.

"*Go* in peace." Again Leopolda ordered the younger woman out of her presence.

Eleanor attempted to distract with questions. "I won't bother you again. Only tell me," she paused, then remembered her notebook jottings, ". . . I've been hoping to question you on the subject of prayer. Have you had many"—here Eleanor stumbled—"results?"

Leopolda huffed with incredulity and muttered, low and furious.

"*Results?*"

She seemed to strangle on the word.

"The prayer is the thing itself! The result!" she finally managed. "Although of course I have had *results*. God requires me! I am fed—honey from the rock—I am fed!"

Leopolda clamped her lips shut. Beside her, on the prickling fan of dry grass, Eleanor sensed the rising wave of annoyance slough off and settle. She gripped her hands together. She could feel Mauser enjoying her predicament and a tide of resentment flooded her.

"Before I came here, long before, really," Eleanor stage-whispered in a confessional tone, "I lived with a fool."

"You lived alone?"

From above them, branches rustled.

"No, of course not. I was married. I lived with a man who

wanted everything from me, who was absent half the time, who loved other women, who claimed to love me, but allowed terrible things to happen and could never be counted on."

"Then you've had practice."

"In what?"

"Loving God."

Eleanor fell silent, wishing for her notebook. *Loving God. So to her He's a faithless husband.*

"What do you mean, exactly? I was talking about *my* former husband. Jack Mauser. What of him?"

"Him."

The nun's voice, stiff with relish and disdain, cracked out like a slow whip.

"What of him? I see a picture of the poor soul, bleeding. He will be crushed by a woman. He'll die screaming in a woman's arms. She'll snap his bones like matchsticks and throttle him with her kiss."

Over them, a shocked alertness held.

"Do you mean Jack?" Eleanor said. "Jack?" She couldn't help but feel alarm.

The old woman seemed to shrink still smaller and to lose some of her vigor. She gave a wisp of a sigh, no more than the shudder of breeze passing through the petals of a flower. A long period of hesitant silence passed.

"Oh, my beautiful and blessed sister," Leopolda murmured, at last, "it is hard to be weak. Hard to be so old. At one time I would have taken up the paddle to the butter churn and given you a whack!" She paused a longer while yet, and when Eleanor made no motion to rise, she sighed and continued. "But now I must bend to your wishes and allow you to pray alongside me. Since you insist on kneeling here, then repeat your request. What exactly is it that you want?"

The sudden kindness in the nun's voice shamed Eleanor, but she sensed it was false sympathy, a bribe, a ploy to throw her off-guard. Nevertheless, she had no choice but to hold her position and, in fact, she decided now to confess her intentions. Her head felt light, uncanny.

"I am writing a book. I'd like you to"—Eleanor took a deep breath—"to be the subject."

"You're writing a what?"

"A book."

"A *book*."

Eleanor waited. "I'd like to write about you."

"Me!" The old nun's vehement rasp faltered away. She seemed genuinely surprised.

"You've seen so much. Wouldn't you like to tell the world?"

Eleanor glanced up at Mauser's massive form, and beyond, at the bushes and vines, so immaculately tended, at the high wall of brick and chipped stucco. It seemed to her suddenly that branches and leaves sprang out against that wall in sharp relief, caught by summery light. Harsh stripped twigs, bitten bark. The patterns were complex, mazy, and full of meaning. There was a flash and then the leaves closed over the skeletal understory.

The old nun's voice was low and personal, perhaps genuinely curious. "What do I have to tell? What do I know?"

"The truth of sacred bonds," Eleanor made the mistake of answering too piously. "You have lived a life of sacrifice and of love."

"Love?" the old voice quivered. "Love?" She considered, then went on in a slowly gathering rage.

"Then ask me what love brings? Can't you see! No relief to love, no end, no wave, no fall, only a continual ascension." She waved a crooked hand, her fingers gnarled like the roots of a wormwood bush. "You asked!" she cried suddenly, then folded back into herself with a high, harsh laugh, the sound of glass scraping glass.

The shrill sobs of amusement hurt Eleanor's ears. She could hear nothing, feel nothing else. She found herself breathing jerkily, as though she'd fallen flat and knocked her wind out. Her chest pinched, an iron band was wrapped around it.

Perhaps she gave some sign of her distress and frustration, or perhaps it was just that the constellation of small events suddenly struck Mauser as ridiculous too. At any rate, Eleanor was certain that she heard Mauser's laugh echo. It was a small, private, almost interior laugh. If she hadn't known him so thoroughly, she would never have been able to distinguish her former husband's sarcastic humor from the nun's hysteria or the wind rattling the grass against the wall. But she did hear it, did know it.

"Will you *shut up*!" she cried.

Silence. The old nun hiccuped. Her mirth turned gradually into wilder sounds so high and penetrating that it ached to listen.

"Hear my prayer! Hear my prayer!" Leopolda mimicked in a light falsetto. *"Day wi kway ikway!"* She turned her head to glare at Eleanor. "My prayer is a tale of burning love, child, but you aren't ready to hear it."

"I am!" Eleanor leaned closer.

Leopolda's voice shook with emotion, broke from her like strings ripping from a harp.

"End this torment," the old nun whispered.

With a terrible effort, as if a tree tried to straighten its own crooked limb, the old nun cocked her head and rolled her eyes upward, strained impossibly, just a bit more, a little farther, to catch a glimpse of the blessed statue. What she saw transfixed her. Just at the moment that Leopolda managed to locate the icon in her narrow view, it seemed to her that the Virgin leaned down off her pedestal, and ever so gently, as Leopolda stretched out her fingers, transferred the carved bundle she carried into the cradle of the nun's arms.

Leopolda's head snapped back to her chest. Clasping the living leaves to herself, burying her face within the boughs, she was overcome with surpassing peace. It was not even the dry wheat by which we live, not grain that the Patroness had transformed, but branches of sweet honeysuckle, which blooms so suddenly and with such intoxicating scent. Leopolda sank down breathing the fragrance of the limp, white petals with such strong and vigorous ecstasy that her heart cracked, she pitched straight over, and was granted her request.

✻   ✻   ✻

As the nun's body fell with a soft thud, her abandoned walker ringing on the stone tiles, Eleanor lunged forward. Mauser jumped lightly off his perch and knelt alongside Eleanor as she checked the old woman's pulse and found it still. She could not absorb what had happened. She continued to pat the tiny bones of Leopolda's wrist and to call her name, gently, as though to awaken her. It was not until Mauser put his hands carefully on Eleanor's shoulders that she gave up.

"She's dead," she softly moaned. "You killed her. Oh, Jack."

She pushed his hands away, overcome.

Jack stood shifting his feet, trying to control his agitation as Eleanor crossed the nun's arms over the blossoms, gently closed her eyes, straightened her twisted legs and feet. With a final look at the beaky, ancient face, mysteriously peaceful in its ecstasy, Eleanor turned away. Staggering until she found her balance, she pushed past Mauser toward the back door of the convent. He followed, ready to deny or accept all blame. But Eleanor strode headlong through the entrance without a sideways glance and was gone, leaving him outside, beside the unpainted wall, too high to climb. The only exit was through the building. He shook his head, drew the cloak more tightly around his shoulders, then opened the door.

Inside, the convent was a surprisingly ordinary place, not that Mauser had been expecting much of anything else. Just not this. The hallway was floored with a durable but inexpensive gray linoleum, and the walls were Sheetrock, painted in neutral grays and tans. Dim lights drew him toward the kitchen, large and airy, filled with storage cupboards. He hoped to find an exit, but instead arrived at the foot of a set of stairs. He climbed—it was from the stairwell that he heard the distant rise and fall of the voices of nuns at prayer—and reached the second floor with its long, narrow hall of sleeping cells.

Once he found himself in the nuns' most private quarters, Mauser's urge to leave the building faded. He still had to talk to Eleanor, decide what to do about the . . . Jack shivered . . .

poor, sick, dead old lady. Her prediction had spooked him. And, too, selfishly, foolishly, he still wanted to explain himself. He still wanted Eleanor to understand, to acknowledge his marriage, his sober self, changes vast to him but surprisingly imperceptible to her. He needed a blessing, perhaps an assurance, an okay. Maybe a little common sense, that was all he craved. The grounded feeling of a connection.

So he began to look. Assuming he would locate Eleanor's room by her familiar objects, her tapestries and antique silver atomizers and African carvings, he entered four nearly bare cells before he stopped to think.

Each cubicle, a simple rectangle with a slanted roof and one square window, held a cot, a small table with a single drawer, and a built-in cabinet. A crucifix hung on the wall and the light fixture was a bare bulb. A tiny bedside lamp. The sameness of the four rooms oppressed Mauser. His vision narrowed.

What could he do? How? He rubbed his chin. The cloak. He crushed it to his face and inhaled lengthily and critically. Then he took it away. He tilted his head backward, considered, touched his nose to the weave again. Not hers. He tried to remember. Not soap. Not any kind of perfume. Just Eleanor. He retrieved a time they had been camping together and he smelled only her—but no, that was smoke of birch caught in her hair. He had it, then, he had it perfectly. The first time he'd kissed her, tasted her. She smelled like . . . apple skins. Not the sweet flesh, but green skins, waxy, tart before you peel them. He started over, now, began with the first room, crept in and then, cautiously, with a delicate excitement, moved to each nun's bed, drew down the cover, and took a breath of the air above the sheet.

He smelled the bottom of a cup of milk in one room, sulfur in the next, he smelled pockets of simmering minerals deep in the earth. He smelled blood, salt, oats, and fresh nails, straight from the hardware hopper. Dough, yeast risen but left too long beneath the towel. He smelled apricots, rough cedar, and mothballs. Wool, and that peculiar sharp sad odor that rises when it is steam pressed. He smelled young hair and old hair. And finally he came to Eleanor.

The actual scent of her hit him with a shock that opened his heart. He smoothed the coverlet back onto her bed, and sat down to wait.

Eleanor had run into the convent thinking to fetch help, but once there, an overwhelming urge to write down what had happened overtook her. The old nun's words turned on a racing mill. *My legacy!* At the same time, exhaustion fizzed in Eleanor's brain, her face seemed to hum with the solid weight of slumber. She was afraid she was in shock and might forget the final words, which might be priceless. Who knew? *End this torment*. Who could forget? What did they mean? She told herself that Leopolda wouldn't mind lying in the grass until she was naturally discovered. It would do no good, anyway, to cause an uproar. Let her rest in peace with her flowers, thought Eleanor as her hand moved avidly across the pages of her notebook. That was the thing to do.

When prayer was over and the incident all but written, Eleanor made her way down the hall. The gears in her brain were stripped smooth. She couldn't catch at a thought. The wind rising outside the walls sounded like the rushing of a powerful river. *End this torment*. Was she really in such agony? The poor old witch. They should have had her on morphine, or maybe they did. And this stuff about Jack—crushed, kissed to death. Appropriate. Maybe this new wife, number five, was overweight? Eleanor smoothed her hand over the taut slope of her stomach. She closed the door firmly behind her as she switched on the dim bedside lamp.

Mauser sat on the bed, the cloak neatly folded beside him, his hands curved tense in his lap. He raised a finger and pointed at the bulb. Eleanor put her palm down on the switch and the room went dark. She put a match to a small votive candle beside the bed and with the spurt of fire her head cleared immediately. She felt the old anger like a jet of hollow flame.

"Get out of here, Jack."

When Mauser slumped, as he did now, as if overcome suddenly with the physical weight of his own body, he lost some of his easy grace, and that made him look affectingly old. Even in the dark, Eleanor could sense the way he shifted into uncertainty, and her sympathy grabbed in spite of her outrage at his nerve.

"I'm sorry . . ." His voice was shamed and quiet.

"She was over a hundred years old, Jack. A living treasure. You shouldn't have done it. Besides, she was *mine*."

Mauser didn't move, didn't speak again. Eleanor put her hand on his for a moment, and when he didn't move, accepting her touch, not overdoing a response, just waiting, she recalled fully and mournfully what it was like to be with him. He kept apologizing.

"It's just that I . . . you know, it was like she asked me when she stuck out her arms, like she wanted the flowers. I wouldn't have done it otherwise. I wouldn't have even thought of it."

Eleanor stared at Mauser without speaking, her expression a mixture of vexed anxiety and the old unwilling attraction. Jack Mauser noted the latter in the downward shift of her gaze. She brushed her lips with the ends of her fingers, put the back of her hand to her cheek to calm herself.

"Should I leave? You can go out again," he said softly. "Pretend to find her."

"No."

Lightning rattled in the eaves, and Mauser and Eleanor met each other's eyes in the sudden glare. The wind had slammed the casement shut. Eleanor walked over and jerked open the window. Fresh air poured in, cooler, stiffened at its edges by that before-rain fragrance of stirred dust. The candle guttered, then the light strengthened. They were silent for a long while before Eleanor spoke, her voice carefully offhand.

"So. Wife number . . . what is it, five now? When's the happy day?"

"Last week."

Just as Eleanor laughed, a jagged branch of lightning whipped the ground, miles off, and they heard the thunder bound toward them. One second. Two. Three. Then the noise closed with a dense, emphatic, comforting solidity, as if a child's hollow block had been clapped over the convent.

"What *did* you come here for, Jack?"

Eleanor struggled out of her overgarment, threw it down at her feet, and stood before Mauser. To compensate for her generous hips, she carried herself in a way she thought was splendid. She had inherited a dancer's lush energy from her mother, and stretched her arms with lingering poise. She held her dark-haired head carefully, raised an upward curve of strong eyebrows, her favorite of her features. Her skin was smooth, too pale. Her face was magnetic, a little startling—the green eyes so deep, her lips so full—but there was something overdrawn about her. Too dramatic. Eleanor always looked as though she was wearing vivid makeup, and yet, she was subject to sudden fits of awkward shyness so intense that it sometimes was interpreted as belligerence. Undersocialized in spite or because of her idyllic little girlhood, depressive as a result of a difficult adolescence, distrustful, on occasion driven to perfectionism and acts of neurotic zeal, Eleanor had always infuriated Mauser and he tried to remember this even as his fingertips burned.

"No one's going to hear us, so we might as well talk."

She was wearing a rough shift and her breasts, heavy, swung as she turned. At the thought of her body within the cloth Mauser ached. He took the fabric tentatively between his fingers and rubbed it, pretending curiosity, but wanting in truth to touch anything that was touching her.

"Cotton."

She shook the material and he nodded and dropped the fold. Eleanor's hair was thick with the stormy air's watery electricity, and his hand automatically reached to smooth it back where it flapped onto her forehead. With a rough gesture, Eleanor leaned forward, knocking Mauser backward like a piece of furniture. She reached into the crack of her bedside drawer and took out a thin roll of toilet paper. Within it, a single cigarette was hidden. She lit it from the candle, inhaled deeply, passed it sideways.

"This latest wife. What's she like?"

Mauser took a short draw and offered the cigarette back to her. He spoke normally, his voice obscured by the restless night. In his own ears he sounded normal, comfortingly like himself again, half drunk with eagerness as he poured out the story. He and Dot had married casually, a weekend thing. Of course he cared about her, in fact they'd gone to the same school once, long ago. Dot was strong-minded. Tough. She loved Mauser, that was in her favor, wasn't it? She'd come to work for him just this past summer. They hadn't known each other over all the years since high school. They had decided, immediately, they were meant—

"Don't say you were *meant for each other*. That's what you always say." Eleanor's voice was acid. "Besides, meant for each other was us. You and me. Meant for each other but can't stand each other."

"I can stand you," said Mauser, gazing straight at Eleanor.

"Don't look at me like that. I know that look." She waved her hand between them as though to produce visual static. Mauser paused.

"Anyway, you would like her," he said. "Dot Adare. Dot Nanapush—though she's not a brain, not like you. She's smart, though. And I'm giving her books," he added with false earnestness.

Eleanor stopped him. "You? Books?"

"Snob." Mauser pretended to be wounded. "Two-bit intellectual," he added, knowing that would make her angry. He felt with satisfaction the sudden tapping of her fingers on the bedstead. She hadn't changed, still so thin-skinned. He slumped against the wall, his whole body sprawling, his legs loose and heavy.

"As for me, the whole marriage thing. It was sudden, I know. Turned out she's part Chippewa too. Coincidence or sign?" Jack laughed, then said more seriously, "Do you think it's a sign, that maybe I'm supposed to do something. Identify? Plus she's Catholic, or was. Convert—back to the church? Except I'm an atheist, whatever. That nun's prediction. Jesus. What do you make of that? And there's one more thing."

Jack paused. "My hands keep shaking," he said, low. "It's like I'm afraid to tell you!"

He held out his hand and his blunt fingers trembled in the intermittent light. In spite of herself, Eleanor was piqued with interest. She leaned to him.

"What was it? Come on. Tell."

But Jack found he couldn't tell Eleanor about the baby. One of their main problems had been children. Neither of them could decide to have or not to have them. She wouldn't sympathize, and besides, she had detested the wife before this one, Marlis. He decided to keep her off the subject.

"I heard you lost your job," he said instead, tactlessly, but Eleanor didn't seem to mind.

"I wasn't fired."

"What, then."

"Let's call it an extended, unpaid leave of absence?" Eleanor stroked her own cheek, and Jack became distracted watching her and blurted out a rude question.

"Who'd you fuck this time? The bishop?"

Again, she didn't act in the least defensive—with Jack, she didn't always have to. With him, she could be herself. Compared to his transgressions, her sins were mere peccadilloes.

"Some kid."

They sat together quietly for some time. Jack gathered courage.

"I had to marry her," he blurted at last, softly. He waited, his breathing shallow.

"I hope you two live happily ever after," Eleanor said, finally, in a light, flat voice.

Brightness froze the air in the room. The words were simultaneous with an attenuated pulse of radiance and harsh ozone filled their lungs. Mauser's face appeared stark before Eleanor—big, handsome, the mouth curved and balanced, the eyes dark, a mixture of Tatar-Slavic, Hun, Ojibwa. Eleanor reclined carefully against him on the narrow cot.

"Forget it, Jack," she warned when he began to trace her chin and throat with his fingers. She shoved him into a position comfortable to her, rustled the covers to hide the snag in her voice, pretended to doze. Jack dropped his hand from her face and held her around the waist. The two breathed quietly together as the rain splashed against the window. It drummed hard and hollow at first, tapered off evenly to just a few drops, then diminished to nothing.

She didn't mean to move her hand, but as she drifted at the edge of sleep the wood smell of him, the tar, the heavy crankcase and elusive blend of grass and soap trickled along her nerves, behind her tongue, her eyes, fired old neural pathways that branched into an elusive pattern of associations. His hand moved so slowly in response that she could feel the trail of warmth his fingers left, passing over but not touching her breasts. He twisted with an otter's suddenness and caught her in one arm so that he was looking down upon her and she, thrilled and wary, opened into his searching gaze. Staring into her former husband's eyes, Eleanor was unexpectedly filled with the familiar and charming peace that lived between them but which was unpredictable, unsustainable, perhaps unreal.

Jack lifted her gown, slid his hands along her hips, to her waist, pressed his thumb to her navel. His blood swam with energy, for he still loved her, he'd never stopped. Most times, except the times they couldn't stand one another, their attraction had been avid and desperate. Their anger as well. Occasionally in the years that passed, they had seen each other on a neutral basis. They kept in communication. Exactly twelve times they had made love. No one knew. They hardly admitted it to themselves. Yet beneath each note, Christmas card, call, the subtext read: *I'm alive. Still here. It's still the same with me. With you?*

They pressed together by fractions. They grew exhausted by the very idea of what came next and lay back, breathing hopelessly, eyes wide. Mauser settled over Eleanor, watching her face in the low and rhythmical lightning that veered around the bowl of the horizon, now and then whipping high a spume of brilliance. His face was grave and concentrated. Hers bloomed with heat. He looked at her almost reproachfully when he entered her, and Eleanor, bewildered, felt her face growing heavy with tears. Her lip lifted slightly. The gleam of white enamel hooked him under.

The storm passed off, all was still outside and so they didn't dare make a sound. Every time a door creaked or a window sighed, the timbers groaned, they stopped moving. Once, when they paused, Mauser whispered all he felt, too low for her to hear. His arms trembled. A slight sheen of sweat iced his chest, his back, and he watched her with a wrenching hope that frightened him. He needed more, a sign. Eleanor's face gleamed with a stilled wonder. What was happening? No time passed. Hours did. Some bird began to sing, five clear notes. They tipped the balance, she on top now, he having forgotten what she felt like on him when she came—light as frost then heavy, crushing the wind out of him, dark as rock and gone.

They moved apart and over the two of them, at once, an oppressing realization settled, a deep mantle of space. What an awful, what a stupid, what an immense thing to have happened. Last time was the last time—they had fought over it, sworn each other off. Their mouths dropped open, panting. Words spun in their mouths like cotton. Thoughts choked them.

"What can I say?" asked Mauser. "What can I do? I've changed, I didn't mean to."

"Like hell you've changed or maybe, I don't know."

Eleanor moved warily beside him, looked into his eyes so deeply that she lost focus, everything blurred. She turned away. Lying next to him in a gathering panic of emotion, Eleanor drew his hand over her face like an air mask. For a long while, until at last he left her, she held it there, breathing against his palm. Had it ever happened quite like this? Exactly? Was it different in some significant way? They had made love and wept before and yet next morning life had swept them on, the path sheer, the ground far below, the marriages and big plans and money worries and careers like mud slides that had catapulted them apart once and kept them from ever meeting, conclusively, again. This time, however, onward from the night of Jack Mauser's visitation, Eleanor began to lose sleep.

Lightning had struck the hydraulic lift as it stayed poised at its highest reach, just beyond the wall. Instead of grounding harmlessly, the spark had leaped, surged toward something in the garden path, probably Sister Leopolda's shiny walker, which was found later—twisted, blackened, and somehow shrunk no larger than a pair of bobby pins. Some of the sisters maintained that Leopolda herself lay next to it, reduced to a pile of ash in the shape of a cross. Kneeling at the empty base of the statue the next morning, Eleanor watched the dust of the holy nun carried off by bees. All of her bitterness turned to honey, stirred one day into a cup of tea. Not everyone was convinced. A few of the sisters were certain that Leopolda had simply wandered away from the convent in the heat of a senile ecstasy. The surrounding fields were searched with no success, but that was no proof, either, that she wasn't somewhere, alive or dead.

The larger consensus, finally, was that she had simply been vaporized by the electrical blast. Of course, there were those who saw a new miracle in this disappearance. The word *assumption* was whispered about until the visiting priest, Father Jude, felt compelled to produce evidence that cases of human combustion and conflagration had been documented before by the North Dakota state weather bureau. Still, behind-hands talk persisted, mounted. Discussions, plans, a decision finalized to fix the remaining ash in place and put the whole site under glass, to consecrate it as a holy shrine. Before the bishop could be summoned and matters arranged, however, a strong, fresh wind arose and swept the garden clear.

Perhaps because Eleanor had torn off boughs of honeysuckle and mock orange for Mauser and now remembered that their bloom was over, their season finished, she was the only one who paid attention to the actual source of the flowers. She noticed, in fact, that for three weeks after the incident the blossoms on the old nun's favorite bushes renewed in such dense profusion and number that the fragrance wafted halfway around the building at night. The odor penetrated Eleanor's window, waking her with its insistent sweetness, loosening her mind, causing her to lie suspended in the darkness, filling her head with such thoughts.

Jack's hands on her, his mouth on hers—she could not relinquish vivid pictures in spite of everything she tried. Days, she turned his image over and over and her mind worked wearily, like an organ grinder, reproducing noises and scenes. She reviewed the text of Leopolda's words and tried to deconstruct, to demythologize, to wreak upon her enigmatic, irritable answers some violence of exploration that would keep them from preying on her conscience. Nothing worked. She kept thinking of Jack. One morning, Eleanor knelt so long before the shrine that birds forgot about her. She watched two pearly, loam-eyed mourning doves fan their tails and mate. Before, and after, they moved the black hooks of their beaks so swiftly in and out of each other's feathers that their heads blurred. When he mounted her, his cloak in a whir, her eyes rolled back behind sudden membranes of metallic blue.

Three decades into her life, Eleanor finally knew who she wanted. Drenched with weakness, she dropped her head into her hands and tried to pray. Her thoughts would not connect. Just one night, just one more night. Would that have been enough? Could she have returned, contented, to her orderly and satisfying refuge? But her peace was shattered, as if the storm had blasted everything. After several weeks, during which her temptation did not abate, Eleanor knew an awful and surprising thing was happening to her—she was falling in love with her own ex-husband. Perhaps it was true, he'd changed. Or maybe she had. His image drenched her. The turn of his wrist, the weave of expressions on his face, the clothes he had worn the last time she saw him, even the cheesy new company logo. All of these things became the articles of faith in the house constructed of her wakefulness. She began to wish she'd made Mauser leave something behind, a souvenir, anything. She wanted his clothing. She wanted his ice-blue shirt. His slacks, which were made of a material rough and tan. She wanted things he'd worn when they were married. His work jacket came back to her, heavy with male significance. She saw it, polished on the cuffs with grease and oiled on the back where Mauser slid underneath his car. She wanted the pockets—his hands had stuffed into them. She wanted the collar that had touched his neck.

After two weeks, sleep entirely eluded her. She dreaded entering her cell, and hated the bed itself, its flat pillow and mattress filled with buckwheat hulls. Some nights she lay on the floor, curled up in the room's corner and drifted. By day she started to unravel. She could feel her nerves, the fibers splitting, twanging off like bowstrings. She could feel her head enlarging. It was stuffed with soft lumps of cotton wadding. Her brain swelled above her eyes, porous, absorbing her experience. She had always feared to go without sleep, and now she was hostage to its loss. She obtained a secret stash of antidepressant medication. Her mother, Anna Schlick, wrote a worried note begging Eleanor to come back to Fargo. She stayed at the convent though, lived on Xanax and Rolaids. There was no diversion. She was only allowed one book in her room besides the New Testament.

What would she have picked a year ago, she wondered, to bring to her desert island? Perhaps Colette, or Tanizaki. A VCR and Madonna videos. Or the erotic journals of Princess Labanne DeBoer. She had been working on an article cataloguing Catholic imagery in contemporary popular culture. Now, such pictures made her shudder. She wanted dry matter, the driest she could find. There were very few volumes in the convent library, but at least they were all harmless stuff. She had chosen the largest, which she kept on her nightstand. *The New York Public Library Desk Reference* became her only reading.

She opened it at random, memorized pure information, as if she could block out Mauser with facts and statistics. She knew the foreign currencies of every country in the world, knew by heart all visa requirements, and became an expert on stain removal. Fish slime? Lukewarm solution of saltwater. Correction fluid? Amyl acetate. Chewing gum? Freeze it. But she never stained her clothes at the convent, nothing clung to her, not even the juice of arbor grapes she squeezed through a cheesecloth to make jelly, not even ink. It was when she had finally used up another month of nights mastering the tables of the nutritive values of food—when she said grace one morning over her soft-boiled egg and thought *73.3 percent water, 12.7 grams of protein, 11.6 of fat, 0 fiber content, 1.4 grams of ash*, and on, down to the last contained milligram of ascorbic acid—that Eleanor began to accept that she was in trouble.

There was "ash" in almost every food, but was it really *ash*, like wood ash, the ash of things burnt way back from the beginning of time, including Sister Leopolda? Eleanor's sense of taste became so keen that she could actually taste in each mouthful the haunted image of things consumed by fire—the spines and floors of houses, piles of yellow leaves, trash of sugar beets, people, dogs, cows, cats, all kinds of trees, hills of straw, newspapers, bags, random garbage. Most days she hardly took two bites. The food crumbled on her lips. The most innocuous substances—oatmeal, almonds—turned on her tongue. She could not untie her throat to swallow, could not breathe except from the livid space around her heart. She trembled at the shutting of a door, and strange notions stole into her head.

Cut your own throat, now. She kept hearing that odd line from the Robert Lowell poem as she worked with knives in the kitchen. Outside, laboring on the convent grounds, she found good resolutions, but also discovered herself hoping that a tree would fall, a snapped limb pierce her dead. And as for the Virgin Mary, the new statue delayed in shipping, Eleanor now imagined in Her the truth of her desexed and virulently demure passivity—a declitorized vessel wrapped head to foot in a goody-two-shoes shawl, carrying within her, for eternity, the miracle of one uncracked egg. Immaculate? Eleanor's heart wrenched from its blue tissue box. She wanted the blood and fire that consumed her to become real. The sisters, amazed at her sudden will to prayer, believed she had found God. Eleanor knew she had found Mauser. But he was married again and she was eschewing all stupid situations, lost causes, and painful attractions. That was over. Work might save. Streams of wild energy flowed through her arms and legs and one night she washed every already clean dish in the convent house, scrubbed every floor and hall the next.

"This," the Mother Superior said, hopeful but also suspicious of such zeal, "could be a sign of the profound love you bear. You are close."

Nearer, nearer.

Eleanor had run out of anodynes and subsisted for one week on the diet of Saint Theresa—distilled water and communion wafers—when she collapsed. She was immediately taken to the small hospital in Argus, where, because no private rooms were available, she took a bed in the ward. There, surrounded by only two layers of tan drapes, in a noisy barracks of women recovering from various ills and minor surgeries, Eleanor at least could sleep.

In fact, she slept so profoundly that the doctors came in periodically to check that she had not slipped into a coma. But it was genuine sleep, the purest rest she'd had since childhood. The sound of talking soothed her, the clank of bedpans calmed her, the groans of other women in the dead of night lulled her into a deeper plateau of unconsciousness. When she woke, she swallowed the lukewarm Jell-O waiting on her tray. When she lay back, sleep stole immediately over her again, a warm blanket, smothering all thoughts.

She dreamed of water. Tons of water. Pounding, rushing her away.

In the end, the summer gone to heat and loneliness and sexual strain, the short growing season nearly finished, Eleanor simply rose, walked out of the ward and down a corridor,

where she used the patients' lounge telephone. She called Fargo
information and then dialed Jack Mauser, who wasn't home,
but in his absence she struck up an uncomfortable conversation
with his new wife, Dot, who expressed concern over Eleanor's
plight and promised that she would tell Jack where Eleanor
was as soon as he came home. A couple of days went by. Perhaps Jack hadn't received the message after all, Eleanor
thought, or perhaps the bitch never said a word. She tried to
control her thoughts, dialed and redialed his office number until
finally she got Mauser on the line.

"Jack."

"What's up?"

"I'm in the hospital. I was sick, but I'm well now. I need
someone to get me."

"Sure."

His voice so calm and full and deep that her heart pulsed
suddenly, as though a match were set to alcohol. He understood, she could feel it, he understood her completely with no
need for an explanation.

"What should I bring?"

"Stop at the liquor store," she managed to say. "Get a good
cabernet. With a cork, Jack. I'll pay you."

"Anything else?"

"A sandwich." Eleanor's mouth filled suddenly, her eyes
watered. "Oh god. Black pastrami, dark rye, hot mustard, and
a kosher pickle."

§

The Meadowlark

AUGUST 1994

Dot and Jack

"*I*f you'd only said something, Jack." Dot sounded more hurt than angry, at least at first, and that made Mauser wary. He still didn't know how to judge her moods, what might set her off, how exactly to placate her, but he knew enough to worry when her reaction was not immediate.

"When she called me I was floored. I didn't know what to say. You never told me about a first wife, Jack. Didn't you trust me?"

"I do trust you."

"Well then, tell me." Dot's voice jumped higher, shook with loose gravel. "What kind of man has a former wife who goes off to be a nun in a convent and has a nervous breakdown? What kind of man keeps in touch with her, takes her phone calls, buys her a twenty-dollar bottle of wine, bails her out?"

Mauser was almost reassured by the quick attack, hoping that would be the worst. He opened his mouth, but before the words came out, Dot answered herself.

"You do nice things for other people. I know that. You pay their bar tabs. You give flashy gifts." Dot waved the sparkle on her hand. "You built me a bookshelf out of rock maple for my new sci-fi books. You carved a plant stand. Now you're making Shawn a tennis racket."

Dot brooded, "We've been married, what, six weeks now? Laminating all those woods, learning how to string— It's kind of scary, Jack, you should be working on your—"

"Don't say it."

"Your tax stuff. With me. I'm starting to wonder what you wanted—a wife or a live-in accountant? Hey, if you would just stop *making* things. God knows what you made for this crazy wife you had! You can't keep track and you won't give anything up. At least Gerry is in jail for life. He can't bother you, call you. You don't know what it's like, how threatening an ex can be."

"Don't be threatened," said Mauser. "Come here."

Dot stood where she was, staring in a blind heat. She had sprayed her hair carefully that day to look both wild and free, and outlined her dark eyes with an exotic-looking shade. Her nose was large, strong, her lips carefully painted, her chin stubborn. Mauser went to her. She made her body wooden. He stepped closer and put his arms around her.

"Don't be threatened," he repeated, in a gentler tone. "You can even come along. Would that make you happy?"

"Happy? Not exactly, no."

Mauser kept holding her until she shrugged him off.

"What can I do? Tell me. In your mind, what can I do?"

Dot hugged herself and looked at the ground. She ran her hands up and down the buttons of her shirt.

"Tell your ex-wife where to get off."

Jack just looked at her.

"You asked," Dot challenged. "What were you going to bribe me with? At least we know for sure it wouldn't be cash."

Instead of the interstate, they took the old highway out of Fargo, main headquarters of Jack's company. It was a good road with swelling curves and deep ditches full of grass. Occasionally, a pheasant flashed by, a killdeer swooped from its nest. The wheat waved, heavy-headed, glowing in the fields. Tall white egrets paced along the far edges, a blue heron or two; blackbirds gathering to plunder exploded upward in great sudden disintegrating spirals, their pattern shattering and swirling in the clear air. About halfway to Argus, a lark flew at them, flashed yellow, disappeared. Mauser started, slowed, looked into the rearview mirror, then settled back.

"I think I missed it." He grinned nervously at his wife.

Dot looked at him. Her gradient-style sunglasses made her face remote and tough. "Tell me one thing," she said. "Was it better, I mean, way back when? Better with her?"

"Christ, Dot, what do you want me to say?"

Dot picked up a pair of knitting needles and began jabbing them in and out of a pastel froth of yarn. She cleared her throat impatiently and then threw the project to the floor of the car.

"'No,'" she said. "I want you to say to me 'no.'"

"No," said Mauser.

"Thank you. Thank you very much."

The hospital was redbrick with white gables and wooden porches. The large asphalt lot overlooked a swift-flowing, narrow brown river. Jack swung into a parking space, and they both got out. Dot stretched her arms over her head and swung her hips back and forth. Jack went around the front of the car to check the grille.

"Hell, I did get it," he said after a moment.

The meadowlark was tucked where the bumper met the curve of red metal. There was no visible damage—in fact the small bird looked natural and comfortable, as though perched asleep, its wings folded flat on either side of the black V, along the yellow of its breast.

"You sure did." Dot scooped the bird from the car in one quick motion, carried it over to the trash can by the sidewalk, and tossed it in.

"Hey," Mauser called to his wife. "You can't just throw a bird away like that."

"Hey, you're the one who hit it." Dot looked at him suspiciously. "Since when would that bother you?"

Since always, Jack wanted to say, but he'd been saying that too much lately and besides, the clarity he'd felt in the few weeks just after making love to Eleanor was starting to muddy and fade. He loved her. There was no doubt. He also loved, or cared for, Dot. What should he do now? Here he was, in the presence of two wives with only a bottle of wine and one sandwich between them. Too late, he realized that he should also have bought something for Dot; she was always hungry.

"What's that?" She nodded at the bag in his hand as they walked toward the hospital. Jack hummed evasively, looking into Dot's eyes for response, hoping she would laugh at the absurdity of it all, but she didn't soften. She asked him again. "Jack, what's in that bag?" He pretended not to hear her and glanced around, uncertain. The ground was tarred, with carefully painted white lines. The sidewalks were bounded by thick mats of clipped tan grass. There was nowhere, actually, to have put a bird, no turned earth—not that he'd want to bury it, but the thing was, he didn't know exactly what he should have done. As they walked through the clear double doors of the place, Mauser took shallow breaths of stale white hospital air. Even the elevator smelled of last-ditch medicines.

"One thing I don't want to do," he told Dot suddenly, thinking of it for the first time as the elevator doors squeezed shut and they ascended. "I don't want to die in a hospital."

She looked at him assessingly. "Who does?"

"I mean it. I'd rather die anywhere else than in a hospital."

"Okay," said Dot. "You got it. Now let's pick up the fruitcake and bring her back to the convent."

"I don't think she wants to go back to the convent," Jack paused, looking away from Dot.

"Where then?" Dot stepped into his line of vision. The elevator parted with a clunk and Jack moved away, walking swiftly. Once on the ward, they approached the desk and

Mauser identified himself. The nurse regarded them searchingly.

"Will Mrs. Mauser be leaving us, then?"

"Yes," said Jack. "We're driving her back to Fargo."

The woman's expression lightened, and she lifted a stack of papers into her arms.

"I knew it!" said Dot. "Fuck!" She exploded, then tried to contain herself. "We're taking her off your hands, anyway," she said to the nurse. The woman lifted her eyebrows and smiled.

"Here she is!"

With a flourish, the nurse swept aside the curtains that hung around the hospital bed. Curled on the smooth coverlet, her back propped on pillows and a pile of books beside her, Eleanor waited. Instead of a hospital gown, she wore a deep, red satin slip. She had lost weight. Her face was gaunt, the stern lines deeper carved. Her rough black German hair curved off her forehead and her eyes burned deep in the sockets.

"God, am I ever glad to see you," she said to Mauser, eyeing the brown bag in his arms. "Hi," she nodded to Dot.

"Hi," Dot answered in a shrill, automatic voice. She put her hands slowly on her hips when Jack drew from the paper bag in question a neatly wrapped deli sandwich, a plastic bag with a pickle in it. But then, Eleanor hardly looked like a rival and Dot felt ashamed of herself. In spite of her fierce glare at the nurse, Jack's ex-wife seemed pitiable. Her thinness was almost shocking, her face so fragile that her teeth stood out. The expression in her great cat eyes was so penetrating that Dot felt invaded, uncomfortable. She shuddered when Jack offered Eleanor the sandwich and the woman snatched at it with greedy claws.

"Let me help you. Here."

Dot moved to the side of the bed as soon as Eleanor bolted the food down.

"Oh that's so good, Jack, *so good*."

Her croon was truly pathetic in its gratitude and Dot

looked away. Here was a woman who hadn't eaten for a long time. Probably she was fasting, something Dot had never, ever understood. Jack uncorked the bottle, poured a little of the wine into a plastic glass beside the bed. Eleanor tasted it with a slow, grateful pursing of her lips that Dot couldn't bear. She leaned away from the two and called to the nurse. "A wheelchair?"

The nurse approached.

"Alcoholic beverages are not to be consumed in the hospital," she admonished, then disappeared.

Jack corked the bottle again. The nurse brought back a wheelchair and then Dot led them through the process of signing out. Eleanor completed release papers and Jack gathered her things. Then the three made their way down the hall. Mauser maneuvered the car to the door, and Dot helped settle Eleanor into the backseat. She tucked an old wool stadium blanket beneath one of Eleanor's arms, and leaned across to buckle her seat belt.

"You're kind to take the trouble." Eleanor looked curiously into Dot's face. "How do you get your eyeliner on so smoothly? It's perfect."

Dot felt Eleanor's sharp, hot breath on her neck. She paused, their faces only inches apart.

"I use a little paintbrush." Dot's voice choked. Eleanor blinked calmly at her, and Dot walked around to get in the front seat beside Mauser.

"She's wonderful," Eleanor was saying as Dot settled herself. "You're very lucky, Jack, I hope you know that. I hope you're taking good care of her, not just in material ways, either. It's clear you made the right choice. I can't tell you how I worried. Congratulations."

"You worried?" Dot looked back over her shoulder as they pulled out of the lot.

Eleanor frowned slightly, nodded, met her eyes in guileless complicity. By the time she answered, they had turned onto the main highway.

"Of course I did. After Marlis?"

"Who's Marlis?" Dot leaned across the seat, her profile keen and motionless as a bird dog's. "What's she talking about?"

"Or don't you know about Marlis? Jack?"

Jack reached over as if to turn on the air-conditioning, but then put his hand back on the wheel with a decisive motion. There was a long beat of silence in the car. The two women hardly breathed.

"I was going to tell you, at the right time," Mauser said at last. "See, there was another wife."

"What do you mean?" Dot spoke slowly, stupid with surprise. She twisted in the web of her seat belt. "Before Eleanor?"

"No. After. It was very short."

"You bastard."

Eleanor put her hands in her lap, and tried to look out the window without glancing toward the rearview mirror, which, she knew, held Mauser's white glare.

"I shouldn't have said anything."

"Shut up, Eleanor," said Mauser.

But Eleanor continued talking as they picked up speed. "Jack met her at a time when he wasn't thinking with a great deal of clarity. Of course," she added, after a pause, speaking over Dot's shoulder, "Jack was absolutely rational by the time he met you, I'm sure."

"Fuck you," said Dot. "And you call yourself a nun."

"You might as well get it done with." Jack spoke loudly, desperately, taking both hands off the wheel. He rammed them back again before the car veered into the ditch. "Tell her everything. Wreck this one too, Eleanor. Why not? You did a tap dance on the others."

"Others?"

Dot swiveled to the backseat, her skin hard and tight beneath her careful makeup, her eyes sharp as darts. "Since he won't tell me, you tell me. Tell me about the others."

"I'll tell you. What do you want to know?" said Mauser.

"How many, first of all?"

"Five." He spoke quickly, before Eleanor could answer. "Five counting you."

"Five? I'm the goddamn fifth?"

Dot tossed her head to the side, as if she had been slapped, then hunched over, seemed to gather herself in, but suddenly exploded in motion. She jabbed her arms down near her legs into the foamy yarn of her knitting bag and pulled out a thin blue metal needle. Mauser saw the flash of it in her hands and ducked forward, wrenching the wheel just as Dot plunged at him, grazing his neck, sinking the needle deeply into the back cushion of his seat. She unfastened herself and began to rummage in the yarn again.

"Jesus!" Mauser cried. "Stop her!"

Eleanor lunged over the backseat and tried to buckle herself around Dot, but Dot easily unlatched her pinched arms. Mauser stopped the car in the breakdown lane. The brakes shrieked. He grabbed for Dot's wrists.

"Calm down," he said. "Get hold of yourself. I was going to tell you—Dot, I was—but I was scared you'd react this way."

"Scared? You were scared? Listen. I have got to know." Dot's eyes were staring, bold. "Are there any children?"

Slowly, keeping his eyes from meeting Eleanor's in the rearview, Mauser nodded.

"How many?"

"One."

"Boy or girl?" It was Eleanor asking.

"A son," Jack said.

"A son?" cried Eleanor. "A baby? Whose?"

Jack turned, his eyes pleading. He took his hand off Dot's wrist and touched Eleanor's face.

"Quit that!" Dot said.

Jack turned back to Dot.

"Turn back around," yelled Eleanor, determined. "Face me! Explain!"

Jack sat staring straight ahead.

The tightness left Dot's face, gradually, and her fingers relaxed. She dropped the second needle. In the backseat, eyes spilling over, lips trembling, Eleanor filled the plastic hospital cup with cabernet and drank it in two gulps, then wiped the edge of her mouth on her sleeve, gazed into her lap.

"I'm still the same guy you married," Mauser said to Dot.

"No you're not." Dot tore away from him. "I don't know you from shit." She turned her back entirely and looked out the side window, resting her forehead against the window glass.

"He's the same man I married, though," said Eleanor from the back. "No difference whatsoever."

No one said anything for a long time after that, and then, finally, Mauser started the car and pulled out onto the road. He began to go faster, faster, up to the speed limit, then past it. The seams in the concrete road struck the wheels hard and angrily. On either side, fields of ripening sunflowers, their heads black and drooping, turned like chains, blurring into the dusk.

"Well, you know what I always say," Mauser said at last, his voice ripping the hum of the air pocket the car moved within.

Nobody asked what he always said, so he shouted.

"I say something simpleminded like 'Let's listen to a little music.'" He slammed a tape into the slot above the radio and a man's velvety hoarse voice looped slowly out. *I'm staring at the wishing well, looking up at a falling star.*

Jack couldn't resist the urge to try his charm or block the women out and he began to sing along with the tape, but as he started a sexy wail Dot punched the eject button, opened her window, extracted the tape, and tossed it into the flowing grass of a ditch. She closed the window, palmed another tape from the side pocket under her armrest, and pushed it into the machine.

"I want girl music," she said, and soon the smoky voice on *Rumble Doll* filled the interior air of the car.

It was not for quite a while, not until the first side of the tape came to an end, in fact, that Mauser noticed, in the interval before the second side began, that both women were weeping steadily and wrenchingly, behind him, beside him, in his own throat, with the same unceasing rhythm and regularity as the sound of pavement breaking against the wheels.

Their weeping did not abate, but continued at the same level of intensity once the tape played out, mile after mile. It was a sighing, beating, tidal sound, and its regular wash filled the hurtling car with subterranean rich echoes that seemed to spur the women on. They wept in unison, they wept in alternate harmonies, they wept as one. They wept themselves into another time, another place, another state of memory. They changed hearts, changed faces, wept with eagerness, persistence, until they came to the outskirts of Fargo, at which point they both stopped, abruptly, and allowed the heavy swish of air to fill the car.

Mauser had been irritated but comfortable with their weeping. *Over me*, he thought. But now, against his left temple, as if it were fixed in telescopic crosshairs, Mauser felt the cocked intelligence of their sudden, dry, and critical gazes.

"What do you want to hear?" he loudly asked.

Neither answered. He knew he was in trouble. "Any requests?"

It wasn't as though they had decided to stonewall him, but rather, that they couldn't be bothered, at that moment, to so much as register the sound of his voice, for they were transforming, reconfiguring themselves. They were becoming a different animal, Jack thought, one he didn't like. He shifted helplessly in his seat.

"Come on," he coaxed. "Talk to me. Ask yourselves this question: Have I ever hurt you on purpose? Either of you? Have I?"

It didn't seem to matter, now, whether he spoke to one or both of them. The weeping had fused unseen connections, circuits had clicked into place, their stories matched cadence by cadence. He wanted to stop the car, to get out and run, to abandon the increasingly forceful complexity beside and behind him. There was a science experiment. Lumps of coal. With the right mixture of chemicals, colored crystals grew on the black surfaces. Blue, white, red, they formed link on link into stacks and cones of intricate needle-tipped bright shapes. It was happening. By the time they got to Mauser's house, he knew that he was in the car with something else, a different shape, alien, brilliant, ultra-female, something he didn't want to look at. He pulled into the driveway, stopped, carefully got out, and walked into the new subdivision house. Only when he was safely behind a window did he look back.

Nothing at all, for a few moments, then Dot, who emerged and opened the door to help Eleanor, shaky but not so weak anymore. She emerged from the backseat, held out both of her hands. It seemed an ordinary gesture and Jack relaxed, took a deep breath, imagining perhaps that he'd been oversensitive. All was normal, he hoped, watching them, or normal enough at any rate. He kept on hoping until Dot clasped Eleanor's hands and spoke. Eleanor looked straight into Dot's face, and then the two of them suddenly laughed hard, together, still holding hands.

Jack knew he was lost.

The next morning, early, Dot wrapped herself in the old brown bathrobe she'd had since she was a girl and went downstairs. Maybe Jack had sneaked into Eleanor's room, slept there. The house was so big she'd never know—still, did she really care? Jack had given Dot a golden silky robe, but Dot couldn't stand the flimsy feel of the material now, the insubstantial weight. She padded in thick socks to the kitchen, sat down in a bar of radiance at the counter of eggshell-pale Formica. Her daughter soon would hear her and come down from her room to eat her favorite foods—toasted bagels, sweet pink cranberry muffins that Dot bought in plastic trays from the supermarket. Dot drank two thin cups and prepared to talk. Her coppery dark hair sprang from her head like blasting wire, and her face was round, both hard and soft. Her body had a wrestler's powerful and cheerful density, but her eyes were sharply sad and coffee brown.

Thirteen-year-old Shawn came in and slumped beside her

mother. She was big, athletic too, and stubbornly resisting adolescence. She clearly preferred being a tomboy and clung to her tattered Indiana Jones pajamas, her worn canvas basketball sneakers. Shawn's brown hair gleamed, straight as her father Gerry's. Her skin was pale olive, her eyes watchful. This morning, she was pouting because Dot had removed the television dials with a pair of pliers and dropped them into her purse. Bored, she'd spent her morning pounding a block of clay into the shape of her own face. Her art project was supposed to be a self-portrait, but because her personal concept changed every day Shawn was frustrated. Some days she was huge, fit for a monument. Others, she was a bug, disgusting, easy to squash. Today, she wasn't even a girl, if she could help it. Her breasts hurt, growing from the inside out, one faster than the other. She'd be a freak, anyway, why fight it? She had bashed her clay image on the table and then, fascinated, sculpted a voluptuous Barbie self out of it for the past hour. Now, she was in a much better mood. She was even happy, so overjoyed in fact that it didn't kill her to be nice.

"Thanks, Mom," she acknowledged the pink muffins.

Her daughter's kindness always touched Dot. She herself had gone through phases that she dreaded meeting in her daughter. She had worked hard to make Shawn as much unlike her younger self as possible. Rude to her mother, hopeless in her dress, smoking constantly, Dot had lost her virginity too early and maybe damaged her self-esteem. Otherwise she'd have a better job, she thought. Maybe she would not have stuck so long to Gerry's memory, or gotten involved with the men she had since, like Caryl Moon and now, even Jack. She was starting to understand him too well, since yesterday.

Jack appeared at the door—shaggy, big, shirtless, in belted jeans. His chest was slightly tanned from summer outdoor work; a few hairs sprang above his sternum and his nipples were pale and pink, fine as a young girl's. His stomach stretched down beneath his belt, still tough with muscle. He was proud of it.

"Punch me there," he pointed.

Shawn doubled up her fist, the middle knuckle jabbing higher than the rest, cocked back her arm, and connected.

"Right in the gut," she cried.

"Hurt your hand?" Jack mocked.

"Don't teach her that stuff," Dot said.

She took a quick drink of coffee, tamped back that question about Eleanor sneaking through the house. The poor woman could hardly walk. And it made no sense at all, but right then she felt jealous for Gerry's daughter on behalf of Gerry. As she watched the two joust and spar, the girl tumbling eagerly at Jack, and Jack catching, the two teasing and feint-fighting, tripping and catching each other in the big square living room with the built-in brick hearth, her stomach hollowed and she felt a surge of loneliness run through her, a watery weakness that made her eyes sting with tears.

She tried to look past her feelings, and focused on the fireplace. She tried to imagine the pleasant fires she would light come winter. She tried to find delight in the big new house that Jack had said he built for her—a lie—what she felt best at doing was leaving it, anyway locking it safe behind her, not having to worry about the paint, the floor, the scratchable porcelain, the groaning refrigerator, and the easily spotted bathroom mirrors.

Jack avoided a conversation and left quickly for the accounts office. Dot dressed, checked to see if Eleanor was up. She wasn't. Dot took her daughter to the grocery store, bought her shoes, dropped her off at a friend's house, where she'd sleep over. She had two pictures framed, one of her mother, one of Shawn. She had photos developed from a day they had spent in Manitoba, and then, she wasn't sure why, she simply could not go back to her house with a car trunk full of bags and completed errands. She both wanted and didn't want to see Eleanor. She stalled. She drove around and around Fargo making small deals, buying fabrics, doing unenthusiastic early Christmas shopping, eating, drinking more coffee. She saw a movie at the Cineplex, lingered in a bookstore, found herself sitting on a bench by the Red River watching it flow—contrary to known natural laws and common sense and most other rivers—due north.

❊   ❊   ❊

When Eleanor woke from her endless sleep, she prowled the whole place, restless, checked through closets and looked in mirrors. Where was everybody? Sitting at the long kitchen counter, she drank a glass of juice. The house was silent, lovely in its off-white perfection and newness. Everything matched everything else so perfectly that the magic overlay of one object on the next almost hypnotized her. Contemplating the furniture of her ex-husband and his new wife, she lost track of time.

I'm desolate, she suddenly thought, and was disappointed that such melodramatic-sounding words had formed in her own head, even after the hospital, sleep, the healing Jell-O. She felt that her eyes were terribly alert, watching to see if someone else had heard her thoughts. She sat up straight, as though something was going to happen. There wasn't even a clock ticking, no brush of wind outside, no sound. She pushed back her hair and took her small notebook from her purse. She called her mother, though in spite of Dot she wanted to stay near Jack. No answer. She called her father's business number, got his carefully trained, professionally sympathetic receptionist at the mortuary, but hung up. She slid the glass doors aside and went out to stand on the redwood deck. Outside, clear air quickened, cooled, came to life.

A wooden chaise lounge. Eleanor sat down in the comfortable old thing, slumped into huge tattered pillows patterned with leaves and flowers. It was the only thing in the house that wasn't new. Maybe Jack, more likely Dot, had found it at a yard sale. Eleanor dragged a hand-crocheted afghan off the couch and brought it outside. She pulled it over herself, and watched the sun strengthen over the greening pond that gave off the thin odor of chlorine and dead bait. In her notebook, she began to write directions to herself. *Talk to new wife, "Dot," gather self, put all the jigsaw puzzle pieces of emotion back in box. Mail the box by surface mail, slow, back to apartment in Minneapolis. Deal with emotions when box arrives.* She felt better. Her love was there, but fury burned through it. *I love him but there's something missing in him. Coward, he's a coward!* She decided. *I'm leaving.*

The dredged murk reflected a pink and gold sunset, a raft of burning clouds. Jack had hauled a million tons of pebbles, stabilized the gumbo with rocks and brick and planted tough grass on top. On the surface, rippling bands of dark blue and silver light broke and refracted as, very slowly, the sun was absorbed by a low wall of slate-gray clouds.

Viewed just at dusk and with her nose pinched shut, Jack's little lake might be very pretty to contemplate. Drawing a shallow breath, Eleanor leaned back into the heavy pillows. Her eyes closed, weighted like a doll's. When she awakened, it was much later. The stars seemed to have swung down close to her face. No street lamps shone in the ghostly subdivision—they were not yet connected. Behind her, the house itself seemed to sigh and shift its bones as the furnace came to life and hot water sighed in the baseboard heaters. A huge weight lay on her chest, a weight of nothingness. She couldn't breathe normally, as though she hadn't the strength anymore to fully take in or push out all of the sadness. Her love for Jack was still alive, disguised as everything. It ached pulled from the ground, it drew the air from her chest, sat on her head like bricks, closed across her lips like the wings of a moth.

It was later still when Dot returned, her step heavy and deliberate in the garage entry. She was sorry that her daughter was staying overnight at a friend's house because she needed the distraction of a child's presence. Eleanor drifted inside and the two immediately sat down together at the kitchen counter. Dot took ironware mugs from her cupboard, ground decaf beans, and poured fresh water into the well of her coffeemaker, all in silence. She set down spoons, plates, a pottery cream pitcher. Sugar in a beehive-shaped sugar bowl.

"My parents live in Fargo," Eleanor said finally, apologetic. "My father runs Schlick's Funeral Home. My mother and I are . . . well, close but too close sometimes, maybe. The usual power struggle." She laughed halfheartedly. "I haven't got her on the phone, not just yet. I do need a ride into town, that is, if you wouldn't mind."

"You don't have to go." Dot sat across from her, clicked her spoon on the table. Her face was pallid and heavy. "Don't run on account of me."

"Why not?"

Eleanor couldn't look at Dot, kept tracing the smooth edge of the counter where the Corian was so carefully finished. "You're married to him. I'm not even his most recent ex-wife. I don't know what's wrong with me—what I said to you in the car, it was inappropriate. I have to, I should, apologize."

"Apologize then."

Eleanor's roundabout way of speaking annoyed Dot, but then, Jack had said last night she was a teacher. Or something.

"I'm sorry," Eleanor said, after a slight pause.

Dot shrugged, then her manner lifted. Forgiveness came easy with her. "It was Jack's fault. He should have told me, right? He set me up. He lied."

"Lies of omission, of indirectness." Eleanor mused out loud. "Are all lies embroidered stories or just the absence of truth?"

"Whatever," said Dot. "I should have known, I mean it isn't as though I didn't have an idea that something was off. He got along so well with Shawn though."

"Kids," said Eleanor. "I had no idea he had a baby by that brain-dead Lolita, Marlis. That was a blow straight to the solar plexus."

Dot looked at her curiously. "A kick in the gut," she finally agreed, shrugging. "My mother likes him. I don't know why. She's usually got a seventh sense about men."

Eleanor glanced up now, sharply, her eyes alert. "Your mother likes him?"

"Turns out they're sort of related and I didn't know it. I should have known a lot more about Jack before I married him. See, it's just that I've been without my real husband for such a long time. He's in prison."

"Too bad," Eleanor said, wanting to ask more. "Sorry about that." She waited, hoping Dot would go on, explain, tell what her "real" husband had done and where he was locked up. Dot was beginning to interest her and Eleanor's hand itched for her notebook, left outside in the folds of the afghan. *Must remember to retrieve it.*

Eleanor asked some leading questions about the first husband, but got nowhere. For her part, Dot had never known anyone connected to a funeral home and she was intrigued. She wondered whether or not they brought the bodies to the house, whether it was disturbing, but she didn't know how to phrase her questions. It might be rude to ask anything at all. Still, she tried turning the conversation again and again to Eleanor's parents and Eleanor kept deflecting by referring obliquely to Dot's first husband, until at last Eleanor tacked quickly over to Jack.

"You met him, how again?" Eleanor inquired as though she already knew and had temporarily forgotten.

Dot sat back. "You first," she said, for, it was true, that question was a bridge, a marker in their conversation. It gave them something in common and somehow lessened Jack's importance, as though he were a minor character in both of their larger and ongoing dramas.

"I knew him for a long time," said Eleanor. "I guess that you might say"—and here she gave a peculiar laugh, and her face shadowed—"he was a friend of my mother's."

Dot nodded at this and seemed satisfied with the picture. In her mind, Eleanor's father was thin, cavernous, and somber and Eleanor's mother . . . who knew what type of women married undertakers?

"Outrageous," Eleanor muttered, as though to answer her. "My mother is an utterly outrageous woman. She's exhausting. Too much for me. Too much for herself. She's sick now, a weak heart." Eleanor paused, remembered. "She used to embarrass me. You know, she was an acrobat once. Who has an acrobat for a mother? A performer?"

Who has an undertaker for a dad? thought Dot, but she said nothing. Eleanor went on.

"Most people like my mother, they don't have children. Yet she had me. Precocious in the wrong ways. I learned to read when I was three years old, but I can't even do a cartwheel. No balance."

The coffeemaker hissed and spat the last drops of the brewing pot and Dot rose, poured Eleanor's mug full, pushed the sugar and milk toward her. She filled her own cup, returned the pot to the warm plate on the machine, and then rummaged in the lower shelf for cookies, a cupcake or two, those pink muffins, a chunk of banana bread, all of which she arranged and set before Eleanor, whose hand reached before the plate even met the table.

"Did she work in a circus or what?" asked Dot.

Eleanor shook her head, threw wide her hands as though exasperated, but she was secretly proud. "I guess. Sort of a crummy circus. After she did the trapeze act she ran backstage and put on the lion-tamer outfit, grabbed her whip. I don't think the lion had any teeth. But really, I don't know where to start with Anna. Maybe you should tell me about Jack."

"Like what?"

"How you met him."

Dot gazed long from the sides of her eyes at Eleanor, and did not withdraw her look for an uncomfortable space of moments. She laughed, short. "He tried to kill my boyfriend."

Eleanor nodded encouragingly, as though the statement was no surprise to her, but she itched for her notebook and at her eager look Dot continued.

"Not really boyfriend, I guess. Caryl Moon is just this guy. A problem. Jack was jealous." When Eleanor's glance did fall, Dot gave a maddened shake of her head, an irritable and resigned swift shudder.

§

Caryl Moon

"**Y**ou have to know Caryl Moon not to like him, that's the thing," Dot began, crumbs sifting from her fingers. "People who first meet him, women especially, think they've met a man worth meeting. His mustache is so *trimmed*, pale brown-blond. He has this reassuring voice. Christlike eyes, clear as scorched butter."

Dot spread flat the pleated paper that had held her muffin, then balled it up. "So Caryl tries to buy me a drink on a night I need one, telling me, *you shouldn't be alone*, his favorite line among many. He likes to lay it on heavy. I've just started my job at Mauser and Mauser and already noticed Caryl Moon. He always wears a clean T-shirt, new-looking, pressed. His forearms are tanned and muscular, the left one tanner from poking out the truck window."

"May I ask where your husband is keeping himself?"
I tell him, although he knows.
"He's innocent." Caryl is so uncharacteristically blunt and sincere I sort of believe him, or at least appreciate that someone

cares enough to put on the act. Mauser and Mauser is the first job I ever held in Fargo.

"I wouldn't insult you by transparently hitting on you, I swear," he says. He lifts one hand, looks at me, all solemn.

"And I'm not going to do anything stupid," I tell him.

He puts down his hand and ducks his head, cranes toward me as though he is looking into a small dark room.

"To be honest ..." He rubs his eyes to adjust his vision, and then puts his fingers to his brow. "I was desperately hoping that you would."

"I do appreciate you coming over," I say. "Really, the beer and all. But anyway, what's new with you? With Mauser?"

All of a sudden Caryl Moon looks depressed. His shirt wrinkles as his shoulders slump. The expression on his face sags. The lines along his mouth deepen and his mouth pinches.

"You might say I'd like to kill the guy," he confides. "Or you might say worse. I can't stand the type. Military minded. Do this. Do that."

"Well, Jack is your boss," I point out.

Caryl looks at me, all puzzled, like what does that have to do with it?

Then he says, in a hushed tone, glancing to either side, "My dear lady, do you *know* about him?"

I almost take the bait and then decide, no, if I start talking about the boss, taking him apart, it will never quit.

"Gossip sucks," I tell Caryl, turning my back.

See what being high-minded gets you into, what shit?

Mauser and Caryl have reached a kind of stalemate. Their horns are locked, they paw themselves deeper into the earth. Mauser has the edge some days, and Caryl's purchase on their turf improves on others. From the outside, the match seems hardly even—I suppose you know. Jack has this streak, a crazy streak, a temper, a flash point.

I joke about liking Caryl before I find out that he's really a laid-back good-time boy with a stupid sentimental streak, self-consciously flowery bullshit lines, high school basketball trophies collecting dust on the TV, and girlfriends, lots of those, besides his wife. Jack has hired Caryl out of some unpaid debt to Caryl's father, the lawyer Maynard Moon. Jack keeps Caryl working where he can keep an eye on him, even though Caryl's only job is to haul gravel, asphalt, sand, whatever is needed. Caryl has this phony eagerness. He makes himself look busy, jumping in and out of the cab, kicking tires, talking long, hard, fast. But by the end of the day, without fail, he has always hauled by many tons the least amount. He would not have lasted a week anywhere else. Jack knows this fact, and hates it.

Jack's candy-apple red Cadillac—you ever see it? The only thing in this world he seems at the time to love. It raises a gray plume of spring dust that hangs in the air, turns ruddy, pink, reflects the morning sky. Everybody, even the payroll clerks, starts work while it is still night and doesn't quit long into evening dark. The push is on. There is so much to do just after thaw that my job is enough to think about. It's the best time of the year, in many ways, for Jack, who forces his Caddy to tricks of quick driving, managing, raging from site to site, screaming at what's to be done as contract deadlines approach.

For Caryl, of course, this time of the year is worst. No one has time to shoot the shit. There's panic in the air. No time to sit and smoke or to drink a Pepsi from the cooler on the passenger's side of Caryl's truck. People keep their ears cocked, their heads turned. Mauser spins out of nowhere, at any time, like Batman or something, a streak of dust and fire.

I do a good job, so I never run foul of him. He and Caryl can kill each other and be done with it, for all that I care.

My office is at the far end of a trailer. I practically have my own bathroom and nobody bothers me past nine, which is when I shut my door to drink my coffee and stare into the screen of my computer. It is maybe noon, a day I am far into the payroll, when the trailer bounces on its concrete blocks and in walks Caryl.

"Can I be straight with you?" he asks. I'm always taken in when Caryl pretends to can the shit. I try to resist, though.

"Not if you want your paycheck."

"I don't care. Here."

He takes a short chain from his pocket, bends forward, takes my wrist and snaps it on. There is a charm attached to the bracelet, a little silver bird. I look at the thing as it rests on my wrist. It is the kind of gesture that just stops you. As I hesitate, Caryl leans over and he puts his lips right where a doctor takes your pulse. I spread my fingers wide and push his face away.

"Get out of here!"

But I keep the charm. It's a *charm*, you know? It helps to have Caryl, so attractive on the outside, turn his attentions on me.

"This thing was stamped like a million others from a piece of tin." I tell this to Shawn that night when I take it off, actually wanting her to admire it. That backfires.

"He's cheap, Mom," she warns me, peering close.

Still, the next morning, before work, I put it back on, saying to myself it means nothing. But from the moment Caryl sees me wearing the little bird, he starts making moves on me. Starts posing. When he knows Mauser isn't anywhere in range he kills the engine of his truck, gets out, stretches. He always does this in front of the window of the accounts trailer. He makes sure to stand within a woman's gaze because it magnifies him, warms him. He feeds, like a bee on syrup, on female admiration.

Given all that, why do I find myself thinking about Caryl Moon? Why, the day before Mauser comes around to check the weights and measurements and sign the paychecks, do I protect Moon? Without letting him know, I change his tonnage. I make him look useful. It is a kind of insurance that he stick around. I do this even though I know the yellow copy of the unchanged original is already over in the files in downtown Fargo. Files that sit around in cardboard boxes or serve as coffee tables, true, but files that are official records.

It gets bad. I wake up in the middle of the night, hungry. Shawn and I are living in an apartment complex by the river. I walk downstairs and open the refrigerator and stare into the cold, bright box thinking of Caryl Moon. Those deep brown eyes, sad, misunderstood, but of course I could light them up. Those smooth arms loaded with muscles. How does he get strong? He never lifts anything.

I am reaching for the milk one night, a glass to calm me down and put me back to sleep, when the phone rings.

I let it ring. But it sounds so loud, so unreal, that I pick it up and hold the receiver carefully to my ear.

"Please, I've got to see you."

"Fine," I say. "Tomorrow."

My voice shakes as I put down the receiver. I wait. It rings again.

"Now," says Caryl.

Is it like I thought it would be? Worse. It is better. For me, those hours are like floating before you've learned how to swim. As long as I hold my breath and stretch out my arms and legs, I stay up. But when I need to breathe I sink in a panic.

"I'm not a person who can afford to get hurt," I tell Caryl.

He turns toward me in a sleep that I know is fake. I lean over him and pin his arm down and speak into his face.

"Don't you hurt me."

"Lay off, baby. You're hurting *me*."

Do I imagine Caryl settling down and us joining till death do us part? No. I just want the chance to touch someone until I can hold Gerry again, to have the pleasure and not the illusions. They are there all the same, though. Somehow I've got it in my head that I mean something to Caryl Moon. Because it can happen. Clichés in love songs. Roses. Violets. Little tin birds. Sometimes, you can't think fast enough to keep that sort of thing from getting to you.

I am in my office around ten, waiting for the boss. I hear the steps, the door opens, but it is Caryl with a can of cold soda-pop in his hand.

"What do you want?"

I'm nervous, shut the door behind him.

Caryl puts the can on my desk and then comes around the side to pick me up. He wants to put me on the desktop. But I slump down, unwilling. He tries to pull me up, to push me, but it's lots of trouble and when I resist he starts to pant with the effort.

"Come on. Help."

I laugh, then I hear the set of footsteps that for sure belong to Mauser, and I twist sideways.

"Let go!"

He doesn't. He holds me in front of him and puts his hands on me, looking over my shoulder in expectation, which is when I see he has decided on the spur of the moment to use me to get to Mauser. I am a prop, a plastic blow-up companion, a partner easily disposed of. His real relationship is not with me, or maybe any woman, but with Mauser, who's like a brick wall.

The door opens. I punch my fists against Caryl so hard he grins in shock. Then I kick. At once, Caryl falls away, doubles over in the corner of the room. I whirl around but the door has shut and already I can hear the red Cadillac accelerating. I don't look at Caryl. I sit down at my desk and rub my arms. They feel bruised and sore, and I am anxious, so very tired. A wave of weariness washes through, the sudden urge to sink against the desk, and it is all I can do to keep sitting upright.

"A thousand pardons." Caryl stands behind me. "It was an immature joke."

He puts his hands on my shoulders, begins to knead the muscles of my back. He leans over, puts his hand on the desk for balance. I grab it like a sandwich and bite down, hard.

"Christ," he cries, shocked, wringing his palm to his cheek.

"That was a joke, too."

Jack fires me fair and square, I'll give him that. He goes back through the files and finds the figures that I've falsified in Caryl's favor. The notice is on my desk on Thursday morning.

Be gone by one. I leave at eleven. I am on the road leading from
the site when I see Caryl's truck approach. I can see it clearly.
The cab is yellow and green, crop colors, garish.

I have a small car, a compact, but I move onto the middle
of the road. I'm not so different from Mauser, or from you,
either. You can drive me past a limit too. This feeling has been
building in me the past two days, a fever that makes me throw
things at the wall and slam the door of the refrigerator so hard
the seal pops. Now everything feels right. It is the moment, I
decide. Caryl Moon has had things too easy in life so far. I jam
my foot on the gas, and keep going. The colors of his truck
blur. The road goes by. Fields. Then we are too close. The
grille of the truck looms and Caryl lays on the horn. I keep my
hands steady on the wheel, lock my ankle, and just like I know
he will, Caryl takes the ditch with a full load of gravel.

"Just a minute," Eleanor stops Dot, puts up her hands,
palms out. "Dot," she says slowly, "let me hear this again. I
want to try to understand what you've just told me. At that
moment you—a grown woman with a dependent child—
decide to play chicken, in a compact car, with a Mack truck?"
"Yes."
"All right, I see."
"What do you mean, 'I see'? What did you stop me for?"
"It's just that . . . how shall I put this? You're nuts."
"Yeah," says Dot, "I guess."

Anyway, Caryl takes the ditch and hangs up on the far
incline. I see this once I stop and remember to breathe. I get
out and walk back. He was traveling slow enough to negotiate
the down side, but the ground is soft where water had collected a month ago, at the bottom of the ditch. His back wheels
sink into that hard muck just enough to keep him stuck where
he is—so he can't escape from Jack's Cadillac, spinning its
plume out at a distance. Approaching fast.

Caryl and I look at each other across the mud and grass.
There is plenty of time to talk, but not enough to think of what

to say. We hear Mauser screaming from his open window before the car is in hailing distance, and then, at the crossroads, Mauser drives down into the shallow ditch. He rides its bottom carefully, straddling the dry edges until he gets to Caryl's truck and swings right up beside it on the driver's side. He jumps out with a crowbar in his fist.

You ever see a thunderhead building in the sky? That blistering rose color? Or a boot camp sergeant in a bad movie? Jack, mad, is a combination. He's a natural disaster mixed with dumb old saws. Dangerous. His voice pops and sings in three pitches. His face goes purple and his neck bulges from the collar of his shirt. He puffs up like a bullfrog. Then he snaps.

Caryl jumps into the cab and restarts the engine, but his wheels spin the ruts deeper. He tries rocking backward, but he is too heavy. He tries forward but the nose of the truck is at too steep a pitch. And as he works, Mauser swings the bar, stamps his feet, and yells so hard it looks like he'll split in half. I edge back to my car. I lean on the back bumper, and stay, so I see it all clearly. I see the thought enter Caryl's desperate head. I see him think that he is simply too heavy! I see him start the dump. The dump bed goes up but the tailgate has banged shut and does not release, so that the load, instead of flooding out the back, collects in the rear. And slowly, I can see it happen, the weight begins to lift the front wheels right up off the ground.

Mauser hops in the air, shrieks like the noon whistle, but the loud whine of the hydraulic dump in Caryl's ears hypnotizes him. Up, up the truck goes, until the gravel begins to course over the top of the sides and then it's too late for everything. We all see it at the same moment, I suppose, but only Mauser moves. He jumps to the passenger's-side door of the truck, and lifts his bar to break the window, but can't balance right as the truck settles back on its haunches and in gradual motion lists sideways, groaning. Its shadow begins to edge over the Cadillac parked snug against it. Then the truck goes with its own weight and topples the rest of the way, crushing the car.

Suddenly Mauser stands on top of the door, which is a solid floor beneath his feet. He looks down. Through the glass he sees Caryl, looking back up at him, sees the buckled roof of clear red. I can hear stuff *give* deep in the Cadillac's interior, maybe the steering wheel or the glove leather seats. There is a thud, a series of smaller thunks, gentler sounds than that first awful noise of metal crumpling. I guess it is the smallness of those sounds that stops Mauser. He stands on the pile of truck, man caught inside, flattened car underneath. Then he straightens up, and looks around as though he's climbed there just to get the view. He squints at the horizon, which is empty and quiet beyond the edge of the field. When Caryl begins to thrash around below him, pounding to get out, Mauser bends over with the crowbar. I think he is going to pull Caryl out, save him if only to beat him up. But instead of breaking in the window, Jack pries the handle off the door. Leaves him in there. Jack then climbs down off the cab of the truck and walks toward me.

Halfway to where I stand, he throws the iron bar down in the yellow grass. Then he looks at me. I don't know why, that direct look I guess, but the space between us shrinks. Goes magnetic. Buzzing with tension. It's romantic, is what I'm saying. All of a sudden, I'm confused, my heart's beating fast. My pulse taps. He keeps the door handle in his hand, as if something might attach to it. We stand across from each other. He extends the handle to me.

I take the handle. I am mystified with hilarity.

"Is he okay?" I ask, trying to pretend like I mean it.

He nods yes then he waits.

"Let's let him sit there," I suggest.

Jack's pleased, I can tell. He walks around to the passenger's side of my car. We both get in at the same time and I begin to drive away from the accident. When we stop at the four-way lights in town, I look at Mauser for directions, and he looks back at me, giving none. So we idle there. One car and then another goes around us, honking, and still we look at each other for a clue.

❧   ❧   ❧

"I suppose you could say," Dot tapped the counter with her blunt fingers, "that was our first real date. I kind of intrigued Jack by leaving Caryl Moon back there, I guess."

"Abandonment," Eleanor murmured. "Being left. Loss. Of course."

"If you try to analyze this or anything," Dot answered, "it could drive you crazy." She stopped, floundered a bit. "Sorry . . . I mean, maybe it *did* drive you crazy."

"I wasn't crazy, not crazy crazy," Eleanor said. "I had a grip on reality, it was just that I couldn't *take* reality."

"Well." Dot was relieved, almost indignant on Eleanor's behalf. "That's not *crazy*."

Dot spilled the dregs of her cold coffee into the sink and poured herself some fresh. She wanted to end the conversation, but didn't know how. "The thing was, though, in spite of myself I got very fond of Jack," she said, tentatively.

"I did, too," said Eleanor in a low, shamed voice.

Her hand was spread, flat and hopeless, on the top of the counter. For a while she just stared at Dot, not meeting her eyes exactly, but looking straight past her into some middle distance encompassing the beige carpet and plush decorator furniture beyond.

Deciding to end both of her marriages made Dot nostalgic. She usually awakened late, on perfect weekend mornings, tasting the salt of her first husband's hands, though Gerry Nanapush was, of course, in prison. Learning about Jack's former wives seemed to open a secret door in her mind that let Gerry through, more real than ever, loving. She had paperwork in process with both men and a lawyer who thought she was crazy. Jack still appealed to her, but the marriage felt wrong. Gerry, on the other hand, was more right than ever, but Dot was trying to be practical though her patience was shredded.

She tried to concentrate on righting Jack's accounts, on living in the new house they would have to sell. *Enjoy it while you can*, she told herself, looking around. Light flooded through the tall windows. The ceiling was high and airy. She drank increasing amounts of coffee, the cheapest she could buy with coupons. She tried to live in the present and think what to do next, but she was constantly traduced by the rich ardor of salt and the bones of memory. Each day attenuated. Time thinned like taffy in the heat.

Dot turned over, and over, in the wide king bed made of solid oak and heavy on the floor of her vast bedroom. Jack didn't like beds that moved. Outside the house, the rich, black sunflower and sugar beet fields were sodded into lawns and groomed. Frail trees were planted, quick-growing poplars with tiny brittle leaves yellow as coins. They cast no shade. When Jack stayed overnight with her and woke, in the brilliance, Dot touched him and they made love, silently, with a businesslike and melancholy reserve developed since Eleanor. Usually, though, Jack slept on a fold-out cot in the storage garage on the other side of town, where he spent late nights tinkering with broken equipment, or vainly juggling accounts and begging off payments with new and cunning strategies. He went to bed during the coolish gray hours before dawn, hoping to avoid his dreams, and perhaps avoid Dot too.

Dot cornered Mauser at home one morning late in an unseasonably hot September week. They made love with their usual efficiency, and now they lay twined together companionably, almost at peace.

"How's Eleanor?"

Jack turned to look out the window, the quiet square of blue skylight. "I don't even know where she is," said Jack. But he imagined her back in the company of the aging nuns who were her favorite people, it seemed—those worn, rare women with perfect translucent skins and quiet, starved, silver voices. Jack jumped out of bed and paced restlessly, then pulled on his jeans and shirt and tied on work boots.

"Where are you going?" Dot had hoped that to speak of Eleanor would vanquish her, but the opposite had just happened and her image appeared in both of their minds. She edged between them, shadowy and sad, a powerful loneliness that spoke to both of them at once.

"It's like there's a time-temperature sign in my head that flashes on." Jack shook himself, sat on the edge of the bed, beside her. "How much I owe. How little I've got." The weird fall air was already heavy and too still.

"I know."

Dot reached up and smoothed back his lank cowlick, touched his ears. She wanted to yank them off. Still, she understood that her jealous impulse was a fleeting reflex. She knew what it was to love someone else indelibly and there were times she considered giving him the simple advice *go to her*. Jack hadn't looked at Dot with softened eyes or turned to her willingly, not lately, but then, it was hard to tell what was more on Jack's mind from day to day—Eleanor or his company's ruinous situation. He was always distracted, tired, consumed with worry. Dot knew he was in serious debt, and yet the bulldozers and the workers were still operating in high gear and the houses in the new development that spread around them were nearing completion, all on schedule. She lifted her hand before Jack's face, let it hover, and imagined that she held a fat cream pie. She'd smash it down. He'd be surprised! But that was not quite fair, not fair at all, because she'd found herself toying with the idea of traveling to the federal penitentiary, to visit Gerry.

She'd bring Shawn with her, clean out her tiny account, disassemble the plastic pieces of a gun and suspend it in a pudding—butterscotch. Who would suspect? With each day she stayed with Jack, her first love increased even as, she suspected, his memories of Eleanor grew more vital to him. Their presences acted upon each other as a mnemonic fuel. They were too close in some ways, like cousins, more and more. Her memories of Gerry grew in vigor, became stronger, more palpable. Her first love was suddenly so real and present that Gerry's absence surprised her. Touching Jack's unshaven face she felt Gerry's smooth chin. Holding Jack's cool, tough fingers, she again clasped Gerry's—thick and warm. Jack's hair was short, Gerry's long and heavy in braids. Jack was big and lean while Gerry ran generous, to say the least. During the years she had concentrated on her daughter, Dot had forgotten her first husband's specific attributes, her memory had mercifully dulled. Now it sprang to life. Sometimes, in bed, she closed her eyes on Jack and instead saw the rapt light in Gerry's eyes as he pressed his face toward her, or the concentrated pleasure on his lips.

Jack's House

*O*n the night his fifth wife left him for the fourth time, the last time, Jack Mauser crawled into bed with a boxed Christmas bottle and forgot the fire burning unguarded in the living room hearth. The top of the box was decorated with a red stick-on bow. Mauser peeled it off and stuck the flimsy thing onto the middle of his forehead. He uncorked the Scotch, single malt, buttered fire, and drank his first drink in untold months. He had cut down considerably when Dot faced him with the consequences — she had made him stop entirely before she had agreed to marry him — so two things were over with now.

It was New Year's Eve, and after four long swallows all Jack wanted to do was go outside and beg the moon for deathless fucking, for Eleanor, but there was no moon. There was no one to look at or even call since she'd moved back to Minneapolis, he'd heard, and unpublished her telephone number. He'd kept the newspaper article on her case, the charges brought against her by some kid, *the little prick should have fallen to his knees, kissed the ground she walked on, thanked his lucky ass!* Jack was so infuriated in his former wife's defense that when

Dot found the clipping and asked him whether he thought Eleanor was guilty, Jack had been surprised. Of course she was guilty!

Eleanor had this predilection, not a problem in most cases. Since their marriage, she'd had a string of boyfriends, a taste for unavailable men.

She likes sex, actually likes sex with men, Jack had thought, but said nothing. He suspected Dot had become indifferent to sex with him.

Jack was now sitting on the satin cover of the solid king bed he'd shared with Dot. He shut his eyes, saw his house and its entire layout from above. Jack's 5000-square-foot model house was situated at the end of a paved cul-de-sac in a high-priced park laid out around a huge dug pond into which, last spring, Mauser himself had poured two hundred tadpoles and a bucket of trout spry. With the displaced dirt, Mauser had raised a hill, and since there were no hills anywhere near Fargo, this one had proved a great attraction to home buyers—until the dirt destabilized and part of it collapsed.

He heard it happen deep in the night, woke to the seamless avalanche of dirt, thick and sudden. He'd thought the cave-in was thunder, and sank back unaware. Now the hill was cordoned off. So was the entire street. His brand-new executive homes went unsold as potential buyers couldn't get loans. There was low-lying panic in the financial community, heavy weather looming in the market. Piece by piece the whole project had self-destructed right before his eyes. Mauser's ex-friend Hegelstead, president of First National, had called the day after Christmas. His voice distant and embarrassed, Hegelstead apologized and asked for payment by the first or it was out of his hands. Mauser slammed down the phone. Then he yanked the cord from its jack in the wall and tossed the phone into the trash. There was no escape though. In the mail came a notice from his Uncle Chuck threatening to repossess and seed the rest of the land unless Jack paid the mortgage due his accounts. Then there were quarterly taxes due in January, too. Cornered. In the previous six days he had at last

understood that his trouble reached so deep and wide, had
sunk itself such a firm foundation both in wasted emotion and
hopeless debt, his problems branched off into so many more
incomplete rooms than he could finish or even count, that the
only way out was to declare himself bankrupt, which meant his
life was over in the only place he cared about or knew.

Mauser lifted the bottle again and then lay back carefully
in the king-size pillows. *Booshkay neen*, he said. *Booshkay neen.*
Where had that come from? Some book? His mother? Sometimes Ojibwa words snared his tongue. Sometimes German.
Sometimes he copied Eleanor. He admired her learning but his
attempts bore mixed results—he was considered strange by his
work crew for screaming lines of poetry or repeating her philosophical maxims in his diatribes. *What doesn't kill you makes you
stronger*, he railed at his exhausted crews, near deadlines.
Nietzsche! Nietzsche! Now, in satisfied self-pity, he removed a
book of Eleanor's, a thin and brittle paperback, from a built-in
reading shelf and read the plaint of Chu Shu Chen over and
over. *Spring flower, Autumn moons, Water lilies . . .* He could not
go on. Where was Eleanor? Mauser almost wept, stopped himself, then wondered. Why should tears—use and relief of
same—be the sole province and property of women? Wet-
eyed, he smiled into the air of the tall ceiling. *Carry away my
heart like a lost boat.* It was such a relief to drink. He had no
excuse to have emotions otherwise. *You can't just have the fuckers,
they have to have you!* He laughed out loud. He was wearing a
pair of soft old jeans and no shirt. That's how Dot had left him,
half undressed, in front of a fire into which they had just
tossed two cheap champagne glasses, one of which was even
too thick to break, after toasting what was, and what was not
to be, with sparkling apple juice.

"Fuck that," said Mauser.

He took another drink. *As long as I am flesh and bone I will
never find rest. There will never come a time when I will be able to resist
my emotions.* Eleanor had given him the book, of course, which
is why he'd saved it, why now he held it to his lips. Falling
back in love with your second wife while married to your fifth

was a sticky, stupid business. He was paying for so many things, all at once, and all the hard way.

He tossed down Eleanor's book, hummed a self-pitying torch song. "Stormy Weather." Another drink. One more.

When you're drunk, when you're drinking alone, when you stop singing, there is a predictable silence that comes down over everything, peaceful and immense. In it, Mauser heard the mutter of the refrigerator as a new thing, as breathing, and the whine of the earth station cables coiled behind the television suddenly struck him as a comfort. Sleet, snow, and the hiss of wind outside enclosed him in a womb of sifting air. He knew that in the morning he would grind his teeth in hurt, sick, but in his bell now the little homely world around him seemed safe. He was already nostalgic for what he had and would lose, so solid.

The walls of his house were a pale color, the pinks and frosts inside a seashell, and the trim on the doorways and baseboards a deeper mauve. Of course, the painters were a bunch of whiners, jerk-offs. They'd done a slapdash job. But how could they completely ruin a palace like this? There was oak everywhere—the handrails, the sills—and stained glass in the doors of the television cabinet. The master bath was like a Roman spa, its tub immense, fitted out with jets and soap dispensers. In the shower, though neither worked, there was a nozzle for steam, one for hot water massage. To complement this luxury Dot had placed small wrapped bars of soap everywhere. She had saved them from hotel rooms, along with tiny plastic bottles of shampoo. She wouldn't buy new towels. He begged her to steal hotel ones, just to feel rough nap. She wouldn't. She brought her old towels from her old life and, Jack thought now, intended to use them until she finally wore them to smooth threads. Then she would rip them up for dust cloths. That was Dot. In order to feel at all comfortable within her grand house she followed strange economies, ritualized salvage operations that made life irritating.

She recycled, kept, saved, mended, wore things out, and used up every bite of leftover food even if she had to grimly spoon it into herself.

He wandered out to the living room, touching the eggshell-colored walls, smoothing his fingers along the dark grain of a sideboard. He hummed moodily, pulled open heavy white damask drapes on a view of the frozen lake. He'd wired lamps into the ground and meant to hire someone to keep the surface clear so kids could skate there. But there were no kids, except Shawn, and now Dot had taken her daughter to live in some apartment, she wouldn't even tell him where. He stood in the soft glow of the hearth for some moments, thinking, before he realized that the fire where he was warming himself was not contained in the tile and brick alcove but was burning in an adjacent place where there had once been a decorative basket of pinecones.

He automatically reached down for the rug, which wasn't there, but anyway it was a nice rug, a good imitation Navajo too valuable to ruin smothering a fire. He remembered that there was an extinguisher somewhere, in the kitchen probably, beside the stove. He watched the fire for a moment. It didn't look all that dangerous. It wasn't leaving marks on the wall yet. The paint wasn't even blistered. Clearly, it was the kind of blaze that would go out all by itself. There wasn't enough smoke to activate the elaborate sensors in the light fixtures, and certainly, not enough heat to turn on the sprinklers. The house was supposed to be wired for everything—intrusion, movement, intercom and stereo, lights of course, dimmers, plus it had a vacuum system built into the walls. The fire-protection alarm would call the department and sprinklers would douse the flames before the trucks arrived. It was a house that could take care of itself, even water its own lawn and guide the way to itself automatically, when the sun went down, for Mauser had installed a bank of lights that ran on solar cells and bloomed on at dusk. It wasn't a house that any human had to worry about, really, besides flipping the right switches. Mauser yawned. He went into the kitchen and began to open cabinets, looking through them, one after the other.

He was annoyed first at the workmanship. It sucked. The cabinets fell open and refused to shut. He noticed that Dot had

stuck wads of paper in the loose catches and he cursed the finish carpenter. Dead drunk most days, missing others. But the
best around Fargo refused to work with him now. Next, Jack
was disturbed by the amount of food Dot had stored. He
blamed all of her bomb-shelter buying on a Depression men-
tality, except that of course she hadn't been through the
Depression. Anyway, she always bought food large. He found
cases of soups, ten-pound sacks of beans, and peanut butter
packed in buckets. She kept every plastic tub and cover, just in
case. *Just in case what?* Mauser thought, put out of patience. He
answered himself. *Just in case I go broke.* She had, it seemed, the
instincts of a contractor's wife after all.

He should never, ever have been hard on her, he realized
suddenly, with drunken self-loathing. He'd been wrong, for
she'd only had his interests at heart. Because of her, he would
be able to eat for months even when the house and all that he
owned was repossessed. He would move into a small room
downtown, maybe at the Fargoan, spend his days quietly taking in the feeble sun alongside retired farmers who still spoke
German and Norwegian and moved their scorched hands
incessantly along the grain of their faded work pants. He
would share his minestrone soup mix with them, his peanut
butter, his giant cans of wax beans. He would count his coins
out of a little blue plastic child's coin purse. Jack looked
around, remembered what he was supposed to be doing,
searched the room twice over, but couldn't find the extinguisher. He knew he'd seen it, and so he sat down to clear his
mind and think of where. The bottle was still in his hands.
Mauser raised it to his lips, to his throat, and accepted another
long and golden drink.

In the middle of his heated swallow, eyes closed, he saw
Eleanor once more as she had been when they were last
together. Her skin was chalk-white in the dusk, her long, fragile face a snowy mask with eye holes cut for the blazing stare.
Her mouth was honed, her lips dry, chiseled in a curve of
irony. If he could get her back, if he could somehow convince
her that he was different, although he wasn't that much differ-

ent—especially now, he thought, tipping back his head for one more swallow, he'd regressed—if he could go after her and fight to win her—from whom? She wasn't with anyone. From herself? His life had gone so wrong for such a long time, maybe since they'd split up long ago. For it did seem to him, now, thinking back, that a fog had descended ever since they'd parted and that, maybe, the clarity of a return to the beginning of his adult life, his first real marriage, might make the rest of things come around.

Impatiently, he reviewed old histories. How laughable it all was. His reasoning so skewed—he'd married each woman out of deep feeling, over and over! Each marriage had presented itself to him as a mirage of perfect happiness. Each relationship had started out that way, too. Happy. Then reality hit one of them—him or her—there was no less pain in leaving someone than in being left yourself (and the latter, too, produced the energies of victimhood, so he preferred it). Self-pity had been stimulating to him, still was. The first reaction always—getting drunk—had obviously set in now. He cranked back slowly, wondered over Eleanor and thought hopefully of their new future. But would it mean, the thought struck him suddenly, in a wheeling fit of humor, that next in turn, after Eleanor, he would be bound on a course to remarry all of them?

He thought of Candice, his third wife. Jack was tethered to a belief that his longest marriage had somehow been sweet, all in itself, sweet and wholesome. *I am capable of something decent*, he said out loud, but no sooner were the words out than what filled his mental screen were Eleanor's old love-charm ways—in a convent, yes, she'd learned a lot! Her perfect ravenous mouth, her lean, full, hungry body crouched right on top of his, searching him out, dragging him back and forth through her world of wants and wishes and tossing him out of it at last!

Used! He'd felt mysteriously weak in Eleanor's presence, but her original fight to leave had paradoxically strengthened him. Resolve. Wife one. That was June Morrissey. Freeze frame. Don't think about her. Back in order. A very definite plan had asserted itself with wife three, that is, with his old high school sweetheart Candy Pantamounty. He still felt guiltiest because of her. It was all falling into place, a pattern, a mosaic of his errors. In marriage three, his wife had defined herself as his victim. He'd made Candice trust him, made her uncharacteristically vulnerable. And then, of course, he'd taken advantage of her bewildered faith and destroyed, ravaged, so she said, the treasure house of her emotions. Here was a question. Were those emotions really such treasures after all, and hadn't he been hurt, too? How could anyone who'd then fled to Marlis Cook, wife four, in bliss and anguish, not have hurt? *I am an emotional man!* They'd all at one time or another accused him of having no feelings, but the opposite was true — his feelings were both vast and too tender.

Was that so bad? So impossible? He closed his eyes. *Feel. Feel.* He felt it all and he could take it!

Marlis had made furious work of him — quick work, insane work. She was, after all, certifiable, a bipolar quick-change heartbreaker who'd simply manipulated him during his own midlife crisis in order to get ahead in her young life. Yes, Marlis frightened him to this day, all the more so because of the way she had fallen briskly out of love with him and, being practical in spite of her psychological problems, moved in with Candice. That was possibly the source of his guilt — the certainty that he had driven his third and fourth wives to distrust him so completely that they preferred to make peace with each other. They should have been rivals, that was it. His pride hurt. These bondings between pairs of his former wives were somehow humiliating.

Mauser raised the bottle, grieving, and unhappily toasted Candice and Marlis's sudden and enthusiastic shift of ground. He closed his eyes and his body spun. The liquor grabbed him, wild, a wicked momentary ride. Eleanor's presence was flung suddenly across him, a light shawl. She smelled like smoke, or was it him? She had loved to put her face to him and breathe the scent of his skin. He felt her breath along his rib cage, her enjoyment, her pleasure as she stretched long and rocked against him with slow pumps of her thighs. He almost slapped his own face. *Shut up*, he told himself. She had not wanted it, nor had he, really, though they must have underneath the façade. The revelation, their emotions, it all occurred so easily. A beautiful frieze shows through a wall of crumbling plaster, a cryptic collage, say, made of beads and chips of mirror. The ground shrugs, a powerful shift occurs, the sequence is revealed. You're left gasping, as he was. Moments afterward he put on his pants and slipped out of a whole convent full of dreaming nuns. He drove back to Fargo, back into his bankrupt life and found that he couldn't turn away, couldn't bring himself to disappoint Dot.

Again, he raised a picture of Dot in his mind. Such longing in her deep brown eyes. June's eyes flashed, sad. But she was laughing at him. Then Candice's blue superiority. Then Eleanor's again and Marlis, pregnant. Why was he being punished?

Because of her? That oil-field woman? June? What I did or what I let her do? Mauser stumped to the bedroom, rolled sausagelike into a blanket. Lurched back on the bed. He opened his arms to the ceiling, kicked the blanket off his feet. *You will be crushed. She'll snap your bones, devour you like meat!* Was this what the weird old nun meant? And was it all because of June? *Hey, could I have saved her now, could I?* He spoke out loud, and then he answered, addressing himself like an old priest. *Jack, you could at least have followed the woman you'd just married.*

I never would have found her. I would have froze.

That's true, he argued, again drinking. *But the hell of it is, I never even set foot off the road!*

In his pocket, he had the note Eleanor had left him, explaining.

Dear Jack,

In spite of myself, I couldn't help but like Dot. Her directness is so refreshing, her honesty such a contrast to your lack of same. And then, there is her

daughter's welfare to consider. I know you're fond of
the girl. As for what happened between us, Jack, I
can't bear it. It is simply too painful altogether. I
wish I could erase the memory, then again, I feed on
it. Anyway, we both know it wouldn't work—it
never did for long, don't forget what it was like to
live with each other! I have to write my book,
retreat, reflect. Perhaps I am meant to be a solitary
creature.

Jack read that last line over. It sounded so . . . what, so
Victorian or something. And then her closing thought. *Let's continue to remain as we've been.* What did that mean—to fuck or not
to fuck?

He wanted her. His heart had been crushed. Then uncrum-
pled and defined in Eleanor's hands. He knew the truth of his
feelings, and all that was left was that old love. He tried to give
her up, over and over, like a petitioner wearing down the stone
steps of a cathedral. His love was that great, that monumental,
he thought.

He was still in his bedroom and the next room was definitely
smoky. He could hear intense snapping sounds and see that
flicker cast by the flames against the white doorway. He put
out his hands and patted around himself until he found the
bottle. Just a quarter of it left. He couldn't feel any heat from
the fire, and still believed that it would simply extinguish itself
once it used up the pinecones, the newspapers, whatever it was
burning now. It probably wouldn't even get hot enough to
scorch the hardwood floor. He sat back dizzily and yawned so
wide his jaw creaked. He shook himself all over, stared hard at
the back of his hand. And then, at that moment, he decided
what to do.

Or rather, what not to do. He decided not to move.

It dawned on him that the smoke alarm was faulty. He'd
forgotten, because he'd counted on the sprinkler system to
kick on. Now he realized that it should have drenched the

place. He looked at his hands, so far away, on the ends of such long arms. He had the awful fantasy that the booze had stretched him out to a rubbery length, but when he measured himself against the size of the bed he seemed to fit onto it the same way he always had in the past. No larger. Reassured, he grabbed the end of a thought that whipped by and held on. He was a bulldog on the end of a bicycle chain, his teeth hurt with the effort of thinking. What could be better? He spoke out loud. What could make more sense? He got up. He closed the door against the smoke that made him cough. Nothing could be better for his hopeless business situation than exactly what was happening right now, in the other room.

His house was burning down.

He was excited, suddenly. His house was burning down! He sat up in bed and started making plans.

Insured, yes, he was insured. He had paid the premiums, in spite of how tight things were, paid them in advance even, just to save the paperwork. He was well insured, but not too insured. Nothing to provoke suspicion, no great change in his policy recently. Last month, a typical friendly phone call from his agent, nothing more than the usual small talk. Jack had even—yes he was sure of it—refused some sort of additional coverage. That fact was sure to be in the records. Actually refused! It was so perfect that Jack could have wept. Things were falling into place, great things, huge problems over which he had had no control now were being solved precisely because he had relinquished control and God had smiled a big hot smile on him. Nothing in the house he valued or cared to save, was there? Except himself of course. He'd let the fire go. He'd gotten drunk. What of it? He'd jump out the window at the last moment, land in the snow. If he was lucky, nobody would notice the house burning and turn in the alarm. Everyone in the whole town was at some party or another—though it didn't matter out here. The whole street was deserted and for sale. It would be too late to save this house and maybe . . . his heart beat fast. He drank. Maybe the next, the next, the whole damn cul-de-sac. Maybe the smoke alarms were faulty all through them and the automatic sprinkling systems too. They were smoke sensing, activated by hard wiring. Someone on his crew had fucked up. God love the guy.

It was a very big and solid house and it seemed to Mauser, after a while, that it was taking a long time to burn. He was at the stage of drunkenness where his vision always narrowed, as though he were looking down a hallway with black curtains drawn to either side. He couldn't hear sounds anymore, he felt them. The walls opened and shut like great valves. The whole house seemed to pulse like the inside of a dark body. A sudden finger of raw heat licked through the space underneath the jamb.

He knew it was stupid, but he opened the door.

Huge heat knocked him back, swelling at him. He could feel his eyebrows shrivel, his hair singe. The Christmas bow on his forehead burst into a ball of harsh light and he smacked out the little flame. The skin on his cheekbones blistered in the instant before he turned aside and threw himself into the master bathroom, escaping the roar of burning heat that flooded the room. That bathroom led out to a small hallway with a back staircase to the basement.

He knew, from his younger days as a volunteer fireman, that there is an odd tension to a room that is about to explode into flames. The air itself trembles and the objects, almost boiling, are suffused with humming tension. Mauser felt the floor buckle behind him, heard the snap of beams as he leaped away and dashed for the stairs. He could have gone straight out, taken a near window, but at the last minute he decided on an image that suddenly popped into his brain. A wine bottle. Cellar. He decided that he definitely craved, required, no *deserved*, one more drink before he left the house. The carpet puffed flames and gathered in his wake. The stairs led straight down to a huge, low, poured-concrete basement, solid as a bomb shelter.

The air seemed thick and foggy in the basement, and he picked up a flashlight from its perch on a shelf, dashed through the open laundry area, opened the door to the wine cellar. No wine was kept in the room anymore, except for that one bottle too expensive and old to drink, yet another gift from a client. That bottle was what Jack wanted now, but it was gone, he saw at once. The room was empty, except for a side of beef that he deduced, with bewildered rage, Dot had bought at some locker sale. Perhaps, he seethed, shutting the door behind him, her aunt had given it to her as some sort of wedding present! Where was that grand old wine? His secretive wife had hauled this beef into the house and stored it here, but where had she stuck that bottle? He swung the huge carcass to one side and sat on an empty, decorative barrel with a spigot in its face. He supposed it was meant to be some kind of planter, since it would obviously never hold wine again. Not here. He turned the spigot hopefully, just in case. Nada. He looked up and down for that bottle he imagined as deliciously aged, covered with webs and dust. There was nothing. Just a few jars of canned whole chickens moldered spookily upon the shelves.

Even without his shirt on, Mauser began to sweat. He took off his jeans, and then his underwear. *What if I just disappeared?* He thought of the buckle on his belt, of insurance specialists and investigators sifting through the debris, of Dot testifying that he'd worn those charred scraps, that very belt buckle on the night they came to the end of their marriage. The air was hotter, hotter, and Mauser knew that it was time to go. He was still disappointed about the bottle of wine, but he tried to be philosophical: he'd turn this to his advantage, leave a clue. He'd had a few of his weaker teeth knocked out playing high school football, and now he painfully tugged free the little piece of porcelain bridgework he'd worn since then, and stuck it into the side of the thawing cow.

The moment neared. He couldn't wait a second longer. Jack opened the door and sprinted across the floor of hot poured concrete to the top of the new clothes dryer. Perched there, he practically died—the air was that elusive and the smoke that thick. Behind him, fire rolling through his tool-room and his workshop, he heard an odd popping sound he knew at once and mourned. He *heard* his collection of carpenter's levels, the spirit bubbles boiling then exploding. They went like firecrackers in a string. He fumbled with the crank on the window, a top-quality Anderson salvaged from a downtown renovation. The handle wouldn't work and there was a slight bend in the sash that made the screen difficult to remove. He got the screen out and then realized in one clear sauceless moment how deep the snow was, pressing down against the foundation.

The window would not crank open against the packed white weight. He pressed his face against the glass. He could feel the house compose itself above him, bleeding shock waves and balls of flame. Of all things to have discounted in a life of tending to material details, snow was the last thing he would have suspected of doing him in. He had always respected snow, watched out for it, figured in its weight on roof and beam. He had always left a way to plow a driveway, an incline, a way for snow to melt away from a house. He had always understood and anticipated snow's treachery in the manufacture of his roads. He had used snow, his friend, as insulation for pipes and sewer systems that were always just to code, no more and no less. Unfair to be killed by snow! All the elements were against him, earth too, water in its purest form. He could feel some difference in the whole configuration of light and heat above him. A boiling drop spat down through the floor and hissed upon his neck. The sprinkler system had all of a sudden repaired itself. The house, burnt down to the wiring, its nerves, had finally acted in self-defense. He could feel the water and the fire, both at once, a torrent thrashing down the basement steps. A wall of sheer steam enveloped him and his brain locked into sudden and complete sobriety.

Jack Mauser flashed upon the picture of himself, naked as a dumpling, steamed to death upon a clothes dryer. He turned back to the window in a fit of determination. The flakes of snow were packed solid as a fine-grained wood. He took a towel from the dryer. He couldn't feel the texture of things anymore, but he was certain he had what he needed in his hands. Water swirled around the floor, rising in a powerful wave. His hands were burned down to the wires also, frozen, senseless with alcohol and hardened by sorrow. Still, he managed to spread the towel upon the window, smashed his fist against it over and over until he was sure the glass beneath was splintered. He dragged down the towel with the pieces of the window in it. And then, using his numb hands as shovels, he threw himself forward.

No. 5429316
NORTH DAKOTA JUDICIAL DISTRICT
COURT, CASS COUNTY
In the Matter of the Estate of JOHN J. MAUSER,
Deceased.
Cause No. 3890–120938475
NOTICE TO CREDITORS

NOTICE IS HEREBY GIVEN that the undersigned has been appointed Personal Representative of the above-named estate. All persons having claims against the said deceased are required to present their claims within four months after the date of the first publication of this notice or said claims will be forever barred.

Claims must be either mailed to Maynard Moon, the Personal Representative, return receipt requested at Moon, Webb, & Cartenspiel, Attorneys at Law, Professional Building Suite #6, Roberts Street, Fargo, North Dakota 58102, or filed with the Clerk of the above-titled Court.

DATED this 5th day of January, 1995
/s/ Maynard Moon
Personal Representative
Moon, Webb, & Cartenspiel

PART TWO

❦

Blackjack Night

§

M e m o r i a

JANUARY 5, 1995

Fargo

*I*t was a winter's day, cold but not bitter, the sky a featureless gray sheath, the snow a crust of lacy ice work on the Fargo boulevards. Cars crackled into their plowed sites and the parking lot pavement of Schlick's—the best funeral home in the city—was clear enough so that the women in high heels did not teeter or skid but stepped firmly, some accompanied and some alone, up the salted walkway. The yard was edged with somber yews grown to an obscuring height. The sculpted plantings prompted the people forward, the packed needles shed a dimming influence, and most mourners were silent by the time they ascended the fan of stone steps and entered through the Victorian-beveled-glass-and-carved-oak doorway.

Schlick's Funeral Home had once been a railroad baron's mansion, one of the first houses built when the Northern Pacific crossed the Red River a century ago and made the fortunes of speculators who had bought land at that exact juncture. Porched and winged, painted now an understated beige, sided with well-grown stands of birch and tall cones of spruce, the house and grounds spread over more than an acre of rich Agassiz dirt.

Once the door breathed shut behind them, visitors drifted toward a parlor lit with lozenges of colored glass. Today a small gas fire flared in that room, projecting even points beneath a mantel of Italian tiles. The casket, into which the remains of Jack Mauser had been sealed, was displayed there, too, resting on a draped table and framed by potted palms.

Eleanor had picked out the casket—wholesale and over-wrought, with brass trim and elaborate handles. Jack's third wife, Candice, had agreed, in exasperation, to split the bill. Candice never had liked Eleanor and suspected her even now of charging her more than the casket was worth. No one knew the whereabouts of Marlis Cook, Mauser's fourth wife. Jack's fifth, Dot, greeted visitors. All present were dry-eyed except for Eleanor, who stood near the door, in the odor of yellow freesia, weeping with hot ferocity into the palms of her hands.

The air around Eleanor seemed humid. Her clothes were drenched and streaked. She repelled all efforts at comfort, slashed at patting hands with nails that raked. Dot found her-self sympathizing with Eleanor's obvious pain over Jack. Standing next to her, Dot became protective. She glared and ground her teeth at any platitude or hint of falsity a friend of Jack's dared offer.

She held the guest book open, offered a fine-point pen with strong and tapered, nail-bitten fingers. Nodding at each visitor, Dot looked suspiciously into their eyes for signs of genuine sorrow. There was little. With some contempt, she registered the thin condolences tendered by the mourners as they entered the room, paused, and then milled forward in a dancing monotony.

First one and then the other approached the impressive shut steel and brass box to stand for a moment, uncertainly, since there was no body to regard, and then back obliquely away. It was almost the same with everyone, and there were many who came either out of curiosity, or hope of money, or honestly to pay respects. There were even a few who liked Jack, for he had occasionally, especially when drunk, been generous and cheerfully lavish with money that did not belong to him. By late morning Dot slowly put away the first guest book—filled—and another was brought out and placed on the ornate side table. The temperature rose at noon and the air turned close. The sun blasted radiance through a rift in the cottony sky and heated up the space between the mullioned windows and the sash, bringing flies to life. The insects spun into people's water glasses, or buzzed sleepily, caught in black mesh of scarves and sleeves. Periodically Eleanor's father, Lawrence Schlick, a big and loose-jointed man, appeared in the room with a red plastic swatter that he wielded, with embarrassed dignity, to poor results. The pests grew more numerous, sprang from the velvet drapes at a touch, and the room grew warmer. Mr. Schlick found that the little jets of flames between the logs of stippled metal in the grate were stuck on high, and while he was in the back room, calling the service salesroom where he'd bought the unit, those near the fire sweated and began to argue.

Death throws people out of whack, forces family to reexamine private interests, brings to the surface all that is deep, chaotic, and fearful in human nature, shows loved ones at their best and worst. The hot room didn't help. Nor the gas fire, such a sham in a house otherwise carefully restored. Perhaps it was inevitable that tensions would surround Jack Mauser in death as they had in life. No one knew that better than Jack's second and third wives, Eleanor and Candice. And yet, these two women, who had once prided themselves on their separate escapes from Jack, were chagrined to become entangled in an issue at once meaningless and provoking: that is, what should become of his remains.

Candice Pantamounty, D.D.S., kept herself in hard focus no matter what the circumstances. Sexually precise, unnervingly well-groomed, clever but anti-intellectual, above all else clean. Professional. She had flourished with or without Jack Mauser. She was blond and petite, pink lipped, and very successful at her job. She was a family dentist. Her self-confidence both reassured and bent lesser personalities like gold. She believed that she could do and think no incorrectness and even on those occasions that she was proven wrong, Candice Panta-mounty—she'd resumed her maiden name at once after her divorce and decided never to change it again—managed to make the admission of her mistake into something admirable, a triumph. In fact, there were times she freely confessed to all sorts of foibles, providing they were of the sort that set off lov-able weaknesses. "I'm a fool for dogs," she might say, revealing her sentimental side. "I can't resist potatoes," she would admit, hinting at earthy simplicity. "I know I shouldn't drive so fast, but I like to be on time!" She made virtues of her small vices, and when she couldn't, she overconfessed. "Selfish? You're right. I am selfish, I admit that. Very selfish!" Giving in to her weaknesses she at least proved that she could be honest.

When it came to her choice—helping out Marlis during the pregnancy and offering to adopt the baby—Candice was uncharacteristically modest. She didn't wave her decision in people's faces, and merely responded with a small and depre-cating smile when people said it was a decent gesture. She con-trolled other people's reactions, concentrated on her choice the way she perfected a patient's bite on a filled tooth. She handed Jack's baby around, liked to see others pleased, as long as she got proper credit for making them feel good. People happy on their own, anonymously and indiscriminately, she ignored, as she did people immersed in any emotion that she could not manipulate.

Although she'd once loved Jack, her main difficulty with his death, the day, the situation, was the uncontrollable nature of everyone else's emotions—feelings that had nothing to do with her. Even carrying the baby, whose presence focused attention, if not directly upon Candice, at least within arm's reach, she felt blurred, almost invisible. But then, this child was already proving less than predictable. He grinned and spat up in an excited arc across her shoulder. Candice handed him to her competent nanny, Mrs. Kroshus, an athletic little green-eyed woman draped in a webby shawl who wore her unnaturally thick hair in a duenna's bun. Stern and competent, she expertly rocked the baby as she scrubbed the cashmere of Candice's suit jacket with a tiny wash towel she kept in her bag for just such emergencies. Eleanor approached, anxious to settle the question of what came next.

At once, Candice's outlook improved. Here was a challenge. Her blue eyes snapped, her neatly pinked mouth tucked at the corners, her hair glistened, filling with light. The two women separated from the other people in the room. Although their coloring contrasted, their emphatic builds were outlined in identical sharp-edged tailoring softened by contrived touches—a signature scarf for Candice, a golden, braided-rope belt for Eleanor. Both wore complex metal earrings hooked and jointed with lurelike swivels that hitched and twirled and caught the light. Their heels were high, their skirts short. Their legs, formidable and flexible, poised as if to kick while their arms wrapped their torsos in false and fluid ease.

"He told me," Eleanor said now, her voice amenable, offhand, "that he wanted to be buried in St. Joseph's Cemetery."

These days she exercised too much, jogged away miles of nervous tension. Her body had become lean with sorrow since her breakdown. She heated up easily, cried hard. The time she had spent doing research at the convent had sensitized her nerves, but although her heart jolted and her throat went dry, she spoke with a professorial ease on the subject of Jack's last wishes.

"Not the Jack I knew!" Candice ran her hands through her fluffy hair, light and frosted as the flocking on a Christmas tree. She had scorned alimony from Jack, and she resented paying for his casket now. An expensive burial seemed more than superfluous—it was a waste, one other instance of Mauserlike excess. Jack had died with drawerfuls of signed lien waivers, with payments way overdue on his equipment, loans on loaned money, portfolios purged of all bonds leaving only stocks that never had rebounded, and a big unfinished project mocking all the optimism about housing markets—it now loomed, vast, worthless, a mass of unsold, shoddily constructed subdivision houses on the edge of Fargo.

"I'm not in the least interested," she'd said to Jack three months before, when he approached her with a deal on a 4000-square-foot home. Perhaps she had refused too harshly, allowed some pleasure at his desperation to show through her mocking sympathy. Still, that hardly made her liable for Jack's ultimate decision, or indecision, whatever had happened in the end.

"Jack told me he wanted to be cremated!"

Candice went on the offensive, spoke firmly and vigorously, without heed for truth. "And so he was, inadvertently! But more than that, he despised the whole idea of stones and monuments and burial plots. It's ghoulish. Let go of him, toss him to the wind!"

Eleanor composed her arms more firmly across her chest. Her black hair, streaked gray and longer since summer, swept around her face in firm withholding wings. With a condescending patience that inflicted itself on Candice's every nerve, Jack's second wife listened to his third and then spoke carefully, as if to an idiot.

"He wanted his *ashes* buried there, Candice. Place, family, history, all of these intangibles held great meaning for Jack. He had a sense of community, of tradition. The urn was supposed to be interred. I'm not imagining this."

She was though. She had no idea how Jack really felt and could hardly contain herself from breaking into fierce tears once more.

Candice stepped back and took control of herself by inhaling briskly, deeply, pulling the air into her stomach as she had taught herself to do when a patient looked terrified or on the verge of bolting from her chair.

"Hold on." Her tone was falsely reasonable and deceptively accommodating when she did speak again. "Let's think about it, Eleanor, let's think what would be best. I'm quite sure that Jack wanted his remains to be thrown to the winds. It was his wish, and it would be symbolic for others. Let's think of others!"

"I am just as sure," said Eleanor, her face now white with strain, "that Jack would have been extremely upset at the idea of being scattered."

Sensing an advantage to be had, Candice lowered her voice to a smooth and clipped attack-dog accuracy. "You've probably got some interest in the family plots in the cemetery. I haven't mentioned the obvious—your father."

The two women glanced automatically at Lawrence Schlick. The flyswatter, useless, was caught up in his fist. There was nothing to be done about the fact that Lawrence Schlick was Eleanor's father, but what of it? The idea that he would even think of profiting from the death of Jack Mauser, whose entire funeral package deal was below cost, upon whose visitation Schlick was at this moment losing money, outraged Eleanor. Her nerves fused in a jet of anger. In life, her father had complex reasons for hating Jack Mauser. Well, who didn't? In death, he forgave. Forgiveness was a natural law with him. Eleanor turned away from Candice, frustrated at the logjam of her feelings, for at heart she was furious at Jack as well as at everyone else. Irrationally, she blamed him, now, for forcing her to deal on this foolish and mundane level with Candice, whom she'd always disliked.

Candice in her own turn smiled fixedly and closed her eyes, blocking out the sight of Eleanor Mauser's sleek and handsome features. Whatever happened, she wouldn't, she refused, she absolutely would not pay another dime. The entire idea was too much—purchasing from her former husband's second wife a burial plot for his own use, if not enjoyment—too much!

Eleanor had never admitted to herself that she intended to be buried alongside Jack if, of course, and when. In her most regressive and morbid mood swings, Eleanor clung to this particular ultimate design. She was, after all and in spite of her dramatic sexual lapses, a deeply conservative person. She hadn't consciously acknowledged her grand plan, but apparently, she craved continuity and family closeness—if not in life, then in some eventual form. Here was an example, she decided, of how hidden wishes come annoyingly to life at unexpected moments, especially in the presence of a great mystery. Death flummoxed Eleanor. She was bad at dealing with endings and good-byes, and knew it, but then, because Candice's too-sharp intuitions made her feel competitive, she gathered her wits to lie and opened her mouth to assert her certainty that she had in her possession a paper signed by Jack pertaining to his intentions. Before she could make her case, though, Eleanor's mother appeared.

Anna Schlick never entered a room without turning heads and causing silences to fall in her wake. Stones in a clear pool, her footsteps sent immediate ripples to the outward corners and doorways. She wore her white hair in a marvelous cloud that blazed and caught the light. Her dress was hot blue, skintight, made of form-fitting material sewn entirely over with scale-thin sequins. Although she moved slowly and turned aside sometimes to sit, and gather strength, for she had a heart condition, Anna gave the impression of unquiet power.

How typical, Eleanor thought, *how annoying of her to come to the funeral of her daughter's husband dressed to kill!* Depressed, Eleanor watched her mother work the crowd. Anna's breasts were pillowy, pushed high, rounded, surging in the glittering low-cut bodice, and her curved torso swiveled in its snaky sheath. *I hate her so much,* Eleanor mouthed passionately, but when her mother caught her arm, gasping, and sat down abruptly, her mind took fire and she melted with a helpless love. And worry. Anna wasn't well, but she spoke uncannily, as though she'd listened in on the conversation between the two younger women, clearly impossible from across the room.

"Jack Mauser couldn't have cared less," said Anna Schlick when she'd recovered her breath. "I distinctly remember him telling you that if he kicked off—he was making a joke, of course—he wanted his ashes bulldozed over along I-29. In the ditch."

Eleanor shook her mother's arm a bit harshly to signal her to stop, but Anna Schlick ignored her.

"He liked this dress," she smiled, her great ravenous eyes lighted with memory.

"What a son-in-law," said Candice, sarcastic.

"Wasn't he? A gracious, good-hearted son-in-law," Anna Schlick thoughtfully agreed. "Plus he was a man with a remarkable fate."

"You call what happened to him fate?" Candice looked at Anna with disdain. "Burning himself up in his own house? I call that stupid."

Anna Schlick's face registered light amusement, her bold features brightened as though Candice had tossed her a bouquet. She stood, cocked a solid hip, and ran her hand along her rounded thigh, absently, loving the rough glitter of her dress.

"He did have lapses in judgment," she agreed, with great simplicity. "You for instance."

She gazed so sadly, then, into the face of the younger woman that Candice lost her voice and flushed.

At the same time, standing at the entry table, Dot watched her dead husband's complex history play out before her eyes. From time to time, she bared her teeth in a nerveless grin. Her eyes were slightly bloodshot from last night's weeping, and her cheeks were puffed from indulging her guilt with half a bottle of red wine. Here she was, a bit hung over, when she was the one who leaned on Jack to quit drinking in the first place. It was embarrassing. Still, she didn't falter and a determined smile flickered on and off her face as she approached the others.

"He wanted a big monument! An angel!" she cried out. "And don't tell me I don't know! He talked about that sort of thing more to me than he did to you, or anyone else here. The last two months were hell and no one else but Shawn and me were there for him. So yes, he talked about death to me. Or bankruptcy. Same thing as far as he was concerned."

Eleanor's eyes brimmed, spilled over, and she clung to her mother's arm. Anna Schlick put her hot, plump palm gently to her daughter's cheek and pressed her full lips to Eleanor's forehead. A fly buzzed around their heads, obnoxious, loud. Suddenly, as if to right things, the older woman turned aside and wrenched the swatter from her husband's grasp as he passed by. She swiped the insect from the air, then breathed heavily, recovering from her sharp movement. Schlick gave her a worried and intense look that changed to appreciation. He smiled, pleased, as though he were at a successful party. Something in the day was giving him an express, deep satisfaction. Anna Schlick ignored him, and ignored all else now as she proceeded to track down by buzz and pause each irritating fly. She stood braced against a chair, smiling enigmatically, swatter held motionless across her chest like an Egyptian scepter. At a buzz, with feral swiftness and startling accuracy, the square of plastic flickered outward past a mourner's head.

Eleanor didn't bother to wipe her face, but let the tears collect along her chin until her face was sheened with water. Dot quieted, struck by the grief Jack's former wife showed. "We should reach some sort of consensus about Jack's ashes," she said in a tentative voice.

Eleanor gulped and nodded her agreement, and then gestured at Candice and the formidable nanny. Mrs. Kroshus approached, stiffly stood her ground, and displayed the cleaned and polished baby to Candice as though he were a wine she'd ordered. Candice accepted the baby into her arms. He was just blooming into awareness, and had discovered faces. He gazed wildly, temptingly, at Candice and spread his delicate mouth in a toothless smile that drew worshipers from among the sober guests. In their relief at this diversion, Jack's visitors overdid the adoration and for a few moments, the sweetness flooding out of Jack's hot-eyed creditors was loud and disturbing.

With a movement so sudden it was almost a shudder, Dot drew close to Eleanor. The two of them couldn't seem to take their eyes off Candice and the child—he was, after all, the only child Jack had fathered among so many women, so many marriages. June of course had died. Eleanor had missed her chance. Candice was physically unable. Dot already had one. Marlis was the only one who had gone through with her entire pregnancy and borne a child of Jack's. The two stared, blinked, looked away, but the baby's face turned upon them over and over again like a flower toward the light.

Eleanor sighed with pure jealous anguish. Why? More tears streamed down her face, unwilled. She was weeping for her own future, for her past with Jack, for the loss of possibility and the memory of that final receding tremble of thunder as the storm passed into the distance. Eleanor marveled at her own capacity for sorrow, her display, and took Dot's hand. Dot's heavy hair was caught up in a beaded clip, then twisted sideways. She looked monumental, larger than life, bursting out of a black velvet Ralph Lauren that Eleanor had loaned her. Eleanor stroked the nap of the material on Dot's arm.

After a while, she gathered enough composure for Dot to ask her questions.

"How are you? You look so thin. Where have you been?"

Eleanor spoke firmly.

"Recovering . . . ," she chose her word carefully and gave it emphasis, "*recovering*. You know more than anyone how hard this is for me. All of the memories, the blinding . . . oh well. I went down to Costa Rica for two weeks and stared at the ocean. Frequent-flyer ticket. Now I'm broke. I didn't tell anyone, though you'll get my cards. I wrote you. I checked my answering machine from there and then flew back." She shrugged. "Thank you for leaving the message."

Dot was anxious to retain the confiding mood they'd fallen into, but Eleanor changed the subject.

"Candice looks happy."

"Scum floats," said Dot. "I used to know her."

The two had drifted near the casket and the frontal truth of it now hit them both. Eleanor felt her blood run thinner, and a hideous weakness surged down her legs, unbuckling her knees. The depth of grief, hopeless as her love for Jack had been, sickened her. She tightened her hold on Dot's powerful arm. They stood raptly, frowning at the garlands molded onto the handles of the box, and then, drawn by the old slide of emotion, Eleanor detached herself from Dot. As she walked toward Jack the room darkened and the floor shook beneath her heels so that she faltered and had to steady herself by leaning on the smooth casket. The hum and hush of voices settled like a cape all around her and when she closed her eyes stormy air flowed, Chinook air, opening the door to the small bare room where last they were together.

§

Radio Bulletin

JANUARY 5, 1995

THIS JUST IN.

THE CRASH OF A SMALL COMMUTER
PLANE MAY HAVE TAKEN FOUR LIVES.
DURING THE TRANSPORT OF FEDERAL
PRISONER GERRY NANAPUSH FROM
PRISON IN MARION, ILLINOIS, TO A
STATE OF MINNESOTA CORRECTIONAL
FACILITY, A FORCED LANDING IN A
DENSELY WOODED SECTION OF LAND
NEAR THE MISSISSIPPI RIVER RESULTED
IN AT LEAST TWO DEATHS. NAMES ARE
BEING WITHHELD PENDING NOTIFICA-
TION OF FAMILIES.

SEARCHERS ARE PRESENTLY COMBING
THE AREA AND THE WRECKAGE FOR
MORE INFORMATION AT THIS HOUR.

Satin Heart

JANUARY 5, 1995

*E*leanor braced herself against the casket, and in a state of intense reverie, smoothed her hand over and over the lid. It was a natural gesture, unforced, even careless in its yearning and sorrow. Dot looked around to see if others had observed. Her friend, for that is how she thought of Eleanor since last fall, not so much in connection to Jack but to herself, often did things that seemed too intimate or personal, too revealing for public settings. In a city as small as Fargo, the accepted way to approach and regard the dead took a more restrained form. As if to demonstrate, Candice now transferred the baby back into his nanny's arms, and approached solemnly, her hands clasped at her waist. Eleanor stepped away and Candice was left alone, standing at demure attention, one foot away from the head of the box.

Candice put a hand to her dry, cool cheek as a haze of sudden thought occurred—for all she knew there was no head or tail to be addressed here—what should she do next? She continued to stand, paralyzed now, wishing that someone would approach, offer sympathies, distract her from the post of regard that now seemed ostentatious. But her very stillness caused those in her vicinity to hush, to cut a wide berth, to leave her even more alone. People would have explained by saying that they did not wish to intrude, but the truth was that no one wanted the responsibility of distracting Candice. She stood, isolated, for as long as she could bear the exposure, and then she backed toward the murmuring crowd in tiny steps, abdicating her place by slow means so that others were able to mill forward, and to her deep relief, surround and absorb her back into the gathering.

And still, once the others had turned away, Eleanor stood rooted on the same square of carpet.

"He was so . . ." she searched, finding no words, ". . . so beyond definition."

Dot found this reasonlessly hilarious, and tried to smother her laugh.

"Very beyond definition," Eleanor murmured, nearly breaking her mood too. "You know, he did say that he would be buried at St. Joseph's," she sounded hysterical now. "He did say that!"

"Give it up!" Dot held a man's kerchief to her face, twisted in mirth. "What does it matter? What do you care?"

"That's the absurd thing," Eleanor went sober, shamed. "I don't know why, but I just do."

The afternoon bloomed achingly around them all, sucking light from the air, then warmth, knocking the flies out and reviving the mourners. A surge of energy flooded into the room as the sun sent late, long-shadowed golden streams coursing through the windowpanes. In that momentary heatless radiance, the subject of what to do with Jack rose once again, only now the argument was dreamier and less deliberate. After an entire day of concentrating on Jack's memory, Candice was losing interest in the discussion.

"Didn't he have any blood relatives?" she inquired of the room.

There was no sign of another Mauser besides his Uncle

Chuck, who came and went early and did not look especially sorry.

What of those ashes? Eleanor's passion on the subject was unspent. She stood apart, in the shadow of dim leafed plants, still weeping, amazingly, with slow and savage determination, like a midlevel marathoner in the last miles. Meanwhile, from time to time during the afternoon, Dot had emerged from her concentration. With a square grip, she had taken up the lavishly decorated giant red heart of chocolate candy that rested on the graven sideboard. This was Jack's last gift to her, ungiven, found in the trunk of his car, a proof of Valentine's forethought, although Dot had never been crazy for chocolate. She secretly felt that she had treated him badly right before his death, and this evidence of his tenderness to have come filled her with shame at her own last words and actions.

Get fucked! She had screamed at him. *You married me so I wouldn't tell the IRS what a mess you made of your books! You never loved me. Never*, she had raved. *Oh well*, she had calmed down. *I still love Gerry, not you.* The chocolates—sign of Jack's true affection—horrified her now.

To every visitor who entered, therefore, Dot offered the candy in hope of getting rid of it all. She held out the box to those who'd been his neighbors when he lived in his own mansion, in a one-bedroom ranch, to his fellow inmates of a downtown residential hotel. Long ago, in a basement apartment owned by an old Swedish widow, Jack had eaten wafer-thin cookies coated with confectioners' sugar and then he had licked the white powder from the daughter's nervous fingers and gloomily asked the girl to marry him. Now Dot offered the same girl, a grown tax lawyer glad she had refused Jack, a chocolate. She accepted, as did the others—the drunk scions of Bonanza farmers, building inspectors he had paid off, or who had refused his money, charitable gambling entrepreneurs, restaurant owners, police officers, big and little uniformly unpaid suppliers, bankers, dissatisfied clients, and most of all, lawyers. Almost every lawyer in the region, including Jack's representatives—Moon, Webb, & Cartenspiel—attended

Jack's visitation. Each accepted a dense cube from Dot, plucking it from its flimsy brown frill of paper, thanking Dot after looking hard at her face.

Blunt, red, doglike, ferocious in its heat, Dot's was not a face to refuse and not a face to trust. As she turned away, the quietly dressed lawyers drifted to the leafy corners of the room, bent to the sterilized earth beneath the palm and ficus trees, and prodded the candy down among the roots. Each of them, every one, had an outstanding bill or score to settle with Jack Mauser and each, in accepting the candy, had felt some diminishment of hope. Dot's stolid grief had some element in it that was implacable, too real to be authentic, overcalculated. As she passed through the gathering, she stabbed a square, hard finger among the satin ruffles. In her attitude they spied a ruthlessness that did not bode well. Her name might be linked forever with staggering debt, Jack's legacy, but the real question was whether any of that money would be collected.

One man tried. Short, freckled and snub-nosed like an overgrown child, wearing a tonsured horseshoe of reddish hair, he accepted a chocolate from Dot and cleared his throat.

"Allow me," he said, "to sympathize."

"Go ahead."

Dot turned away. The man popped the candy in his mouth and, wiping his hands together, stepped in front of her. With his mouth full, he couldn't speak quickly enough to capture Dot's attention. He had to gesture. Waving his hands and blinking rapidly, he signaled.

"What now?"

The man held up one finger and then drew a paper from the inner pocket of his suit jacket. Unfolding it, he showed Dot the invoice and payment schedule for a diamond ring—a shockingly expensive one. Balancing the chocolates on one arm, Dot took the paper and read the fine print. Three smallish payments had been made by Jack but there was obviously no point in putting up an argument.

"Okay," said Dot, "but before I give the ring back, I want store credit for the amount Jack paid you."

"With all due respect to the sad occasion," said the jeweler, "I can give you half credit, and that only after I examine the piece for damage."

"Damage? Half?" Dot had needed a place to focus her rage. Now she had it. "Half store credit? What's this *half* shit? You think you can screw a bereaved wife?"

Rattled, the man threw up his hands.

"It says so right here." He showed the paper to Dot again.

"Well, change it," Dot snarled.

The light died and blue shadow bled deeply down the heavy tree trunks, staining foundations and driveways and the sills of garages. The lawyers retreated and even those who needed the money worst wearied, until by four o'clock the only people who remained were the former wives of Jack, the Schlicks themselves, and one solid-looking and intense mixed-blood Indian man. Dot recognized him.

Lyman Lamartine rocked on his feet, alone, in the corner of the room, regarding each mourner or creditor with a shrewd and assessing look that either dismissed or filed each person for future use and reference. He was the youngest half brother of Dot's first husband, Gerry, and he was well-known for reasons completely unrelated to Gerry's notoriety. Dot had never known Lyman Lamartine very well, and so she offered him a chocolate as she passed by with only the most perfunctory pleasantry. Still, when he waved his hand, palm up, politely refusing, she gave the box a menacing shake, rattling the paper frills beneath his nose.

"How much did Jack owe you?" She couldn't help herself. The jeweler had frayed her nerves. "Over ten thou? Take two."

"Actually, nothing. We're square."

"You're kidding."

Dot lowered the box, put the cover on. "Then you're the only person here he settled with. I thought you hung around thinking maybe you'd get paid if you were the last to leave."

"Like I said, he didn't owe me."

Dot tipped her chin up, watched him thoughtfully. "Jack

mentioned you recently," she remembered. "He said something about your big casino."

Lyman stepped closer, his voice intense and low.

"When?"

"What do you mean, 'when?'"

"I mean," Lyman looked around at the others in the room, murmuring or dull, lost of focus, preparing to leave but not quite ready for the effort of good-byes. "Is he really dead?"

The question startled Dot. An abrupt sound of disbelief escaped her, but she composed herself. "What the hell do you mean, 'Is he *really dead*?'"

Lyman Lamartine's broad face closed, and he stepped back a pace.

"Gerry's out," he whispered.

Dot's mouth tightened and she stared tensely at Lyman, trying to take in the sense of what he'd said. She stepped closer, searching the man's face. Gerry *might* call him. Might, even though Lyman was as straight an arrow as she'd ever known. Gerry out? Dot slipped back again. Had she heard right? Her brain hurt, the connections faltered, a white buzz started up between her ears. She saw brilliant lights blinking, blinking. Overloaded, she tried sitting. There was no chair. She tried leaning. There was no wall. Swaying, she tried to question Lyman, just as Lawrence Schlick approached and stood within earshot.

"Poor Jack," Lyman Lamartine's smile changed warningly, all secrets and pretend rue. "He and my big brother were pals way back. In fact, *I* owe *him*. Jack. Jack. Jackie. I just mean I can't believe he's gone. He was the kind of guy you thought he could survive anything."

"Well, he couldn't." Dot was panicked at Schlick's smooth timing. She willed him to leave, but instead the funeral director stepped even closer, as though drawn by empathy. "Poor Jack, yes. A whole burning house caved in on him." Her eyes began to water at the thought, at the larger questions now stirring in the room.

Lyman Lamartine casually nodded Lawrence Schlick

away, assessed the other mourners, and then swiveled back to Dot. His expression became chastising and playful, fatherly although he wasn't any older. He all but wagged a finger.

"Gerry's out," he swiftly repeated. "Don't ask anything. What I want to know is where you're keeping Jack—"

"Jack's dead!"

"Brand-new houses don't burn," Lyman admonished her in a whisper. "Insurance come through yet?"

"No, they're still . . . "

Dot's eyes instantly dried. She regarded him thoughtfully now, splayed her fingers on the top of the box. "I know what you're saying. But they can tell those things. Gasoline burn marks and so on. They never found any. Not that Jack would."

Even to Dot her defense sounded falsely pious.

"Torch his own house, I mean," she said, just to be clear.

"Of course not, of course not." Lyman rocked back on his heels, hands in his pockets, and for a time he stared at the floor and was lost along with Dot in speculation.

"Maybe it's just wishful thinking," he said at last, and at the fake tone in his voice, so similar to her own, the corner of Dot's mouth turned. "Just this hope in me he's somehow living. And I don't know if you'd consider, but here. I'm giving you my business card. If I can do anything. If you need anything."

Delicately, Lyman extended his card. With his other hand, he lifted the edge of the Valentine's heart. He placed the card inside.

"Where's Gerry?" said Dot, not taking the card. "How do you know?"

Lyman ignored her questions, lifted the lid higher, and read the diagram on the underside of the cardboard.

"Why don't you read the card?"

"Sure," said Dot. She thought of slamming the box shut on Lyman's fingers. He was so mysterious, so frustrating. She hated needing information from him and resented the pleasure he took in controlling a situation that affected her so deeply.

"Figures, somehow," she clenched her teeth. "You're the only one so far who's used the key. To the fillings of these things, I mean." Desperation and hope surged up in her. "Just take one! Take a handful. Live on the edge!"

Then she realized that he was talking about his business card, snatched it out of the box, and read the letters B & B on the back of it.

"I hate marshmallow," Lyman said, pursing his lips as though he didn't notice what she was doing. His hand hovered, the fingers blunt and avaricious, until he found a dark center.

A short, uncomfortable and quizzical silence held among the women before everyone spoke—together and all at once, in relief. Now there was laughter, nodding acknowledgment of Jack's temper, the difficulties he'd been drawn into by his pride, his too-lofty ambitions and misplaced energies. Mr. Schlick flicked switches and dimmers throughout the first floor, and the women who had been close to Jack Mauser understood the signal as notice to take final leave. They stood beside the casket in a state of summary. This unstudied contemplation, disconnected, wordless, linked them and gripped them until Dot broke it.

"I want to see Jack," Dot stated.

Eleanor waved off the syllables because she couldn't believe, wouldn't believe what she was hearing. She'd got hold of herself, but she was treading thin comfort. Soon she'd break though and again be swallowed by grief.

"So do I," said Candice

"You can't be serious." Eleanor twisted her hands together, repelled by the idea and at the other women's cold attitudes. A look of despair crossed her fox-thin features. "Leave him alone!" she said passionately.

"In all honesty I don't think," said Schlick, opening his hands to them all, "anything in particular would be gained. Still, there are those who need to view the body. Different ways of mourning. Not that there is a body, exactly, you understand."

"Well, what is there?" Candice's tone was thoughtful, almost bargaining.

Although Lawrence Schlick tried to keep his tone neutral, there was a hint of gratification in his voice that only Eleanor was tuned finely enough to recognize. She glanced sharply at him.

"Ash. A bit of organic matter. What there was, what we could determine, in the vicinity of his dental work. It's taken, you realize"–he tried to lower his voice–"great skill to sift him out."

Eleanor shook off Dot's hands as Mr. Schlick used a screwdriver carefully and then, with professional detachment, lifted the lid. The women held back for a fascinated moment. Dot was the first to take a step forward. She had to crane a bit to see down into the bed of gray satin, and when she located the bundle that lay on the pearly fabric, a square the size of a book wrapped with waxed butcher paper, carefully tied with a twinelike black cord, she squinted hard.

As she straightened, her stare turned back upon them all.

Schlick explained that a special waterproof urn had been ordered from Minneapolis but had not yet arrived. Dot shook her head. The sprayed red strands of her hair stuck out and almost glittered as the false light caught their points.

"What's it like, this urn?"

"Roughly the shape of a large vase. Of course, it is constructed of a high-tech material, a water- and fireproof cement-based type of malleable stucco."

"Fireproof?" Dot laughed low, a little wildly, then her voice strengthened. "I won't let you bury Jack in a damn pot!" Before anyone could move to stop her, she reached into the coffin and removed the white parcel, then carried it over to the sideboard along with her Valentine's box. With an impatient gesture, she lifted off the top of the box, glanced at them all in warning as she shook out the remaining fluted wrappers, and placed the container carefully open, on the surface of the old wood.

"I'm still his wife."

She dismantled the package of Jack's ashes, breaking the knots with her fingers, and then with great care, as if she was transferring a precious spice or drug, she folded the sides of waxed paper into a cone and shook the ash and crumbled bits of boney charcoal, the lump of belt buckle and porcelain, into the empty heart. She put the box together again, patted the ornate lid, and then she refolded the white paper and handed it to Schlick.

"Somehow it fits," Eleanor spoke loudly. A jealous outrage gripped her, uncontainable, at the sight of the velvet bowed heart. "Jack's last, cheap gesture," she muttered.

"Who cares, really," said Candice, a twang of envy in her voice, too. "He never gave me chocolates. Just those cheap little hearts with slogans on them. *Kiss me. Hot Mama.*"

Dot's hands shook as she lifted the box of ashes now, but with the great red heart in her arms she stood before them visibly charged, directed from within. Her square face was firm.

Candice, not to be outshone, spoke with blunt authority: "Before we decide what to do with Jack, we should talk to Marlis. We've taken a sort of poll here. Marlis is the only vote left out."

There was a vivid and immediate sense of recoil from Eleanor when the name of Jack's fourth and most problematic wife was spoken. Marlis! Marlis! The name itself seemed infused with low-rent disgust and her mouth twisted.

"She never so much as sent *flowers*," cried Eleanor. Her head hurt. She couldn't think. She heard herself saying absurd things, becoming protective of Jack now, when it was too late. And she was displaying her jealousy of that baby. Still, she couldn't stop her words. "Marlis never even called! What's going on with her? I'm sure she never reads a newspaper, but she's got no excuse. She *knows.* Not to mention she never even showed up! What do we owe her? Marlis! She's simpleminded and she's mean, plus she's not so much a wife as something else—why beat around the bush—I've heard things. She was Jack's slut. I know there's a marriage certificate floating around, but I've never seen it! Jack needed

AA—nobody stopped him. Nobody cared. Eventually, Marlis snatched him."

"There wasn't really anything between them!" Candice was cold and furious and half strangled. "Except that she helped him live out his dream, express himself, his talent. . . ." She was too filled with conflict to say more.

"Talent?" Eleanor hollowed to a near screech, embarrassing herself. "Third-rate lounge-lizard singing voice? *Talent?*" She tried to gain control. "Marlis is probably on a bender again. Reason in itself not to seek out her opinion."

"She's bipolar." Candice spoke definitively. "But she's definitely turned a corner. She has the problems of any bright woman trapped in a dumb job. We're still sharing our baby, and she's back dealing blackjack out at the B and B."

"The B and B?" Dot started.

"Our baby?" said Eleanor. "*Our* baby? Ours who?"

Candice's face pulled stiff around the edges and deepened in color. She made no answer, but looked to Dot for what was next to come. Dot, however, was staring down at the buoyant satin bow and voluptuous curves of the candy box cradled in her arms. She considered it for so long that the others grew quiet in their contemplation and rested their eyes on the dark red lobes. A half-opened plastic rose was taped to the cover, the lettering was looped gilt, there was a metallic threaded ruffle, a spray of baby's breath.

"Whoever she is, in her own weird way she probably loved Jack," Dot said at last. "We all did, right?"

§

Caryl Moon

*F*inally, after all the shit and drang, a fluke of freezing air worked in Jack's favor. With flames at his back, the house above about to collapse, a snowbank in his face, with true fear guiding him, Jack threw himself at the white window and popped through. The wind had given him a break in fortune. Blown air had scoured out a well in the side of the snowbank nestled near the house. He toppled, naked except for the singed bow stuck fast to the middle of his forehead, into the empty spot.

Jack sprang up, alert, figuring he hadn't long before he froze completely, or at the very least, did some permanent damage to himself. He didn't even think of staying close to warm himself in the thrill of his burning house. At a dead run, down the iced boulevards, he headed for the highway, for the turnoff where there was an all-night café. He thought of the blessed shelter of the men's room, of the phone. As he ran, he cupped one hand and then the other around his penis and testicles. The cold was unpleasant, with an edge of bitterness, but not severe, at least not at first. As he passed the empty houses on his dream street, he thought that the temperature was deceptive. He could feel bits and patches of himself turning numb, turning off.

He ran faster, worked a little heat down to the end of his limbs, thought twice that he might knock at one or another of the model houses in the next subdivision, or the next, but shame prodded him onward until he reached the lighted intersection. Desperate to get across, he sprinted.

The dark box of a delivery van slammed along so near that the wind of its passage rocked Jack off his feet. He flew back against the curb and rolled twice over the frozen points and peaks of black slush. The driver tried to stop but skidded and then swiveled the truck awkwardly until it halted. The door opened, slammed, and the driver jumped out and ran back to Mauser.

"You okay? Oh my goddamn fuck, *Mauser*!" The driver, a young man, heavily built and possessed of a smug square-headed chubby handsomeness, was dressed in a drab, padded uniform.

"Yeah," said Mauser, recognizing the voice of the man from somewhere. He rose in an embarrassed crouch, tried for insouciance through numb lips, chattering teeth. "Moon! You working for this bullshit outfit? I'm fine, I think."

"No doubt a wonderful time had by all?" Caryl Moon's voice was strained with mockery, though he helped Jack up.

"You could say so."

"God, you thoroughly reek. I suppose you could use a lift."

"What do you think?"

Caryl looked to either side for witnesses. Giving rides was against regulations and he was late in his deliveries anyway. The truck was full of champagne flown in from Seattle, roses from Hawaii, and he was past exhaustion, working long overtime that night and all of the nights before. He hated the holidays—no breaks, no windows of opportunity. Mauser swayed, unsteady, patted his hands out to brush himself off and again realized that he was naked.

"Sorry about the, my ..." Mauser's speech slowed. He

couldn't catch the kite strings of his sentences. ". . . catchease-over, courtnet, condition."

"Allow me."

Caryl eased out of his mud-brown jacket and draped it over Jack's shoulders. He had on a T-shirt underneath. Kiss My Glass was written on it in small block letters. Jack wanted to say something funny, because he knew after he'd fired Caryl he'd worked in window repair, but once he got inside the cab of the truck, he began to shiver with uncontrollable violence, so hard the windshield shook before his eyes and he tried to steady himself against the dashboard as they turned and cornered and began to head back into Fargo.

"Direct me, oh mighty master," Caryl said after two stoplights, his teeth clenched in a fading grin. "Where to?" He was beginning to remember, through his fatigue, how much he had against Jack. Still, was this rich or what?

The heated air blowing on him hadn't in the least warmed Jack and he felt his throat shut, too cold and parched to form an answer. He pulled the jacket tight around himself, tried to gesture at the dashboard.

"If you don't mind," said Caryl, "don't stretch that jacket." He was heavier, Jack now saw, swollen through the middle, almost pregnant-looking. An extra chin lapped beneath his first, but his teeth were white and even. He bit his lip and frowned as he cruised down NP Avenue.

"Did you think of it?" He spoke urgently. "Where you want to go? Destination? I been up three nights, way behind on work, see."

The light was black, crystalline, falling in slow sparkles around them. Jack's voice box still wouldn't produce any sound. He opened his mouth. Nothing. He was drowsy, falling back, unable to catch himself, falling forward.

"Okay," Caryl said, loudly, all of a sudden. "Should I take you to the cops? You want that?"

"No," said Jack, his voice too low to hear. But he couldn't think of what came next.

"I can't drive around all night! Where do you live? Where the hell's your goddamn big fancy house?"

Caryl Moon's voice snagged, harsh.

Jack looked over at him and a raw and nameless emotion jolted him alive. Surprise came over him. Stripped to his skin, he was nothing, was he! In Caryl Moon's eyes, he, Jack Mauser, was a big-time loser, pathetic, less than a nickel, lighter than a dime. He was erased. Here was the truth of things. The feeling enraged him and Jack's voice surged in his throat, warm as whiskey, but clear and clipped.

"Take me to the Radisson!"

The van stopped short.

"Forget it. You're not my problem," said Caryl. "For your information, I'm working this *bullshit* job because you never even paid me severance, asshole."

"I paid you for what you did."

"You ruined my life. Just get out, now. And give me back my jacket."

"Plus, you wrecked my car," said Jack. "Negligence. I've got an attorney."

"He's my fucking dad, idiot! Out!"

"Take me to the Radisson!"

Caryl Moon spoke low.

"I don't take orders. I don't take orders," he repeated, as though to calm himself.

"I'll order you." Jack's anger smiled in him, now, for a heated interval. "I'll order you," his voice built. From somewhere he pulled the strength, the old words. "I'll tell you where to go. Move, you dumb shit. Drive!"

Caryl grabbed the keys from the ignition, jumped out the van's door.

"Wanna go? Come on! Let's go!" he screamed, beckoning, open-handed, at Jack.

Jack stormed from the cab, stumbled. Anger had steamed him hot but his legs didn't work. His arms didn't work either. He was incapacitated, weakened, and understood this, suddenly and simply, when the younger man caught him hard in the chest with a punch. He tried to balance but went over like a big wooden doll and still his anger poured, waves of it coming out of him as he went down, useless vapors. Caryl grabbed Jack, stripped off the jacket, put it on himself and began to kick, drawing his heavy haunch back, swinging his arms up in a big arc when his foot connected.

"That's for us little guys," Caryl groaned, drawing back.

He was wearing soft-soled running shoes, Jack thought at first, and he laughed out loud because nothing hurt. He caught a glimpse of the foot once, smashing toward his face, and it surprised him that he was wrong—the foot was cased in hard, unjointed, and sober leather. The sole connected and in the dazzle that swirled up behind his eyes, Jack saw sunflowers. Caryl kicked harder, now in a kind of dreamy lust, and moaned with effort, with the hard work of pounding Jack. Once, twice, Jack felt an astonishing pain, a deep black shock. Then nothing again. He grew drowsy as Caryl Moon's feet touched him, turned him over, revolved him, worked him across the pavement, this way, that. As he fell asleep Jack saw wheeling petals, tossed high, shooting off fierce sparks. Sunflowers turning, spokes blazing in the heat.

§

The First Draw

AUGUST 1992

Jack Mauser

I never expected her to keep on walking!

Jack's hands were deep in the oiled workings of his uncle's Steiger, a piece of farm equipment they were fixing together, as they always fixed things, with bread ties and duct tape and spit and every now and then the right bolt or screw. It was August, not the dog days of heat, but clear and cool. Years had passed since the woman had walked from his arms into the snow, and yet, when his mind emptied to a mechanical task, Jack's thoughts often returned to Williston.

Whether that bar wedding was legal or not, he'd grown to think of her as his first wife. He felt that the least he could do was claim her.

"The hell!" Chuck delicately fiddled with some flattened threads he'd forced. "No way this is gonna work."

The two men were lying on purple plastic toboggans from Kmart, sliding themselves up and down underneath the bellies of various machines in an orange Quonset garage. Sweat and grease coated Jack's neck, plus a dusting of grit, but it all felt good. He had always liked the fixing and the tinkering, but not Chuck's winter paperwork, the frantic harvesting, the dependence on weather. He hadn't liked the money, either. Lousy after the payments on the big equipment. Nothing left. Farming made him think of getting away from it. He thought he should return to the construction site. Just wanted to see his uncle, that's all, but as usual he'd come to visit and got caught up in a small endless job the way he always did with Chuck.

Jack's uncle stared at him with a pulled-long expression, but then sighed and said so long. *Get the hell out of here.* Jack wanted to tell him that moment, right there, about the development and the land, but he couldn't. A few years back, when dirt was still cheap and Chuck got in over his means, Jack had bought out his quarter section just west of Fargo. He'd leased it back, and Chuck had put all that acreage into flowers. Sunflowers. They were now in bloom. Tomorrow, Jack would draw his first payment on the line of credit he'd been finessing and politicking and begging after for so many years. He would have to tell Chuck that those fields would be a subdivision, a good one, *unique and high quality*, he thought of saying, as though that would matter.

The next morning, early, Jack accepted the bank check, stiff and clean in its plain white envelope. Hegelstead had made it out himself to "Mr. Jack Mauser" and signed it with pompous ceremony. Now Jack pinched it in his fingers, lifted it to his face, and inhaled the sharp odor of the paper. But then—and this offhand decision was the one that fucked up his life for the next two years—he did not deposit it. With the envelope in his hands, Jack walked out the doors of heavy glass and polished steel. He went to his car. He put the envelope on the dashboard.

Jack drove back out to Chuck's place with the rich white rectangle reflecting in the windshield glass. As he drove along, houses going up to either side, new ones, his beliefs were easy, his thoughts simple: *I am the luckiest of lucky sons of bitches.* He had formed an idea, a plan, and it was going to work. Jack Mauser would finally put something big into operation.

Mauser and Mauser, Construction. Jack twice. There was no other Mauser, no partner, just himself. He had doubled his name because he thought the title looked more stable, as though there were generations involved. Of course, there was only him. Over the years, he had built up the cash, crews, and equipment, by himself, from nothing, from a secondhand Cat and a couple of boys who couldn't get their high school diplomas. He'd had luck, but his main secret was he worked himself just as brutally as he worked everybody else. Plus, he could crawl and connive with the best and worst. Jack had patched together his own company by scraping money off the cash edifice, the limestone façades of banks. He knew how to wear a suit jacket and a tie, how to shake hands and look a banker in the eye and promise on a schedule he had no hope of meeting, but did anyway, or almost, by killing his crews.

Oh, and the very last secret of his success—Jack routinely paid his best subcontractors just enough of what he owed to keep them stuck with him on the next job. Of course, he finessed, apologized, strung them along. He kept them hooked in and never let them get too far away. He never paid any invoice in full, never squared his accounts. Smart contractors didn't do that sort of thing, Jack thought, so he kept a keen balance of debt and walked a knife's edge. Now the practice was catching up with him. Some suppliers, the best, wouldn't do business with him. But there were still others to take their places, always would be. Bound to be.

Jack was convincing and he was smart. He barged through doors of black glass, through the tinted lobbies, over rich-wheat carpet, over sugar beet wealth and desks of polished oak bought off the interest on loans to sunflower farmers like his uncle. He went in with the grit of digging septic systems under his nails and he came out, time after time, with that dirt turned miraculously paper crisp and green. Every day was a ground-floor day for Jack. The local boom was always just about to begin. There was a big road to build. Local crews hired on by the government. Jack didn't bid too high and didn't bid too low, and he held where proper, a knack he had learned at the keno tables.

All that hustling, and he now had this. Too much, almost. About to start his biggest highway construction project to date, an overpass and access road down near Argus, his loan comes through. Huge draw, first draw on the biggest sum of money he'd ever landed. The check. More zeros in a string than he'd ever seen. *And here he was*, Jack faltered. *Here I am.* He was about to think *in Fargo*, but instead he thought *an Indian*. That part of his background was like a secret joke he had on everyone. His crews. His banker. Asshole clients. Even his own wives. He'd thought, strangely sometimes, when walking through those bank lobbies, *the hell with all of you. Your doors would swing the other way if you knew who I am!* But who did? He was a mixed-blood with dark eyes and dark hair and a big white German grandfather and a crazy mother. He never thought of her. Or him, either. Both eaten up by time.

Jack turned down a dirt road between two of his fields, parked, opened the car's windows, and let in the day of perfect sunflowers. Their leaves brushed in the still air, dollar bills in a vault of blue sky. Their fat chock-full faces, surrounded by petals, reminded Jack of legions of rich women in fancy hats. He sank back in the warm seat, let the sun shine hard, stretched and yawned until his nerves hummed. Cannons popped, set to go off on small timers so the hungry swirls of blackbirds wouldn't land. Chuck Mauser had tied balloons to his fences, too, and painted them with eyes to look like owls. The fields looked jolly, circus bright, and of course the blackbirds weren't the least afraid. Jack could hear them pecking, flapping, talking, feeding noisily and full of joy.

Chuck Mauser happened by, stopped his truck when he

saw Jack. Jack stepped out of the car, walked with his uncle into the field, and then the two men stood together moving clods of dirt back and forth with the toes of their boots. Jack was uncomfortable. His face burned. There was a buzzing in his ears. He thought about getting underneath the seeder again, fixing that fuel pump in the old John Deere or goofing with the new Steiger, but he also wanted a drink. So Jack and his uncle talked about the crop, the value, weather, and then Jack told Chuck that his first draw was through, showed him the check. Chuck did not look pleased. He did not in fact look at Jack at all. He just stared over the bright blank-faced flowers. Jack hadn't thought exactly what his good fortune meant for his uncle, but now he grew irritated at Chuck's lack of interest. The truth was, Chuck Mauser only had those fields on a lease which was up four months ago. Chuck knew and had agreed on what was coming. Naturally, Jack intended to let him work the fields until he broke ground next month. A farmer had to obtain his yield. But those fields were the first open land past the last mall, between the DollarSave and nowhere. Any fool could have figured.

Jack's uncle narrowed his gaze and screwed his mouth sour, scratched his chin. He had a bad shave, all nicked. But he had the guts to bring up the subject.

"So, you're putting in what . . . a new development?"

Jack nodded.

Chuck nodded. The two men stood at the edge of the field nodding with the nodding heads of sunflowers. They were posed in a vast surround of serene and unthinking agreement, but they were bearing different thoughts. Chuck looked keenly into his own distance and said:

"These are good fields. Rich dirt. Too bad."

Jack took a step back, swayed, put his thumbs in his belt.

"Location, location, location," he mumbled.

Looking down at the ground, they both saw money. They were both pragmatic Germans, Jack partly at least, of the soil but not of the romantic earth. In Jack's case, to be exact, the Ojibwa part of him was so buried it didn't know what it saw looking at the dirt or sky or into a human face. Jack did not see land in the old-time Ojibwa sense, as belonging to nobody and nothing but itself. Land was something to use, space for sale. It did not occur to him that the ground he put his houses on was alive, could crumble, cave in, betray him, simply turn against him, or in any way fail to return his investment. Land didn't do that. Land seemed dead to Jack. To Chuck, land was living stuff.

Chuck thought of rain. He thought of water. He looked up the way a farmer looks into the sky—not to see the weekend ahead, but to see his whole future. Just a slow râin, a soaking rain, a careful rain, no hail. Please no hail to beat the flowers flat. All right? Just water. Jack thought of water, too. Well water, for instance, that he could pump to the surface of his development. It did not occur to Jack that just to drill his wells through that lush crust of black dirt, to suck the sinking aquifer into his faucets and underground sprinkling systems and to pipe it through his showerheads and into his dishwashers, was a temporary luxury that would last only as long as the water down there did. Water dries up. Topsoil blows off. Trees topple. Land lasts, but only farmers know how easily it can turn against you. Since the Ojibwa part of Jack was inaccessible, he was a German with a trapdoor in his soul, an inner life still hidden to him. Both men saw money when they looked at land. It was just that they saw the fields delivering the wealth in different ways, as dead, as alive, as more and as less autonomous or powerful.

"You'll get a lot of money from this crop," Jack went on. "It's a bumper. You'll buy a big damn house right at the end of this cul-de-sac." He smashed his foot against a clod of topsoil. "We'll build it here. Every one of your grandkids will have their own room. Your next wife will have a dream kitchen."

"I'm not going to get a new wife," Chuck informed Jack. "And your aunt won't come back. Women ditch us. Something in the genes."

There was an underlying implication. *She ditched me the way you ditched me, Jack.* But Jack felt no guilt toward his uncle.

Only irritation. He never said he'd be a dirt farmer, had he? Never so much as hinted!

"Your grandkids will cook, then." Jack laughed, shrugging off Chuck's malice and loss. "We'll make everything the right height, their bathrooms, the dish sink, whatever, so they won't have to always stand on stools."

"Kids grow," Chuck said.

"Bless 'em," Jack agreed, but there was a note in his voice, a mean little edge, and Chuck stopped talking, shifted nervously. They stood in silence and then Chuck Mauser gathered himself. His voice grated, almost shaking in low rage at the sky, at the horizon, at the creeping façades of the edge of Fargo.

"The more you fill it up, the emptier it gets."

Jack stepped back another foot or so.

"People have to live somewhere," Jack said, and he managed to keep his voice mild enough, but inside he was setting to boil. He and his uncle were too much alike, maybe. Candice, deep into the pop psychology she used on her patients, had counseled Jack to memorize a trick that would help him keep his temper when he was in that no-man's-land between feeling normal and letting go. She told Jack to mentally image a wire cage, to visualize himself putting up the chain link, and then to get right inside the damn thing like an animal. She told him that he could pace inside the cage, he could go wild, he could let off his steam as though he had just been captured in a jungle. The only thing was, he had to stay in the cage, not jump the fence, not ever let himself out until he knew he was good and ready.

Jack was not ready. He got into his car, backed out and drove away without saying good-bye. His stomach was turning over with the frustration of it all, because he wanted to celebrate, to raise the roof with someone, not deal with a farmer's problems, a farm boy's mistakes. He tried to step back, unheat, look at life through his uncle's glasses. Chuck probably needed those fields to get himself over the edge; he probably felt like shit when he thought of a new house that he never could afford in this life anyway, in this world, and Jack had pushed it in his face. He drove to town and wished he could get Candy and go to their favorite bar, which was called the Library, but Candy was probably in a real library. She was back in school taking another class on some new dental technique that she said would stop pain with little electric jolts.

I want some of those, thought Jack, *or maybe that drink*.

Jack drove past the bar, then doubled back, pulled into the lot, went in and sat down. The room was dim and calm, the talk quiet. No music played, no pool balls clicked, the television was a muted natter. It was only eleven o'clock.

He ordered and drank two beers. Ate a hamburger. Two beers more. He considered what next—go back to the office, or the current work site. There was plenty of work pending, pressure, hordes of details, but he felt that this day should be experienced differently, out of time, out of his regular life's routine. The more he thought about it in the quiet of the morning tavern, the more it seemed unfair. He recalled the hard work he'd done and anticipated all of the work that was in store, and with that in mind he felt righteous about enjoying the zeros on the check he held against his chest within his inside pocket. He thought of driving to the lakes, fishing, eating out, taking simple enjoyment in the cash, the fat roll he'd taken out of his account against the big deposit he would feed it later on.

"I should I should," he muttered to himself, tapping the ashtray with the plastic rapier that had held his hamburger together. "I should go back to work," he said decisively, and then instead, as the waitress approached, he ordered his fifth beer.

The fifth was the one that always sent Jack. He weighed 190. He could handle four and then he'd skate in the sky. He promised, as he poured the Blue Ribbon, that this was his last little gesture. But then he saw Marlis and the gesture became part of a roadhouse dance that went on and on.

One afternoon passed. An evening. He slept. He woke. Needed a jump start. Raw egg in a glass of cold Pilsener. More of latter. Morning flowed into another afternoon. A night. The winnowing sky, wild dark and Marlis, too young. Trapped and passive, he let things happen. A long trip to South Dakota. Morning fell. Again the need clamped down but Jack was broke and stank and couldn't find his check.

He decided to go home.

He'd had his car keys all along, but couldn't recall where the car was parked. Now he walked over to the Library lot to see if it was there. It was. Plus his clean, trim, blond, tooth-pulling former wife, Candy, sitting in the front seat, reading a book. She had kept tabs on Jack. She was still taking care of him.

Jack leaned over beside her, at the open window.

"I'm sorry," he said.

She waved his breath away.

"Get in."

"Where are you going?" he asked. His voice was so small, so unnoticeable, so guilty, that she was able to brush it away the same as she had his apology.

"I'm driving you to work," she said.

"I haven't done anything to you!"

For some reason this just made her laugh, and her laugh was surprising, free, as though she enjoyed his wit. She stopped abruptly and drove in silence for a mile before she finally spoke. Her tone was pretentious, as though she'd thought out this phrase in advance.

"Your capacity for screwing up is far beyond what I can help you with."

She hummed a little tune to herself, and it occurred to Jack to tell her it bothered him, to stop, but he didn't. He thought maybe if he kept his mouth shut she'd turn the car around and bring him home, to the house they'd once shared, make some lunch. She pulled into the construction yard. Her car was already parked there alongside the bulldozer and a couple of tractors, so he guessed she had a friend in on this scheme. He felt it coming on then, as she indicated with a neutral wave that he should go. He felt the hot place in his stomach, the empty place that sent the anger up his arms like cold jelly, the rage into his head. The sudden feeling was so blinding and futile that it scared even Jack. He tried to stop it from happening, and he put himself into the cage the way Candy had advised. As soon as he was in the wire enclosure, in his mind, Candy walked away and got into her car. Before he could jump out and catch her, he was alone in the dirt lot. Her car was already raising dust on the road to town.

And she took his car keys. Maybe by mistake, but they weren't there in the ignition.

He stumbled out of the car, wheeled around, went looking in the windows of the other cars, the equipment, finally climbed up on the bulldozer. He was in luck. The silver key was in the ignition, he turned it, started the thing up and went bouncing after Candy at full throttle thinking he would catch her somehow, cut her off before she took the turn to town. He would yell at her, reason with her, weep, pull his hair, and throw himself down at her feet or beneath the black treads of the dozer. He'd humble himself and start all over just as soon as he stopped being mad, which he was as he moved, as the thing surged forward. It was as though the power of the machine, the throb and heft of it, the things he could do with a lever and a switch, were part of his anger then.

It got too big for him, too big for the wire net he put up to contain it, too big for anything. It roared over him and he grappled with it weakly for one moment and then he was out of the cage, bigger than life, rattling iron on iron down the road with his blade in the air and looking for he didn't know what, until he saw it—fields.

His fields. The flowers looked at Jack, all fat and frowsy, full of light.

"Harvesttime," he shouted, sweeping in with the blade lowered, and he kept on shouting as he cleared swathe after swathe, as the air above him filled with swirling petals and excited birds, as the seeds rang down on the hot metal, as the seeds poured down his neck and shirt, as the heads of sunflowers bounced off the fenders and rolled under the cleated treads and the dust flew everywhere, a great cloud that hung around him in the air of a cool and dry September.

I'm not a truly destructive man. I've built about anything that you could name. You look around Fargo—banks, half the hospital complex, the highway, Vistawood Views, the nursing home, most of the mall, house upon house—you'll see it's set up and hooked in and put there to stay by Jack Mauser. I do things from plans. I make them real. I could do it for myself if I could get a guy that could design me. But since that's not possible, I've always relied on women. Somewhere inside I think— they're women, they should know.

And that's how trouble starts—you plant all your hopes in another heart. Then, if you're like me, you just leave them to grow, as if the woman you've married is a hired gardener.

Jack stripped most of a field down before that cold strength stopped flowing through his arms. He was breathing hard and his eyes were fixed upon the gauges and dials of the machine's control panel. He couldn't hear anything around him, anything outside himself, and then gradually his heart slowed and the adrenaline that had flooded him turned so mellow he lay back in his seat. He surveyed the crushed welter of stalks and plants on which the birds were already lighting with enterprising cries. In the distance, he could see people, his construction crew, coming at him. Candy's car wasn't in sight.

The heat of noon lifted off the fields like a gleaming veil. He'd always intended to build the best house in the whole development for Candice. She wouldn't want one, now, he thought. But as he sat there, he saw them rising anyway. He saw stone trim with clerestory windows, the Tudor look, or Colonial homes with shutters, plantationlike spreads with columns to either side of the front door. He would set the mailboxes into little brick hutches that could not be knocked over by a teenager with a baseball bat. He would sod in big lawns, plant seven-year-old maples. The garages would be double, triple, some with arches, and all would open automatically to accept their owners. Executives would buy these places, school superintendents, the owners of local businesses, wealthy farmers who wanted a town home in the winter. He would name the place the Crest. Just the Crest. Not Crest Park, Crest Acres, Crest Ridge, Crest Wood, or Crest Go Fuck Yourself. His development would speak class through simplicity, like it just meant the top of something, the place we all want to get.

§

The Garage

JANUARY 1, 1995

Jack

*J*ack sped to the edge of his life—a wide, treeless field—and from there, in the fresh wind, he looked down at himself flung on the sidewalk, arms stretched across the snowy grit and dead scarp of the boulevard. He was crushed of importance, pathetic in his fetal ball, naked, gray, same color as the pale gray snow, stuffed with unspent anger, almost dead. He had known, hadn't he? Something was going to happen—he had been warned by that nun, by Eleanor, by Dot, by Marlis, by everyone.

Disgusted, mystified, he rejoined his body and considered going to sleep on the tough grass, against a giving rock, where the pavement was so comfortable and the fizz of faraway traffic a pleasant drum of tires. He would have, too, but a loud pain blasted through his body like a horn and rescued him. It was wracking and unprincipled pain, an anguish so intense it threw him to his feet, howling, dancing to fling it off.

He could see clearly through one quickening eye that the

street narrowed to a green jaw. At the hinge there was a gas station, a bright ball of screaming light. If he should travel to the right, treading on the agonized lumps at the ends of his legs, he'd eventually reach one of his own heavy equipment garages. He thought of it—the smallest of his four twice-mortgaged properties, the one with an office and a coffeepot. No night watchman, no access, but there was, he plotted desperately ahead, a second window he could break.

He took a staggering, rending step. Another, and thought it was the last he could force. Managed one more. A fourth. Almost fell. In this way, Mauser dragged his body through a terrible mist that was worse every time it became bearable. For strange clear moments the pain eroded and bright waves of pleasure flooded him. Rushing cushions of agreeable dreaminess made the gray beams of snow and garbage bags piled on the boulevards appear soft and inviting. When his feet quit he reached down and moved them with block hands. Through the tunnel. He took one halting step, another. He didn't think about the distance, didn't think ahead at all, but concentrated his entire effort on consoling and praising his feet.

June Morrissey. Had she cursed him to die this way because he hadn't even told her his real name? One step. Another. He didn't like to think of her by name. Summer lady dead in snow. He kept on going—slow, impossible—but once he touched the brick side of the garage, a numb energy suffused his limbs. He broke the glass behind a barred window, reached in, turned a dead bolt, and gained the cold interior. At the end of the garage he broke another window and stepped over shards of glass to snap on a space heater he used while he juggled his accounts.

He could feel nothing, all of him dead as firewood. He stood in the glow of a street lamp that faintly washed the room with pallid streaks of luminosity. He didn't want to arouse the suspicions of police or passersby, so he didn't turn on the lights but found his desk chair by feel. He shut the office door, groped along the wall until a pair of greasy padded coveralls fell off a hook into his hands. It was like dressing a store dummy. He shoved his legs into the pants but couldn't clasp his fingers yet to zip. He put his frozen fingers into his armpits to thaw and then fell back into the padded chair and sat, watching the red heat. Every time a ball of current shuddered through the coils, Jack drew a deeper breath. Watching the square of the heater's screen slowly redden, he began to think he wouldn't die. He smelled the dry and homey scent of ironing. A cage of wires scorched the air.

The B & B

*A*t five P.M., the indigo dusk rushed into the funeral home's windows and with practiced solicitude Lawrence Schlick herded Jack's wives from room to room until they reached the front door, where he was able to eject them, all except for his daughter. Eleanor stood for a moment in his arms before she patted his smooth shaved cheek and said good-bye.

The temperature had dropped and the melted surface of the roads had begun to freeze. Ice clung in small patches to the trunks and boughs of trees and made the walkway treacher- ous, slowing the women as they emerged. Having at last decided to drive to the B & B, where Marlis worked, they fit themselves into Jack's car without speaking. Dot pulled out of the parking lot with the Valentine's box on her lap. She was belted in, the box was not, and as she slowed for lights she put her palm onto the heart protectively.

The floor of Jack Mauser's new and about-to-be-repos- sessed red Explorer was already stained with the grease of engine parts; and the recesses between the seats were stuffed with flyers and old newspapers. Empty soda cans rattled. Tangled balls of shirts and jackets that he'd put on in the morning and torn off by noon lay heaped underneath the women's feet. An interior smell clung—the day's hot winter sun, spilled gas, sweat, and spicy aftershave—Jack's lingering aura.

Eleanor sat in the passenger's side front. Candice hugged one backseat door. All sorts of things Jack had kicked aside or his hands had touched were bunched around her and she folded her arms, leaned away as if from Jack himself in a rigid silence.

Half a century ago, the land to either side of the road was cropland, tedious and sweet. In those old days only a few houses of Minnesota timber, some barns, a cooperative elevator, stood against the spare horizon. Some of the very first mud-tamped shacks still sag there, caught up in the drift and shag of old split cottonwood that no one has bothered to clean out from behind the press of farm implement and car dealerships. New stores and companies line the highway: Williams Pipe Line. Sexauer Seeds. Hokum Insurance. Red River Valley Homes offers mobile log cabins. The Sunset Motel boasts water beds. There is a Mattress City. A miracle mile of places to eat. Kelly Inn. Taco John's.

Just past the sand pile, the windbreak, and the train tracks, West Fargo. The sand is for the roads, so slick in the winter. The tracks of course bear away the grain, seeds, beets, and cows. The windbreaks do not break but comb the wind into a long thick tail of air that flows down Main Avenue with great force straight through Fargo and then Moorhead, and on across the frigid, feminine, waist of Minnesota.

There is a bar on Main Avenue that conducts a little charitable gambling. The B & B steak house–bar–casino–lounge is a dimly lighted place, all on one level, with a Styrofoam tiled ceiling and a cement floor covered with stained sheets of chemical fabric. Still, there is a flavor to it of the West more than the Midwest. This is where the regions meet, where the tallgrass once shaded into mixed-grass prairie and from there the short-grass plains. This is where the rain slackens and where the men's slacks turn to jeans, where the women of the eastern seaboard and the ladies of the next few states over, as well as tender young females, turn into gals, gals, gals. In West Fargo, at the B & B, where chicken meets steak, there is a settling and a blending of farm and ranch. Here a western-wear shop and there a farm implements dealership. In the window of one store a carefully painted Holstein, on the roof of the next a fiberglass quarter horse. Still farther on, Herefords. An ad for bull semen. A sign: Milk. North Dakota's Official State Drink. Then a test patch of Sunco sunflowers. The B & B, too, is a cautious amalgam. The package store stacks cases of Grain Belt to the roof, fewer Coors.

The sign outside the B & B, a square of white, glowing plastic, begs Canadians to enter, offering par on their dollar for drinks. The front door is battered and has been rehung so many times that the pins have pulled from the wood, and inside, another door, this one of insulated glass, is duct-taped together in a broad Y. There is a steak house, windowless, just down the hall, and to the left stretches half an acre of carpet scored with three linoleum walkways, studded with small, black chairs, and tables, on the top of which candles in red bowls burn low, casting wedges of feeble light into the faces of the bingo players. The players are mostly friends and neighbors. The ceiling is low and there is the sort of illuminated case full of stuffed toys that will appear from now on in every Town Pump and bar until you fall off the western edge of Montana.

Marlis Cook scared women, snowed men. She had an eye-focusing quality, matched a swimsuit-calendar ideal, her smile was a fast print film that invited instant response. Hair: streaked pale brown, frosted, pulled to one side in a thick tail. Eyes: big, periwinkle blue, black lashed, and void. Figure: medium. Jeans: tight. Heels: high. Age: maybe. All of this was strictly worked out. From her twelfth birthday on, with teenage persistence, Marlis had imagined herself in the spotlight, though she couldn't sing. She took piano lessons, planned her look with grids and stacks of magazine articles and hairstyle booklets, with fortitude and desire. Starvation, peroxide, and manic devotion to the cause of herself had transformed Marlis, born plain, into a stare-gathering creation.

Once she had achieved the desired visual effect, though, Marlis usually concentrated on drinking everyone around her stone-blind. It was good to forget, she believed. Forgetting was the talent. Memory is overrated, she told Candice. People with satisfying and beautiful memories are, of course, the ones who harp on the value of retaining a detailed picture of the past. Marlis on the other hand was more interested in erasing hers. Tonight, the first time in at least a year, she knew she would drink too much. If she was lucky, she would wake with a calm black patch of forgetfulness covering the events she had lived through. Like a person piecing together a blanket, she relied on those patches. Some quilts are beautifully colored. Hers was made of darkness.

Marlis was on the verge of giving up—on herself, as a mother, as everything. It was too painfully obvious that Candice was better, more stable, an influence for the good on the baby. Jack was dead, the unwilling father. Panicked, Marlis had decided to ignore Jack's death as a fact and treat it as a stupid joke. By drinking, she thought she might succeed.

She could work the twenty-one tables in her gathering quilt of darkness, drinking in the ladies bathroom from a bottle of Cuervo hidden in the toilet tank. Her condition was never evident, her hands never faltered. The least conscious part of her was the most expert dealer at the B & B. Already, upon entering the bar, she'd lost the memory of the day and so as not to retrieve it, not to restore it, but to continue to forget, she took the hall at a fast clip, entered the bathroom, and locked herself into the second stall. Her breasts stung, milky. She could hear her baby's cry and hesitated, but she couldn't stop herself from lifting the porcelain tank's top. The worm at the bottom of the bottle glowed. She took two vivid swallows, and then, hating herself, took three.

Marlis replaced the bottle. As she emerged from the bathroom, she realized that she was slipping away, that this night was a test she was setting herself up to fail, that she should go back while she had a half a brain left and pour the tequila down the tank and flush. Marlis stopped. She stood outside the chipped pink door waiting for the booze to take hold so what she did from then on wouldn't matter. *I won't be sorry*, she promised, but then her breasts felt so heavy. Jack burned to ashes in his basement—once upon a time she had been in love with him and couldn't take it. She would not believe it, just refuse. No. But the third shot of tequila hadn't taken. She wasn't drunk yet. She would have to go back and get another half a gulp.

She did. Carefully, she entered the ladies room, latched the door behind her, and again lifted off the top of the toilet tank and set the heavy rectangle down across the sink. The bottle lay in the water, cradled and still. She picked it up by the neck and the cap fell off. *Oh shit*, she hadn't screwed the top on all the way or something. The fiery tequila was now cut with toilet tank water. Marlis shook the dripping bottle. Here was the question. She turned the tequila side to side—toilet tank water. Just water. It was just water, wasn't it? There was no spillover or connection to the rest of the toilet, right? Like regular water. She put the bottle to her lips, took it down without drinking. Here was the question. Here was the question. That's when she had one of those thoughts she hated. Sometimes her brain would betray her into doing something right. *If you don't drink, Jack will not have really died, it will all be a mistake, and he will help you get your baby back if Candice goes to court*. Her mind set this up. Superstition. That's all it was, and then again, how could she mess with it? She tried very quickly then to get the bottle to her lips, but instead her foot kicked up the toilet seat. Her arm poured. Tremendous sadness welled in her as she watched the liquor tumble down.

❖　　　　❖　　　　❖

Outside, the onstage microphone amplified the clear and self-serious drone of an old man hired to read the numbers off the Ping-Pong balls that popped from a clear plastic box into his hands. They were playing the last bingo card and soon she would have to open her table for business. Marlis saw Candice, right there in the hall, and knew that she didn't want to deal with whatever piece of the funeral she had to face. She paused restlessly, watching the slim blond woman, her freckled and complacent, hard face. Marlis lit a cigarette and put the match out with an impatient wrist snap. And there. Another of Jack's wives, she couldn't recall the name, a classy tough-looking woman who frowned in fixated blankness, fishing for stuffed animals in a lighted plastic case. She was pumping quarters into the slot, working the miniature hooked crane, slamming her knees at the steel base. She liked stupid games, like Jack. The expression on her face was pure concentration as she worked the controls, and Marlis began to softly imitate the way she shifted her hip into contact with the box, bumped, and ground.

"Hey," said Marlis to Eleanor.

Eleanor turned, recognized Marlis from a picture that Jack had once shown her, and was overwhelmed by a sudden flush of confused anger. She regained control by shoving her hands deep into the pockets of her down coat.

"Where were you today?" Her voice was cool.

"Nowhere." Marlis was forced but pleasant. "How's Jack?"

Eleanor shook her head, suspicious.

"Dead."

"Oh yeah. Right." Marlis stubbed out her cigarette against the wall and tapped it onto the floor, then she ground it flat again with the tip of her toe. "Geez, I'm up. I gotta get back to the tables. See you." With a slight wave and a floating motion of her hips she was gone, her walk a fast flow that took her swaying between the small, black, round tables of the bar floor and across to the back room with the counter of glass pull-tab jars and tables of green felt—half circles where customers already sat on bar stools buying chips and pondering the shallows of their billfolds.

Blackjack is an unenlightened game that fools and drunks play well but never win, not in the long run, through mesmerized evenings. In the course of a night, a table of strangers betting idly together can turn passionate about one another's welfare, or resentful because of some irrational habit of mind. People's faults glare. Players sitting elbow to elbow close ranks against newcomers, sometimes, if their entry breaks a streak of hopeful wins. They mentally kick out a player whose dour caution brings bad luck, and draw close to someone else who wins with no letup on the averages. The dealers at the B & B were women, all blondes, all secretive and hardened but professionally good-natured—as they had to be, for a table can unite in a wave of feeling against a dealer whose fingers move too fast, whose eyes are too cold, who shows no compassion for the horseshoe of small disappointments spread before her.

Now, as Jack's other wives approached her, Marlis smiled, cool, benign, and asked if they had come to play.

"The more you play, the dumber you get," the man on Eleanor's right stated, warningly.

"Speak for yourself." Eleanor took a tall chair, ordered a martini, and winced when it came in a water glass with a spear of pineapple chunk and a maraschino cherry. She doubled down, bet low, and took no chances unless she felt the prickle of luck. She counted on her patience to outlast the dealer's odds. Dot's personality, on the other hand, ran to flukes, and because she was aware that she tended to bet high and fast on instinct, she hung back. The Valentine's box still sat squarely in her lap. Marlis raised her brows and widened her grin.

"I'll just float with the tide," Dot said, her voice low, stubborn.

Candice approached the table with a margarita in her hand and stood watching, a confident smile flickering off and on. Before she and Marlis had come to an understanding she sometimes had felt humiliated. There had been times, overcome with jealousy, when she'd fantasized violently and obsessively about choking, poisoning, or shooting Marlis Cook. It was no use telling herself that Marlis was her own punishment—for one thing, Marlis didn't seem at first to be suffering from her personality as much as she should be. That had changed. Now Candice Pantamounty found herself increasingly consumed by worry and tenderness. New themes in her life. Marlis was having trouble with postpartum blues, but she was determined to persist in nursing. They had agreed, though, no booze. Was Marlis drinking? Candice couldn't tell.

For weeks now, the two had been fighting over the baby. Candice had legal adoption papers drawn up and ready to sign, but now Marlis didn't want to sign, to share. In a fit of anger, Candice had told her to leave. Marlis refused. She'd taken a job as a substitute blackjack dealer, though, and allowed the nanny Candice hired to care for John Jr. on the nights she had to work. Candice watched Marlis's hands, so smooth and well cared for, so adept with the cards. She had a light touch, the natural touch of a piano player, and her hands passed the cards from side to side, righting and smoothing, gathering, her face impassive, that of a priestess.

"You okay?" Candice asked, stubbornly offhand.

Marlis let her eyes drift quickly upward and then back to the cards. Her eyes went almost navy, smoky, violet-blue. In that one short glance Candice was sure that she detected the intimacy, the shared and secret knowledge that she craved. She breathed deeper, in relief, and let herself drift away. Then she recognized something she understood in Marlis's look — tequila. They had to talk. It was wrong, what was happening. All the time, up to now, Marlis swore she had stayed on the wagon. How had she, Candice, let her lapse? Or should she take responsibility? Shouldn't Marlis discipline herself? It was Jack's fault, Candice eventually decided. Dying, especially at so inconvenient a time, right at the New Year, had given Marlis an excuse and had diverted Candice from her usual careful cataloguing of her habits.

After the visitation, the nanny had taken their baby home.

He was safe now, at any rate, and Candice was free, arms empty. She was much more a suitable parent than Marlis, thank god. There was no question, in Candice's mind at least, whom the baby preferred. No question whom the authorities would consider a proper custodian. A dentist. A professional! Still, Candice worried. She hadn't planned any second thoughts, but now a wave of sadness passed through her and she gulped her drink. The liquor knocked a sudden optimistic notion into her brain. It was nice, wasn't it, to have an evening out—even if it was a funeral that she herself had half paid for!

Eager, feeling the leash of baby-need fray and then snap, Candice tossed her drink down too quickly, bought five one-dollar chips, and took a chair. Although she was shrewd and careful in her work and business, there was rarely a purpose or strategy to Candice's gambling, and tonight she was even more erratic than usual. She blew her chips in quick succession. A morose man in a blue tractor hat sat next to her, losing quietly. Now he pushed his glasses onto the bridge of his nose.

"Help me out here. Come on. Gamble," he invited Dot.

Dot laid down a ten and carefully piled her chips in front of her.

As Marlis smoothly shuffled, she focused on the women before her. "Hey!" Her voice was bright, her hands moved. "Hey, how did it go?"

She dealt, and played out a hand. Dot hit a natural on the second pass.

"So you're Marlis." Irritated, she scraped in a pile of chips. "I'm Dot, the last and final wife. It went terrible, it was a goddamn funeral!"

Marlis dropped her eyes, faltered, went bust, and paid off the table of customers.

"See," the sad weasel-thin man said. "Picking up. Things are definitely picking up."

Eleanor, staying even in the game, played five more hands as cautiously as Dot and then split pairs, bet everything and fished until she came up with a pay-off hand and a twenty.

"What are you, lady?" The man in the hat, excited, drummed the counter.

"A nun," said Eleanor.

"Wow." The man pulled a wrinkled fifty from the emergency pocket of his billfold.

"She won't bring you luck!" Candice said. "Forget it."

"A nun's a nun." The man kept his money in.

Within two more passes, Candice bet and lost all of her chips once again. She stared at the circles in the green felt, blaming Marlis, her face rigid with frustration and the sudden infusion of alcohol. She'd drunk too much, on an empty stomach, and she was losing control. She could feel it happening — as though she wore layers of paper and they were lifting off her, burning, disappearing into the air until she was exposed, raw, ready to jump.

"Why can't I win?" She almost wept. "Just one time. This one's for Jack!" She threw down her hand, had a drink, and then another. After drink number four she took a dollar from her purse.

"One chip?" said Marlis.

"Two fifties."

"Big spender." Marlis gave her a tiny, shy smile and Candice's heart lurched, tears burned behind her eyes and she put each chip in an adjoining circle.

"See?" Her voice attempted the clipped smoothness she used with frightened patients to still their fears. "I'm tipping you half my bet."

Marlis knocked, then tossed the money in her tip cup when the hand was played out.

"I just contributed another buck to the house," said Candice. "See?"

She raised her hand in the air and twirled the yellow chip off the ends of her fingers.

"All right!" She suddenly screamed into the lull of the band's song. "Fire up!"

It was a loud scream, disturbing. The power and volume of

her voice was shocking. People sitting in the unlighted section of the bar turned, tipped back in their chairs.

"God," she screamed. "This wasn't such a good idea!" Candice pitched forward, slamming into the rail of the table, and the other women bent over her, rubbed her temples, soothed her, and sat her carefully upright on the stool.

"Here." Eleanor offered a chip. "Bet. This will be your last drink if I hit right off, on this hand."

Candice shook her head, vehement, and then slumped in a dizzy rush as the cards fell. "And there it is," she said softly, squinting at the table. "The ace of hearts. The goddamn queen of spades. That's you." She tapped the queen, put her head back down on the edge of the table.

"It's all part of the grief process," Marlis stated, snapping her gum. The repetitious patterning of her own cards and fingers seemed to have thrown a switch in her brain and she was momentarily rational. "I'm on break," she said to Dot. "Let's sit down a minute, talk."

Dot nodded and raised her brows at Eleanor, who stood up and helped her support Candice in a wobbling stagger between them. The women settled themselves together almost ceremoniously, and waited silently after they ordered their drinks, looking at the fake plastic grain of the wood under their hands, at the television, at the drinkers slouched at the counter, anywhere but at one another.

Finally Dot spoke, her voice quiet and slow, addressing Marlis.

"Listen, Marlis, we came to get your vote on what to do with Jack."

"What to do with him?"

Dot tapped the Valentine's box, which she had brought into the bar and kept close, on her lap. Now she centered it upon the table. "He's in here, actually."

Marlis stared at the box, turned her head side to side.

"My candy," she said.

"No." Dot's voice was patient, her words slow and reasonable. "Marlis, this is Jack, this box contains his ashes."

"Marlis!" Candice came to and put her arm around Marlis's shoulder and shook her roughly, as if to wake her from a feverish sleep. Marlis opened her mouth wide and then gulped, bent over in a sudden and private fit of humor. "Last time I saw him, I said he should bring me a box of chocolates." She pointed at the box. "Those are my favorites. He knew."

"That was a long time ago," Candice said, her tone so soft it was almost a reproach. Marlis held Candice's gaze and then glanced away in confusion, but their small moment was lost on the others, especially upon Dot, whose eyes narrowed into the distance. She removed her hands from the box.

"What the hell are you talking about?" Her face was all steel, lined and pointed.

"I *said*," repeated Marlis, shrugging away Candice's hand, "'Those are my favorites.'" Her voice was light and musical. "He left them for me. Said he would every time we got together. Always did. Last time, though, I forgot to collect."

Dot seemed to condense, to square herself into a hard and solid mass. She closed her eyes, concentrating inward before she ground out her words.

"I believe you." Dot's eyes opened, fixed on Marlis. "He knew I hated chocolate. I just thought . . . well, fuck what I thought." Dot pondered, her mouth moving in a low-pitched growl, she argued with herself until she reached a decision. "As far as I'm concerned, the problem of where to scatter Jack has just been solved."

Dot took the box into her arms, held it up dramatically, and then threw open both halves of the red heart.

Simultaneously with her gesture, both doors to the bar cracked open with such force that the duct-taped pane popped out and rang on the stiff linoleum. A freezing blast of wind in which sleet and the smell of a thick perfume were mingled whipped through the low room. The blast caught the ashes as they fell from the box and whirled them into a fan of grit that suddenly and immediately doused and covered each of the four women at the table. The powder polished their faces, drove itself into the nap of their scarves and coats, lined their tongues, sifted down their necks, up their sleeves, into their hair, stung their eyes, and caught in their throats. The wind blew harder. It crashed around with such force that papers and cards flew from the tables and a bird of cocktail napkins flapped toward the dark ceiling. Women shrugged their coats onto their shoulders, men stood up and stamped their feet, swearing, dealers scrambled to pin down their cards, wildly counting tens and aces. When the door slammed closed again and the swirl of icy air subsided, when everything had fallen into its place and new drinks were poured, those who looked back toward the door saw that a massive Indian woman stood alone in the entryway.

Her face could hardly be seen beneath the mask of ice that covered her head like a helmet, but there was something about her that emanated the stark quiet of dead bones. Her hair flowed down across her tattered coat in thick and sinuous streaked tails, and her hands, in woolen mittens, were clasped around her waist. She lifted one thick paw and knocked away the ice from her brow, took a long, wide step, then stopped herself, hunched over a bit, and shuffled into a corner, where she kicked a little table sideways and sat. Her feet were big, encased in black rubber boots. Her head bent suddenly over the tiny round logo of a coaster, and her face was shrouded by the stiff, uncoiled hair. She seemed about to fall asleep, or perhaps just to retreat from human contact, but then, just before she vanished entirely into herself, she cast a quick glance toward the back of the room and Dot caught the gleam of a wolf-white smile.

Dot gave no outward sign of her shock, but the blood drained away from her head, her heart faltered, and she nearly toppled from her plastic chair. The other women didn't notice. Eleanor, Candice, and Marlis had jumped up and each, in her own maddened frenzy, brushed, plucked, and beat at herself, but so fiercely had the wind blown that the particles of ash were impossible to dislodge and the taste of it, the tone of it, the dry rub of ash upon their fingers felt fixed and permanent.

Dot was the only one who hadn't moved. Now, she dropped her gaze and began to riffle her purse in seeming distraction. She found a key ring, a tissue, a roll of mints. She looked carefully at these objects in the dusky gloom, trying to ground herself, and she counted to ten, evenly, before she dared look at the corner of the room again.

The woman was still there, frowning at her empty hands, and the cocktail waitress stood near, violently gesturing in some obscure argument with the manager over whether the woman—drunk, confused, or in such complete possession of herself that no one dared approach her—ought to be served or not. The scolding ended with the waitress flouncing sideways, banging down the metal tray she carried. The manager winced and retreated as Dot pushed forward. She leaned across the bar and announced that she wanted to buy the lady at the corner table a coffee and a pizza. The bartender was instantly alert.

"An entire pizza?"

"Large. Supreme. She's got a big appetite," Dot said evenly.

The manager bent down to the small refrigerator, and took out a frozen pizza. He extracted it from its wrappings and set it carefully in the microwave oven. After Dot paid him, she stood absently, watching the other wives who brushed more slowly, staring at their clothing in dismay. Dot disregarded them and turned her full attention on the newcomer, whose hair was now a mass of melting ice. The woman tipped the coffee into her mouth with a motion fierce in its delicacy, and, as soon as the pizza was set before her, downed the whole thing slice by slice with such quick movements that it seemed to vanish by itself.

After no trace of food was left the great woman rose. Without a word, Dot stepped away and walked down the long hallway that led to the rest rooms, the back storage rooms, and the employees' parking lot. Six paces after Dot, the formidable stranger moved, in an aura of monumental calm but with a spring and heft to her step. The two paced together until they entered some door or aperture and vanished to curious eyes. A short time later, it must have been half an hour, Dot emerged from the storage gloom and made her way slowly, musingly, back to the other women and the nearly empty bar.

§

The Owl

Jack Mauser

*L*ight was greasy gray in the windows when Jack woke, curled in the smoky sleeping bag that he sometimes took hunting. He rubbed his hands across his broken face, recoiled at the pain. Thinking of Dot, of Eleanor, even Candice and Marlis, he became uncomfortably agitated—it took him some time to discover that he was bothered by the idea of their grief. Would it be safe to telephone one of them and tell her that he was all right? Alive, at least. And then, what would her reaction be? Relief or disappointment? Which? That thought twisted. The bad paint on the wall was a watery tan. Skin tan. Jack wanted to howl at it as soon as he moved. Every muscle, every tendon, every bruised inch of skin came alive. In slow agony, stopping to breathe hard, Jack raised himself and swung his legs over the edge of the army cot. His feet touched cold cement and he tottered toward the heater, stubbed his toe. The shock moved up his leg. There was a toilet with a tiny scrap of mirror in the corner.

His face was puffed into an ugly jack-o'-lantern. New shades, new colors, continued to rise all day as Jack lay low, eating candy bars from the broken vending machine, drinking iron-brown water mixed with coffee and hot chocolate he boiled with a plug-in kettle he found in the closet. Sleeping. He slept hard and long, as if—should he only stay unconscious long enough—he wouldn't wake to stumble into the shape of his trouble.

Each time he came to, Jack had stiffened a little more, his limbs like sprung boards. His brain itself had hardened in its helmet of bone. Each part of his body ached. One toe then the other ballooned and throbbed, passively subsided. The knee took over, the lower lip, his eyelid. A storm moved down to his wrist or, worse, the kicked muscles in his back. His body gave up and put him to sleep again. Sleep rushed into him powerfully, a dam-burst. He was sleeping like a newborn, it occurred to him. The way Marlis's baby must have slept at first. Punched. Bruised. Shocked. Shutting out the world.

On the next morning, useless window light again. He hurt so badly he began to laugh, feverish, turned over on the cot, in his sleeping bag, moaning, leaking tears. Shuffling to the toilet he got the dry heaves, collapsed on the floor, slept there. He wondered if women felt this way in labor, if Marlis had, bearing his son.

On the third morning, he felt better.

Maybe it was all the hot powdered chocolate—the taste brought him back to his Aunt Elizabeth's house in Minneapolis and the little ledge beside the kitchen window where birds landed for the crumbs and seeds his aunt piled there evenings, after dinner. His aunt on his German father's side, his *Tante*, kept him while his mother took her cold-water treatments— the physical shock that was meant to break the rigid silence she fell into every autumn. His father, the big Mauser, the copy of the original John Mauser, brought six-year-old Jack up the tiny stone walkway, by the hand, and then left him there. In the morning his aunt stirred a stingy wedge of Mexican chocolate into boiling milk, added too little sugar, and let him sit without her—the best treat of all—drinking it while he watched the chickadee peck up a seed and dash away to crack and eat it on a twig of dark yew. Watching the birds occurred during those long blank periods while he waited for his mother and father to return. His aunt tried to starve him in the meantime. All that candy and puppy fat—*Tante* said that Ojibwa mother spoiled him!

All that was left after Jack had blown his aunt's money in the 1970s was the other chunk of railroad land he'd bought from his uncle, and that house in Minneapolis, which still stood and which would be his, theoretically, though his aged aunt still haunted it with her presence as gray as a smear of smoke on the wall. He had some options, he had some options. He could go back there and drink her watery-pink chocolate, or he could die right here with a mug of instant in his hands. He could sit in his own garage until he was found and then he could undergo the loss of everything he stood for, the bankruptcy proceedings, the crazed feeding frenzy of his creditors, all that he was in for soon as they began to seize his equipment. He could vanish, and he knew just where, he'd always fantasized it anyway. He could simply drive due north and still north until he passed the border and then roared through Winnipeg and then still drive north, north to Churchill, and still north, farther yet.

Time pressed on him. Each of his wives passed through his mind and his thoughts hung on them all with varying degrees of guilt or unkilled love or sorrow. The worst thing was dealing this dishonest blow of grief to Eleanor. He could not get over the image of her face in shock, but what could he do? He imagined calling, hanging up if she did not answer, but where would he call? The memory of Eleanor was like the edge of a pit—he consistently fell in and climbed back out. She popped up. He threw her over the edge. Grabbed her back. Fervently, sorely, he still loved her. Time only doubles the emotion, time fixes it in place, time builds. He despaired at his useless wishes. There also appeared to him, at a bitter hour, the tiny light of his new son. His son. As morning hardened in the windows and then grew dim, he began to think about the boy, to wonder, his thoughts insistently returned to the first moments that Marlis had allowed him to hold John Joseph Mauser— for some reason, even Candice had been unable to sway Marlis from naming the baby after his father. There was satisfaction in that, at least.

After the baby was born, Jack had briefly rocked him in his arms. He was surprised at how bird-boned, how passionate the baby's worked-up cry of hunger, how direct in rooting at his chest, mouth twisting blindly for a nipple. Jack had a feeling of unreality, a thrill of fear when he knew the infant would cry, and then a sudden calm took hold when the baby seemed to accept him and lay back blinking into the middle distance, squinting, staring directly into Jack's own face.

The next day Jack began to acquire some strength. He shoved a billed cap low on his head, a disguise, though he was almost unrecognizable, his face so swollen. He broke into the cash box of the vending machine, emptied it of quarters and then went out and bought a newspaper and a thick meatball submarine sandwich. Better than painkillers, that sandwich fortified him and renewed his spirit as he read the *Forum* through and through. Certainty gathered in him, and a low form of joy. He was beginning to understand what he had to do. He took small bites, unlike himself, made the food last for hours, watched the light sift gray to black in the wire-pattern of industrial windows.

As he sat there, chewing in an odd, cheerful, vacant funk, he heard a slight scraping sound and then, with no warning, Hegelstead, bank president and purveyor of prime-rate interest loans to Jack, the man to whom he owed everything and everyone, Jack's personal line of credit, appeared in the room.

Jack jumped, it was so abrupt a sleight-of-hand materialization. The sudden plummet of a stock. Grain futures going bust. Gone money. It was all there in the person of Hegelstead.

The bank president shut the door at his back and stood gaping sternly at Jack's sunset-colored face. Hegelstead's skin was hearty, white around the ears, and a seared-steak red on nose and cheekbones. He was wearing a heavy black topcoat with a plush astrakhan collar and warm black deerskin gloves. His hat was thick, a clump of Russian-looking fur with earflaps. His voice was thin and reedy, but he spoke with precise assurance.

"I figured I'd find you here." Hegelstead leaned against the desk. "Moon called me, told me that he'd seen you New Year's Eve, the night of the big fire. Very alive."

"Not so very," said Jack.

"It stinks in here."

"What do you expect?"

"I expect to get my money."

In his voice, as he settled into a folding chair and drew from his inner pocket a sheaf of papers, there was an intense bankerly energy. Numbers clicked through the air, open-ended and hollow. Hegelstead unfolded copies of Jack's loans and lien waivers, promissory notes and displayed them to Jack one by one.

"What am I supposed to do with these?" Jack tossed the papers on the cot.

"Think of something," said Hegelstead. "Quick, or as of tomorrow night you're trespassing on Norwest property."

"Does anybody else know that I'm here? Alive?"

"Just me and Caryl Moon, who's paid off for now. Oh, and I got a call from that reservation guy, too. Lamartine. Friendly. Too friendly."

"It would be better for me if I really was dead."

"Monetarily speaking, yes."

"In other ways, too, better for a lot of people." Jack spoke morosely, but inside he felt hilarity build. "Don't tell me." His mouth twitched. He wanted so badly to laugh. "You have a gun. I write a suicide note. You shoot me and put the gun in my hand. That way you don't have to deal with my subcontractors, lawyers, or my wives, either."

Hegelstead gave him a disgusted look, though he conceded, "It's a thought."

"Or how about this?" Jack sighed. "You forget we talked. You never saw me. I go up north, get hooked in with a few people that I know. A couple of them in the casino business. Lamartine, okay? I'll be his indentured servant. What choice do I have? He knows. He's sharp. He's got his reasons. Meanwhile, down here, you make a few inquiries and in a discreet way you satisfy the worst of my subcontractors and suppliers. We forget about prosecuting me—all you'll do is rack up huge legal bills. End up with nothing. Because I've got nothing. Plus I'm no good to you in jail. Let's just say I take a leave of absence. I travel up north and you get me a big project where you'll make back big money—take a cut, a percentage of the profits. You know the future. Call Lamartine—from a pay phone. Get in touch with him. I know him from way back. Get me involved in his mega-project, Hegelstead. It's our only out. That way, instead of screwed, you eventually get paid!"

Hegelstead sat back, his face impassive, arms folded.

"It would be worth a lot to see you locked up," he said, his voice wistful.

Jack tried to laugh, but his face felt strange and heavy, as though a plaster mask had dried onto his features. He touched his nose. Maybe it was broken. He was having trouble breathing.

After Hegelstead left and the night was still, Jack tottered into the concrete-walled bathroom, pissed, rinsed his mouth with ice-cold iron-tasting water, drank a great draft, swallowed, spat, gulped down three aspirin he found in a truck's glove compartment. He painfully and finally wiped more cold water against his face, then at last crawled into the sleeping bag. He was getting used to the routine of it, the quilted bag and army cot were almost comfortable. As he fell into sleep, exhausted, unable to worry about the money, about the future, something happened to him that hadn't happened for a long time.

Jack thought about his mother. His memories were usually so vague and so painful that he avoided them. But that night, she appeared.

Big—he remembered her as huge. He hadn't seen her as a grown-up though, so he didn't know whether she was really that huge, towering over, hair full of leaves, or whether he had been so small that she seemed treelike to him, massive. His mother, Mary Stamper, came of some wandering people who joined right in with Ojibwas but might have been created out of a lot of different other tribes—Crees, Menominees, even some secretive Winnebago knowledge might well have been hers. Who knew? She was listed as a full-blood on the tribal rolls but from somewhere in her background French blood paled her skin to the warmth of brown hen eggs and also freckled her face with childish dots of deep brown.

As Mauser drifted down toward sleep, her face crashed into his emptied vision. Stark-boned, filling up the wide screen of his consciousness, she smiled. An owl preens its young with the finest touch of a beak sharp as a razor and strong enough to open cans. Her touch was like that, so tender, of stanched power. He opened his eyes to darkness, closed them. She was still there. Hovering. She flew over him with spread wings, hollow-boned, enveloping. And there was something so familiar about her expression. Wild, troubled, silent. She had periods of catatonia in which, it was told to him later, she reexperienced the loss of her parents as a child. For hours, whole days, she stared at Jack as though she would eat him.

He remembered that stare. As though she would chew him up. A stare of hungry fascination. It was, he now realized with just the tiniest spark of connection crackling as he drifted down, lower, into sleep, the same stare and expression that animated the face of the saintly old nun in the courtyard, lit with lightning in the glittering air. His limbs trustfully loosened, more sleep and the aspirin undid the knots and wrinkles of pain throughout his chest, his back. He went deeper, still deeper, under his mother's protection.

He *was* food to her, he sustained her, lovingly, with his presence. She craved him. She loved him with the secret, wild, despairing love that mothers bear their boy children, an ardor bound up in loss and foreignness and fury. She adored him and could erase him. Just at the instant he entirely surrendered to sleep he saw her once again, swooping down, his earliest memory. She was the shadow of a bending tree that springs up, snaps toward heaven, and you in the branches, curled against the live heart, shouting!

§

The Hitchhiker

Dot, Eleanor, Candice, and Marlis

*T*he first blizzard of the new year was predicted by no one, not the television weatherman who did magic tricks with scarves and eggs, not the state meteorologists, not the *Forum*. Not even the local farmers guessed what was in store. No one read in the satellite photos or the infrared maps of the Upper Midwest the fact that snow to the depth of three feet would be dumped on the Fargo-Moorhead area in as many hours. Among the old Scandinavian and German grandmothers of the present generations, there was once a vague and widespread rumor that the world would come to an end in the middle of a terrible winter. The Great Doom would commence in January, the month of the conversion of Saint Paul, who had so long ago approached Damascus breathing threats and slaughter.

On that day, of course, the unbeliever was blasted from his horse by a mighty radiance. Midwinter is marked by Paul's vision ever since, and bears close watching. "If Saint Paul's be fair and clear," the saying goes, "it promises a happy year; but if it chances to snow or rain, there will be dear all sorts of grain; or if the wind does blow aloft, great stirs will vex the world full oft." The latest stir was, as the local TV meteorologist commented, a lollapalooza. All through the broadcast he referred to it as "she." She was the sudden, frontal, take-no-hostages drop attack of the low-pressure system that caused such impressive damage. She was the lingering depth of cold that killed.

Tiny glittering points of ice had stuck to the ground and frozen to a sheet. During Dot's disappearance with the powerful-looking, mysterious pizza-eating woman, Eleanor and Candice lost about thirty dollars each to Marlis, and although they had been absorbed in their games they were relieved when Dot returned—and curious, too, though Dot's face was such a study of concentration they did not dare ask questions. She gave them no information, but simply insisted that they should start off immediately before the blizzard grew worse. A light, wet snowfall was covering the ground now, and as the women emerged from the B & B they huddled into their coats and crossed their arms against the gusting wind.

Eleanor's boots were soled with corrugated rubber and lined with a thick synthetic pile that trapped warmth and held it close. She dressed warmly, for she was always chilled, riddled with bone aches, perpetually chafing her hands or stamping her feet even in above-zero temperatures. She had been refused an extra blanket at the convent, and told that this deficiency was her cross to bear. It was, now, a physical shortcoming that would save her, for on winter retreats she had learned to be practical. Kneeling on cold floors had taught her to value warmth. She wore a cream silk thermal slip, a turtleneck of the same under her suit. A greatcoat quilted past her knees. Because the head, like the flame of a candle, gives off the body's warmth, Eleanor always kept the hood zipped onto the back of her coat although she knew it made her look a bit childish. Oh yes, the two layers of socks and gloves lined with Thinsulate didn't hurt, either.

Poor Candice! Poor Dot! Warm coats, but, underneath, thin tight cotton sweaters and silky shirts. Pointed boots. Light wool pants and skirts—they had both dressed for the funeral.

Candice Pantamounty staggered out of the B & B in her high-heeled snow boots and nearly pitched face-first into the wall of a fresh drift. Surprised at the change and force of the wind, she wiped a blast of snow from her face, and peered out the door frame at the parking lot. It was so cold that she could feel the tears freeze in the corners of her eyes—that tiny stinging pinch that means the temperature has dropped below zero. Snow whipped through the air in frosty patches, and the streetlights wore obscuring halos. Marlis needed a ride, and Dot had agreed to take her, too. The two women stamped out the door together.

"We'll get through!" Dot insisted, but her eyes were shining too purposefully as she led the others into the parking lot.

Stepping beneath the yellow lights, pressing their collars to their ears, turning their backs to the sharp wind and gritty snow, the women held on to one another's sleeves and shoulders, groped along the parked cars, and finally made it to Jack's vehicle. They stood for a moment, a secret-looking huddle around the door handle. The wind slammed and boomed, tore letters off the B & B's signboard and sent them swiftly into black sky. As Candice blocked the wind, Eleanor managed to pull open the jammed catch and one after another the women tumbled into the freezing shell.

"Let's get the hell out of here." Candice was dizzy with the cold, still under the influence, lost to her own control.

Dot smiled into the rearview mirror. She loved storms.

"We're dropping you and Marlis off first." Her voice was pleasant, excited, as if this were an ordinary excursion. "We'll take the airport road."

Dot started the Explorer and the heater breathed frigid air onto Eleanor, who clutched the warm lapels of her coat to her cheeks. Dot was so affable, so decisive, so firmly in possession of herself, that none of the other women questioned her. As a matter of fact, Dot thrived on emergencies. She prepared for them. Although she had never actually been caught in a storm of this particular magnitude, she'd used Jack's car often and had stowed an emergency space blanket, a pie tin, emergency candles, and a bag of kitty litter—good for spreading under stuck back tires—in the backseat. These small preparations afforded her a dangerous overconfidence.

Once the motor throbbed smoothly and warmed, she proceeded forward. The iced-over ruts of frozen slush from earlier that evening gave traction beneath the snow. There was enough visibility to read a sign or two, at least to see their outlines, but she hadn't counted on the number of other cars that had slipped off the road. Here and there the hulks loomed, staggered, blown down the smooth incline of snow. They hadn't traveled a half mile, at a slow and steady clip, when a shape suddenly defined itself, arm out and thumb up, silhouetted in a sudden cessation of wind, in the frosty radiance of a streetlamp.

Dot downshifted, crept toward the hitchhiker in first gear. Snow spun in a blanket around the figure and then, all of a sudden, fell to its feet. As if a cord had been pulled on a drop cloth around a statue, the dark shape stood revealed. Dot pumped the brakes. But the devil of snow had twisted into a whirling cone again and totally obscured their vision. The Explorer fishtailed, slid sideways, swiveled once, came to a halt, and stalled not two feet from the steel post of a lamp.

Eleanor flew against the dash, though it was a fairly gentle stop. She had forgotten to buckle herself into her seat. While she was still gathering breath and force, ready to blast Dot, the rough shape materialized at her window, a shadow in the headlights. Eleanor opened her door to the scream of snow and a blanket-wrapped figure leaned down. Eleanor saw dark lips, the long strands of webby black scarf, the heavy lenses of a pair of frosted eyeglasses. Then the cowl of material shut and the face was deeply muffled.

Candice made room in the backseat and the figure in its tatters and coverings tumbled in beside her. Light on its limbs, quick and powerful, the hitchhiker bounded over the seat into the small back well of space where the spare tire was usually kept.

"There's a sleeping bag back there," called Dot. Through the rearview mirror she could tell that the hitchhiker was scarved, mitted, and swaddled in dark coverings.

Dot restarted the engine and put the car into reverse.

"Are you hurt?" Eleanor called. "Are you okay? All right?"

"I'm good." The voice was oddly pitched, paper dry.

Dot's hands clamped on the wheel and the engine balked.

"Come on, come on, baby."

She revved up and moved back into the nearly invisible tracks that led to Fargo. She continued steadily but with growing tension to follow the ruts grooved into the ice, filling quickly with hard and drifted snow.

"This is absurdly dangerous!" Eleanor came to a sudden decision.

Marlis shifted in her seat, wrapped her arms around her knees, teeth clicking. "Probably the airport road's drifted over by now, too."

"I doubt it," said Dot. "The crews have plowed it out already. For sure."

"Better to sleep on the B and B floor," said Candice. "Come on, Dot!"

"I've got a winch and a steel cable." Dot gave a strange, hearty laugh. "I owe Marlis a ride home. Those chocolates, her chocolates, took away my last pangs over Jack. If she hadn't told me they were hers, I would have felt guilty for ditching him. Now that's done."

Marlis shifted herself deeper into the seat. "Turn on the heater again. High. I'm cold."

Eleanor's voice rose, sudden and urgent.

"Dot, you're being totally unreasonable! Turn around!"

But it was too late. Great volumes of snow swelled, blew across the highway in thick and even ribbons. Pockets of whiteness fell against the windshield. There were long moments in which the road was almost totally obscured. Hypnotized, Dot entered the bell of her own concentration and advanced at a slow crawl, alert to each twitch of the wheel, buffeted, traveling at a calm, steady speed through the twisting sheets and blankets, nudging the wheels out of momentary skids. In the backseat, Candice laughed once, stopped herself. The hoot of her voice sounded vacant in her ears, a sign of growing self-consciousness and waning drink. She was slightly less drunk. Even Dot, who hadn't realized that she was actually high on the adrenaline that poured into her blood when she had narrowly missed the lamppost, was beginning to grasp that only the sheer momentum of their passage kept them on the road, breasting drifts and continuing steadily in some relation to the invisible center line. And yet, in this remarkable way, they continued forward, as though pulled by an unseen towrope. Eventually they entered the glow that marked the extreme edges of town.

In a sudden flash of understanding, it came to Eleanor that she was trusting her life to the same woman who had played chicken with a Mack truck.

"Let's pull over here, don't you think? Stop!" She cried out in a loud voice, but Dot didn't respond. Eleanor saw the faint orange radiance of the city manifest before them and longed for the safety of the lobby of a Burger King, a gas station, or a Taco John.

"We're almost to the interstate!" Dot was breathless, obsessed, too sure. "They've got big trucks to salt and ice. Once we cross, we're fine. No way they won't have kept the lane to the airport clear."

They took the turnoff, Eleanor's stomach hollowing with fear, but the car slid smoothly down the on-ramp, careened around the curve, and shot onto the four-lane without hesitation. They continued through blowing drifts, obscure whiteouts, shuddering jolts of wind. They went on, fell silent when the glow around them faded. The snow came down thicker, ceaselessly, beating at the side of the car. When at last Dot urged the vehicle onto the airport access road, each woman took a deep breath. This was the last stretch of the journey.

The car climbed the ramp and bucked onto the road. At first, the surface seemed more stable than the highway, but a few yards farther and it was clear that the pavement was almost entirely drifted over. The lane was surrounded, as they all knew, by a couple of experimental North Dakota State University farms and several fields that fed into the runways.

Dot felt for the path with all of her senses, kept the window open so she could crane out and try to catch a hint of the asphalt. Gray patches were visible here and there, but with no consistency. Dot drove on instinct, her throat dry. Behind her, the snow closed like the waves of the sea, like earth. There was no retreat. Just as she sensed this, Candice's voice rose in horror from the back. "It's a total whiteout." And it was. The snow buried them in motion. They inched through it, under it, like winter moles. The wheels still dug through snow and met road. Dot could feel the shock of paving in the calves of her legs, as though she was connected through the mechanism to the tires. She could have progressed indefinitely if the road hadn't dipped beneath the old railroad overpass, but there, in the depression, so much snow had collected that when the car rammed into it they sank. Dot felt the solid presence of the road give beneath her feet. The wheels instantly lost purchase. The hitchhiker was squeezed tightly against the cargo door, but the other passengers flew forward and their seat belts slammed them back when the car stopped.

After a moment, Dot turned off the ignition. She left the lights on.

"Let's not panic." Eleanor spoke automatically, her chest tight with fear.

"I have a shovel," Dot cried out. "Under the backseat. I've got kitty litter, maybe some rock salt."

Candice curled up and shut her eyes.

Eleanor began to laugh softly now, along with Marlis. "Kitty litter? *Kitty litter!* You're so intense about getting rid of Marlis that you had to drag us all the way out here. And the car's not even . . . you don't even have a cellular."

Dot's regret was muffled. "Shit, I can't believe this!" She slammed her hands on the wheel and silence held until, with sudden energy, she tried the door, wedged shut with snow, then pondered a moment and hoisted herself out of her open window. The last the other women saw of her, for long moments, was the edge of her fancy black parka, one shoed foot. Then a knocking sound was heard on the hood.

Eleanor unrolled her window, reached out and grabbed Dot's coat and held it tight while she struggled back into the car. She fell into the front seat—her hair, her cap, her eyes and brow grained with white beads.

"We're wedged in, up to the headlights, I think," she gasped. "There's no use in trying to shovel out."

She rolled up her window, turned off the headlights. The world went utterly dark, and in that black moment, Eleanor put out her hand and touched the sleeve of one of Jack's old denim jackets. He owned several because he kept leaving them in bars. She dragged it over to herself and lay it carefully in her lap, held the cuff to her cheek. The heavy material had a comforting closeness—dirt, smoke, an animal scent, as if he'd slept with it rolled beneath his head. It had been rained on, dried, rained on again. It felt like the quietest part of him, and as she hugged it closer her spirits lifted. He was too much alive, too with her, too compelling to have disappeared, and she couldn't believe, suddenly, that the ashes in their hair and coats and on their skin were all that was left of Jack Mauser. He was with them, he was someplace else, and thinking of this, Eleanor smiled out the window, into the dark and moving snow.

"It's about midnight now," Candice calculated. "Seven hours or so until dawn."

"Three quarters of a tank." Dot congratulated herself, silently.

"We're fine."

"We should conserve the battery."

"We'll be all right."

Eleanor put her hand across the face of her watch and the

darkness that closed over them was complete. The cold seeped through the floorboards and the seals around the doors. It entered the car with the smell of raw dirt, of iron. The wind flowed beneath the train tracks and its low moan enveloped them.

§

Secrets and Sugar Babies

JANUARY 6, 12:15 A.M.

*I*t took some time for the women to accept the reality of their situation, but then, such narrow circumstances are never easy to embrace. The hitchhiker seemed to have fallen asleep. Low snores were audible from the back. As for the others, their position was so precarious that none of them could confront it at first and they found themselves arguing about a stupid matter, which hadn't the least bearing on their danger.

"He was at least a full seven, maybe even *eight* inches—" Eleanor stated.

"You're off by—" Candice leaned toward Dot.

"He was small, please. Undersize. I should know," protested Marlis.

Still addled, buzzing, hung over, Candice disparaged Jack Mauser's natural endowment, while Eleanor defended but made light of it and then referred to his attributes with a shamed and superior coyness that privately enraged the others. All of this raw talk didn't in the least affect the hitchhiker, who breathed on in a slow pulse, a rasp that emanated from the space behind the backseat. A quilted sleeping bag covered and disposed of this chance responsibility that Dot against all common sense had taken on, and, as the women were avidly focused upon the question at hand, no one even paused in argument, at first, to consider the stranger. After a while, more and more immersed in one another's opinions, they wasted no more regard than they would have upon the spare tire.

Eleanor hid her feelings in pedantry, and argued her apprehension that Mauser was exactly the national average—no more, no less. "Six then. Except," she said, "of course I am petite so I would experience him as—"

"Shut up," said Marlis.

"Intelligence," Eleanor continued. "We know he had brains, but he let them atrophy. Otherwise, fair looks. Huge fluctuations in income. No unusual identifying marks. No crimes, of which he was convicted anyway. He was mentally and emotionally normal, if not entirely healthy. He had the usual slight oedipal hang-ups, but no real neurotic tendencies. Temper was his shortcoming, but underneath that crazy bluster . . ."

"You'd call his temper his one shortcoming?" Candice spoke suddenly from the backseat. She gave a harsh laugh. "I'd say five wives is a warning sign of something."

"That's not as strange as it seems at first." Eleanor took on a fussy air, though she was secretly humiliated by the embarrassing turn her grief had taken. She was desperate to talk about Jack and she turned to her professorial mode in threatening situations. "We've all had a number of relationships. More, in fact, than five. We just didn't marry every Tom or Dick."

"I wouldn't call Mauser every Dick," Marlis spoke up.

"I wouldn't call us every Tom."

"Mauser married every Jane."

"Perhaps he was actually, though we all deny it, more comfortable with some type of commitment than most women," said Eleanor. She was beginning to miss him again. Shooting pains stabbed lightly through her heart, and in spite of her controlled, argumentative demeanor, the corners of her eyes burned.

"Quite a theory." Candice tapped the seat in front of her with the ice scraper. "Jack was comfortable with commitment. Oh yes, he was so comfortable that he could actually commit himself to several women at a time."

"He never had another lover while I was married to him," Dot asserted, forgetting in her extremity her suspicions of Eleanor and, as well, the Valentine's heart.

Marlis had set the box down on the floor and now rested her feet on the crushed bow. She moved her feet to wrinkle the bow a little, and then hummed softly to herself. The effect of her off-key action was a kind of underhanded jab—a sudden reminder of perfidy that Dot couldn't quite absorb. Her breath came fast, shallow, and yellow spots blipped from side to side as her vision corrected itself in the darkness.

"Thanks for reminding me," she said calmly, after a time, remembering that Jack's betrayal absolved her.

Eleanor spoke mournfully into the blue night. Although her words were hard, her tone was regretful, caressing.

"How is it that we all, constantly, apologize for that womanizing, weak-spirited, failed contractor, our husband? Did we all love him so, were we blinded, did we—" Eleanor's voice broke, for she was inwardly furious and hurt at the other women's heartless discussion. "The real question is this: if he was so ultra-normal, so banal, so pathetically male, why did any of us agree to marry him?"

Abruptly, the women in the car fell silent.

"He had kind hands," Eleanor whispered at last. "He had kind, slow, forgiving hands. I loved him for what his hands knew—more than he knew, sometimes. Jack had a wise touch."

"He had a wise ass," Marlis said sideways. "Not wise enough."

But no one contradicted Eleanor and for the next few moments the only sound to be heard was the deep gnashing of the wind as it roared and flexed over their vehicle.

❅   ❅   ❅

Dot suddenly reached across the dashboard to the glove compartment, hit the latch, and pulled out a thick white candle. She struck a match from her purse and touched the wick, but it did not light and the match burned down to her thumb. She spoke enthusiastically anyhow. "Look here—you put it on a pie tin and the warmth spreads. There's a few of each underneath the backseat. And there's a space blanket, too."

It was obvious to everyone that Dot was desperate for some sign of forgiveness, some little touchmark, a signal of kindness that would alleviate the burden of her impulsive and dangerous action. But no one was ready to give that to her, not yet, and in a kind of black alienation the women sat firm, each waiting for the other to decide the tenor of Dot's present status among them. But just as, it seemed, Eleanor had begun to make a small overture, no more than a tiny sympathetic sound, Candice crushed the possibility of immediate reinstatement with a small emotional explosion.

"What a bunch of goddamn whiners! We're here, ladies, stuck. And if we don't make the best of things . . ." Her voice faltered.

"Thank you *so* much, that's *so* helpful!" Eleanor's professional air dropped and she tripped over her own words in eager anger. "Our lives are on the line and you're blaming Dot because you're terrified to accept responsibility. She didn't hold a gun to your head to force you into this car!"

Dot's voice rose, defensive. "Hey! I'm stuck too—I mean, I didn't do this on purpose."

Candice should have said something, forgiven her then, but instead Marlis moaned childishly.

"Like that matters."

The black air in the car seemed to vibrate now, cold and sugary with anger, with delicious feelings they all harbored and saved in private. The initial moment of the argument was to them all like the first cut into the crust of a perfect pie. The knife went in, the filling oozed up over the metal, rich and dark. Each muttered to the woman that she hated most in the car, who answered at a slightly tougher pitch.

"Still the same whining stuck-up bitch you were in Argus," Dot hissed to Candice.

"Loser!" Candice choked out.

"Go ahead," Marlis pushed Candice. "Yank her chain like you yank mine."

"If you hadn't been so *pigheaded* . . ." Eleanor finally said to Dot.

The exchange tightened down and suddenly they were screaming. And why not? They had all at one time been married to the same man. Each woman had seen the others as usurpers and killers, as thieves, as sluts driven by the same lusts that she treasured as sublime in her own heart, but despised emanating from any other source. They had boiled their hatred to a dense jam, enriched and condensed it over years. Nothing could contain it now, even the curved metal walls and breath-sealed windows of the car. Ripe fury had escaped and it was delicious. Hot, wholesome, filling.

"You're such slime, you fixed my medication," screamed Marlis to Candice. "Admit it!"

"I didn't, of course I didn't. You're a pathetic *nutcase*, Marlis. What I've put up with! You swore you wouldn't drink and nurse!"

"And you were sleeping with him all the time," Dot pounded the side of Eleanor's seat, then reached back to pound on Marlis, too. "Sleeping with him all the time!"

"What if I did?" Eleanor cried out, overwhelmed with sudden longing. "I *loved* him, which is more than any of you did. *I loved Jack Mauser when he was broke and poor as dirt!*"

She slapped vainly about with both hands.

"While you, while you"—Eleanor breathed—"you wanted his money and then tried to dump him when he lost it all."

"I was loyal! I was loyal!" Dot raged.

The women lobbed slabs of imprecations at one another, smashed jealousies. They clenched their fingers into thick, furred claws and clung fast to the zippers and hoods of one another's parkas and coats. They were all too closely seated to actually fall upon each other and attack, but between the two seats, back and forth, the screech and ardor of murderous intent and righteousness flew in scalding arcs until, gasping, empty, eaten up and filled, scored with adrenaline and thoroughly warmed, they suddenly, as one, remembered that they were in danger.

Silence fell, and it was Eleanor who broke it to speak at last. In her voice there was a deep thrill of conviction. "I've heard that in a large family each child experiences essentially, different parents. Perhaps that is also true of Jack. To some of you, he may have been a perfectly adequate husband."

The atmosphere in the car was still thick and stormy, but the sudden gap of realization had cleared a space around Eleanor and the other women paused longer to catch their breaths.

"I can't say that he was a terrible husband to me," Eleanor went on. "But the circumstances under which we married were so strange, so abrupt."

In the velvet darkness, Eleanor became impersonal, once again, in her assessment.

"As I say, Jack probably showed a separate facet of himself to each one of us. Or we brought it out in him. Made him as different as we are different from one another. In fact, it isn't entirely far-fetched to say that we each married a different man. And if we can agree to that"—Eleanor slowed to make her final point with emphasis—"we can safely feel, I think, that no one of us has a quarrel with any woman in this car. No more so than if we'd all had different husbands."

The stymied attention from the other women was palpable for an instant, and then, as this new apprehension sank in, Marlis gave a loud saw of a laugh.

"I went to school with nuns," she said. "But you're a goddamn televangelist! That's *twisted!*"

"I don't know," said Candice. "Maybe she's right, in a way. Why victimize one another?"

"Jesus, I lost it," Dot apologized.

Eventually, among the women there occurred a shift from antagonism to tentative sisterhood, and in that, there was a sad wisdom. Sometimes, if two women who have shared a lover can abandon old jealousies for the denser bread of analysis, they can generate a closeness, an intimacy that rivals any lover's union. After all, they have, between them, every one of his moods, mannerisms, and betrayals to conjure with, and there is no private joy like that of figuring out and disposing of a man who has caused you pain. Candice wavered in and out of drunkenness, and now the anger snapped her alert and relaxed her as well so that she was the first of the women to become objective, to understand this shift in their passions, and was the first to connect it to their situation.

"I don't know whether or not any of you have noticed," she said in a dry, taut voice. "But this car is getting goddamn cold."

"These candle contraptions don't work for shit," said Marlis. "Let's put this Jack stuff on hold and figure out what we're going to do. I can see the headlines, WIDOWS FREEZE IN GRIEF-STRUCK SHOCK," she gloated. "It's definitely *National Enquirer* stuff. I hope I survive so I can get on TV."

"You, on TV?" Candice laughed.

"Yeah, me. And write. I could do better than your patient alerts—floss daily, floss nightly, floss in your sleep!"

"Well, I do try my best to keep people from suffering unnecessary gum problems. I don't enjoy people's pain."

"Implying that I do? Lay off. We have all agreed and made it clear that the baby was conceived *after* you and Jack broke up. *Just* after, but definitely after. I had no intention of even going out with Jack, but he was *starving* for it."

Candice abruptly laughed at this, surprising herself, and suddenly she and Marlis caught each other's eyes, gleaming in the dark, and held on and held on, staring until Marlis looked away, down at Candice's hand, and touched her.

"How's our boy?" Her voice was small.

Candice put her arm around Marlis's shoulders. Marlis gripped Candice's tightly, then tighter, said nothing, crunched herself into her coat. Her stomach growled and she sank still lower into herself, embarrassed, all the more so when Candice noticed and said, "Do we have any food in the car?"

There was a sudden galvanized attention given to this problem, and each one of the women scraped through her purse and pockets. Eleanor undid the hinge on the glove compartment and spread out the take on the little tray it made above her lap. From Candice's pocketbook, an old bag of airline peanuts and two rolls of Tums, then an apple and half a granola bar, chocolate covered, and a plastic square of breath mints. Marlis had a box of Cracker Jack. To her surprise, Eleanor had half a sandwich and a carrot strip—she could not remember where she'd picked up these items. But then, she was confused by grief. As for Dot, she cracked through resentment, stilled blame, by opening a huge, padded mailing envelope full of Halloween candy that she'd taken from Shawn's overstuffed sacks in this, her last trick-or-treat year, and placed underneath the front seat of the car.

"Peanut butter kisses!" Candice scraped a handful into her lap, jammed a caramel into her mouth. "God, this is good, I think it was the tension, and then we didn't eat out of sheer grief. I was starving."

"You were drunk," Marlis said. "Who are you kidding?"

Dot turned on the heater to normalize the temperature and a state resembling contentment held for several minutes.

"Remember when they used to give out popcorn balls?" Eleanor pawed hopefully through the bag.

In the light of a flickering candle Dot chose a tiny yellow box that contained six Milk Duds.

"Hershey bars!" Temporarily calmed, Marlis spoke with lucid authority. "You ladies, you don't know the first thing about me. I live outside of what you know. One thing, though. I'm a survivor. I'm going to get us out of here."

"Oh, good," said Eleanor, half sarcastic, half amused. "An hour ago you didn't even know Jack was dead. Now you're the survival expert. I can put my mind at rest."

"Can it, Eleanor," Marlis snapped. "Unless you can think of something that will get us out of this mess."

"We do need a plan," Candice tried to slow her aching jaws. The caramels were frozen stiff and stuck to her teeth.

"Like I said," Marlis thought slowly, aloud. "We don't go out of the car. We don't form a human chain or anything like that, I mean, where would we go? Which direction? Obviously, we stay right here. We run the heater every fifteen minutes or so, every half hour if we can stand it." Pleased not to be interrupted, Marlis continued. "I've heard that you should, like, clean out the tailpipe when you're stuck like this because snow is liable to clog it, and a tasteless, odorless poison can build up in the car."

"Would that be carbon monoxide?" Eleanor inquired, stuffing back her irritation. *Why am I stuck here with illiterates?* At least she had her notebook in her purse, somewhere. She could jot things down even though she couldn't see exactly what she was writing. That's my survival tactic, she decided. Taking notes. And this way, if we die, I'll have the last word. Rummaging in her bag, she drew out her lined record book and pen. *Marlis. You can hear the wind whistle in the space between her ears. And shallow? I guess. You couldn't wet both sides of a penny in that pool.* As she wrote, Eleanor's hands warmed and her heart rate increased.

Dot reached down, tugged loose the crinkly, metallic space blanket from beneath her seat, and passed it into the back. Marlis took it from her and wrapped herself in its foil. For a long fifteen minutes, the women sat in the waning flicker of Dot's first candle. They ate their candy, and for the first time, as though the sweetness on their tongues gave them fool's courage, they were able to think ahead.

It was cold, burning cold. Every time one of them sat still too long, or in the slightest of breezes that managed to sliver its way in between the sealed edges of a window or a door, the bitter knife of the wind that enclosed them stabbed and numbed in quick succession. There was no ignoring the bare truth of their predicament anymore, and with each slow bite of thick toffee or bleak cream of marshmallow, acceptance stuck in their throats and slunk out to their nerve ends so that their blood hummed now with whipped sugar energy.

"God, we could all die together," Candice whispered. Her

skill at dentistry useless! Her patients scattered to hands of less painstaking care. Her new life, her baby. "What do we do, what do we do?" Her heart banged for herself and strangely, as if she were somehow a third party, watching at her own autopsy, she heard the solemn words intoned in a low male voice. *Her last meal was candy, the kind that sticks to your teeth.*

"No, no, no," she choked out. "I will not die this way!"

"Me either." Marlis, irritated at the hysterical note in her voice, shook her hand away. "Not in present company."

"You'd be lucky to kick off in the company of anyone with a phone, not just a beeper number." Eleanor spoke dreamily, as if from a distant height. She was preoccupied with imagining her obituary, complete with photograph, in the *Star and Tribune*. There was so much about her that would sound impressive. Foreign publications and diplomas and certificates from exotic panels and workshops. She hated to share the space! And the last line? That should be something special, spectacular, lonely, and definitely quotable.

"I've got big plans for my death," she decided. "Bigger than getting gassed in a stuck car."

She saw herself at ninety, hang gliding off a cliff in Vermont's Green Mountains, or at 100 years old, trying heroin for the first time in her life, or say 108 years, surrounded by flowers, like Leopolda, breathing their scent as her soul rushed to its freedom like an unhooded falcon. *Not yet though*, she wrote all in a jumble. *I'm not ready.* Eleanor spoke suddenly in a voice low and vehement and bereft of control. "Let's make up our minds here and now that we are going to get out of this," she said. "Let's be positive."

"She's right," said Dot, with a decisive slam of her palms upon the dashboard. "We've got to be positive. We've got to talk."

Marlis spoke with a heavy rush of abandon. "Talk? I'll talk! Dot, you fucked over me who fucked over Candice who couldn't have cared less about Jack's first wife, that Indian he met in Williston. And then there's you, Eleanor. You're headlines already, you sex harasser. Why the fuck are all of us fucking each other over? We're women. Was he worth it?"

Although stung, Eleanor quickly gathered herself. "Of course he was. In my experience, you come across three or four people worth having sex with—that's over a lifetime. I've had relationships—many—just to test the odds! But three or four, at most, would I consider time well spent—"

"In your considerable experience," Marlis interrupted, "having slept with everything that moved—"

"Having made a judicious survey." Eleanor gave an infuriating trill of laughter. "You wouldn't understand. And yes, Jack was worth it. Not because he had some sort of magical technique. No, it was the . . ." Eleanor snapped her fingers with such panache in the dry cold that a spark leaped from her fingers to finish her sentence.

"Resolved." Eleanor went on, she would not be stopped. Her voice was all of a sudden so strong and enveloping that the other women all leaned forward, as though she were a source of warmth, and then they stared, for the snow light and the glow of the guttering candle changed her face. In the hollow of her ruffed hood, Eleanor's eyes had deepened and blackened. The planes of her face were silver, and serene, like a beautiful and white-haired fox. Her streaked mane tipped up around her ears. Her mouth was as dark as an opened flower.

"Let's tell all," she grinned, breathless. "Pretend this car is a confessional."

The candle nearly gulped out and Dot took it, dripped some wax upon the glowing pie tin. She fixed the candle into the wax, held her hands to its warmth for a moment, then carefully passed the contraption to the women in the backseat.

"We're not going to die," Candice stated, softly.

"No fucking way," Marlis assured her. The January night swirled and whistled at her back. The cold was squeezing in, pinching off the feeling in her feet, fingers, face. She took the candle from Candice and in its low light her face bloomed again, harsh. "We have six hours, maybe seven, to go until dawn. We'll set up a watch system, each be responsible for those hours."

"Responsible how?" Candice nearly whimpered with the cold. "What are we going to do, sing campfire songs? Roast marshmallows? Torch the tires? I'm cold already. I have never been so *miserably* cold and it's going to get worse."

Dot turned the key, started the ignition.

"The battery sounds strong," she said. "As Marlis says, our main problem is simple: we have to stay alert. If we fall asleep, we're headlines in the *Enquirer*."

No one spoke, absorbing this. Eleanor went on. "We *have* to stay awake all night. The one responsible for her hour has to keep the others from dozing off. We should set some rules."

"Rule one," Dot volunteered. "No shutting up until dawn. Rule two. Tell a true story. Rule three. The story has to be about you. Something that you've never told another soul, a story that would scorch paper, heat up the air!"

Marlis laughed out loud, her voice arcing. "We've each got secrets. Anybody does." She tossed her head, wrapped her arms around her chest, and bent into herself to conserve warmth.

"Where do we start?" said Dot.

The heat tapered to a spent wheeze in the vents, the candle flickered and died. Nobody had an answer and so, at last, Eleanor commented that it might as well be her. She locked her coat around her and began. Her voice was low, of the dark that surrounded them, a blackness of eye-troubling intensity that sprung green forms of twisting smoke behind their eyelids. She spoke formally but with a rapid-fire lecturing passion, just under the blast of the wind.

PART THREE

The Tales of
Burning Love

§

Eleanor's Tale

JANUARY 6, 12:55 A.M.

THE LEAP

⸙

*A*ll of our love stories begin with our mothers. For although it is our fathers, we are told, whose love we seek, it is our mother whom we imitate. If she was a huntress then we beat him through the woods, out into the open. If she was a temptress we are standing in the clearing as he emerges, slowly removing our clothes. A whiner? We draw him toward us through quick tears. Strong. We dominate. If she was equal, if she was one of those souls who stood beside him, naked to the core and unafraid, more is the luck.

Anna Schlick is all of the above.

My mother is the surviving half of a blindfold trapeze act. You saw her at the funeral moving easily through the room. She never falters, in spite of her big, square feet. Her arms are soft now, but she never makes an unnecessary gesture. Perhaps she looks a bit clumsy, overblown, her thighs so bold, her clothing tight. But she never upsets an object or so much as brushes a cobweb onto the floor. I have never seen her lose her balance or bump into a closet door left carelessly open. And even though I owe my life to her agility and courage, there are times I can't help resent her irritating sense of balance.

Her poise still tempts me. As a child I once tied string on a dark stairway to catch her feet—I could have killed her! She neatly stepped over, sensing it in the dim light. The catlike precision of her movements is instinct now—the result of her early training in the family of Flying Kuklenskis. She was a Montana barrel rider who ran off young with a circus. An ancient family of third-rate Polish trapeze artists adopted her. Artists? The old master had dropped a daughter and his son a former wife. My mother knew this, but had her name added to the stage posters anyway.

My father doesn't like to see the photographs or advertisements from that part of her youth. He let me play with her brilliant costumes until I wore them to shreds. There was very little left at home to remind us of her life in the air. I would have tended to think that all memory of double somersaults and heart-stopping catches had left her arms and legs, were it not that sometimes, when she and I sit sewing and talking in the same little room that I slept in as a child, I hear the crackle, catch a whiff of smoke from the stove downstairs. Suddenly the room goes dark, the stitches burn beneath our fingers, and we are sewing with needles of hot silver, threads of fire.

I owe her my existence three times. The first was when she saved herself. South of Fargo, there stands the replica of a cracked and splintered tent pole, cast in concrete. It commemorates the disaster that put the town on the front page of the tabloids of that day. It is from those old newspapers, now historical records, that you can find information, not from Anna of the Flying Kuklenskis, nor from any of her Montana relatives, or certainly from the other half of her particular act. In the news accounts, it said, "the day was mildly overcast but nothing in the air or temperature gave any hint of the sudden force with which the deadly gale would strike."

I have lived beyond the trees, where you can see the weather coming for miles, and it is true that in town we are at something of a disadvantage. When extremes of temperatures collide, a hot and cold front, winds are generated instantaneously and crash upon you without warning. That, I think, was the likely situation on that day in August. People probably commented on the pleasant breeze, grateful that no hot sun beat upon the striped tent that stretched over them. They bought their tickets and surrendered them in anticipation. They sat. They ate caramelized popcorn and roasted peanuts. There was time, before the storm, for three acts. The White Arabians of Ali-Khazar rose on their hind legs and waltzed. The Mysterious Bernie folded himself into a painted cracker tin, and the Lady of the Mists made herself appear and disappear in surprising places. As the clouds gathered outside, unnoticed, the ringmaster cracked his whip, shouted his introduction, and pointed to the ceiling of the tent, where the Flying Kuklenskis were perched.

They tried to drop gracefully from nowhere, like two sparkling birds. Sometimes they rode down on a gleaming, painted moon that jerked and rocked. Blowing kisses, they doffed their glittering helmets and high-collared capes. They skipped to all sides of the ring to accept applause, and flirted openly as the moon hauled them up again on the trapeze bars. In the final vignette of their act, they were supposed to kiss in midair, pausing, almost hovering as they swooped past each other. On the ground, between bows, Harry Kuklenski lithely bounded to the front rows and pointed out the smear of Anna's lipstick, just off the edge of his mouth. There was a small rouge pot hidden on the pole of the trapeze landing, but who was to know? They made a romantic pair all right, especially in the blindfold sequence.

That afternoon, as the anticipation increased, as Harry and Anna Kuklenski tied sparkling masks onto each other's faces and as they puckered their lips in mock kisses, lips destined "never again to meet" as one long breathless article put it, the wind rose, only miles off, wrapped itself into a cone, and howled. There came a rumble of electrical energy, drowned out by the sudden roll of drums. One detail, not mentioned by the press, perhaps unknown—Anna was pregnant at the time, seven months and hardly showing, her stomach muscles were that strong. It seems incredible that she would work high above the ground, when any fall could be so dangerous, but the explanation, I know from watching her, is that she always lived comfortably in extreme elements. Perhaps too comfortably. It astounds me to see how she is becoming one with the failings of her age, her sick heart, just as the air had been her home, familiar to her, safe, before the storm that afternoon.

From opposite ends of the tent they waved, blind and smiling, to the crowd below. Then the ringmaster removed his hat and called for silence, so that the two above could concentrate. They rubbed their hands in chalky powder, then Harry launched himself and swung, once, twice, in huge calibrated beats across space. He hung from his knees and on the third swing stretched wide his arms, held out his hands to receive his pregnant wife as she dove from her shining bar.

It was while the two were in midair, their hands about to meet, that lightning struck the main pole and sizzled down the guy wires, filling the air with blue heat and light that Harry must certainly have seen, even through the silk of his blindfold. The tent buckled, the edifice toppled him forward. The swing continued and did not return in its sweep. Harry went down, down unkissed into the crowd with his last thought, perhaps, just a prickle of surprise at his empty hands.

My mother once told me that I'd be amazed at how many things a person can do in the act of falling. Perhaps at the time she was teaching me not to fear the inevitable grounding of my designs, or my own emotional plunges, for I associate the idea with the drift of reason. But I also think she meant that even in that awful doomed second one could think. She certainly did. When her hands did not meet her husband's, Anna tore away her blindfold. As he swept past her on the wrong side she could have grasped his ankle, the toe-end of his tights, and gone down clutching him. Instead, she changed direction. She chose herself and in so choosing, me. Her body twisted toward a heavy wire and she managed to hang on to the braided metal, still hot from the lightning strike. Her palms were burned so terribly that once healed they bore no lines, only the blank scar tissue of a quieter future. She was lowered, gently, to the saw-dust ring just underneath the dome of the canvas roof, which did not entirely settle but was held up on one end and jabbed through, torn, and even on fire in places from the giant spark, though rain and men's jackets soon put that out.

Three people died including Harry, but except for her hands my mother was not seriously harmed until an overeager rescuer broke her arm in extricating her and also, in the process, collapsed a portion of the tent bearing a huge buckle that knocked her unconscious. She was taken to the hospital, run by Franciscans, where she must have hemorrhaged, for they kept her confined to her bed a month and a half before her baby was born without life.

Harry Kuklenski had always wanted to be buried in the circus cemetery next to the original Kuklenski, his uncle, and so she sent him back to Milwaukee with his brothers. The still-born child, however, is buried at the edge of town. I used to walk across the unpaved field there, just to sit. The child was a girl, but I never thought of her as a sister, or even as a separate person, really. It is egotistical, an odd defense, but I always considered her a less finished version of myself.

When the snow fell, throwing shadows among the cemetery stones, I could always pick hers out easily from the road as I passed on my way to school. Her marker was bigger than the others and it was the shape of an actual lamb at rest, its legs curled beneath. The carved lamb looms larger in my thoughts as the years pass, though it is probably just my eyes, the vision slowly changing—the way it has for my mother—as what is close to us sifts away and distances sharpen. In odd moments, I think it is the edge drawing near, the edge of everything, the horizon I did not have to confront in my parents' closed yard. And it also seems to me, although this is probably an idle fantasy, that somewhere my sister's statue is also growing more sharply etched as if, instead of weathering itself into a porous mass, it is hardening on the flat field with each snowfall, perfecting itself.

Early during her confinement in the hospital my mother met Lawrence Schlick, then known as Fargo Businessman of the Year, personally delivering flowers to the circus victims as a goodwill gesture. He stayed, sitting at her bedside, then came back week after week, at first telling himself that it was because he was something of an armchair traveler, and had spent meditative hours reading of the places Anna had visited in fact — Kansas City, Chicago, St. Paul, New York, Omaha. The Kuklenskis had toured the big cities before the war, then gradually based themselves farther and farther into the boon-docks as bigger acts including elephants and raging tigers drove them into small-town territory.

It was in the hospital that Anna began to read passionately, a way of overcoming the boredom and depression of those months. It was Lawrence Schlick who insisted on bringing her books. Between them, they read aloud, speaking into each other's eyes. Falling. I sometimes wonder whether as he fell in love my father had time to think. For he went down fast. He plunged. He would never be the same.

I owe my existence, the second time then, to the two of them and the hospital that brought them together. That is the debt I do not ever take for granted. None of us asks for life in the first place. It is only once we have it, of course, that we hang on so dearly.

I was only six years old the year that our house caught fire, probably from standing ash. It can rekindle, and my mother, forgetful around the house, probably shoveled what she thought were dead coals into wooden or cardboard containers. The fire could have started from a flaming box. Or perhaps a buildup of creosote inside the chimney ignited. The blaze started in our living room, and the heart of the house was gut-ted. I woke to find the stairway to my upstairs bedroom cut off by flames.

There was only one staircase and that was gone. My parents were out and the baby-sitter, panicked, had run out the door to the neighbor's house. As soon as I awakened, I smelled the smoke. I did things by the letter then, was good at memorizing instructions, and also I was happy. Never to be underestimated, the pleasure I took in existence probably helped to keep me calm. For I knew, completely trusted, that I would be saved. So I conducted myself exactly as I was taught in the first-grade fire drill. I got up. I touched the back of my door before opening it. Finding it hot, I left it closed and stuffed my rolled-up rug beneath the crack. I did not hide beneath my bed or crawl into my closet. I put on my flannel robe, and then I sat down to wait.

My mother and father, returning in their formal coats and thin shoes, stood below my dark window and saw clearly that there was no rescue. A fire truck arrived, but flames had pierced one sidewall and the glare of the fire lighted the mammoth limbs and trunk of the vigorous old oak that had probably planted itself a hundred years, at least, before the house was built. No branch touched the wall, and just one thin limb scraped the roof. From below, it looked as though even a squirrel would have had trouble jumping from the tree onto the house, for the growth of that small branch was no bigger than my wrist.

Standing there, Anna asked my father to unzip her dress.

When he treated her too gently, as though she'd lost her reason, she made him understand her intentions. She stripped off her stockings, stood barefoot in bra and half-slip and pearls. Then she directed one of the firemen to lean the superannuated extension ladder up against the trunk of the tree. In surprise, he complied. She ascended. She vanished. Then she could be seen moving easily among the leafless branches. She made her way up and up. Along her stomach, she inched the length of a bough that curved above the branch that knocked on the roof of the house.

Once there, swaying, she stood and balanced. There were plenty of people in the crowd and many who still remember, or think they do, my mother's leap through the ice-dark air toward that thinnest extension, and how she broke that branch in falling so that it cracked in her hands, cracked louder than the flames but gave her the necessary purchase as she vaulted with it toward the edge of the roof, and how it hurtled down end over end without her, and their eyes went up, again, to see where she had flown.

I didn't see her stretch through air, only heard the sudden thump and looked out my window. She was hanging by her toes and feet from the new gutter we had put in that year, and she was smiling. I was not surprised to see her, she was so matter-of-fact. She tapped on the window. I remember how she did it, too; it was the friendliest tap, a bit tentative, as if she were afraid she had arrived too early at a friend's party. Then she gestured at the latch, and when I opened the window she told me to raise it wider, and prop it up with the stick so it wouldn't crush her fingers. She swung down, caught the ledge, and crawled through the opening. Once she was in my room, I realized she wore only underclothing, a tight bra of the heavy circular-stitched cotton women used to wear, an abrasive scapular, and silky half-slip. I remember feeling light-headed, of course, terribly relieved and then embarrassed for her, to be seen by the crowd undressed.

I was still embarrassed as we flew out the window, toward earth, me in her lap, her toes pointed as we rushed toward the striped target of the firefighters' tarp held below.

I know that she's right. I knew it even then. As you fall there is time to think. Curled as I was, against her stomach, I was not startled by the cries of the crowd or the looming faces. The wind roared and beat its hot breath at our back, the flames whistled. I slowly wondered what would happen if we missed the blanket, or bounced out of it. Then I forgot fear. I wrapped my hands around my mother's hands. I felt the brush of her lips, and I heard the beat of her heart in my ears—loud as thunder, long as the roll of drums.

Eleanor slumped forward, loaded with peculiar optimism.

I won't freeze to death, she thought. *She'll save me. She always does.*

"Turn on the heater," said Eleanor. "I'll continue with my story in a moment."

Soon the women were so dreamily comfortable that they had trouble staying alert. Dot turned off the heater and as the chill entered the seals around the doors Eleanor resumed her tale.

JACK'S COAT

My grateful father joined the fire department. As with anything he tried, he soon made a success of it and was named the chief. But fire had changed him twice, and was to yet one more time. The first fire gave him everything, in Anna. The second gave him me. The third fire, however, was to take everything away.

On the coldest night that ever went on record in North Dakota for the month of November, there occurred a devastating blaze. Around dusk, the railroad hotel that had stood downtown in its place for over one hundred years caught fire and began to burn with such an extravagance that there was no hope of saving it or the men and women trapped inside, although every trick was put to use. During these attempts, the temperature continued its remarkable plunge, dropping more than forty degrees in two hours. As the firefighters sprayed the building with water they were surprised to see the streams shoot high into the air and crystallize. The water fell upon the steaming bones of the hotel as ice, while, in the tanks of the cars of volunteers and rubberneckers, gas turned to syrup, and still elsewhere, approaching Fargo, a train froze fast to its tracks. The municipal water mains were suddenly in danger and all through the city the drains and pipes of home owners and renters began, inevitably, to burst. Still the temperature continued its steep descent, and in the chaos my father, Lawrence Schlick, ordered an overeager volunteer back to the firehouse. Jack Mauser. Attempting to make a hero of himself, Jack had cranked the nozzle of a hose too far and thoroughly doused himself. In danger now, Jack was sent back to the fire-house to change his clothes.

In that same blue sequined dress my mother wore to Jack's funeral, she returned from a party and put together food for my father. I had pestered my mother to let me deliver my father's dinner in a covered pan. So she drove me to the fire station and waited outside while I proudly made the delivery. I put down the pan on the firehouse counter and was just walking toward the front door when the back door slammed open. I jumped aside, startled, and hid. Jack entered. I heard him stumbling, knocking around in a peculiar wooden way. Afraid to confront him, I slipped into a closet across from the gas heater and watched the cold room through a crack in the door.

I saw Jack for the first time, then, a hulk of a young man in a big rubber coat that stuck out around him like a bell. His hair had frozen in short spines all over his head. His face was covered in white frost, white shadow. He stopped before the heater, his hand moved as though turning up the gas, and perhaps he imagined, dreamily, that warmth spread into him, quieting his shakes. He stood there for a long time, calm, as though basking in imaginary heat, but the firehouse was freezing cold. Then he coughed suddenly, bent to stare into the face of the glass dial and apparently saw that there was no flame. The pilot light was out.

A box of kitchen matches lay near the latched-open valve, but when he tried to grasp for it, his senseless hands bashed it against the wall, spilling all of the wooden sticks. His coat was big and clumsy as an armor on him, so solid that there was no hope of his bending to retrieve them. I watched him fiddle madly with the useless dials, his hands knocking like iron. He seemed to drift, walked insensibly back and forth through the cold building. I was freezing, too, but his odd behavior made me so wary that I remained concealed until he finally lost his balance and toppled slowly, falling onto his back against a pile of coiled canvas hose.

He didn't move. I finally walked out into the room and

stood over him. That's when I realized he was a cascade of ice. Water and mist on his thick yellow coat, black hat, and boots had frozen to a clear and solid cast. I ran for my mother. She left the car idling and sped back with me into the firehouse. Immediately, she grasped the situation. She took a hammer from the tool case and smashed the ice off the buckles of Jack's coat. When she could not tug open the hardened shell, she hunted through the toolroom until she found a small silver bow saw. Using that, she cut away Jack's slicker in pieces. She wrapped him in her own coat, but kept on her gloves. She sawed a piece of hose the right length to wrap under his arms, and across his chest, so that, using all of our combined strength, we were able to drag him out to the car, still idling, the heater going full blast.

My mother propped him in the front seat, in the warm air, and drove him home. As I have said, nothing ever threw my mother, nothing ever caught her by surprise. She only raised her eyebrows slightly when I asked if he would live, and said that he would, of course, and not to worry myself. When we reached the house, she strode around the car, yanked open the door on Jack's side, and checked his pulse. She prodded him awake to ask him his name. He could not pronounce it.

"Disoriented," she concluded, and hauled him out. Between us, we brought him inside. She called the hospital, but there had been so many cold-related traffic accidents and fire victims that the emergency rooms were jammed.

"Hold the phone," she told me, while she tended to Jack.

"Immerse in warm water," said a harried doctor. I passed the phone quickly back to my mother.

"I can't do that . . . ," I heard her say. "I don't have a sleep-ing bag. . . . Plus, I'm a grown woman. . . . He's a young man. A stranger. . . . Right. . . . Right. . . . We'll try the bath first, then, yes."

We guided Jack up the stairs and then down the hall to the bathroom. He was faint and confused and did not register our presences, but automatically began to strip himself of clothing. My mother gestured me from the room and ran him a bath, into which she had already dumped her usual spartan capful of Ivory dish soap.

If it had ended there, if Jack Mauser had soaked in reviving water and thawed out, then dried himself and left, things would have gone on simply—or might not, for the truth was that my mother was unhappy. Her marriage, though safe, kept her grounded. Her position as the wife of one of Fargo's leading citizens was both gratifying and constricting. As Mrs. Lawrence Schlick, her every action was reported as local news, her turn-of-the-century house was envied, her leadership cherished in the acquisition of funds for the library, for night shelters, for theater, for the nascent North Dakota opera. She was known for her original, even eccentric arrangements of flowers, winning entries in the garden show, for her published recipes, for her work on the bitter problem of drunks who died upon the railroad tracks, and for her newspaper columns that squarely faced such issues as housewives' legitimate fears of botulism in their canning. Since her rescue and my near escape, she had become, in short, an admirable woman who had done everything she could to preserve from herself the knowledge that she had not yet evened the score with death.

She was owed two lives and had retrieved but one—mine. Jack's stood in the balance, though I had no doubt at all that she would win. Over the years, I had seen how the tough shield upon my mother's feelings resulted in a formidable restlessness. She cooked, gardened, wrote, chaired meetings, and volunteered incessantly, almost maniacally. Her house was ferociously clean, her yard a marvel of trimmed hedges and iris beds. On windless summer nights when she couldn't sleep she might mount a ladder to clean the gutters, or shampoo the carpets on her hands and knees. She sewed my clothing, using expensive designer patterns special-ordered from the fabric stores. She did too much, took her failures hard. I once found her weeping over a failed orange cake, flattened by humidity and uneven oven temperatures. She baked another and it came out perfectly, of course. There was a military passion to her domesticity. It was as though the precision and athleticism of her performances as a Kuklenski were transferred into the mundane.

I am sure that most days she told herself that the ardor and transport she brought to small tasks were normal. Perhaps that night, she didn't understand that her own actions, which seemed at first so unlikely, rose in reality from the deepest part of her nature, which was acting to rescue itself by saving Jack, thereby flouting the robber of one more grave.

For my mother hated death, did I tell you that? More than any other thing. She was outraged at having to die.

She had shut Jack in the bathroom and gone downstairs. I knocked softly on the bathroom door, received no answer, and opened it. Jack lay against the bluish porcelain, his lips spread. A dreamy light played about his face, and his expression riveted me in its glow, for it was an inscrutable mixture of alertness and dreamy pleasure. As the blood flooded back into his pinched nerves, deadened vessels, his limbs burned and loosened. It all happened before my eyes. I grasped the curtain, unable to tear myself from such an open display of feeling, and as I watched, slowly, he slid underneath the meek froth of bubbles.

My mother entered the room behind me, reached down and grasped Jack's forearms, an acrobat's catch. She lifted him toward her and as he streamed out of the tub she crooned to him as to a child or lover, though he was neither.

After she helped Jack from the bath, she rubbed him dry. He swayed and started again to shake, still with that wild look in his eyes. Suddenly, his legs went out from under him. He collapsed, naked, whimpering and shivering so violently that my mother couldn't hold on to him. "Get some blankets," she ordered. "Then go to bed."

She rolled him in a heavy blanket and brought him into her bedroom. She put him under the covers and piled the quilts with quilts. Nothing helped. He continued to shake so hard that the bed jumped. Finally, with dispatch, in the half-light of the open bathroom door, she took off her exquisite dress and covered his body with hers.

❀   ❀   ❀

"How do you know?" asked Marlis.

"I didn't go to bed," said Eleanor.

"It is, after all, what you do for hypothermia," Dot interrupted. "You warm the person with your body heat, bring the . . . ah, victim, back to normal temperature gradually."

"That was her reasoning, of course," Eleanor quickly agreed. "But of course, he *was* a man, however else she treated him. And so it was that everything changed.

"I was still a child," Eleanor went on. "Remember that! I had to know! Plus, the night was deadly. I jumped from my bed about an hour or two after they had settled, and made my way down the freezing tunnel of the hallway. I crept so softly into my parents' room and slipped beneath the covers so gently that my mother did not wake. She usually wore flannel, smelled of coconut hand oil, and gave off an even glow of warmth. That night, I leaned a bit closer, and as she shifted her weight, heat seemed to pour off of her skin along with the deeper smell of fresh bark and dish soap. She sighed, rolled away from Jack, and flung an arm around me without waking."

Astonishment, fear, outrage, and grim satisfaction swept over many a former friend of ours the next day when it was learned how Mr. Lawrence Schlick, owner of furniture warehouses and funeral parlors, of the city's largest car dealership, of grain futures and no less than three historical town landmarks, stumbled into the master suite of his own restored house and found his wife sleeping with her lover and their daughter curled just beside. Without waking them, he walked out of his magnificent home and trudged straight through the frigid backyards of Fargo's most prestigious neighborhood to the door of his banker, then to the house of his lawyer, and finally, since it was broad daylight and office hours had begun, to the desk of his accountant, where he drank fresh coffee and fortified himself with nearly an entire box of glazed maple logs as he feverishly attempted to make certain that nothing his wife could do or say would pry from him another dollar.

Later, still wearing his oilcloth jacket and fireman's boots, but now carrying his hat with the large golden-crested badge, he sat down at the desk of a local realtor, a cousin. By noon, he had rented himself a new place to live and put his showcase mansion up for sale.

After all previous disasters, both large and small, Lawrence Schlick had always slept at the firehouse. He hated to expunge the odor of burnt things, seared paint, smoke, which tasted to him of the heroism so elusive in the daily turn of men's lives. He preferred to sleep and shower there before returning to his work and home clad in his everyday guise. Just this once, because the furnace was frozen solid at the firehouse, he had violated his custom, but my mother was unaware. Things happened with such speed that her day was just beginning even as her life was both saved and ruined.

She had no idea that the walls around her were a discount bargain, that her name had been expunged from bank accounts and property holdings and a complicated will. She did not know about the story that had been told with frank vindictiveness to the editor who printed her newspaper column, as well as to the members of a ladies' circle so self-important that it had no name in Fargo, and to everyone, in fact, who met her husband on Main Avenue, whether or not he knew them personally. My father told his story on both sides of the velvet ropes in bank lobbies. Customers who entered his glass-windowed dealership looking for a good used car heard instead the blistering personal tale. And as the day wore on, he embroidered it, in spite of the usual quietude of his imagination. Perhaps because he was known as such a literal man, the desperate inventions of his grief and shaken faith were taken seriously. His wife had been deceiving him for years! With many men! She frequented bars, the notorious Pink Pussycat, the Roundup! She picked them up at high school pep rallies and in her rounds through the Greyhound bus station! Minneapolis! Anna actually went over there, and much too often!

Meanwhile, in her soon-to-vanish home, my mother was undergoing a strange set of unexpected sensations. They began when she attempted to leap from the bed that Jack Mauser had just vacated, and found herself unwilling to rise. She was an early-morning person, usually up at six. I woke in the warm shadow that her body cast. A radio announcer told us school was called off—this was a snow day. Everything was stalled in a cruel, supernal peace.

I got up, but my mother found herself unable to travel farther than the master bath, which she ran at once. I heard her upstairs as I made my own breakfast, and she was singing. It was an odd, amazing, unlikely tuneless sound and it meant something I could not fathom. I had never heard her sing before. And in the bathtub! Her voice, magnified, swelled powerfully from behind the door. An unprecedented pile of clothing littered the immaculate hall floor. Thanks to opening those spigots the night before, the pipes were all intact. Hot water streamed from the spout, steam rose between her thighs, and my mother dumped an entire expensive vial of perfume upon the water. The scent floated through the upstairs rooms, exotic and sharp. Soaking herself in as much depth of sensation as she could manufacture, my mother, too, was coming back to life. The night's encounter had broken the spell, melted through her veneer of capability, caused her to sing.

By saving Jack my mother erased the past. She was herself again, her original self, and to my surprise it was already apparent that she was extravagant, messy, had an awful, loud, unmelodic voice and knew the words to dozens of songs.

It has since occurred to me of course that she and Jack might have had sex, wild or romantic, during the hours I slept. She acted as though something shattering had taken place, it's true. I have asked, she has denied, but of course she would. I can't be sure, but I think it more likely that the act of salvation was for her the snap of the hypnotist's fingers, the wake-up kiss, the magic that freed her from the hex of guilt and catapulted her into a genuine, though problematic, life.

The phone did not ring—she told me later that she noticed the silence as the morning wore on, but so thoroughly immersed was she in her own thoughts that she was glad for the lack of distraction. She decided that my father was too busy at the firehouse to send a message and did not call the phone company, as she usually would have, to ask that they check the line.

It was cut off, anyway. My father made sure of that. He would have cut off everything—gas, heat, electricity, water, air if possible. He would have taken the wood from the hearth, the food from the kitchen cabinets, the clothing out of my mother's admirably laid-out closets and fragrant cedar chests and moth-proof attic. He would have taken me, too, except now he couldn't bear the sight of his previously doted-upon daughter. He would have pulled the house apart by brick, by board, by joist and screw and fixture, but he had to content himself with what he could do. Everything had changed for him too.

Though my father wasn't a truly vindictive man, he was surprised to find he was a passionate one. His love for Anna was a terrible and driving flame, a wound, a need. He hadn't known. The shock unhinged his balance and he tipped into a torment of jealous actions. One led to the next: and so, as my mother at last dragged herself out of bed and cooked her hus-band's most loved meal in anticipation of his late arrival, he booked himself a trip to Haiti. As she was kneading homemade yeast rolls, then rounding the bits of dough between the circle of her thumb and forefinger, he was getting his papers in order. As she mashed a large squash she had baked with sweet butter, he was trying to repossess their car. She washed and tore up lettuce for a salad. He called her family in Montana with the news. She cradled and salted the last thick roast of beef she would be able to afford for years. He withdrew from all of her tiny bank accounts the modest sums of cash that she believed were hidden from his eyes, and which she had drawn on in the past mainly to buy him surprise gifts. She pried the lid off a jar of pepper berry jelly, her husband's favorite, and looked at the face of her expensive watch.

My mother frowned, tapped the watch. She thrust a meat thermometer into the center of the beef and then forgot every-thing and gazed out upon the lawn, within the deep brown barriers of planted hedges and the stiff dried balls of uncut hydrangea. I watched her, thinking, her hands drumming on the carved armrest of her chair, excited, letting the beef go hard, dry, and brown.

"Your father hasn't called yet," she told me softly. "Something's wrong." And then she smiled in such a joyous way, free and easy, that the prospect of something going wrong almost enchanted me.

What would she do? Where go? What of me?

In the long sweeping rush of her feelings, she took me into her arms and rocked me. As she moved back and forth in that quiet rhythm a penetrating sweetness assailed me. She was happy, tremendously happy, and I could feel her lightness. The two of us were floating in the chair. The intuition of her joy came on as a kind of blue and oceanic feeling, but it was sharp, as well, and it flashed through each nerve and left me lighted, as though I lay in a dry electric field still pulsing with friction. Before birth, in just this way, our mother's joy translates into us, sinking cell by cell into the body, forming mind, providing the hinge of differentiation.

And what about Jack Mauser, whose body she had brought back to life only to be wrecked herself? He was an NDSU engineering student and part-time fireman who spent his free time at his uncle's farm just outside of Fargo, raptly tinkering with the engines of tractors and expensive foreign cars. Jack himself told me he worked the next day, lost himself in the mysteries of an old Mercedes. However, the woman who had pulled him from the bath in his thrilling agony, each muscle flaring new, my poor blissful mother, was beginning to realize her husband wasn't coming home.

From the window of her childhood bedroom, she'd watched the grave mountains over Hungry Horse tack themselves upon the sky, their outlines at dawn a torn ribbon of gray construction paper. So, too, perhaps her impressions now seemed drawn against a vastness upon which there was no other discernible thing written. I sensed a movement in her, something profound and wild. I crept within her magic circle. Joined her exquisite peace, and again the two of us slept the sleep of deep satisfaction that night. It was a lucky thing my mother did, because she needed to have her head on straight to keep her balance when her husband jerked from under her feet that ankle-deep money rug, that shag carpet of good living.

Her life, as the patrons of the bar where she eventually found work, would have said, went completely down the tubes. It was rapid, irreversible, almost joyous in its slide to ruin. Once she knew what she was accused of, pride gripped her. Pride gripped me too. She refused any settlement, refused even a divorce, for she was and is devout, a Catholic who picks her way across the great stream of life on stones of dogma. Of course, she only steps on those that do not wobble underfoot. She believed in marriage, kept her vows. The two of us simply drove away from the Schlick house with what we could pack in the car, which my mother would shortly sell. We brought nothing much along except our clothes.

With a sound that echoes even now in my thoughts like the shout of a sledder careening off a cliff, our old life abruptly vanished. It happened in one month, and there was to the process a certain excitement, a novelty. From the loveliest old house in town, we moved into a two-bedroom apartment on the second story of a crumbling complex that was so badly built in the first place that its floors ripped out of their grain and plaster chips shook loose alarmingly when the Empire Builder swayed in from the west. Every night, just as my mother got home from work, she braced herself against the stairwell and waited out its passage. From the greenhouse and the huge yard planted with every flower and shrub that would tolerate the short North Dakota growing season, my mother and I were reduced to raising a few geraniums in coffee cans. From the grand kitchen, to a galley, from the king-size beds and flowered coverlets to a bunk in my room and a rock-hard fold-out couch in hers. No bathtub anymore, just a shower that sprayed crooked. The windows rattled and rang when the wind hit and in the summer the aluminum siding would retain heat and bake us like bread in a tin can. We left behind the wedding china and ate off mismatched commemorative plates bought for a dime apiece at the New Life Mission. We still had our expensive clothes, of course, but nowhere to wear them and no prospect of buying more.

And yet, for my mother, there were tangible benefits. She didn't worry about what to write for the newspaper, what to stir up for bake sales, or when to hold auctions for the Red Cross. She didn't march with the auxiliary or chair civic strategy meetings with the other wives of prominent men. She didn't host big cookouts at the lake cabin, or have to think about the motorboat. She didn't have to keep up the huge house or give people orders or pick up after a pack of girl scouts. No girl scouts were allowed within a mile of her, and that was all right, for she realized that, except for her own daughter, she detested the face of every middle-class girl-child raised in Fargo, and most of their mothers, and fathers too, and in this hatred there was something so satisfactory and liberating that she was transformed from an attractively kept, rather solid, nice-looking, middle-aged woman, to a creature completely stunning in certain lights.

What made her so was that there was complete truth in what people said about her. She had no shame. Perhaps she was the only woman in North Dakota in that state of grace.

Pausing here, Eleanor sank for a moment into her own thoughts, gathering her sense of the rest of the story. She shifted herself slightly toward Dot. The exhaled breath of the women already coated the window in white velvet. Each word that Eleanor spoke added to the icy fabric. The image struck her. They were, all of them, enclosed in the spoken words, both saved and cut off by the narrative trailing into the dark and shaping itself into the larger, flatter, patterns of crystals collecting on the glass windows of Jack's Explorer.

Must remember this, she wrote. The ink in her pen was frozen and left no visible mark, but in the dark she couldn't tell and so she wrote across the ruled lines, jaggedly, in a fit of intensity. *If so, to breathe upon that window, opening a black space, is to erase, to forget some portion of the past. Perhaps when all is said and done and we are rescued, this cathartic account will help to lay undone feelings for Jack to rest.*

§

The Red Slip

JANUARY 6, 1:27 A.M.

Eleanor

I blamed Jack Mauser for our terrible situation. Every time my mother bounced a check, every time the landlord called with suggestions on how to pay our rent without the use of money, every time our phone was disconnected, I blamed Jack Mauser. I blamed Jack Mauser for the tree that dropped a limb right through our window. I blamed him for the scrabbling brown rat that lived inside our wall, for the whine in our refrigerator, for the lack of a piano, and for the slow and relentless stiffening of my mother's hands, the result of early arthritis brought on by the wretched bar-cleaning work.

I decided that justice must be done. Every Sunday, at Mass, after Holy Communion as I knelt beside my mother, I prayed for a solution. Perhaps Jack would stumble before me stunned to freezing. Next time, I'd let him die. Each Saturday, in the hushed afternoon, I confessed my wish and was absolved of its weight.

By the time I was a teenager, I had vividly imagined Jack

Mauser dying in a thousand, a million, ways—he fell through ice, he ate a poisoned cake, he was devoured by a rabid lion escaped from a circus boxcar traveling through Fargo. I didn't always let him die by accident. Sometimes I shot him or I hit him with a black hammer. I ran over him with a street sweeper, with an asphalt packer, with a John Deere tractor, with a combine, with a corn picker. Is it any surprise that such a hateful backlog should turn to love?

At any rate, I had murdered Jack Mauser so often that in some way I almost began to believe he was dead. So it surprised me on a slow afternoon, while I was walking through DeLendrecies, pretend-shopping, to see him, so alive after all, approach me down an aisle of crystal glassware. I tried to divert myself. I continued picking up small items, looking at the bottom for prices, testing them for flaws against the light, as if I could afford them in the first place. I was holding a pearly vase when Jack stepped close and said hello.

"Hey." His voice was pleasant, neutral, innocent of any pretense. He didn't actually recognize me, only thought I looked familiar.

It seemed to me wrong that, as the two of us stood only feet apart in the vicinity of so many breakables, everything around us stayed intact. When Jack Mauser smiled at me and began to make some unremarkable comment I opened my hand. The vase dropped with a crash that seemed to shine in the air, a high ringing unmistakable sound that made people's heads swivel. Jack jumped in surprise and looked at me strangely. In that thrilling instant, my breath stabbed, the rusty knife of my girlhood's end, and then I breathed from a deeper, hotter place. It was a small act, but it seemed to me the first thing I had done as a grown woman.

And yet, the act was still incomplete.

Jack bent over automatically, politely, to pick up the pieces. As he arched his hand above a set of shards thin as shaved ice, I stepped down hard and crushed his palm against the glass.

He gazed up at me, his mouth open, handsome in his shock

and pain. It was as though I were another person suddenly, as though I inhabited my old skin but was bursting out of my personality with surprising power. A vigilante thrill trickled down the center of my chest and then the icicle lodged there, crooked and gleaming. I had never caused another person intentional suffering. What I was doing was so bold and strange it wasn't even forbidden by the Ten Commandments.

My mouth went dry. Excitement. I couldn't speak.

He was angry. "Get your fucking foot off my hand!"

I pressed down, pressed harder until he made a noise. For him to drag his hand backward would have hurt worse, while to lift his other arm would have flipped him off balance. A store clerk and several customers had come near and stared at us now, mystified.

"Let up, let up," he ground between his teeth.

"We saved your life, Jack," I said to him. "My mother and me. You just left, never even said thank you, never even called or told my dad what didn't happen. Just went your own way."

"No, shit! Get off my hand!"

"You're gonna help me. Call my dad!"

I made him promise twice, three times, while the manager tried to drag me off.

Abruptly, in the middle of her story, Eleanor began to editorialize. "It was an expensive hand-blown vase, too! If only I'd chosen something cheaper to drop! I had no lunch money all that week—and the crystal was completely shattered, of course."

"Do you still have the pieces?" Dot wondered.

"In a little bag," Eleanor answered.

"You're sick." Marlis approved. "I knew you were. I can identify."

"Neurotic," Eleanor corrected her. "The word is 'neurotic.' I don't claim to be in perfect mental health—I'm Catholic. In this day and age how could I be one and be perfectly normal? I adapt to life, to other people, develop coping mechanisms. Sadism was a coping mechanism."

"That's what they all say," Candice yawned. "Suppose I was your dentist and I used that as an excuse?"

From the silence of consideration that followed her remark, Candice was gratified to think she'd made a point.

"As weeks went by," Eleanor continued, "Jack did not call Lawrence Schlick. From time to time, through the years, I had written my father anonymous letters telling him that nothing happened between his wife and Jack Mauser, but my father knew my handwriting, even disguised. My mother wouldn't say a word. The two were stubbornly entrenched in separate lives. I attempted to blame my father for the suffering that his stubborn behavior had caused my mother and me, but I was unable to, in the last, because beginning on the night that he found Jack Mauser in his bedroom, my father began to fail incrementally, then with almost intentional slow drama, in his own life.

"Lawrence Schlick started with plodding and thorough indifference to lose things, not small things, but, for instance, whole shipments of brand-new cars. He made bad purchases, speculated in water beds. He stockpiled inventory, forgot it. One windy night, he froze the entire warehouse of king-size mattresses that he'd set up and filled with water. They burst, and when the heat switched on flooded half the stock of Karpet Kingdom, which floundered through the next few years and then collapsed. His business sense went haywire. He couldn't sell or keep up his house and he didn't care. Only the dead did not desert him, it seemed, for the Schlick funeral business continued to flourish in spite of all else that went into the red. Perhaps the mortuary did so well because, in fact, it was the only aspect of his business edifice in which he took any interest. He had an advice column printed in the newspaper. 'Funeral Questions. Living Facts.' He oversaw the setup of family viewings, and dabbled with the notion that he should go back to school and learn mortuary science. At last, when virtually all he had left was his own house and the funeral home, he decided to consolidate the two.

"My father hired a crew to do a final restoration and

repainting of the grand Victorian house that my mother had hated, a place whose deep entry path was bordered by yew grown to a sober and unusual height. He instinctively knew that the lovely walk could serve to comfort the bereaved. My father let go of more that had once meant everything to him. He had the fancy mahogany and lead-glass parlor made into a viewing chamber, and felt the rightness of that small decision. It was part of letting go. With each loss, he felt so much lighter, so much freer to move toward the unthinkable."

At the same time, an obvious plan of attack was forming in my mind. I had waited long enough. If I seduced Jack, it would prove to my father that there was nothing between Jack and my mother. He would beg to take her back. Skewed. Indirect. But that is how my mind works. All I had to do was call Jack up and apologize about the department store, my foot on his hand, the glass. All I had to do was make myself available because I knew from his look, from his approach, from the way he had walked toward me down the aisle of glass, that he could be interested in me. I knew. That evening, I called Jack's uncle's number at the farm on the outskirts of Fargo.

Jack answered on the fourth ring.

"It's me, Eleanor Schlick. I'm sorry I stepped on your hand," I said. "Are you okay?"

There was static on the line. Either in our first meeting I'd got his attention but good, or else I scared him off forever. But he was not afraid, not Jack.

"Are you like that all the time?" His voice was low and clear, full of wary curiosity.

"I could be."

I felt his interest intensify.

"Do you go out much, have a boyfriend?"

"I've decided on you," I said.

There was a strange almost mournful pause from his end, then more interest. Then plans.

In a way it was as simple as that—I met him on a street corner. By eight o'clock we'd driven out into the squares of fields that bounded the city, interconnected section roads that led off nowhere, gravel roads sheer with ice and very lonely. Sometimes a car approached from far away. The headlights sank briefly over the interior roof. We used Jack's Silverado, a pickup he had bought with summer construction job money. We turned on our lights in the blossoming heat. If the car didn't veer off but continued to approach, we drove, still naked, until we found a place more secluded but also secure enough so we wouldn't get stuck the way we are now.

Here Eleanor stopped talking. The others waited.

"Details?" inquired Candice.

Eleanor hated the prying tone in the other woman's voice and did not go on. "It's getting stuffy in here. We'd better make sure the pipe's clear. If you others make a chain, hold me, I'll go first."

The other women roused themselves and Eleanor forced her way through the front passenger's window, holding on to Dot's hand. They groped along the side of the car, the wind a roar, encompassing, to Candice's side of the backseat, which Candice opened and out of which she stepped, holding to Dot on one side and Marlis on the other. Marlis called down behind the seat, but the hitchhiker, huddled in a softly breathing lump, was impossible to rouse, so Marlis hooked her arm onto the inside window of the car and held on as the women unrolled the chain of themselves to the tailpipe. Eleanor, at the very end, dug at the snow with her mitten—there was an opening there, at the base of the fender. She was able to kick snow away from the opening and bent to feel for the pipe in the utter darkness, to clear it as best she could. But while she was doing all of these difficult things to ensure their survival, she was thinking. She was remembering the details that she wouldn't share.

When the car stops and he cuts the lights, the stars rush down. Gradually the frozen fields seem to light up from inside, like iridescent panels, as our eyes adjust. It's not as though we're here for anything else, so we quit talking.

He is inside of me and he comes. We have to start that way, almost in greeting. We put our heads together and we close our eyes. He thinks about the kind of sex he wants to have with me, plans it, so that by the time we are together he has worked it out, and the sequence is locked in his mind. I kneel over him, cradling him, start touching him, gliding over him, stopping when he says to stop.

Eleanor stumbled against the car and was flattened there by wind as by a sudden, invisible hand. Dot managed to roll and push her. Slowly the women edged along the side of the car, back inside, and flung themselves into their seats. The interior seemed colder than outside, but enormously quiet after the roar of wind. Dot started the car and let the engine run for a few minutes in park, then put on the heater.

He turns me on my back carefully and kneels, his thighs just under my hips. His head is pressed to the vinyl ceiling. He holds my waist. He smiles, his eyes slanting, dark with hidden thoughts, the dash lights glowing on us in their false colors. From under the mats and through the seals of the doors, ice-cold air seeps in and we're partly hot and partly numb. I would do anything. He comes into me, comes again, quietly and emotionally, looking into my eyes. "You're the one," he says. "I know it." I answer. Even in a big front seat there is not enough room and he's tall. It is impossible for him to stretch completely out without bending somewhere, and after a while this limitation bores us. We push the seat back as far as it will go and sit naked. Warm dry air is blowing like a balm. Soon he will ask, and I will answer, we will talk about our love. Our Love. We discuss it like it is outside of us, pinpoint things about it, clinically, under control, and then we fall together and we keep going, we fuck ourselves stupid, again and again, until we're both crying, until it's time to bring the pickup home.

Sometimes, afterward—I like this almost as much as parking on the farm roads—we go to the restaurant. We have a favorite, a real one that's not a chain, that stays open all night. It's small, long, narrow, lined with mirrors. The booths are wooden and the smell inside is rich with the smells of crackling grease, fried onions, coffee, and cigarette smoke. His roast beef sandwich comes on white bread with a fringe of lettuce and the meat is always slate gray, fibrous. Breakfast is what I order. He pays. The long, thick, white, oval plate, slippery hash browns and over-easy eggs dotted with circles of melted butter, dry toast, ketchup. I eat it fast, stuffing every bit down, swirling the toast in yolk and butter, silent. Sometimes he watches me, the prim dry triangle of sandwich on the plate, untouched. Then, when I'm finished eating, he stuffs the whole sandwich into his mouth, chews still watching me, swallows. From the way we eat together it is clear that we are very, very much in love.

How could I have those feelings without wanting them to last, mourned Eleanor. Her heart pinched. I sent him away once, again, and again. He went out west, stayed a year. Maybe sex was too new. I didn't trust it, didn't value the fact that we're beholden to our bodies, after all. Or perhaps, since I'd originally gone out with Jack to get my parents back together, I was shocked by the unexpected love I felt for him. More likely, here is the truth. How stupidly selfish! I thought that if sex with my first man was this good, other men would be even better. What greed! I didn't want to commit before I'd tried them all, sampled everyone!

"What happened?" Dot broke into Eleanor's thoughts. "To your mom, your dad, to Jack? What happened when you told them about him?"

"Nothing at first," she said. "They didn't react at all. Frustrating. I decided to push it one step farther."

Eleanor rubbed her face, hard, to wipe away those memories. Her heart sped in a panic of sorrow—he shouldn't be gone, shouldn't be! Get back here! She was angry with longing. All of the ambivalence she'd felt while he was alive had melted now into direct desire. As Dot waited, though, slapping her gloved hands lightly on the wheel, bouncing in the seat to generate more warmth, Eleanor took up the place where she had left off in her tale.

I was carrying a bag of groceries through the back doorway when I saw the faces of my mother and father. Calmly, as though from grainy portraits, they stared. They were sitting at the kitchen table, arms crossed, together for the first time in years. They knew. They had that stunned, suspended, wary look of people who are about to ask you something painful. I preempted them.

"Did Jack tell you we were getting married?"

My mother paused. Her deep eyes met mine, full on.

She saved me once. She saved me two, three times. This time I'd set up such a complicated plot that she didn't know how to react. She paused midair, put out all of her feelers, used every instinct to try to understand.

"Then it's true?"

Her voice was light and genuine, but questioning.

I dropped my gaze from hers. Desperate for her to disapprove so I could feel justified in what I was doing, I lied. "I'm pregnant. He's the father."

For one instant, I thought I saw her composure crack. Her eyes opened very wide and a flicker of lightning challenged me, running up and down my flat stomach. Her face strained as though it were about to break, but once again, she composed herself.

"You'll be a good mother," she said gravely, and in that instant, my heart hollowed with dismay. The moment she approved, I wanted to be rid of Jack. He was drinking too much since coming back from the oil fields, saying strange things when he was loaded. I wanted my mother to forbid me, to tell me I was making a mistake, that I wasn't pregnant, that she knew. If she set up some opposition, I could get angry and justify my behavior with a burst of rebellion.

"You'll be a *grandmother*." I was desperate.

Once I said that, however, as though in punishment for my attempted cruelty, which only made her smile, I felt a sudden faintness. An eerie wash of morning sickness flooded through me, and I sat on the floor. My father knelt and checked my pulse.

"I'm all right," I reassured myself.

I was amazed at my body's reaction, since of course I wasn't actually pregnant. It was late fall, and I wore a heavy blue jacket lined with dark violet satin. The cloth fell around me in an evenly rumpled circle. I looked like Holy Mary, or some kind of passive martyr. A wave of profound boredom suddenly crushed me. I didn't want to get married, didn't want to have a baby—the truth was I loved Jack one minute and the next I couldn't stand to be near him. I had woven myself into such a corner in my feelings that I didn't have room to maneuver. Yet it seemed almost in spite of myself that I set my course.

Even though I'd made up the baby, I felt the pretend pregnancy progress rapidly all the next week. Sometimes the baby seemed to kick, pushing off, a tiny swimmer. I riffled through my feelings, needing something true. When you drift in ambivalence, there is no place to touch down. No certainty. I hated that shameful instant of falsehood that had hit me in the kitchen. But when I came to that place in myself where a woman in my situation would naturally get to, the question— why don't you tell the truth?—my heart beat faster. I couldn't wait to find out what would happen if I did nothing. Maybe I *was* pregnant. Why not after all the times we'd parked? Why shouldn't I be, after all? We'd used foams, condoms, more than once nothing. Besides, pregnancy got me things, gave me the upper hand. After the surprise, my parents came to terms with the idea in a sudden rush.

Forgiveness happens, shocking in its emptiness. My father didn't know it. Revenge is fuller, rounder, more human somehow. Acceptable. Wandering downtown after a particularly stunning set of financial conversations with his friend the bank president, my father one day found himself standing before a taped and shattered door. He stayed there as people walked in, walked out. Three times he was approached. First, by a drunk who asked for a quarter, next by an eager missionary, and last, by his wife who touched him on the shoulder, smiled, and walked past him to begin her day's work. He felt the shiver of her presence, and his bones ached. As the door closed incompletely behind her, my father swayed forward, swayed backward, and then followed.

Anger turns into its opposite, but what is that? An oil, a smoothing emollient, a general radiance toward others, a fortified goodness, a non-anger. Maybe even something that resembles love. My mother and I moved back into the renovated upper floors of the Victorian house, and began a new life with my father, a life that took place between walls of sandblasted brick and brand-new pastel Sheetrock. My expectancy had them both edgy and solicitous. My father kept thinking of what could go wrong. He read medical texts, and put me on a strict diet while my mother baked food to tempt me. When I was entirely comfortable in my childhood bedroom, set beneath the eaves of the roof, looking out into a forested backyard of wealthy neighbors, I relaxed. I began to think. I still harbored my angry dreams but soon they were mixed with other thoughts, visions, attractions. No true plan of revenge had ever motivated me, just a subterranean fury, thick in its lazy rush. Now I wondered about my true feelings, my ambitions. Take away my parents and my manipulations and anxiety, and what were my feelings for Jack?

I was home by myself, reading, bolting down wheat crackers as fast as I could, when the doorbell rang. I had to sneak them into my room or my father would gently pull away the box, reminding me the baby was growing bigger too. I hadn't heard a car drive up, so I went to an upstairs window and looked down to see who it was. If it was someone in black, I decided that I wouldn't answer.

Jack was watching me watch him through the upstairs window. His face was tipped back, his skin golden, eyes dark and hair mink brown. He arched one brow, held out his hands. Would I let him in? I sighed. Here it came. I let the curtain drop. Before I opened the door, I brushed my hair from my face with my fingers, bit my lips a little. Still, what I had decided was this: He'd done the job of getting my parents together. I'd paid him with sex. Paid him too well. It was time to fire him even though I'd grown attached—maybe fallen in love. Still, no sooner that I decided he was for me than he suddenly said something stupid and I changed my mind. Conversely, the moment I decided that I hated him he warmed my heart with a perfect gesture. He had physical grace. He won me effortlessly and at the same time he drove me crazy.

I knew Jack's basic history, his football career, his decent grades, his careless string of girlfriends. His big move to the outskirts of Fargo, then into the city itself to get his engineering degree. All normal enough, too normal for me! He told me he'd been married once, for a short time; he was a widower. I didn't believe him. He worked with insane energy and on weekends he sang lead vocal in an awful rock band, throwing his hands high and rocking side to side on the balls of his feet. Although his voice was mediocre, he was tender and unashamed, with an outright joy or sorrow that affected people in the audience. He often sang off-key to loud cheers.

I tried to turn him from the door.

"It would be rude not to ask me in," he said with smooth confidence I found annoying and also hard to resist.

I took a deep breath, opened the door wide, and nodded toward the living room.

My voice was as neutral as I could make it, but the edge was there. I wanted to get back to my little study, the safety of my stacks and piles of books and mail, my earnest little typewriter, my gloomy journals, my Thomas Merton paperbacks. My *Castle of the Interior*. He wouldn't let me. He settled immediately into a heavy old chair, and drank the Coke I brought him. When the glass was empty, I didn't offer him a refill, but still he sat there, looking at me. I was anxious to get it over with, then uncomfortable. I steeled myself not to feel his feelings but just to get it over, clean.

"We're finished."

"The hell we are."

I hadn't expected him to resist.

"Through," I said forcefully.

He leaned forward and put his hands in his lap—big hands, square and muscular. He rubbed his chin, clasped his fingers together. He obviously had something more to say, but

I didn't want to hear another word drop from his lips. I held my arm toward the door and gestured that he could leave anytime he wanted. He remained seated. The sudden confusion and antagonism in his face ignited in me an odd surge of power. I fixed a cold smile on my face and pointed directly at the door.

"Your bum's rush, it's above standard. Elegant," he said.

I slowly let my hand drop.

"I'm tired of you." I sounded unconvincing, so I tried to be crude and simple. "Leave!"

To that he had no answer, and there was no grace to his sudden, stunned, uncomfortable shame.

"What do you want?" I asked, impatient.

"You."

"You can't have me. I'm sorry." My voice turned falsely soothing, syrupy.

"Now fuck off, right?"

I shrugged.

"Oh," he said. "It's useless. I'll never . . . here."

He unbuttoned the flap of his breast pocket and he drew out a photograph. He looked at it for a moment and then he turned it toward me. It was a picture of me that a girlfriend had taken, an art shot. In the photograph, I was lying on my side on a couch, in a Manet pose, watching television and wearing a red satin slip. I'd given it to him. He flapped it toward me.

I refused to take it back.

"I don't want it."

"I don't want it, either."

That made me furious.

"Keep it!"

"No." He sensed he was gaining the upper hand. "It's yours."

"I gave it to you."

"Well, I'm giving it back."

"I don't want it back."

"Okay." He watched me carefully and then he raised the

photo to his lips. "I love this picture of you," he said softly. "I love you to the end of everything."

Sometimes, when our eyes met, I crept right into the space between us and I sheltered under our exchange as beneath an intimate roof. I almost settled there now. But then, Jack looked straight at me over the edge of the paper and put the photo back in his pocket.

"You're pregnant."

I put my hands over my ears.

"You're pregnant," he repeated.

He said the word again.

Obviously, my mother had told him and I hated her and hated him right then with equal force. Jack looked full into my glare and flushed.

"You and me," he spoke as though it didn't matter. "We weren't exactly made for each other, except physically. You can't change. I know. But what about the baby?"

"There isn't one!" I cried. "It was a stupid mistake, one of those things, you know, I just said. I'm going to college, it's just deferred. I'm going to Carleton College where you'd never get accepted in a million years. I'm sick of hanging around here."

"Now you're lying. You *are* pregnant." His voice was rough and passionate. He wouldn't listen to me and he started talking too fast, babbled about going to Florida.

"I've got vacation," Jack said, "two weeks. We'll go down, have some fun, maybe we'll get married or something."

"No."

But he kept talking, talking, until I finally said I'd think about it. That was just to get rid of him, but by the time two days had passed, the photo turning over and over in my mind, I'd become restless.

"I'm taking a trip," I told my parents that night after dinner.

"Where to?"

I had a girlfriend in Minneapolis, and I told them I was going to visit her. My father hated the idea of my traveling, but I worked on him for hours, telling him I needed a change of scene, promising I'd snack on celery sticks, drink my required milk, and do the light exercises his books recommended. I finally stood up and smoothed the lines on his forehead. I took off his glasses and cleaned them on the end of my shirt.

"I just worry."

"I'm fine."

He took my hand down and held it between his palms, but it cooled there. Raw guilt sank my stomach, hollowed my bones. He usually had a flat, cool, businesslike touch, but that night I thought he sensed my lies.

"I'll be all right," I said, twice, three times, so many times that I started to doubt it.

We stayed at a pink hotel, a huge rich cake of a place, made all of stucco. Jack was using up the money he had earned in the last year—he'd worked construction, in the oil fields, out in western North Dakota, and he was trying to impress me with the luxury he pretended he could afford. The place was surrounded by enormous ropy trees, hibiscus, and everywhere fountains, seats with roots gnarled around them, tile courtyards. Florida kites, huge black birds, circled through the air in weaving patterns. We were ushered into our room on a low second floor. The window was alive with palm fronds.

"Here we are." Jack's voice was flat, tired. We were stiff from the long train ride. He walked over to the bed and threw himself face down across it. He kept trying to impress me. I'd seen him flip through novels on a rack and in a fit of cruelty I'd bought him a copy of *Finnegans Wake* and said earnestly that it had been my favorite book ever since I got it for my tenth birthday. His eyes crossed every time he opened the pages, and his head soon fell to one side. The book numbed his brain, put him instantly to sleep. Now, I untied the little bow beneath my throat, the thing that held my collar together. I began to undo the buttons that led down, then stopped, sat in a chair across from Jack, and fell asleep, too.

When I woke, he was gone. I took a cool bath, dressed myself in blue cotton, and went out to sit on the low balcony.

As the dark lowered around me, I looked across the courtyard. Directly below, about eight feet or so, there was a newly turned flower garden and past that a fountain, two tiers of water musically dripping, overflowing, spilling out the small openings in the rich mosaic. A large tree grew beside the fountain, touching the glowing pink walls above the balcony where I sat. Its leaves drooped, thick ovals of shiny black. People passed, nearly close enough to touch, floating along the walks. When darkness had sifted almost entirely through the sky, the other guests vanished into their rooms to dress for dinner in rich clothes, glitter, diamonds. There was nothing below me but the splash of water, and before me the barrier of the balcony rail, iron lace. A small breeze blew. White curtains billowed out of our window like a mist and sagged back.

Jack returned.

I turned away from him. We were silent, uncomfortable. I finally spoke. "We're going home tomorrow. This was stupid."

"Maybe."

He reached around me and put his hands under my breasts, began to stroke where the baby was supposed to be, but I was indifferent at first, distracted. I was used to soaking in my own sorrow as the light faded. He opened my blouse. I did nothing. He pulled it down my shoulders. I felt the air sweep across my throat, and then suddenly, as he put his face beside mine, I felt the shock of what we were doing. I saw him as he saw me. From his eyes for a moment, I watched as he arched back and put his arms around me, saw as he showed my pale body to the leaves, to the steady fountain.

I made some sort of protest.

"Let 'em look," he said, but there was no one to see. The palms and black leaves were a ragged screen. We made love standing up until the ornate bars rattled, and then he knelt before me and kissed me—but I was too nervous, worried that someone would see us, to lose myself. Jack looked around, murmured softly that I should be the sentry, and then stood up and entered me from behind. When I lunged to grab the iron bars, leaning our combined weight on them, we kept going. A bolt probably loosened the first time, gave out the second. I went straight down with the grate, maybe eight feet, that was all. Jack flew over me. Branches snapped and fell with him. I landed with a soft thump in a bed of begonias. Jack crashed into a yucca and rolled through some prickling shrubs but we were both up in a flash buttoning on and smoothing down our clothes so that it would have appeared to anyone attracted by the snapping and the thumping that two people had simply fallen from, not fucked themselves straight out of, a balcony.

I began to feel strange the next morning, aware of the heavy knot of blood that was my normal period. Now I could get rid of Jack, a thought that both relieved and frightened me. As soon as I told him, though, Jack decided it was a miscarriage and got a doctor through the hotel. But the man only told me to rest.

"We're not going anywhere," said Jack, "we're getting married right now."

"Forget it."

He sat beside me on the bed, stuffed pillows around me, stroked my arms, brought iced tea and magazines. I paged through the photographs of women with pursed lips and thick eyeliner, threw them down. "You don't know," I cried out once, muffling my voice with a towel. Storms built in me, small pockets of whirling violence, tears. I wept round damp stains into the pillowcases, and then laughed and talked and shoved away Jack's solicitous face.

I sent him away and ordered up two breakfasts from room service. When the waiter left, I took the pancakes right off the plates and ate them like big pieces of bread. I had never been so hungry in my life. I stuffed myself with sausages, eggs, fruit. When everything was gone, I slept hard through the afternoon. Jack came and cleared away the plates so quietly that I never woke. I stayed in bed, and watched the leaves of palms, of oak, the black ovals, touch and cross out the window. The sky was dark blue. The walls a warm peach. Maybe there was some purpose to my lie. I kept seeing myself pregnant, growing big among my dolls and stamp albums. I couldn't see myself in childbirth, though. I didn't think I could get through it. Still, I would not let go. This pregnancy was the first complex thing I'd invented, and even then I knew it was the closest I'd ever get to having a baby.

I had just bought myself a notebook, to record my impressions, my self-pity. I filled two, three, four pages with the word "empty." Then I turned from thinking about myself to thinking about food. *Hungry, hungry!* The wind moved through the room in a tranquil swirl. Shadows descended, a faint turquoise, swimming across the wall. After dusk, Jack came into the room, sat next to me.

"Jack," I said, almost apologetically. "I need food. A lot more food. Seafood."

"I'll go order it."

We had cocktails of sweet, pink shrimp, then a salad with rich poppy-seed dressing. I had a rare steak, very tender. I covered two baked potatoes with melted butter and sour cream. I sprinkled pepper flakes on everything. I wanted cake, dessert. Strawberry shortcake. Orange ice cream. Baked Alaska.

"You pig!" Marlis broke into Eleanor's story. "Will you shut up with this grocery list? Where's that bag of Halloween candy!"

"Don't stop," Candice said. "What happened?"

"I ate *everything*," Eleanor bragged hungrily. "Jack was surprised."

"How do you feel?" he asked me when I was finished, the room cluttered with utensils and silver domes and heavy napkins and plates.

"Still starving," I answered.

I went into the bathroom, but left the door ajar while I brushed my hair, ran a bath, and filled it with bubbles. The hand towel I'd held between my legs all afternoon was red and I knew that it was over, that no matter how much I ate the food wouldn't hold back my body's simple rhythm. Once I had my period the fantasy was over. I'd be free and Jack would can the tender solicitude. I eased into the warmth and fragrance, closed my eyes tight. Jack sat on the edge of the heavy tub.

"Do you know or don't you?" he said. His eyes were soft with anxiety. "About the baby," he hesitated.

"There wasn't one. I told you."

We stared into each other's eyes until his grew shiny and slowly filled.

"I'm just this guy, Eleanor." He clipped his words. "I'm from North Dakota dirt farmers, Indians, a railroad executive, big-shot and little-shot people. I grew up isolated and I really was married — several hours. She died, but that's not why I'm after you. You're smart, I know that. I wouldn't take that away from you. Marry me and I'll give you everything I have." He paused, he stood up. "I know you better than you think. I've read your mind over and over. I knew you weren't pregnant. I'll marry you though. I'll do it."

"Don't force yourself."

His face came down next to mine, lower, insinuating. He tried another tactic.

"If you don't take me, Uncle Sam will."

"Let him," I said, indignant at his ploy, which even I knew was a scam. There was no way he would join the army.

"You'd send me to boot camp!"

His voice rose, strained and passionate, and now he paused, regarding me, looking for a sign. I kept a poker face until I made him so uncomfortable that he laughed a choking little laugh.

"We didn't. We didn't. Me and your mother," he added to make sure I knew.

He had the photograph folded in a piece of cardboard in his shirt pocket. Right there, he took it out, held it above the bubbles and let it slip out of his fingers. The piece of paper caught, then sank, swirling along my ankle. I looked up at Jack and our stares caught, unblinking. We looked at each

other too long and got lost again. Jack stepped into the tub
with his clothes on and bent, the water darkening his chinos
and then swallowing them as he unbuttoned and went to his
knees and fit my hips and legs around him, secure, like a yoke.
Underneath the bright froth, there was a thin stream of color.
Me or the photo. By the time I let the water flow out and
down, the slow blood, I was erased, my body just a pale
shadow on a background of grain and mist, and only the dark
outline of the slip.

I slept on the floor, woke, and wrapped myself in a thick terry
robe. I began to walk through the room, touching things, looking at them as though I had never seen such objects before. I
had to let my body think for me, do exactly as it pleased. I was
surprised at the amount of energy I had, the buoyant restlessness, the sudden apprehension that was nothing I could put
into words, a purely physical sense of purpose. Several times, I
slipped off my robe, turned from side to side in the mirror, ran
my hands up and down the slope of my breasts, my stomach. I
rubbed my fingers in coconut tanning oil and massaged myself
in slow circles and then stood before the back window over-
looking the glittering tiled rectangle of the swimming pool that
stretched below, down a steep slope.
From far above, I watched Mauser approach the edge of
the pool. He threw down his towel. Without testing the water,
he dove in, his body long and pale brown. He began to swim
laps, stroking awkwardly but calmly, eating up the distance.
The motion of his monotonous crawl hypnotized me and I fell
into a thoughtful mood. After a while, I leaned closer and my
stare burned through the glass. I could not take my eyes off
Jack. I almost felt him move beneath my hands. He must have
swum a half mile before he turned over on his back and rested
way down there, under me, keeping himself afloat with small
hand motions, flutter kicks. My heart squeezed in one convul-
sion after another, as though a hand was pumping it to life.
Jack was so far away, so defenseless, his body any body, his
shape so humble and buoyant in the water. He was so alone, so

unexpectedly frail underneath the deep sky. Maybe I was prepared to care for someone. Him. I moved closer to the window, and then I stepped up, stood on the broad pink sill. I couldn't see down the sheer edge of the building and it almost seemed that I could swoop down over Jack Mauser like an angel, like a woman in a Chagall painting. I stretched my arms and held on to the edges of the window. The white robe with the crest on it spread like soft wings and then we were floating, flying, heart to heart, through the water, through the blue air.

We married in Florida, quickly and with no ceremony. In Plato's theory of our loss of innocence we search for our other half. We are one body cut off from itself, rolling wild, a wheel of longing for the other sex. I often believed that with Jack I had found the other half of my wheel, the match, all of my body's missing pieces. However, his mind drove me crazy. If I was the woman in the Chagall, then he was a Magritte landscape, one of those skies with holes punched in it. I would step through suddenly and find myself completely lost in an unplanted field. Jack wasted his intelligence. He had a high IQ, a good memory, but wouldn't go the extra inch to learn what he was talking about. He knew a million facts but not one truth. And then, too, past a certain point Jack froze. You know what I mean. He'd play the ice man. He could harden himself somehow, or maybe it was that he couldn't stay tender. He waded shallow where nothing too dangerous could sneak up on him. We made out constantly, to shut each other up, but in the interims between erotic events, we found that as well as loving, we hated one another with an intensity so bewildering it was almost an exhilarating rush.

We fought constantly over all that was large and small. We fought over the meaningless things and over the big things, over the color of the couch in our Florida hotel room and the size of our bed, over the definition of God, over peace, over war, over the hypothetical name I'd give our baby, if we ever had one, Leda. We fought over how Jack froze me out. How, if he had the chance, he'd treat a child. Whether to let the unborn Leda cry or pick her up. We fought over the story of the swan, over who Zeus was, over the definition of a metaphor. Back in Fargo-Moorhead, we moved into a small apartment, which I hated, and where I hadn't enough privacy to rage properly over Jack's habits—his lazy reading, TV watching, his drinking, his hunting, the buck he brought back into our tiny yard and hung up in a tree and gutted. We fought over coffee cups, whose was whose. We had screaming fits over the way the carpet had flipped up by the door. Whose fault? We fought over how we couldn't fight, sometimes, because we were too much in love. We fought about whether we really felt good about sex or whether it was all pretense. We fought until we couldn't talk, until we lost our tongues, our words, until we couldn't remember what we fought about. We fought until I walked out on him and went back to my parents, who shut the door in his face. We kept on fighting until I went to college, where I would never hear the name Jack Mauser. We continued fighting through the mail, through letter after letter that he wrote and I burned, or I sent and he burned, or refused and had returned. We fought so hard that neither time zones nor distance could divide us. We couldn't agree on a divorce, even that. No sooner would one of us decide than the other would be against the whole idea. At all hours, for a year, in all states of mind, we shouted at each other over the phone. I drove back to Fargo for the summer and after one good month we fought so hard that I took a year's exchange in London. Only when I put the whole Atlantic between us as well as half a continent, did the fighting between us stop.

§

T h e   B o x

WINTER 1983

Lawrence Schlick

*D*uring the cold hours that Lawrence Schlick prepared the dead for morning viewings, an owl often roosted in the deep arms of the pine outside the shaded window of his renovated, tiled, and fluorescent-lighted workplace. He felt less alone, welcomed its solemn, hollow call, and was reassured by its continual return. Though he never actually laid eyes on the bird, he imagined that it was small and of an unusual gray softness. Lawrence Schlick found a feather that he slipped into the frame of a mirror.

Familiarity with death had connected him to all of life. He was intimate with human brevity, which intensified his lover's yearning. The yews outside his house, clipped and coddled, were dark expressions of his own thoughts. Birds at his window feeder absorbed his attention, and the raucous squirrels. Everything around him was a portentous sign. He had turned from being a social, gregarious small-city speculator to a thinner, more serene type of man.

Often, he felt a human presence hover in the room and he was careful with what the spirit left behind. At other times, the smoke of evil twisted. Too much knowledge came to him, and questions. Suicides made him uneasy and his job difficult—they had to look peaceful, not blaming, but their faces were so often set in the stubborn mask of their triumph. They always seemed, to Schlick, to have died in the act of uttering one word that he could not quite catch . . . although he stooped to hear . . .

Ever since he had resumed their marriage, pleasing Anna had been his guiding star, but she looked upon that occupation with a reserved indulgence and concentrated on her own work with the church. She fed outlaws, drunks, addicts, fools and artists, her friends. She let Lawrence Schlick see to the dead, so found and final, while she cared for the living lost. As between them they had divided up the universe, their marriage went along in such smooth and simple routine that he was mostly able to shrug off his intuition that Anna might not have given up her feelings for the man he believed was her lover, Jack Mauser, even after his marriage to and divorce from their daughter, and that Jack's visits, though occasional and rare, had not ceased.

Lawrence Schlick hadn't ever caught them, seen them, heard them. He had only the cry of the owl to go on—nothing more substantial, just a floating vowel. Jack Mauser's presence in their life was soundless as the bird's flight, his power no more than weak suggestion, and yet it remained.

One night in late winter, Lawrence Schlick purposely returned to Fargo two days before the annual Minneapolis funerary trade show was scheduled to end. He drove straight home, in darkness, all the while pretending to himself that out of courtesy, unwilling to disturb Anna, he hadn't called to tell her of his plans. It was not until he cut the lights, pulling into the driveway, until he tried to mute his entry, that he admitted to himself in any way that he was acting from small and suspicious motives. At that point, he felt a tinge of embarrassment, and having picked up his suitcase, he purposely slammed the car trunk, hard, to prove that he wasn't sneaking home. In the silence following that sharp sound, however, he stood quite still and could not determine, heart tapping wild, whether or not he heard or morbidly imagined the sounds, in a ratcheting series from the inside of the upstairs bedroom, whether there was a clatter of footsteps, whispers, a door shutting, opening.

A light flickered on, and off again.

Jealousy is a rich emotion. It takes undreamed-of forms and burns away conditioned and acquired intelligence. It is a sieve, a net of flames through which only the ash of sweeter longings drifts. Blind, undiscoverable, witless, true, it swells so suddenly and dangerously that the human body cannot properly contain it. The brain seems at first to have lost its own name. The soul is not organized to so quickly regress.

As Lawrence Schlick fumbled with the key to the house, he found himself at the mercy of that wind of feeling that had swept him before it on the morning after the night of the fire so long ago, the night that still held records for the quickest November temperature drop occurring in the tristate region. He turned the key, paused, opened the door softly, and stepped into the unlighted kitchen. His shoes in old-fashioned rubbers stuck and unstuck to the floor as he crossed to a door that led down a short hall into the main storage room, where he kept caskets, plant stands, urns, and rollers. The back staircase from his and Anna's room led down into that private warehouse.

He now entered, switched on a low bulb.

Absolute quiet gripped him and his heart went numb. A veil of yellow sparks dropped before his eyes. The air seemed to have been sucked from the room, and he gasped and pulled his tie loose, sat in a folding chair sometimes brought out for weak-kneed customers. Nothing. No one. Of course. And yet there was the flight of the owl. Those steps and sounds. He sat directly across from an expensive black-lacquered hardwood casket and as he sat there and sat there and sat there, an impossible and absurd suspicion took him by hot storm. He leaned forward, stared at the box.

Was Jack Mauser hiding inside it?

Gripping his knees as if he'd otherwise fly apart, he glared at the wood and frowned. After some time had passed, he relaxed, dropped his head back. He noticed his thermos of coffee, poured himself a cup. Forgot to drink it. His thoughts softened into further questions and he extended his hand, withdrew it, self-consciously cleared his throat. Still the box, on the elegant hinged rollers that were used to move it where it needed to go, the box made no reply. He watched it carefully for a sign.

The brass snap locks, which always went down after the viewing was completed, hung open. Schlick could not remember if he'd kept them closed, open, closed, open, closed. His heart muscles pinched. Possibilities, sensual, violent, tender, flickered on in vivid mental scenes. Anna, her body warm and shadowy, her breasts moving against him, her hair loose and whirling. Anna flying. He pressed the soft cushions of his palms to his face, his eyes, pressed harder, harder, until pictures were blotted out in red dots. He came to, leaned confidentially forward again, but did not speak. He folded his arms, crossed his legs, continued to stare.

At two A.M. he heard Anna rise. Something heavy fell, perhaps a book. Then silence. At three he told himself to shift his weight, to move, because his arms and legs were losing sensation. The owl, at four in the morning, began calling and did not stop until the dark went iron cold at five. At six the sky grayed. Seven. Seven-thirty. Seven forty-five. It was eight o'clock when he finally rose, walked briskly over to the box, and snapped the brass locks shut.

He left the room, then, and went into the kitchen. By nine, he had a full breakfast steaming on a tray—pancakes in a light stack, real maple syrup, pats of butter cream. Orange juice, shaken hard, ice in the glass. Coffee in a silver thermos. He was wild with elation, giddy. He brought the tray upstairs, sat down with Anna on the edge of the bed, ate his own breakfast, too, from her plate, and blurted out that he had planned a surprise excursion to the city of Chicago.

She answered, looking at him until her face glowed the way he loved to see it, "What made you think of it?"

Lawrence Schlick felt his smile falter, and he looked down at the surface of the tarry coffee. He tipped the cup to his mouth and closed his eyes. Darkness rinsed down behind his eyelids. Putting down the cup, he felt his lips form an odd new smile. Bitterness. Tender lust. The softest feathers brushed his throat.

§

Funeral Day

*D*ripping light penetrated the cave of Jack's hideout office.
It was his funeral day. The hours had been printed in the
Forum and Jack had torn the announcement clear, along with
the notice to his creditors. Once or twice he started a truck in
for repairs, listened to the radio. Late that morning, curiously
and grievously for Dot, he heard a brief account of a light
plane crash in which Gerry Nanapush had, presumably, been
killed. He pondered the chipped metal of the old clay-green
surplus army desk where Dot and then only he and no one else
had spent futile nights willing balance out of chaos. The numbers, though, had long ago tipped and the desk had taken on
the hated aura of a savage encounter. Money had disappeared
there, at a great velocity. Jack looked away from the desk and
the fresh clipping, and out the office window to the vaulted
windows of the concrete garage, where pale lavenders and
golds of a noon sun trembled through the industrial-glass ripples and floated, cold splendor in octagons of chicken wire.

Now sweeter, redder fires flared into the sky, and shafts of cathedral intensity, bold and strange, held for long seconds in Jack's vision a fractured emblem.

My son!

Clouds passed. Jack rose planning how he should accomplish a visit to his baby boy before he left Fargo, heading north—perhaps in Candice's second car. That car would be hard to trace at first—he'd leave her a note so she wouldn't report it stolen. She wouldn't, then, would she? If she knew it was him? Jack cast his mind into the drama of his own demise. Now that his guilt over causing grief and shock was diminished, Jack took some satisfaction in picturing the arrangements.

He imagined that Lawrence Schlick was at this moment rolling out the fake grass. First the sidewalk, an Astroturf walkway, then another blanket of shaggy green plastic to cover the earth at the cemetery. Schlick would be pleased, thinking that at last he'd gotten Jack into his clutches. Schlick's eyes followed Jack with calm dead killing regard anytime they happened to be in the same room. Jack had thought of making a provision in his will that his funeral should be handled by a concern other than Schlick's. Of course, he'd had no intention either of dying or pretending to die. Now he reminded himself that when, if ever, he had a lawyer willing to represent him again, he would attend to that detail. This death was a practice run.

He returned to the fantasy—what *would* they do with his supposed remains? Who would cry and who would pray? He saw it all—wives and wives and wives approaching—waves of women marching like the sea toward his casket! He touched the space on the left side of his mouth. His bridgework would be the center of controversy, plus what they found of *him* in the ashes, petrified cow?

Meanwhile, disguised as an ordinary backhoe operator, Jack would leave his own garage and walk two miles to the home of his third wife, the dentist who had lovingly fashioned the very bridge that used to fit perfectly and painlessly into his mouth and who would, might, possibly, *could* wonder where the rest of her careful dental work had vanished in the inferno that was supposed to have engulfed Jack. He dressed as warmly as possible, swathing his feet in ancient stinking socks and crumpled newspapers, padding the jumpsuit with a worn lap blanket. He found a greasy sheepskin hat with long ears and a chin snap. Work gloves. He gathered the money he'd weaseled from Hegelstead and pried out of the vending machine.

Outside, the goofy shock of freedom! The day was so short that the afternoon light was already growing dull. He could smell the snow around its edges. His senses had grown fine, really too fine since not drinking. It was annoying to sense much of what he'd numbed himself from feeling—even weather. There was a lot of weather to become aware of and so many other things he'd tried unsuccessfully to shield himself from in the past few months. Lucky thing, too, about the congested bruises because they did disguise him along with the scruff of beard—a wizened fringe of a half-breed beard, a voyageur's beard, nothing to brag about—but hair enough to obscure the line of his jaw. He took the streets straight on, walking as though toward some destination like a normal person, a soiled workman. Carrying a lunch pail even, one left under the desk, scrounged, to look as though he was heading home after some shift, any shift. And the raincoat—that he'd found, too, and the odd pair of shoes that were big and oddly stylish, grunge boots for a workingman, but which the long cuffs of his overalls hid.

As he approached Candy's tidy little house, the one into which the postpartum Marlis had moved with all her mental and material junk, Jack tried even harder not to look suspicious—but how could he not when he was supposed to be dead! What would the baby-sitter, whoever she was, make of him in this crusty getup unless, maybe, he said he was the baby's uncle, come to the city for Jack's funeral, wanting to see his little nephew. He'd try it.

Jack knocked.

An older woman, muscular and slim with exotic green eyes and raven hair pulled strictly back, opened the main door and stood behind the storm glass.

"What can I do for you?" she asked.

Jack's hand reached out to try the door just as her finger snapped down the key that bolted it fast. Her face changed quickly.

"Good-bye," she said.

"Wait, I'm Jack's brother, the baby's uncle. Just wanted to see him!"

"I'll call Dr. Pantamounty." The baby-sitter's voice was muffled as she shut the door and turned away.

"No!"

Wildly, Jack scrambled off the front porch, remembered where during their life together he and Candice had hidden the extra key near the back door. He vaulted over the low dog fence, grabbed the key from the underside of the second lattice on the back porch, and let himself into the kitchen, quietly, just as the baby-sitter picked up the phone. She whirled, smashed her fingers down on a 9 and a 1.

Jack put his hand down on hers, stared into her face, trying not to look menacing.

"Please," he said in as gentle a voice as he could manage. "I just want to see my little nephew, I won't hurt him. Please. And by the way, I'll need the keys to Candy's car, you know, the white one in the garage. Now listen. I'll leave a note for her. It will be all right. We're very good friends and she'll understand. What's your name?"

"I'm not afraid of you!"

"I was just trying to put us on a more . . . familiar footing."

The woman's round eyes hardened, her sharp face narrowed and paled, the mouth, perfectly lipsticked, shut in a reptilian clasp. Her rich hair was beauty parlor exact, curled and sprayed into a dense upswept knot. She wore small flat shoes and fashionable stretch pants, a glittering sweater. She stood in the doorway with the light from the kitchen windows gleaming all around her, off the white knit of her clothing, the flaring lizard sequins of the flowers on her breast. In a way he'd never before noticed in a woman of her age, his son's nanny was quite attractive. He couldn't help it—she was beautiful, though her face was lined and stark with determination. There was no fear in her hooded and upturned green eyes. She was not intimidated by him at all.

He had not expected this. Already, too, he understood that no charm of his would work. This woman knew exactly what was happening.

"What was your name again?"

"I am Mrs. Tillie Kroshus!"

The elegant knob of hair on her head cocked forward a little.

"May I see my nephew?" he asked, hoping that she might relent, that something in his face, some resemblance perhaps, might sway her. She thought for a while—her face strategically blank.

"Well, I suppose I have no choice," she at last said. "I'll fetch the keys to the car."

Could it be this easy?

"Where is he?"

"Upstairs," she gestured, sighing in a pantomime of defeat, leading the way. "Last door at the end of the hall."

Eagerly, Jack climbed to the landing, ran down the hall. He opened the door to a bedroom in which—he knew it instantly, saw it, understood it—in which his two former wives slept together as lovers. Jack stood in the doorway and could not set foot inside. Confused nostalgia smote him. There were a thousand tiny signs. He'd lived with them both, known them intimately. The pillows. Candy slept with hers rolled up, Marlis on hers flat. Candy combed her hair, impatient. Marlis spent hours with her brushes, her rollers, and slept nude. Candy wore the sweetest little flannel . . . oh shit. Shock overtook him. The nanny, the fox! He remembered again the telephone in the kitchen and tore back—she was not in the kitchen. He stood still. She was nowhere, then, a rustle, the soft snap of a lock. She had obviously had the baby downstairs somewhere, sleeping maybe, and in that split second, Mrs. Kroshus had spirited him out!

Jack jumped through the side door and into the garage and there was the nanny, strapping the baby into Candice's white car!

"Oh, Mrs. . . . !"

She turned, her features even and decided. Her black topknot rose. "Kroshus," she firmly said. She glared at him, tossed the car keys skittering through the open garage door far down the driveway where they tinkled over and over sliding down a patch of ice.

Jack put out his hands in a pacifying gesture.

"Now look, all I wanted . . ."

With a swift motion Mrs. Kroshus grabbed a staple gun off the side bench for equipment storage. It was powerful, a pneumatic model Jack had bought to install a rug. She held it in both hands, poised. "Halt!"

Jack took a step. A heavy carpet staple zinged over his head and stuck in the door's lintel. He evaded the next. Then there was a thick swarm, one that stuck in his cheekbone just underneath his eye.

"Ow! Christ!"

Jack tried to wrestle the tool from her grip and in the tussle her dark hair sprang off in his hands—a flowing wig! Denuded, she poised on the balls of her feet, lithe and calculating as a trained Ninja. Beneath the wig, the nanny's hair was a soft, gray, bristly crew cut and her unframed features stood out in bold and determined relief. She held the staple gun with both hands and peppered him until he dodged and danced. Then she ran out of staples. The trigger clicked. Empty! They gazed in speculation at each other. Without a word she threw the gun at him.

What a pitch! Bells and stars.

Somehow he got to her and then put his hand over her mouth when she began to holler with vigor, *Help, Help, Help! Murder! Murder!* He dragged her back inside the house, or at least he started to. With the swiftness of a lightweight wrestler,

Mrs. Kroshus ducked beneath Jack's arm. She tripped him with her sculpted ankle, and then bolted back toward the baby. Exhausted, Mauser still managed to tackle the nanny, but she elbowed him in the gut and got free. She unlatched the car door. He dragged her back with both arms around her waist. It was really a surprise by now that no one had heard her shouting, for she did not let up as he tried to gather her into the house. *Kidnap! Kidnap!* She jabbed at Jack's old wounds with bony, sharpened joints, stamped on his feet. Inside the house, she broke free again, grabbed a spatula from the kitchen, walked toward him vibrating the blade in the air. As he reached to take it from her hands she dropped it suddenly, lunged to jab her thumbs in his eyes. He grabbed again, blinded. She cast about, scratched like a wildcat with strong and polished nails, then bit. Eyes streaming, Jack finally tied her raging and bucking into a chair with the cord of a flimsy lamp, then another cord ripped from a toaster. He rummaged through the kitchen junk drawers, found duct tape, secured her ankles, and then stood back to regard his labor. She looked down at herself, too, at dangling cords.

"You're not skilled at this," she observed.

Jack sat across from her. She did look clumsily wrapped—the broken neck of a reading lamp hanging down one arm. The duct-taped ankles. He was whipped, though, his old interior wounds bleeding, his bruises sore, his face stapled. He did not dare remove the piece of metal but glared at Tillie Kroshus over it. Formidable! A tiger! He didn't see any reason for a gag, though—she could yell all she wanted, indoors. He'd be long gone, but now he had the baby! He was stuck with the baby! This wasn't part of the plan, not at all. Jack's face smarted horribly. He studied and thought. The moment she was free she'd call the police, but if she wasn't free she couldn't care for his son. He needed the car. He'd only wanted to see his son—now his son was in the car. There was suddenly so much to think about, his brain was crammed full.

He almost consulted the fettered nanny about what his next move should be. She wheezed in the chair, and he felt guilty.

"Can I offer you something to drink, to eat?" he asked. "Before I go."

"Not me, the baby. Bring a bottle. Don't do *anything* to hurt him," she implored, her voice pitiable now, trembling with true sorrow.

"Look," said Jack. "He's my son, to tell you the truth. I won't hurt him. Where's that bottle?"

"In the fridge."

Jack walked over, peered in, and removed a couple of baby bottles. One of juice, one of weak-looking bluish milk.

"There's a bag, his diaper bag, in the backseat, too," the nanny volunteered grudgingly. "He gets a rash. Change him every hour on the hour."

Jack stood before her, holding a bottle in either hand.

"I *am* his father, I promise you," he swore.

"Then you're supposed to be dead," Mrs. Kroshus said sternly.

"I know," said Jack, suddenly ashamed. "I'm sorry."

"I am too," said Mrs. Kroshus.

"I'll write Candy a note," said Jack. "Explaining."

"Meanwhile I'm supposed to wait here, trussed up like a chicken?" Mrs. Kroshus fixed Jack with a reproachful stare. "Until Dr. Pantamounty returns from *your* funeral?"

"What else," said Jack feebly. "You're dangerous."

He couldn't help but say this in a mildly flirtatious voice, but the nanny was neither alarmed nor gratified.

Jack wrote a note on the top page of a pad of tooth-shaped white stationery.

Dear Candy,

I can explain! Please don't call the police. John will be safe, I swear on my life. I still love you.

Jack

He anchored it underneath a candlestick on the kitchen table, then took shrugging leave of the woman tied into the chair. A sudden anguish of protection gripped her. "Don't forget to snap him in tight with that seat belt!" She cried after him, her voice a howl.

Out in the garage, Jack tossed the telltale wig into the front passenger's seat along with shawls and blankets. He made sure that the car seat was precisely engaged. The baby, covered and warm in a snowsuit, stirred drowsily. John's face was taking on a hint of stubborn character, the mouth both full and firm, a line. His violet and pink eyelids were relaxed in a sleep of exalted bliss—he had no idea that he was going for a ride. The sweetness of his son was magnetic, frightening. What would Jack do when the baby woke up? He walked out the driveway, gingerly plucked the keys from the cement, and then eased himself behind the wheel of Candice's car. He backed out, started down the tree-lined, silvery streets.

He was six blocks from the edge of Fargo and the burnt ruin of his old house before he realized that Candice most surely *would* mind his taking the baby. Her face hovered before him—implacable, eyes hard as the tips of her drills! She'd supply a full description and her license number, have him picked up and arrested in her car. This was no good. No good at all. It was starting to snow, too, flakes falling in steady spirals. He'd have to find another way north. He pulled against the curb. First he thought of the airport, but no planes landed near where he needed to get. Besides, he would have to leave the white car in short-term airport parking. Next, he thought of the train. A former employee of his worked there now, a stationmaster. Amtrak still headed northwest on off days, its service reduced.

Perfect. Jack headed for the station. No one gave him a second glance in the shelter of the driver's seat. He pulled in close to the offices just as a train was arriving on track, hissing and sighing passionately as it slowed. If only—his heart jumped. He could hop on this very train with the baby and then get off at some small town, heading north. From there, he could call Candice, make her understand the predicament that he was in. He left the car idling and fought his way into the small new building. People streamed past him, loaded with bags of food and blankets and suitcases. He caught the eye of the man who had worked for Mauser and Mauser, but the guy didn't recognize him, apparently took him for a bum. He waved Jack off, whistled between his teeth, kept on writing out tickets. Jack was waiting impatiently for the other customers to disperse when he had a sudden and sensible thought—leaving a baby alone in an idling car wasn't a wise idea.

He turned, went out to check on his son. The car was . . . *gone!* Jack tracked it with his eyes, saw it easing through the parking lot toward the street. He leaped forward in a jolt of terror and managed to vault onto the back of the car's fender. Jack clung spread-eagled to the trunk as the car pulled out of the station parking lot. Just for a moment, clawing higher, he caught a glimpse. A young man sat in the passenger's seat and Candy's Honda was being driven sedately by an older man whose face registered in every dimension—from the long-ago past, recently from the framed photo on Shawn's bureau. Over the years, a mental printout of Gerry Nanapush had filed itself internally.

A nightmare determination gripped Jack. He screamed and shouted as he tried to hang on to the car's back end, straddling the roof until Gerry sped the car up and veered around a corner. There was no hold. The metal was slick underneath him. When the car turned, Jack lost all purchase. He flew off, tumbling over and over in a standard acrobatics' crouch. Landing in a dreamlike surge, he knocked down a small formation of people set like bowling pins upon a street corner. They sprawled. He popped up chasing the car, and when that disappeared, chasing air.

§

Surviving Sleep

JANUARY 6, 2:22 A.M.

Dot, Candice, Eleanor, and Marlis

*I*t was nearly two thirty by the lighted digits of the dashboard clock, and when Eleanor stopped talking the women's bodies filled with a torpid drowsiness. One after the next, they dropped off, came to, dropped off again. Only because one or the other of the women periodically stabbed awake filled with adrenaline, desperately shook the next, slapped and jogged another before she herself succumbed, only because they took turns panicking, did they succeed in eluding this dreamy and most pleasant of deaths. But each in turn would not let the other rest, and so gradually, as though sleep itself were a weather through which they passed, they regained their alertness.

Once they had ascertained that they were all conscious, shaking and prodding at one another, pulling at each other's hair and ears, they paused in a state of desperation so intense that none of them dared take charge of the moment and speak. Finally Dot switched on the heater and yelled, filling the car with her voice. She ordered the other women to slap themselves, to make noise, scream, stamp. When the pandemonium died down it was Candice—after all, the most lightly dressed and farthest from the heater—who regained her strength of mind.

"There's got to be snow clogging up the tailpipe. Open the windows, then let me out. I'll go first, it's my turn."

Candice's teeth were clacking together and her head was pounding. Her blood felt thick and poisoned. The women pushed through the door and slung themselves against the car in a human chain with Candice at the end. Spitting icy driven flakes she managed to kick and clear away a drift that had blown hard against the rear of the auto. When her job was finished, the women folded themselves back into the car, brushing the snow off as best they could, stamping, complaining.

Dot called back to the hitchhiker.

"You okay back there? Hey, say something!"

"Leave me alone." The voice was a sleepy grumble.

"Would you mind telling us," Marlis said, huffy. "Hey, don't go back to sleep—who are you?"

But the monotonous windy sighs and snores began again and even when Candice reached back and tugged the hitchhiker only groaned.

"It's a woman back there, right?"

"No way. Sounds like a man."

"Probably smashed, sleeping it off."

"I don't think she's drunk," said Marlis.

"You'd know," said Candice.

"I'm the expert," Marlis agreed.

"I've been thinking . . ." Candice paused. Reaching for words, she questioned Eleanor. "What's your percentage? Your take on an afterlife. I want to know!"

"An afterlife!" Eleanor gathered energy to expound. She clapped her hands together and blew on her knuckles. "I can hardly feel my feet anymore." She clumped hard on the floor of the car. "What I want to believe and what I actually do believe are different. I'd give human life a ten percent chance of continuing after death. I mean, in any recognizable form."

"Our same body or same personality?" Dot asked, hushed.

"An intact memory? Something of the self? Ten percent odds."

Marlis laughed, but the sound was strained. "You like percentages?" she said. "Try these. You're born. *Hey sucker, welcome to the casino!* Just remember, the house *always* wins in the end."

"I would have said fifty-fifty only a decade ago." Eleanor resumed with a pseudoscientific air. "But now, with all I read in the papers about one human function, then another and another, reduced to a biochemical process." Eleanor shrugged. "The numbers go down. I've heard emotions are neuropeptides. That's depressing. Still, what more can one ask of a god whose indifference to most goings-on is continually proven? Into each life there falls some providence, some pain."

Eleanor was gathering energy into a flowing lecture — Marlis understood the warning signals now and tried to divert the river.

"We're just stuff," she said roughly. "A bunch of cells. Minerals. Not worth a ten-dollar chip. Who's kidding who?"

"I am a firm believer in the sciences," Eleanor went on. It was impossible to stop her. "In our advance as a species. Now that medical progress runs our physical evolution, we will have to put our faith in the sciences — I am quite convinced that one day we'll genetically engineer ourselves into immortals. We will become beings capable of giving birth to and nurturing our exact cloned selves time and time again. As I say, I put my faith in science, a form of religion. When science and religion merge, we will reach a new evolutionary level. We have to realize that we're part of an interconnected net of life. We're the most intelligent, we say, but that's by our measurements. We haven't the longevity of the pine or the endurance of stones. What we do have is the wit of the rat."

"The wit of the rat." Marlis considered. "You're onto something. In other words, the ability to eat shit."

"If necessary, yes."

"In order to survive," Marlis continued. "I've got that.

That's me. I'm already where we're evolving in a thousand years."

"Well, *I'm* an optimist," said Candice, crumpling the space blanket a little closer to her chest.

"Yeah, how so?" drawled Marlis.

"I like the computer model," said Candice. "Even when I'm unplugged, dead, I figure maybe some form of my software survives. And then there's the supernatural—I've never had a direct experience, but you hear about things. Phenomena. Nobody can explain everything yet, right? Maybe there's more than our senses take in, more than this one dimension, more than this one life. It's just a feeling. But are feelings, are instincts nothing?"

"They're bullshit!" Marlis cried out, surprised at her own fury.

Eleanor ignored her. "Why are we conscious if not somehow to go beyond our bodies in death just the way we live beyond our bodies now in life? How can consciousness and curiosity be solely the product of physical evolution?"

"Consciousness!" Dot was excited, suddenly. "What's the point in creating something so complicated?"

"Of course it could be a mistake—consciousness that is," said Eleanor. "A mistake of natural selection, a glitch, a dead-end mutation."

"Just like the exquisitely sensitive, and unnecessary, nerves in our teeth," Candice finished.

"Maybe evolution just overdid it. What's the point in dancing bees?" Eleanor was regretful. "Insane complexity is evolutionary. Staghorn beetles. The octopus. Bowerbirds. Ever read about their nests? There are lots of creatures overevolved in one area or another. Dogs, for instance. Take the dog."

"Don't get Candy started on dogs," said Marlis. "Don't even mention a dog to her, please."

"Their sense of smell is a form of consciousness," stated Candice. "They should survive death. Besides, I don't want to go to a heaven that has no dogs."

"She's weird on dogs," Marlis explained. "She likes dogs better than people."

"Most people," said Candice. "Not all people. Not you. Not our baby. But dogs are not just easy love, simple gratification, adoration, ego strokers. They have higher forms of emotion. Until you have been personally betrayed, you don't understand the depth and comfort of a dog's loyalty. You don't know how deep a value to put on trust. Dogs don't give that out as easy as some people think, either. You can't be one-sided with a dog. You have to think like a dog, give the dog what it needs, give the dog's life a shape that includes loyalty to you, and certain tasks. Just like husbands, dogs have to know where they stand in your affections."

"Where did Jack stand in yours?" wondered Eleanor.

"I gave him grief," Candice answered. "But when he was first he was first and only. At least I never deceived him about a pregnancy. Never lied. I had my hesitations, but once in I was in. It was a dog that drove us together, though, and a dog that drove us apart. Not a dog man, was he, Jack."

"I never knew him to have a dog," said Eleanor. "He had this stray cat once—it followed him around like a dog."

"He didn't get along with dogs. Ask yourself this. What kind of man does not like dogs?" Candice was serious, thoughtful. "A guy who's heartless or just too driven? A guy who's not in touch with his emotional self? A guy who's deaf to all other forms of life?"

"So he didn't like dogs, really." Eleanor was indignant. "What's wrong with that?"

Everything, Candice's silence clearly indicated. Only after a long pause of contemplation held between the women did Candice Pantamounty pull Marlis close to her beneath the space blanket and begin to speak.

§

Candice's Tale

JANUARY 6, 2:44 A.M.

THE LEVELS

*Y*ou could say that I literally put myself into my work. My reproductive system financed my medical future. I wasn't with anyone, not serious, but I dated all the time. So I was fitted with a Dalkon shield in the midseventies. The thing nearly killed me—perforated uterus, quick infection, hysterectomy. I felt fortunate, at first, that I only ended up sterile. I pooh-poohed it. I hadn't wanted children in the first place, I reasoned, otherwise why would I have used the thing? It took me six months to get furious, and by then, there was a class action lawsuit. I got the materials from a friend in Baltimore and joined the other plaintiffs. Two years passed, I graduated college and went straight to dental school. By the time I got out I had both my D.D.S. and my settlement from A.H. Robins, a check in my hands that I used to put a down payment on a house, an office space. I made do, turned calamity to opportunity. That's who I am—I don't get beaten, I keep going. I have never stopped, not for loss or tragedy or sickness or embarrassment, not for Jack, not for anyone.

We all survived Jack. What's a blizzard, ladies, compared to him? He could snow a heat wave.

I talk about survival like it's easy just to do it, but of course it's the world's toughest assignment. Sometimes you need an angel, just a little bit of grace, a visitor from another dimension.

Sometimes you need a dog.

I was dealing with the aftermath of the shock of understanding, really getting to the heart of what it meant that I couldn't ever bear a child. I was working it out in all sorts of subtle ways, like overbooking myself with an impossible patient load, then swimming a mile in the tiny health club pool, lifting weights, reading every self-help book in the Fargo library, sleeping four hours and then back to the first appointment of a long day that started at seven and ran until eight. That's the Norwegian way to get through tough times—denial, hard work, more denial. Then straight bourbon got involved. Seeing Doctor Hakula, a therapist, I went into a twelve-step program and got in touch with my higher power. Then my higher power fizzled on me and my lower power came back, strong. I drank, but less than before. I started concentrating on my patients. I got obsessive about their well-being. I traveled, saw the fjords, saw Bergen, Hammerfest, the midnight sun. Then I came home. I count my life as before the shield, BS, and after the shield. AS. One day, I read my horoscope. *Get outside*, it said. I sat in my cozy new-built carpeted house and looked around. Out there, the grass was growing. The grass was so tall it had flopped over. Time to mow!

This big, huge lawn that went with the two-bedroom house had a riding lawn mower to take care of it, and that's what I used. I rode for two acres, great therapy, and then got off the thing and bagged the grass. I put the bags in the back of the car and I drove to the dump in the smell of fresh clippings. There was this compost area. I brought the grass there, stopped my car, and was hauling the bags from the backseat and trunk when my eye was caught by a man getting out of a pickup truck. He was a big nondescript sort of guy, it struck

me at first, dressed neutral. Out jumped a dog, a rather plain
sort of dog, too, but with an alert rakish air I liked. Nose up,
the dog sprang around, testing his surroundings. He trotted
over to the edge of the pit, glanced down, pleased as anything.
Looked back at his master, who was loading a gun.

The sight of it, the dog, the man loading up the pistol,
didn't register at first except that I was shocked they let people
in here to shoot rats. I mean, that's what I thought at first.
Such practices were dangerous. I wasn't about to interfere, but
then I didn't recognize Jack from high school. He spoke
sharply, commanded the dog. The dog gave him a disdainful
look, walked over, and lifted its leg against Jack's knee. When
he kicked at the dog it sat down in front of him and looked up,
expectant.

"Fine," said Jack. "Fine. You s.o.b. Just sit still, doggy
boy."

Jack gave the dog a biscuit from his pocket and then, while
the dog was eating it, he crooked his elbow and steadied the
pistol on his forearm. He took a step backward and sighted.

I leaned into my car window and I honked. Jack looked
around until he saw me and I waved at him to wait. I got into
my car, drove the sixty feet over to him. Keep the car around
you during possible tense moments is my theory, a metal skin,
a quick getaway. I parked beside him but I didn't get out, just
opened my window. That's when I recognized Jack as the
Jack I'd gone out with in high school. I called him over. He
seemed astounded, distracted, awkward the way you are after
so many years but not the least embarrassed about what he
was about to do.

I asked him what he was up to, pleasantly, and he told me,
just as pleasantly, that he was just about to shoot his dog when
I'd interrupted, and how was I these days?

"Did the dog do something wrong?" I asked.

In answer, Jack came over and put down the gun,
thumped it on the hood of my car, just over my head. Then he
rolled up his pants leg and showed me the long gauze wrap.

"Fifteen stitches."

The dog looked damn proud of itself. It had a kind of grin, a curious unsettling expression.

"Tell you what. Instead of shooting it, why don't you give that dog to me?" I proposed.

Jack just laughed. "That dog is vicious." His voice was like a pat on the head. "Showed up begging at the construction site, so I tried to tame it for a while. You don't want it."

I dug in my purse and held out ten dollars.

"No way," he said. "I can just see the size of the lawsuit."

"Try this: ASPCA."

"What's that?"

"Old times' sake?"

He stepped closer.

"Forget it," I said. "I see I'm going to have to get tough."

I always kept a hundred-dollar bill tucked into the photo section of my wallet—something I learned when traveling—and now I pulled it out and waved it with the ten.

"You're going to sell me that dog."

Jack eyed the money, but shook his head, grinned.

When he showed his teeth, I saw decay invading the very top left corner of his right incisor.

"Open your mouth," I said, dropping the charm and putting away my purse.

"Wha . . ."

"When'd you brush last?"

"The hell."

"I mean it. I'm a professional dentist now."

Meekly, only halfway mocking, Jack bent next to the car, the gun dangling from his grip. He stretched his jaws wide. I examined what I could see with the naked eye, the dog watching us.

"I've got a deal for you," I said.

He shut his mouth, stood, asked if it was what he thought it was. I shrugged.

"There's no telling what's going through your brain, but what I'm offering is this. You give me the dog. I fix your teeth. I'm painless. I swear if I hurt you then you can just walk out. I feel sorry for you, Jack, I really do!"

He finally nodded. "You bought yourself trouble," he warned.

"It usually comes cheaper." I looked down at his leg again. "Fifteen stitches?"

"And this."

He held up his hand to take my business card, the sleeve fell away from his forearm — scarred with chew marks.

I took the dog home, and it's true he was a fear-biter. He tried to get his teeth into you before you got yours into him. I understood that. We had some go-arounds. Times I would be gripping an ear in each fist and he'd have his fangs bared and ready to go for me, but he'd have to lose his ears first if he did. Or I'd just step down hard on the choke chain if he lunged. I had that dog's number right from the beginning, and when he finally got mine it was a perfect relationship. Pepperboy was made to give unspeakable devotion. I was made to get it. But then, of course, life got more complicated.

Jack made his appointment, came in one morning, late. Opened up his mouth and my hygienist, Andrea, tried not to react and just took the X rays. We took about twenty. Six teeth needed root canals. He had a threshold like you wouldn't believe and had treated what he did feel with Jack Daniel's. Said he couldn't tell where the sensations were coming from, all sides. Said he hadn't slept much for months, that the trouble dated way back, years and years. When he laid his head on the pillow it was like his head made an electrical connection — like all of his teeth clamped onto his nervous system, pulsed on, wouldn't quit.

I had Jack stretch out in the big chair, got him all numbed up. When the pain in his teeth turned off, tears filled his eyes. I felt so sorry for him, this big guy, former boyfriend of mine and all that, whipped. A puppy. I treated him with extra care and then told him we'd be seeing quite a bit of each other during the next few months.

During those visits, while we waited for the Novocain to

kick in, we talked. I heard about his life since high school. Once he told me he'd gone through a divorce, the teeth made sense. Divorcing people usually neglect their teeth. After you, Eleanor, during you as well, probably, Jack chased and netted every woman who came near him. During that time, of course, he let his dental hygiene lapse completely. Not to mention he'd always had a taste for sweets, handed down from his father.

We had a date, my first one with Jack since I was a junior. It was just a lunch date. I'd put the last crown on the last tooth—it was supposed to be a sort of celebration of Jack's mouth, right? In fact, it was a celebration of Jack's other favorite part of himself.

The first thing he said to me?

"I have fucked *everything* in Fargo."

He told this to me in a tragic tone as we studied menus in a cute antique booth decorated with brass railings and frosted glass. Old Broadway had large salads, which was why I ate there. I watch my weight.

"That statement right there is the main problem with you, Jack, if you'd just take a minute to analyze it."

When he had started coming to me, it was just teeth, and over the course of the visits, as I said, he had begun to ask for more serious assistance in his private life. At first, I had responded to him with deep suspicion. I knew who he was and what he was, as you only know men you've shared with girlfriends in high school. Jack was worse than transparent to me, he was invisible, a kind of child-man. I watched him eat, no, I X-rayed the rest of him I hadn't yet looked through—I almost saw the progress of his meal like in a science diagram. It made me dizzy. Jack ate a big, solid club sandwich that came in a basket with French fried potatoes. He had one or two drinks, Bloody Mary, a beer, and a creamy dessert. He was big but not at all fat, just tough and heavy and muscular, and his energy those days was depressed but endless. He said he could go for nights with only an hour or two of sleep, working round the clock, exhorting and screaming at his crew and bullying the workers on his building projects into mad efforts that sometimes nearly killed them with nervous exhaustion. He was known, already, for completing work on time and within estimates. In construction, you only had to do that once to become a legend.

I suppose, too, I saw him in those days as a man who'd make a lot of money—not that cash swayed me emotionally, you understand, I just sensed the crisp feel of it sliding off him when he cranked his shoulders. New ink. Paper. But his smile was a counterfeiter's press.

"Jack dear," I said that first time, trying not to sound as though I had any personal interest in the matter of his love life, which I honestly didn't want to touch with a thirty-foot pole. "Maybe it's time you realized that you're a sexual Neanderthal."

I let that remark dangle for a moment, but Jack had turned his sad dark gaze out of the booth and now it rested with gloomy clarity upon a solid-hipped waitress who flipped her middle finger at him.

"You're right," said Jack decisively, biting hugely into his triple-decker sandwich. "I have made an enemy of everyone I've ever touched, except you. Let's get engaged or something, Candy."

I put down my fork.

"Look at me."

Jack obeyed, stopped eating, and opened his face to me across the table. I know what I can look like, how good, especially having kicked the sauce. I'm a sturdy woman with straight, short hair and a freckle-dusted face. People call me sweet. Fine. I'm glad I give that impression. I have excellent circulation. I'm always rosy, warm. Underneath it all, I'm tough bone.

"I am the sort of woman who will immediately let you down," I informed Jack. "Treat me right, and I'll make you miserable."

Jack held out his hands. "I don't get it!"

"Let me put it simply. I'm not interested, Jack. You're just desperate. But you do need someone stable and strong and, most of all, forgiving."

Jack started eating again, pushing the food steadily and carefully into himself.

"You're probably right," he said. "I'm sure you are. But the thing is, I don't want the kind of women that I should love."

"Take my advice, don't take it. No skin off my nose."

Jack took the bite of coconut cream pie away from his mouth, lowered his fork carefully, focused on me clearly for the first time, and frowned.

"I'm sure it's not," he said gently. "But what about you? I've been through the mill, and maybe I have actually learned something about my limitations. Maybe you can't give me credit because you knew me when. I take young love seriously. I think about it. Did you ever wonder that maybe we were meant to be? Has it ever occurred to you that maybe you know me so well that you're completely blind to how I've changed? Of course you don't know me, entirely, not anymore."

"I've forgotten all about that."

"No, you haven't."

We stared across the ruins of our lunch, all the littered plates and clouded glasses. I watched him very carefully for any sign his speech was sly or underhanded, but he did not meet my eyes. He did not gauge me, watch any longer for my reaction, but devoted his attention to the varnished grain of the tabletop. As I waited him out, I felt that tiny shift, that gear grinding, and suddenly there was something that had not been there before, a hint of speculation, a scent of the unknown, curiosity, that essential component of sexual sympathy.

"Don't mess with me." I think my voice faltered, just a little.

Right there in the booth, then, with people wheeling around us, not even noticing, Jack reached over calmly and pulled the throat sash, the tie of my red silk blouse. I had something black and intricately lacy underneath it, and when the neckline fell open I felt Jack register the fact of the garment. I let him look, my face cold, then retied the collar.

"That's as far as you'll get," I said. But I was shaken.

It was the way he smiled at me, both penitently, after the bow was perfect, and unabashedly, knowing we would have to know more. *Knowing.* It was the way he dug back into the cream on the top of his pie, the way he eyed me above the crust. It was his hand square on the fork, the shadow at the base of his throat, the pure inch of worry between his eyebrows. What convinced me was nothing that I could name or that truly had a rational basis in understanding, and yet, suddenly, there was no rescue. None. With each of my relationships I have experienced something similar to this moment of clarity. Everything seemed much too real. My apprehension of the future pressed in on me with all of its weight. My hands shook and my clothes seemed too small and tight. I could feel the lines in my face, a burning sensation in my temples, a pressure on my skull. I couldn't breathe, couldn't fill my lungs. Annoyance covered me, and desperation, and then finally, sheer love, a mantle of amnesia and of hope.

It was a triangle from the first—me, Jack, and Pepperboy. Our wedding day. Jack was standing in a cluster of people dressed in pastels. He swiveled around, a drink in his hand, looking for me over their heads. He caught my eye across the room and raised his brows, moved his hand to indicate he had a question. I remember shaking no, to whatever it was. Jack tipped his head to the side, further mute consultation. I bent over and fed Pepperboy the first piece of wedding cake. Jack looked away. We had argued over bringing Pepperboy along and he had lost that one, just as he had lost all of the arguments about my dog. He'd brought us together, after all. What could Jack say to that? I walked over, entered into the conversation pleasantly enough, took Jack's arm. I knew he didn't feel like drinking. Partly, it was Pepperboy. The dog was sobering to Jack, perhaps because it didn't drink. Jack said he never felt at ease pouring a shot for himself, taking a beer from the fridge. Pepperboy was always there with a bound, ears perked, staring. Even now, at his knee, the dog was focused on the drink in Jack's hand. Jack held the glass at arm's length. Pepperboy knew when he was being toyed with, turned to me, and calmly licked my leg.

Jack composed himself, knocked back the rest of his drink without looking at the dog, then left the party without me.

Left our own wedding reception party! I guess that should have been an omen.

Jack left me without a ride, too. He was bad at details, although he was well organized in many other areas of his life, including sex. In that regard he was like a cat. From me, Jack wanted complete sexual devotion, but on his terms, his schedule, and he responded with bored indifference when I began to pet him without permission. I had gotten used to our every-third-night regulation center-ring event. It was something else, I guess we all know, when Jack was in the mood—that is, until about a year or so after.

Maybe it was the fact that Pepperboy felt so alone in his doghouse. After a few months, Jack had made me promise to keep the dog in the basement, but I sneaked him upstairs anyway when he started to beg and howl. I woke up just before dawn, remembered that it had been three days more or less, and started to move my leg against Jack's. He put his hand out across the warm expanse of bed between us and he touched the hem of my silky T-shirt. Whenever I touched his hips, any man's hips, but especially Jack's, soapy smooth and buoyant, my pulse beat red. I rolled closer in a rush of heat. Jack stretched and sighed. I touched him softly, asking, and after a while he took me into his arms. Soon we were moving together, quickly, easily, with promise, when from under the bed a threatening rumble sounded.

"What was that?" Jack stopped.

"What?"

He began to move again. The dog growled.

"Shut up, Pepperboy," he said.

We were making love crossways. Beside him, I stiffened. He felt the bolt of my outrage, and it curled him down to nothing. My blood hummed with confusion and we lay there, suddenly opposed, magnets with switched polarities. The space between us had turned into a band of live repulsion.

I sat up straight.

"Don't you ever say that again."

"Say what?" Jack propped himself on an elbow. "That dog is underneath my bed. I'll say any damn thing I want!"

"No, you won't!"

"Just listen!" Jack leaned over the side of the mattress. "Hey, garbage dog! Beat it."

Slowly, rustling along the carpet, Pepperboy emerged. He shook out his fur and stood beside the bed. In the gray predawn light, his eyes gleamed, baleful.

"It's okay, Pepperboy," I said.

The dog backed away without taking its pale gaze from Jack. I loved how it had the stealth of a wild animal, a coyote, a thing that depends entirely upon its wits.

"Hungry?" I took the word between my teeth.

"Who, me?" said Jack to himself. "I must be hearing things."

I got up and began to make the bed with Jack still in it, then he got out, began moving about the room in that trained and groomed clarity of violent motion by which men display their fury. He threw things. Whipped his pants overhead. Snapped his shirt at a chair. The dog pit-patted after me, out the door and down the stairs. Its nails clicked on the hardwood, on the tile, as I poured breakfast Kibbles.

"Choke!" Jack yelled from above.

"You're jealous." I came back to stand within the doorway. "Jealous of a poor animal you would have killed."

"He knows. He knows. He hates me. He's possessed. Besides, you never make *me* breakfast."

I turned to the dog. Ears cocked, Pepperboy stared back at me, not adoringly, but as a kind of partner might, as though he were asking, 'What do you wish of me?' So I told him.

"Say you're sorry," I said. "Go apologize."

I nodded Jack's way.

"Go on. Go say you're sorry."

Pepperboy hunched, dropped his head. Jack watched, fascinated. Slowly, the dog moved toward him. Again that light, hypnotized stare fixed Jack. When he reached the side of the bed Pepperboy turned back to me with a look that said, 'Must I?' I switched my hand in the air.

The dog groaned, lowered himself onto all fours, and rolled over onto its back.

"Supplication behavior," I informed Jack. "Now pat him on the stomach. Go on. That way he'll know you're his alpha."

Jack leaned over and scratched the thin hair and frail pink skin of the dog's stomach. Through his fingers, I could tell, he felt the weak electric voltage of the dog's disgust, but Pepperboy didn't dare move under my gaze. Too bad I turned away, too bad the dog snapped at Jack's fist, left a deep tooth track, then bolted.

After that, it seemed to me that I did the same. My body had always risen to meet Jack's, somehow weightless. Now I felt passive, solid as dough, so unresponsive I wanted to turn myself upside down like a cut-glass paperweight and shake myself until I snowed. Jack distracted himself with work, with plans. His new company was embarked on its first big job—a huge, cheap, low-budget motel out of town. He took me out there every day to look at the finish work, such as it was. The doors were hollow core and the fixtures flimsy.

"This is not how I'd do it," he'd say, rattling a light door handle. "This stuff is crap. It's all they paid for. Don't ever spend a night in this place. You'll never sleep. All the pipes are plastic. So damn noisy!"

I batted off his hand and went into the motel bedroom, the dog heeling me. Jack followed. Anywhere, in sight of any bed, the dog growled.

"This is ridiculous," Jack said, his voice low. He turned to Pepperboy and kicked hard, suddenly tense. "Bite me again and I *will* blow your brains out."

I held my breath, let it out slowly. Every time Jack threatened my dog I felt a rage bubble up in me, a darkness so intense it felt unreal, as though I were swimming out of my skin. I had never hated anyone before, and didn't realize then that I was drinking from a black well, that I'd tapped a profound source. I despised anyone who'd pick on a thing more helpless—animal or human. I did not respect Jack once he'd hit Pepperboy.

There was too much that I wouldn't say, couldn't say, refused to say, and because Jack couldn't see or even imagine the words, the air around me filled suddenly with sharp inky marks. He stepped closer to me, and my face shut against him. I was back in English class, where I'd always had good grades although I couldn't parse a sentence. I punctuated all I wrote by feel, and sometimes I thought I understood and sometimes I had the sickening impression of a tiny window opening upon a landscape of thick and roping paragraphs that I would never untangle. It was like that now, in the space around us—the emotional messages flew so thick and fast I couldn't read them as they whizzed by and my brain felt pricked, torn by the hooks of question marks and darts of commas.

I held my hands out to Jack, a gesture with no feeling behind it, and was relieved when he turned away and it was just me and Pepperboy.

We—me and my dog—drove home and went downstairs. Jack kept his workshop neat on one side and messy on the other. On the neat end, he had wooden cabinets and pegboards with hooks on which he hung his tools. There was a wall with the tops of jars nailed into it and different sizes of screws and nails and washers in each jar. He had a wall of shelves on which he kept his collection of favorite things: a few hand-planes, old handsaws with lovingly scrolled handles. What he really cared about were the levels. His oldest one was a pale wood with brass fittings, and he had a French model, the spirit in the glass held by two flying angels. Next to it, a number of antique Swedish levels and some odd homemade ones he'd restored himself. I liked Jack for his levels, the fact that he kept them, and sometimes I went down there just to sit near his shelves. That night, my dog slumped on the floor at my feet. I pictured the ethereal little tube of lime-green fluid fixed inside of me where no child would ever grow. My heart was shaking in my ribs, my fist was clenched, but I breathed deeply until the air bubble was centered between the double black lines.

§

The
Wandering Room

Candice

*J*ack taught me how to use my hands as tools, in a different way, I mean, than fixing teeth. He taught me how to strengthen my hands, how to keep my fingers steady, how to work big, work fine, how to build arrows. We used a small wooden table in a cleared-out corner of the basement. I sat beside him in a creaking chair, and kept his things in order, lined up his tubes of binding cement in rows, kept jars of orange and yellow nocks sorted out, the vanes in rectangular boxes—green, gray, white, and red. We sat in the light of a little black adjustable lamp, just him and me. These times were intimate—us working in the basement. He sighted down a light Serpent shaft and cut it to the right size for the draw-weight on his bow. He carefully lifted a three-blade Broadhead from a special wooden container, and began to build. We'd work for hours in the little circle of intense light and when we had half a dozen balanced shafts, all matched, all ready, all perfect, I handed them to him one by one and he fit those arrows into a rack high above the shelves of levels, just underneath the ceiling tiles, to dry where no one could accidentally touch and slice themselves upon the razor-sharp blades.

I can't help laughing, see, because around that time I got some advice: share his interests. Okay, I think, what are his interests? Other women! *Yeah, right. Think again.* Well, there's hunting.

"I'm coming too," I said one day.

"Oh, sure."

He did not believe me. I was just about a vegetarian, such an animal person. "No way you're not going to hate me if I slaughter Bambi."

That made me think.

"I'm not so simpleminded," I said. "Hunting's the natural order of things. I see that, Jack. It's fattening and butchering pathetic veal calves that I object to."

Okay, so he decided I could go along. I developed hopes from this. We might bond on the trip. He might fall in love with me for real and ever. I'd melt him, warm him, fill him with cheese sandwiches and heat him up with thermos coffee.

Some people like to hunt on days of good weather only, but Jack liked threatening skies. He woke me one cold morning in November and we went out with the smell of grit in the air, the clouds low and sullen even in the ink-dark of five A.M. By seven, the sun would glow behind them like a feeble bulb, the light would grow and spread until the cut fields, the roads, the sloughs and land along the river exuded an even grainy radiance. Jack drove carefully, and I dozed beside him, strapped into the passenger's seat of the pickup. In my dreams, I felt my head roll against the seat belt, back and forth. The metallic cloth belt landed on my mouth like tape again and again. Jack's army jacket, on the seat between us, had deep pockets I'd packed full of candy bars, sandwiches, and apples, for me, and for Pepperboy, Liver Snaps and two big milk bones. Pepperboy curled on the floor of the truck. I could feel the tension running off his fur, warming me.

Jack always started hunting on the huge old farm he had bought out from under his uncle—half developed, half up for collateral. He was gambling that someday it would be a prime development parcel. Then, as we know, he tried developing it himself. It was beautiful land and I think he shouldn't have touched it. An oxbow of the river ran along the eastern corner and there was, in the tangle of brush and downed trees, enough shelter for a few deer to haunt the edges of the neighboring fields and live off the missed corn and the crop stubble. Jack wasn't a successful hunter. He used a left-handed Martin Recurve, a classic, and rarely got a clear shot, but there was an uncertain understanding between the two of us about going hunting today.

According to me, this was about togetherness, not meat. Even though Jack said I couldn't come unless I went with the flow, I was sure that with me along he'd botch any shots he took, on purpose. Since he had started using a bow, Jack had never hit a deer anyway. He said he didn't care all that much about whether or not he got one, in fact, because hunting was just an excuse to walk in the woods. A focus. As for bow hunting, that alone made him superior to those who killed by looking through the sights of a powerful rifle. What did they know, he had said to me once, what intimacy did they feel with the animal?

Intimacy? We turned down an almost unused section road, and steered for the river, lowering the front wheels gently into the deep washouts and ruts, calmly managing a few impossible spots where the road fell away entirely. I looked at the twist of leafless box elders, eased my feet out from under my dog. I flipped the passenger's mirror down to make sure my eye makeup wasn't smeared. We stopped, got out of the truck. Jack took half a ham sandwich from his pocket and placed it on the step-up board. When Pepperboy snatched it, Jack grabbed his collar, tied him onto a piece of nylon rope, and secured it around the fender. Then Jack nudged at my dog with his foot, teasing, growled back when Pepperboy growled at him. I grabbed Jack's arm, diverted him as Pepperboy lunged to the end of the tether. Jack turned away and took his bow from the quilted camouflage printed case, bent it, strung it, and then took one arrow from the rack attached to the handle and carried it loosely along with the bow, the nock between his knuckles on the string.

"How come you're carrying that arrow out?" I said, mocking him.

"Always be prepared," Jack said. "That's my motto. What's yours? Carry floss?"

He had teased me, with affection, and I was gratified. This was how it should be—us joking together. Us companions. We started down the dwindling road, me following carefully, and didn't speak as we passed into the sudden growth of woods just past the plowed-under stubble of wheat. No branch rasped. It was just dawn, the light breaking in red streaks under a low inverted bowl of thick gray-blue clouds. The breeze was not yet up and every step and breath rang hollow. We followed a thinly worn trail into the deeper underbrush along the river and when that petered out, and the river ran on to make an oxbow farther west, Jack headed for a copse of tall trees on its bank where I knew he had nailed up a little stand last year.

The tree was just on the edge of a field of corn. The dried stalks were still neck-high and now, as the light broadened, the wind gathered enough to blow the flat blades of the leaves. The rasping lisp of their noise was a relief. We could hear, faintly, Pepperboy's barks, a low, odd gurgling noise of complaint, from behind us. The tree where Jack's stand was nailed up was across the field directly, and there were probably, he felt sure of it, deer even now stopped silently in the uncut cover, ears turning, gathering each sound. He stopped and in a crouch whispered my instructions.

He would double far around to reach his tree. It would take him about half an hour. Jack put his watch on my wrist and marked the time. In exactly thirty minutes, I was to walk slowly through the cornfield toward the tree that he pointed out. I was to walk one step per second, One Mississippi, two Mississippi, three. I would put out my hands and brush the stalks as I went forward, not to make a lot of noise, but enough to simply move the deer. They wouldn't be driven, Jack said, but they might be coaxed, encouraged to move by the sound of the dog and my presence. They would only flow from one area of cover to another, preferably denser, and in that nearest place of cover he would wait.

I looked at the face of the heavy black diver's watch, my heart tapping regularly. Looking into my eyes, he ticked the end of my nose with his finger.

"Here I go," his voice was hushed. He touched his wrist to remind me of the watch, and walked sharply right to begin his wide circle. I saw him tread noiselessly as possible through a thick shelter belt of wild plum and evergreen, melt along the sides of trees, avoid fallen branches, slide his feet carefully along the edges of the pits of brush and grass. I lost sight of him on the edge of the next field over, blackened sunflowers curved like gooseneck lamps, then saw him briefly as he took the edge and swiftly found his way through the back side of the strip of woods that faced onto the river. Then he disappeared. His tree, he'd told me, was the second largest oak, with a big low limb to use as a step and a nail banged in to hang his thermos of coffee by the strap.

Now, I imagined, he'd thread his bow and rack through the leafless twigs and make his way up to the platform he'd built. He'd find his posture, put his arrows in exact reach, prepare himself. I was wearing a bright pink jacket. He'd made me wear an orange cap, too, fluorescent, and so the moment that I stood that cap would be a beacon.

I still see myself, through his eyes, the orange-pink dash wavering across the field into the furrow as I began walking, half hidden as I entered the nearest row. I couldn't hear my dog or see any deer at all yet. On one knee, balanced, ready and sighting along the margins of the field for the first nervous buck to step out, I knew Jack bated his breath and counted with me, stepping along with me, One Mississippi, two. He kept me, brilliant, in the corner of his eye, and never lost me as he scanned the field for moving shadows. Gray as sand, sifting, soft as swept powder, they would appear without announcement, materializing almost, as though the air took shape. There, now. I saw two. Does, both of them. Another. It was a medium-sized buck. I stopped suddenly, hoping that the animal wouldn't step into Jack's range. It had a small rack, and his sides were filled out with corn. Mentally, I called it away from the pale stalks where Jack sighted above the stroke of the blade.

My heart pumped. He could get it with one shot. I willed it to turn. It was deaf to me, though, and moved slowly and magnetically toward Jack through the restless leaves all around. Every so often, it stared testingly, hung back behind the does, froze and studied the air. *Turn, turn,* I begged. Twenty Mississippi. Thirty. Forty. I saw Jack draw the bowstring. Quiet, even, slow, with all of his strength, he pulled back and poised.

I watched the buck so hard that I felt the trembling of its planted hooves.

Jack's arrow slammed into it.

The buck exploded upward. I thought I heard, impossibly, the animal laugh in surprise. A wild laugh like a little girl on a Halloween street, running. Then it flew as high again on springs, and bounced straight over my outflung body. I had thrown myself down and now I came up running. The buck, mortally hit, bounded straight back into the corn cover.

I looked up. Jack hadn't moved, his mouth was open, and his bow, dropped from his stiff fingers, caught in a lower branch. I knew in one part of my mind that he hadn't known I was so close, nor had he seen me. I stood below the tree, looking up at him, right underneath the suspended rack of arrows.

"Step back slowly, careful," Jack said to me in a calm voice.

When I had, he retrieved the bow and climbed down the tree and then set the bow in the grass. He stood before me, but he couldn't look at me. My arms felt heavy, my face fat as the moon. I shook my head, then shook it harder, to scatter my thoughts. I took a deep breath, groaned, and again the weight of that shot creaked through that living body, squeezing my heart shut. Tears flushed behind my eyes, salting the edges of my lids.

He suddenly walked into my arms, buried his face against my neck, beneath my collar. I smelled cold grit from the field, the faintly sour wool of his scarf and mittens, a teasel breath of sweet soap. His arms closed tighter and hopeful thoughts composed in sentence strings, balanced on wires looping through my mind. How worth it this was—the danger. I had frightened him into feeling something. Something. There was a new alertness toward me in his body.

His voice was a slap, though. "That buck's probably gut shot. Shit, Candy, why?" He stood, all business now. "I have to go after it."

I patted my mittens together, desperate to keep him.

"I'm going with you." Maybe I could salvage that moment. He didn't answer, just walked forward, bending down to the little trampled place. He touched the edge of a leaf and walked a little farther down, rubbed his fingers in the livid spatter of purple blood.

"Paunched it, oh fuck."

I stepped behind him, tense now and focused as he was on the trail of blood and deep split moons of hoofprints that led back through the field and into the gnarled swatch of trees and rigid tip-ups on the riverbank. He said that the thing to do would have been to wait for a couple of hours and let the deer go until it lay down. But the wind had deepened, gone raw with that choking dust smell of oncoming snow, so we had to follow. A little sleet swirled out of the trees and down along the edges of the field. The buck was taking the riverbank and heading west toward an area that was overhunted and where Jack was sure that someone else would put a tag on his buck if he just left it. He looked again at me. I stared right back at him. We kept on tracking.

Every so often, he bent down, put a finger into the side of a print, or showed me the blood sign. I was careful, spotted details, pointed out the waver in the side of the hoof that marked our buck from other deer tracks. Sometimes, I caught the trail where he had lost it and we went on, the snow swirling up at us now, a couple of inches deep, the blood unfrozen once, before the buck caught our scent and bolted across a field.

"We're going to find it, over there, dead," Jack told me, and we started across the field at a diagonal. He could sense me lagging, trying to keep up, slowing down and then galloping at him. The wind had gone past raw and stuck at freezing. It lay a prickling band on my brow and scraped my cheeks. My hands had shut in my sleeves, wooden blocks, and Jack said that when we reached the trees we'd stop and build a fire to warm up before he dressed out the buck. Then he looked back more keenly, and met my eyes for a moment. I was blank, empty and stopped of will, except that I was bound in desperation not to quit. He paused, waited for me, and when he saw me close, cheeks slashed with white, his face changed. He sucked in his breath and put down his bow.

"Remember where I put this," he said. As if we could, in snow that began to fall.

He lifted me against him, staggered as I molded to his chest. I balled my fists against his jacket, kept my face at the opened zipper of his parka, taking in the warmth of his chest and scarf. The snow fell thicker, in waving bands that met, until the world was white around us, ghostly. We almost seemed not to be moving. We tried to test the air for direction, but lost bearings. Jack thought he had made it to the edge of the field, but there was no shelter belt. He muttered, thought he'd turned, heading toward the highway, but the highway did not rise beneath his feet. There were no fences, no boundaries, no features in the landscape, just the whiteness that enclosed us in a wandering room.

I was afraid then and I'm afraid now, the same way. Only I have got this feeling Jack is here somehow, leading us to safety the way he did to me then. When Jack was pressed to the

limit, he always made things come out all right. He didn't stop,
he knew better than to stop. He kept his arm around me, made
me match him step for step. Sometimes, he carried me. I say
the worst about him, but when I think back to who he really
was, he was that man. He was that man in the whiteout who
refused to leave me, or to lose his way. In this blizzard, this
storm now, talking about him gets us through! He's leading us!
Back then, he kept walking and we made it along the river
where the snow let up enough so that, eventually, we found
ourselves on the road near the pickup truck.

He bundled me right into the door, took his parka off and
packed it around me, then jumped in and turned the key in the
ignition. The motor caught and after a few moments he swung
into reverse. Glancing over my shoulder, I looked straight into
Pepperboy's muzzle at the back window. I'd forgotten him, the
first time.

"Jack, stop," I said.

He wouldn't.

"He's tied, Candy. The rope's long enough so your damn
dog can sit on the pile of tarps."

As Jack eased the truck backward, Pepperboy disappeared. I opened my mouth but my voice came from somewhere far away. *Stop, stop.* I was shaking deep in his jacket.

"The heat should come on," Jack said.

He moved the wand to red and the roar of air filled the cab
as we swung off the two-rut road onto highway. There, the
snow squall had finished and blown straight off the asphalt,
dusting the ditches and fields. The sky came back in blowing
patches of blue. Jack fished a sandwich from his pocket and
ate it wolfishly. I threw myself across the seat and wrung my
hands in the air while my toes and fingers unthawed, but when
I was warm I sat up, remarkably and suddenly all right, and I
unwrapped a sandwich and began to eat with Jack. Perhaps
because the heater roared so loud, filling our heads, or maybe
because we were so intent on devouring every bit of food we'd
brought, neither one of us noticed that, when we stopped at
the town's first light, Pepperboy jumped from the back of the

pickup. Tied to the tailgate, my dog tumbled end over end once we started again, tried to skitter to his feet, got tossed down, lunged once at the collar and the rope that held him. Then, for about a quarter of a mile, he gave up and went entirely limp as the truck dragged him to the next light.

We heard the car behind us honking but the sound did not penetrate until the frantic drumming on the back wall of the pickup box. A man's face appeared in the window, mouth open in a long shout. Jack rolled down the window, flipped the heater off so he could hear, then killed the engine. I jumped out the other side and ran back to Pepperboy. Stretched long, legs folded and curled beneath, Pepperboy lay at the end of the rope, the collar bound tight beneath his ears. Jack bent down with me, put his arms on my shoulder, to spare me I suppose, to turn me away. But I resisted. I would not let myself be turned. I pushed Jack aside and undid the collar with my own hands. I don't know how long I knelt there, for when my dog's cold eye opened, blinked wide and fixed me in a flat beam of understanding, I saw deeper than the moment. Wider than the street. I saw farther than my marriage, straight to its end, into the heart of helpless things.

§

Marlis's Tale

JANUARY 6, 3:38 A.M.

LUCK

*T*here was deep silence, hollow noise, freezing green air at the end of the story. The wind bashed against the car. A cradle of empty words, a muscle of air, it rhythmically jolted the women back and forth. Marlis had crept close to Candice as she spoke and she shivered and shuddered, drifting in and out of sleep. Candice shook her awake, frantically, rubbed Marlis's hands in hers.

"Talk," Candice insisted. "Please, you know you have to. This was your idea."

Marlis was sunk in a bitter state of cold and had trouble rousing herself. She turned over and buried herself against Candice, stubborn as a child.

"Leave me the fuck alone," her voice was slurred and belligerent, but Candice refused to let her sleep.

"Talk, talk."

"What!"

"Tell where you came from, how you met Jack. What happened after."

And so Marlis began. Her mouth, her lips, her brain, all felt stiff and frozen at first, and then, as she continued she warmed to the story of who she was and how she met Jack and married him, just long enough to wreck his life.

For a while, I live off accidents. Man opening his car door in traffic clips me. We settle out of court. I eat this raw egg with salmonella. Sue the farm. I am sitting in the park in downtown Fargo watching the reflection off the pool water when it hits me—the idea, the sometime notion—that my small-time liability mishaps are only warm-up ploys and practice for the big accident on which I will make my fortune.

At this point in time, I have my clothes, three dollars, and a place to live. I live underneath a trailer house. I live in a nice foundation. There is a trouble lamp and lots of black plastic in sheets. I have a mattress. I think I might hook up a TV set, for evenings. True, it is not a home you can stand up in. It is a place, though, while I am getting my life together, where I know I am fairly welcome. My sister-in-law, who divorced my brother, lets me sleep there although her new husband doesn't like me.

I can hear everything that goes on up above. The floor magnifies their voices. Sometimes it seems like it is all happening right inside my head.

"Her being down there, it keeps out the skunks," says my ex-sister-in-law.

"I'd rather have skunks." Her husband, Dane.

"Come on."

"At least skunks warn you before they bite. She just stinks all the time."

"She doesn't bite though."

"All right. But she's not harmless."

"Where is the harm then, what?"

"She's underneath the goddamn house. She's always *there.* If we had kids, they'd wonder."

Silence, as though they both were thinking, looking at each other. Then Lindsay's voice is shaking.

"Dane, you know it's the only place she's got. The shelters they put people up in, they can be dangerous."

"I know. All right, I know. But this house isn't even paid for. What if the bank loan officer just happens to come by? What if he sees your little sister-in-law Marlis crawling out from under the foundation?"

"We can tell Marlis to make it look like something else, like she's working down there."

Suddenly they're laughing. Their laughter is bursting out of them. The linoleum floor takes it, spreads it like a sheet over me.

"Right." Lindsay's voice is lighter. I can hear her stacking dishes, putting them carefully into the cupboard. "I know. Dumb idea. But it's dry down there, and fairly warm this time of year. We'll get her out by winter. And she does come up and take a shower. You know she doesn't smell. She's clean enough."

"Oh I'm sick of arguing. I'm tired of it."

It is true. Dane hates controversy. But he brings it on all the same.

"Why don't you go lie down," says Lindsay. "I'm sorry."

"I think I will."

I hear the bed give way down in the corner of the house. The legs creak gently as he folds himself into the comforter. I think he sleeps on his side, his hands pressed together between his knees. That's how I picture him. He doesn't like me, but I feel sorry for him. I understand him. Credit. Here they don't own this place even though they poured a nice foundation, set it on the edge of the lot by a ragged grove of trees. They have small jobs, shaky jobs. I'm not the only one thinking beyond her means. Everything is borrowed. Even our bodies. Those most of all.

If I can't get a job singing, I'll go to work on a switchboard, as an operator. I think I would be very good at answering the telephone. But then after several weeks of it go by, the phone ringing in my ear, me picking it up, speaking in a mellow tone, there would be one last time like always. I'd lift up the receiver, shout into it, "Yo! Fuck you!"

I think maybe I should be a zookeeper, work with animals. I can't decide. I am thinking I'll mow lawn in the park and then, when I go to look it over, I see the ducks and geese, the Canadian honkers, have shit green all over the stretches of sidewalk. I decide I can't get myself to clean up after ducks.

I am watching the water shake the light on its surface, like an animal. It is as though the water is one being when it is held like that in walls. I wonder how it fits together, one end to the next. I wonder how water stays together, lets people in and lets them out. If someone came here from an alien planet, they would be startled. Here is this substance. A thing goes down into it. Disappears. A moment passes. Another. Nothing is disturbed.

So with an accident.

It can happen soon, I hope, at any time. There is a way of thinking it might happen without expecting it. I don't look for luck like that. Shit happens, like on the bumper stickers. Doo-doo occurs. But here is the thing: I have to put myself into the path of events. I won't do what I'm going to do if I know what will happen next. Would I have stepped off the curb? Would I have eaten the egg? It is the result that matters, the settlement. I have to let go of small things, and allow myself to be surprised by the unexpected. Shocked.

And that's what happens.

One thing I like to do is walk around in big stores and I can get to them easily by going straight out of the foundation through the trees. I make a beeline through land that is undeveloped, walk around the back parking lot and in. I do not want anything I see and they have followed me around enough to know I don't steal, never have yet. It is just that I like to see what is being manufactured. The things they sell! Nail buffers. Like I would have time to do my nails! Humidifiers. Things that put water into the air. All styles of curtains, washcloths. I am walking through the bicycle section where they are doing some work. Remodeling. The ceiling above is open and long electrical cables and connections are dangling right through like spaghetti. The thing I do is instantaneous. It happens. I grab a cable. It is not a bike cable. Bam. I am knocked over.

I am looking straight up at the ceiling of the discount center. The charge is so great I guess that both my lungs collapse. The air is going up, up through metal beams, up through tin, through foam. It goes up through the tar and shingles. It continues. I am not afraid but I am thinking to myself, *Now is the time to take a breath.* It doesn't happen. I have no other thought.

That is how I meet Jack the first time. He is the guy who saves me, but who saves me wrong. I black out. Jack sees me pitch down while he is buying switch plates, and he runs over and he gives me mouth to mouth. Only thing, he is so rattled that he forgets to hold my nose shut. So I lose precious oxygen, which gives me a twitch. I end up with features of my face I can't control—my mouth sags, something's wrong with my eyelid muscle. Nerve damage. Hard to get a job with nerve damage, in the future.

I hire my attorney off a TV ad.

"All right," he says. "I think we've got a suit."

I think that I'm onto something with this guy, but later on, I find different.

"Against the discount store?" I ask the lawyer.

"And the Good Samaritan."

"Whoa."

"You're going to tell me that you feel sorry for the guy even though your face will never be the same?"

"Well he did try to help out. He didn't have to."

"He fucked you up, Marlis."

"Right." My eye blinks rapidly, like moving wings.

Dane and Lindsay won't let me stay underneath their trailer anymore, but my attorney is even more sure he has a case so he puts me up for the month in a downtown rooming house. It is an old place, a hotel once, but now it just rents by the week or longer. Seven dollars a night or one-fifty a month. My room is orange with handprints on the ceiling and a sick smell, like someone took a long time dying there. Death got into the walls, the floor, the mattress. Even the water tastes flat and sad. The other people are mostly veterans and retired farmhands with no pension. They leave the doors of their rooms open, hoping that company will drop in, which I do. I sit and talk to these guys for hours, on every subject. There is only one television for the whole place, in the lobby, which is dark and disinfected.

We are talking, me and the oldest guy there, who is eighty-seven, when another man, a big man, walks into the room. I don't recognize him.

"I'm Jack Mauser," he says, "I'm the guy who saved you."

I invite him to sit down. What else?

"Look," he says, "I'm going to be out front. I'm asking you to drop the case against me. You won't win it, anyway, because there's protection laws for people who try to help others. Besides, your attorney just realized the Samaritan is his firm's biggest client. Me. You have to get someone new, and, well, it's just that I don't need this shit."

I can't process it. My eyelid starts going up and down on me like crazy.

"I can't do that," I say. I point to my eye. "Look."

"Oh yeah," he is embarrassed, almost. His hands clasp in his lap. "I know I could have done better, but I wasn't prepared. I knew about pinching the nose shut. But I had things on my mind. You would have died if I hadn't done something, though. Why doesn't that count?"

I don't have an answer. I don't know what to say.

"I can't help you," I say. "I can't call it off. Too late."

"No, it's not. Of course it isn't."

I sit there and think about it. The guy's features are rugged, almost handsome, but bitter and cold. He has the kind of face that never did look young. You cannot imagine how he ever was a baby, I mean, there is no softness. His hair is brown and his eyes dark, but I'm not scared.

"Get out of my face," I tell him.

"No," he says. "I won't."

"I'm just doing this for the money," I say.

Like, his mouth shuts hard then. He just looks at me. He can't believe what he is seeing and so I tell him.

"Nothing. I'm nothing. But I've got you by the balls."

"Yeah."

He can't stand me then. He turns his face away, sitting there. Hunched over, his fingers laced, he bobs his head in little nods.

"I've got a kid," he remarks, quiet, reflective-like. Even then I know he doesn't have a kid, a wife only. Instinctively, I know he's lying to me. "I've got a wife. She wants things. I'd like to get them. I was in that store doing some early Christmas shopping, you little weirdo, till I saved your life."

The way he says "weirdo" it comes out eager, like he wanted to say "bitch" and didn't. He bites his lips, and then his foot juts out and he kicks the leg of my chair. A little kick. He's huge though, jumping up in front of me all of a sudden, his coat flapping out to the side.

"Okay. You want to sue me for damage. Nerve damage. I'll fix your goddamn face."

Before I know it he has knocked me over and he's sitting on my chest with his knees on my arms. Maybe he took wrestling in high school or something, he's that quick. I can't get up. You won't believe this. He Dutch-rubs my face—not hard, not gentle either, but deliberate. He takes my nose in his knuckles, pushes my eyes back so far I think I'll go blind, tap-taps at my temples and my cheekbones. I'm so surprised I can't get out of the clinch. I lay there. At last, he vibrates his fingers all over my face, really fast, one side to the other, back and forth. Bappity, bappity, bap. Finally, nobody else has seen this, he just gets off. And it is strange, I feel okay, even better. It is like I have been massaged.

I don't know what to say—it's both disgusting and cool that he did this. It could be abuse. Then again, some places you would pay for it. Exotic. I'm confused, and of course it's just my luck, what happens then.

I go back to my attorney the next day to tell him of the outrage, and at first he's real pleased. He puts his hands on the table.

"Well, Marlis, well, well. I'll have to refer you to someone else, of course, but there are, we call them *compensations*. I can provide solid proof, under the table of course, that Jack has done this sort of thing before."

"Yeah. Is it not fucking amazing?"

"Let's see your face. Let's estimate the bill."

But when I look at him it turns out, I hadn't noticed, but the twitch? It is entirely gone. Gone! Gone! Jack's face tapping has cured me! I blink my eye, but it's a normal blink. The fact takes a moment to register.

"C'mon," he says, but there we are.

We are both stunned. Not a bruise on me. No witness, and a total cure. We talk. I look into the mirror. But no, there is no getting it back and I can't fake it. Me and my attorney, we part as friends. We shake hands first, kind of slowly, regretting this, but then we go our separate ways.

A few weeks later, just weeks, right? Things have looked up for me. A job and Dane leaves so I live upstairs. To celebrate my new future, I walk into this bar.

I am wearing a black shirt with the sleeves sliced off. I have raided Lindsay's closet and my arms are full of silver bracelets set with water-colored stones, turquoise, agates. I've got on little round movie-star sunglasses, and I keep them on although the room is dark because first off I see Jack.

He looks back and doesn't recognize me. I've got my hair fluffed up, ratted out to there. It curls, stands out in a bush, as though just chopped into this shape with nail scissors, or messed up in the backseat of a car. A lot of makeup, too. Four-inch-heeled black leather boots.

I stop where he is sitting.

"Baby, I've been waiting all morning for you," Jack says, loud enough. He's only kidding. He doesn't think I'll take him up on the line or take him seriously at all. He tosses back his beer, throws a five on the table just as I turn and cock my hip and look at him, just look. Then slowly, very slowly, just to let him see my twitchless face, I begin to slide down Lindsay's sunglasses. I change my mind, shift them back to the top of my nose. I put them back up before Jack can see my eyes. He's attracted, doesn't recognize me yet. I can see that. It is in that moment that I decide to take him for a ride.

I sit down. Jack drinks me in.

"Skipping school?" he asks.

"I'm not in school," I tell him. "I'm twenty-one."

"What do you do," he asks, "for work?"

"Play." I smile. I look away. "Piano." I turn back.

Then he smiles back and things get more complicated. I'm in trouble and I know it.

Jack's smile tears right into me as though he has been looking for it all of his life. I am his goddess, I can see that already! And Jack, he's a man stuck down at the bottom of a well, a drainage ditch, looking to me to save him from the pit. We're sitting in a bar, two people across from each other. I see Jack down there, okay, where it isn't very pleasant. But I don't stay up in the blue sky where it is safe. I climb right down to keep him company, and suddenly he finds that he is not getting shit-faced lonely. There are two of us getting drunk at noon now. Two. There are two of us to look at the row of zeros on the check he shows me—first draw from the bank. Loan day. Celebrating! Two of us all day! There will be two of us to go to bed. The room feels warm and close. Jack looks older, suddenly, yet full of high school coach's charm. I bend slowly over the table and Jack is forced to think about my breasts. Heavy? Light? Delicate? Big? I can see very well that he can't think. He can feel them in his hands as he sits there looking at the sliced low front of my T-shirt.

"What do you want?" I ask.

Jack doesn't say what his hands want. He says a different thing.

"Another beer."

"You got it."

I go over to the bar and pay for one and carry it over by myself.

"Now you're going to have to buy me one," I tell him, "fair is fair."

So we sit there for a while, talking, and as time goes on Jack stops thinking of me the way he thought of me at first. Something happens to Jack that he isn't sure he wants to happen. I can see it, feel it. He starts thinking of me as someone too young, and looking at me makes him sad.

"What do you really want?" I ask him, a little later, grinning as I say it.

Jack doesn't answer me for a while. He just stares at me, his face full of conflict—not exactly the face of a man about to have a good time.

I lean over, grab Jack's chin in my hand.

"What the hey, you're here, aren't you?"

"Yeah," he laughs at himself, "I was going to say something strange. You want to hear it anyway? At first, I was going to say that I want you. The thing I want, though . . ." He thinks awhile. Then he says it offhand, as though he's joking. "I want to be real."

"Real rich. What you want is to be real rich," I decide for him. "I know you better than you know yourself. You think if you're rich you're more real. My dad was rich."

"I'm rich, too."

"I'm poor," I say. "My dad kicked me out." I touch Jack's collar. "Maybe we need each other."

We start laughing, and the hell of it is, Jack remembers, now, who I am. He remembers! We can't stop. We just keep on laughing and laughing until we are asked to leave. And I know the bartender.

"Please," I say, "just let us get our shit together."

"Someplace else," the bartender says, not unkind.

We do go elsewhere. We go down the street, and Jack stops drinking as the day wears on. Then starts again. He gets serious. He tells me that he's just gotten divorced. We keep on walking. We started near the bridge and in the warmth of

August and the length of light we make every bar in Moorhead once and end up at the Treetop. Jack enters the place and looks around himself with drunken affection. Roses in small vases on the tables. Big menus with gold tassels.

"Good evening, Mr. Mauser," says the host.

Jack puts two fingers up.

"Pour deux."

I can tell by the way the host looks at us that he hopes that I am Jack's niece, some kid relative. Still, the guy finds us a table by the window, where we can look out over the city and see the lights come up softly in the dusk. All day Jack has been asking me about myself, but not until we are sitting up on top of the twin towns looking down at the river and the Hjemkomst Center do I tell him any details.

"Marlis from Sobieski," I say, very loaded. "From the pierogi belt. Marlis made of the left thighbone of her father. From the clay her mother swallowed. Marlis found in the nest of a fat white hen, dragged in blue from a snowdrift, stuffed underneath a pile of chopped cabbage for the rest of her life."

Jack looks at me like he's alarmed. I cool it.

"All I mean to say is that my mom died young. Left me. I'm fresh out of Catholic school," I tell him, prim. "I went to Saint Bennie's for a year."

"Sure you did."

"No shit!"

I laugh a little, and then my mouth sags down on one side, as Jack is watching, and it is not as though I've made a face or am constructing any kind of expression at all. It is involuntary, like a mental patient, like my fucking twitch is back. It's back! It is something that I can't help, and I keep doing it. I do it again.

"You're making that face," Jack tells me. "Are you okay?"

I slap my hand onto the place my mouth fell and hold it there, as though I'm wearing a mask that keeps slipping off.

Jack orders a straight shot and then the two of us forget my face and we eat big rare steaks, seared black, potatoes slit down the center, pats of butter going transparent in the cleft and sour cream thick with cut chives. We eat salads with fancy roasted walnuts, served on regular-sized plates. Two kinds of cake—brown, white. We get fortified. There is a piano player sitting at a grand piano. It turns out we both like the old tunes, love to sing, so we close the place together and we're not too bad. Not too fucking bad, I think.

Later, we find ourselves way down the end of Main at last. We are in a motel called the Sunset. Jack is standing at a pop machine, and it is dark. I watch him from behind the curtain, inside our room. He fumbles change from his pocket and he buys an orange soda, drinks it in the cold light. When he has drunk the can dry he takes out his pocketknife. What the hell is he doing? I get very still. He glances over his shoulder, can't tell I'm watching. I see him enlarge the keyhole until it is big enough for him to stuff in his car keys and what remains of his cash. As for the check he showed me, he wraps that in a piece of plastic from the garbage, and puts it underneath a rock in the landscaping.

I let the motel curtain fall shut. So much for trust!

"Marlis," he says as he walks in the door. "You have to take me as I am. I'm poor. My hands are empty, see?"

I turn to him in the light of the bathroom fixtures. My shirt is off.

"Your hands aren't empty, Jack," I say in a purring voice when he touches me.

I am in a little alcove of sobriety, the kind of clarity that is a smashed-out window in the long hall I walk as a drunk. He holds me against him as we lay in the rotten bed. Even half passed-out, I can tell how uncomfortable it is.

"Look," I say, "this makes no sense. We're going downhill fast."

He starts to laugh at "downhill," the understatement of all time. I lower myself onto him and then, it is unclear to me how it starts, we are making love. I feel too sober. I am moving on top of Jack, the whole bed shaking on its flimsy metal rig, the nonacoustic ceiling magnifying the sound of our breathing until I am sure everybody on the east side of Moorhead can hear it. I am double conscious of everything around me. I put Jack's hands on my hips and it is a kind gesture, not a sexual one. I am just trying to keep my balance! I am just trying not to completely embarrass myself.

I begin to move faster, faster, until it feels like we are taking off. It's very boring, repetitious. I flip him over, get underneath. Even worse. I'll fake an orgasm, I think, just to get it over with but then the noises I make, I guess, are too exciting to him finally and he lunges forward, missing me, and smashes his head into the wall over the pillow.

"What's that word, you know when one thing reminds you of another thing?"

"Association, symmetry, serendipity," says Eleanor. "I suppose you're thinking of the balcony. He could be clumsy, I mean, enthused! There's nothing wrong with that."

"Who said there was? But whoa, I mean, not to mock the dead," says Marlis, "but he wasn't exactly a sharpshooter!"

Anyway, it was a cheap Sheetrock wall Jack knocked into. Where the studs are set too far apart. But wouldn't you know it, you can never get a stud in the right place to hang a picture, but Jack goes and finds one with his skull. After the crash, he sags down on me, practically breaks my ribs. I roll out from under him. At first, I don't know what to do—give him mouth to mouth, give him oxygen? And it comes to me that I sued him, so why wouldn't he sue me? If I do the wrong thing, I'm stuck. So I do nothing but lay him down on the bed and prop his head up and let nature take its course. He breathes. His chest goes in and out. He mumbles.

Me, I put on my clothes. While he's still coming to, I take my purse. I go outside into the courtyard where I watched him hide his money. I lift the rock, slip the check out of its Baggie and take it and fold it into my bra. I replace Jack's check with a blank piece of motel stationery. I leave the can where Jack put it. I don't touch his wad of bills. I go back inside, and find that he's staring at his own hands, so I sponge his face with ice wrapped in a wet washcloth. After a few minutes, his eyes question mine.

"What happened?"

"You knocked yourself out."

"Holy shit," he says. "I've never done that before."

"Men go unconscious on me all of the time," I say in a soothing voice.

"God!" He sits up, mad or embarrassed, in awe maybe. Probably because I'm nervous, my mouth sags on one side, the way it did in the restaurant. I go into the john. Pull myself together. When I come out I think Jack looks a little guilty so I decide to interrogate him. I take off my clothes, throw them on the bed. I make my voice hard and slip my feet into those heels. It's all I'm wearing.

"Did you look through my purse while I was out? Feel free. Here."

I turn my back to him, bend over, slowly and straight from the waist. I pick up my heavy denim shoulder bag. Then I turn around, I reach in and draw out a plump little brown envelope of leather. Jack's having trouble refocusing his vision—he waves it away, but I insist that he has to look because, I say, he has already looked. I open the wallet, my money's there.

"Well, at least you're honest." I throw it at him. "Open it!"

"Okay," he says, wary, "if that's what you want."

He turns my wallet over and dumps everything in it on the bedspread.

There are six credit cards, three gold, three platinum. I'm not stupid—I know if I use these I'll get caught. They're souvenirs. There are five crisp one-dollar bills and change for a twenty. There is a picture of an elderly woman and a picture of me, Marlis. There is a lucky four-leaf clover encased in plastic.

Jack doesn't know what to say. He looks at the credit cards, all in different names, male names.

"I didn't steal them, just in case you're wondering."

"I was."

"I'm actually twenty-five," I say. I turn on the light beside the bed and let it shine on my face.

"You look about fourteen," Jack whispers. He can't figure. He isn't drunk anymore, and he doesn't want to be. He just wants to get out of the room. He has a feeling that he has stumbled against someone he has underestimated. He's right. This whole thing is very wrong and he isn't attracted to it in the least, not at all. Maybe he thinks of his wife, safely divorced from him, out of reach. He thinks of his company, Mauser and Mauser, his line of work, his project, his check stowed underneath a rock. He feels like a fool for putting this complication, this girl or woman, into his life. Clearly, I am not someone who will just go away!

"We're going to hang out here," I tell him, "get some sleep. Then you're going with me tomorrow. You're going to be my dad, buy me some clothes and a car."

"No, I'm not."

"You wanna bet?"

I unzip a little pouch in the back of my denim bag and remove a card, a driver's permit, the kind that farm kids can get when they need to drive the equipment. There is a birth date, my half sister's, but how is he to know? In black and white. All official. He subtracts. Fifteen years old.

"You just told me you were twenty-five."

"I lied."

"I'm getting out of here."

Jack grabs his things and starts to walk out of the room.

"Have you ever heard the term 'statutory rape'?" I call after him.

He understands, he sleeps the night on the floor. He tries not to wonder what is going to happen in the morning. He can't decide whether or not he deserves what is in store.

"I suppose you want a sports car," Jack says, weary. The next day, we are sitting in the booth of a sunny diner near Pioneer Mall. It is like having the devil for a daughter all of a sudden, and none of the good parts, none of the sweetness, the growing up. There is suddenly me, this grasping menace he has to appease. But so what? I've had to appease a control-freak father all my life. That *is* life, or so I think at the time. Making men feel good, important.

"First the school clothes, Dad!"

Jack nods and picks up the breakfast check, pulling the bills off the roll he's fished out of the orange soda can. They are stuck together from the sweet pop. Across the polished tiles and planters in the lobby, there is a long low teenage kind of store stuffed with clothes, flashing neon, playing loud rock music, trimmed with glass and chrome. We go in. I touch things all over the place, unrack things, take them off their hangers, and pile them in my arms.

"Pretend we had a fire." My mouth sags, I'm so happy. "I need new things, a whole new wardrobe. Pretend that you and Mom got a divorce and you're trying to win my love back by spoiling me. Pretend we're lovers." I lick my lips, and then I feel my face sag in that funny way, again. Suddenly, with all my true feelings in my voice, I speak.

"Jack honey, Jack, pretend we're insane about each other, really."

Jack has never seen someone try things on the way I try things on, the whole store goes in and out of my dressing room, along with belts, shoes, clothes pulled off the mannequins, socks, underwear. I have the store manager in there with me, helping me, eyeing a big fat sale. At one point, though, in the frenzy, I forget to watch Jack and I hand him a size eight and say I need a ten. I tell him to go get it at the last rack on the right. My mistake. Jack walks over to the rack and hangs up the pants and keeps on walking. I peek out of the dressing room, see him, and know that I have no choice. I run out of the store in my underwear, down the center of the mall. I don't want him to leave me for real, and I'm not inventing my tears. I'm choking on my own sadness when I scream.

"Dad, don't leave me! Don't leave!"

My voice is tortured in a continued wail I cannot stop. People stare. I run toward Jack through walls of shoppers, wearing only my bra and underpants and socks. I run howling until he turns. He stands still. What can he do? There is a look on his face that pleases me. He understands, I can tell that. He is starting to realize.

He can't get away. There's nowhere to hide. I will do anything to keep him.

§

Best Western

Marlis

I never hold grudges. My memory is bad. I forget how Jack tried to ditch me and I forgive him overnight. I can afford to because by afternoon I am made over. I am entirely a new person and Jack has paid for the works. The look I'm aiming for is a combination of Thelma and Louise, the two in one body — and younger, my age. I think I get it just perfect. Threat and innocence. The slut next door.

Fate always has my best interest at heart. I meet Jack at a vital jumping-off point in his life. There he is, with this big new project and like he said when very drunk, he is potentially in deep shit with a trail of unpaid subcontractors stretching all over North Dakota. So fine. He has other talents, other things he's always wanted to do. Places where I imagine he fits with me better than he fit with his tooth-puller ex — sorry, Candice!

I let Jack rearrange my face and I let him try to leave me in a clothing store. Then I take my revenge. Holding that fake license over him, I make him come and sing with me at my job.

Wearing Lindsay's prom dress, I now play piano weeknights at the Elkwood Lounge. It's not like he's totally opposed, anyway. I can tell that he's starting to like me.

I learned the basics from the nuns, and never knew how good I was until I left Sobieski. As for Jack, leaning over my shoulder he croons "Bye Bye Blackbird." We're off. He enjoys himself, in spite of our rocky start. I never would have thought it, expected it, but it turns out the two of us have everything in common. Once upon a time, Jack was lead tenor in his high school choir. My voice is adequate, that's all, but I am a fair piano accompanist. Jack has a drink, another, three, and then four. Either he forgets I'm holding the end of a very short leash, or he likes it. I can't tell which. Anyway, over drink five we decide to form a duo, the Midnite Specials. It's my plan. It's my dream. I convince Jack he needs a leave of absence. Of course, I know it's only what the Krauts call a *schnappsidee* and he'll forget it in the morning. Therefore, after number five I keep on pouring.

"We'll get an agent," I plan. "We'll book ourselves to play hotel lounges, wedding dances, and live-music bars. From Oregon to those sad, black forest towns of upper Michigan. I am a clear alto, Jack. My voice has no range, no upstairs, but I know just how to dress for the spotlight!"

It's true. I wear zircons on my fingers so my hands, on the keyboard, glitter. Teen Hints taught me where to vertical-stripe and where to drape, showed me accent points, the tricks of choosing costume jewelry pieces to draw attention toward good features, and shift the eye from others. I am what you'd call a visual asset. Jack's voice carries us, though. He's got an Irish lilt from somewhere, a floor of solid German dirt, a touch of Hungarian soul, even moments of clear falsetto. His voice has everything, all of the whole of Europe, a world about which Jack doesn't know any more than I do. When he sings, he gets this haunted, heavy-haired look. "Volare" is his passionate number. He throws his head back, arms out. At the same time he can make himself wholesome-looking with that big square face and preacher-clean smile.

I never take appreciation for granted. In high school, I was that kind of girl who'd go on a date that consisted of six rounds of miniature golf. I fall in love all the time, I can't help it. Movie stars, rock stars, even faces in commercials. Football captains, all the assistant coaches, civics teachers. Obsessed, you might say. That's what the school nurse called it. The counselor. Once I get a thing it crushes my heart to pieces, it steals my brain.

I suppose I knew I was getting a thing for Jack. Someone real, at least! And we have so much in common. He had a strange childhood, too, or so he says. All through grade school he was the one the others herded out, the chubby boy who'd get beaten up, cry, tattle, eat dirt. His aunt had stolen him from his own mother, that's what he said. He couldn't get over it. I felt for him. Who couldn't? He got tough, let the mean aunt have it, ran away to her brother who was farming down near Argus then, and finally one year he blossomed into the class hunk. He joined the football team and paid people back. He had no friends, exactly, yet everyone was awed by him. By the time his senior year was over, he'd run through all the girls, down to the little sway-backed sophomores. This is all by his account, of course.

I keep pouring. We go back to the Sunset. The night is heavy and he is too drunk to make love to me but I don't care. I listen.

He talks on and on about eloping. Then he changes the scenario and dreams of putting together a big wedding, asking everybody from his company and all of his ex-wives, getting wineglasses engraved with our names.

"And our birth dates?" I ask.

He goes quiet and shifts around, uncomfortable.

"I don't know about that, honey babe. I just don't know."

"South Dakota," I say to him, all of a sudden. I get our clothes on, put the shoes on his feet. I drag him out the door of the Sunset. It is time now. That night as I drive Lindsay's car, all the way down there, the air so fresh and cool, I feel as though we are traveling the very top of the world. I take the superhighway, the one Jack says he worked on. He's slumped beside me. I'm fresh. I'm decided. There is no way he's backing out.

I kiss the air every time he wakes up. He just groans and goes back to sleep. Although I've already planned a Princess Di dress in white satin, with a tiny sophisticated diamond of a hat and a long lace train, I know that running off is my best and only chance. At seven A.M. we get married in South Dakota by a justice of the peace with thongs on her feet. She's yawning. Her house smells of just canned pickles.

I throw sparks. I feel it. Once we're man and wife we go back to Fargo. I drop Jack off at the Sunset so he can sleep, and while he's out I get breakfast, mark time drinking coffee. I'm so excited that my hands shake, the coffee spills into the saucer. I can hardly wait! At last I am standing at the counter of my bank with my personal savings account checkbook in one hand. I have the wedding license in the other. Jack's check is before the teller. I have chosen the exact right ink to add an *s* to Jack's Mr.

The teller's eyes widen a little as she takes in the amount. She examines the wedding license with its embossed circlet.

"Notarized," I say.

She deposits the check.

"Would you like to have the name on your account changed?"

"Of course," I smile.

She directs me to a desk behind a wooden panel and then she turns to the next customer. I sit down, then I have a long pleasant conversation with the bank officer about the possibility of a car loan. I get papers to fill out, wave them at the teller as I leave. I throw the papers in the trash once I am outside.

The day is beautiful! It is mine. He is mine. The money is in my name. Just like Jack said, *more zeros on a string than you've ever seen.*

We hide out for a month at the Garden Court in Eugene. Jack's in trouble about the money, and I promise myself that some day when he has been extra nice to me I'll take it out of the bank and hand it to him in a wad. I'm not interested in that money first and foremost, see, that's not it altogether. I want Jack to depend on me, to live out my dream and his. Getting my way is more likely if he's dodging his crew, out of town as an excuse for not making payroll. He's delegated all the work and things are going fine back there in subdivision land. Besides, there's another piece of the loan coming in a month, he says, muttering in hope when he gets off the motel phone.

I rub his shoulders, lick his temples, and tell him I believe in him! And I do!

He just looks at me, morose, and doesn't even try to smile. But he's my husband, I think, stubborn, hating his guts for not laughing at a single joke I've ever made.

We hole up in a room with a narrow balcony, pictures of pots of flowers on the rough tan walls. The double glass-door windows look out on a parking lot. We don't care. And I can tell that toward me he's getting fonder and fonder.

One afternoon we get in, real beat, from a live audition. Sitting in our twin captain chairs, we pour ourselves hot coffee to get warm. Jack spikes his. We're silent. Actually, the day has not gone well. In Jack's baby-boy refusal to meet my eyes, I see blame. I hit a few bad notes. He sang over my mistakes. Now, he stares moodily down at the side of the fish restaurant next door. Suddenly a young long-legged blond girl in a tight little parka and jeans rounds the corner carrying a violin case.

"That's sweet," says Jack. He's number one looking at her legs and number two wondering if she will practice. Since we've gotten together, I can tell unexpected things are bothering him. He has gotten so touchy. Noise bugs him.

Behind the girl Jack watches as a boy, also carrying a violin, pops over a hedge. Then a dozen, some with cellos, and then more girls with all sorts of instruments in cases of molded leather. French horns, trumpets, tubas, drums.

"It must be some sort of convention," Jack says uneasily. We watch as they come toward us across the lot, laughing, screaming, showing off. They stream toward the Garden

Court. We hear them on the stairs. They plunge up, down, thundering. In their rooms. Doors slam. Out of their rooms. Doors again.

"World's just one big animal party, babe," I say to Jack, throwing myself on the bed, across his line of vision.

"No, no," Jack's voice rises, an edge to it. "I *need* my *sleep.*"

Sleep is not mere routine to Jack. I never think much about sleep before I share it with him. Love is the thing he takes for granted, adoration. Sleep is the thing he has to court. At the motel desk, he always asks for the quietest room. Walking into it he puts down the bags and turns his face intently, from side to side, checking for the roar of traffic, cries of pleasure from the outdoor pool, thumps overhead, or the whine of television from next door. Even in the most dreamless quiet of the night, however, he has trouble sneaking up on his own oblivion.

I sense him beside me, those first weeks. He hums to himself a little, trying out new arrangements in his head, or replays the day's tensions, the fights he often has with bar managers, arguments I pick that he tries to smooth over. As I drop off, I feel him flexing and relaxing each part of his body in a kind of yoga exercise that he learned from Tarzan books. Sometimes he screws in foam ear stops and some mornings, when I wake, I see that he's won his battle only by putting on a black eye mask he bought at a drugstore. He claims that lack of sleep destroys the timbre of his voice, and whether that is true or not, it sure wrecks his mood. I begin, very quickly on, to try and get him a full eight hours. Not my style, as you can imagine, to baby a man like that, but I am Polish after all and in my family the old women used to say the man is king. I answer *the man is king shit,* but I try their method anyhow, with Jack. I try to be responsible, try to be adult. And so that afternoon in Eugene, when he turns to me, his sleek brows wild, his mouth stuck half open, I am already thinking.

As always, we are in the No Smoking wing. Since he's been trying to quit, he hates smoke. All of a sudden, he's superior. Breathing cigarette smoke, he says, is our only occupational hazard.

"Let's move to a smoking room," I say. "They're teens. They're not allowed to smoke, right?"

I can see him weigh the noxious alternative. He gives in and that night, in the blessed and stale-odored quiet, his nerves soothed by the white noise of a blank station of the radio, Jack falls asleep in my arms. It is such a rare thing, sleep overcoming him with his neck crooked at an uncomfortable angle, that I don't dare move although his head on my chest is a weight I have to lift with every breath.

That night at the Garden Court is a high point. I should have known we were heading for a low. The only nature I see in those days of our marriage is landscaping. It comes back to me so clear sometimes. Moments. Places. There we are at the Knight's Inn, Detroit, in soft, fresh snow. I am looking at the boulevard, at the plantings around the parking lot and pool, at the way the flat yew bushes grow between the clumps of sculpted pine. I am looking at the soft shapes of evergreens, when I suddenly miss central Minnesota. Central Standard Time. I'm off because I've never been out of my time zone until this trip. Never. My inner-clock spring's broke. I want so bad to just lie down somewhere real, in a snowbank or even a fucking ditch. It is midday, the parking lot quiet, but Jack is in our room, in the bed underneath the crossed spears on the wall. He is catching up on sleep. I need sleep, too, but I don't want to go back in the room and wake him.

The pines are six feet tall, maybe more. Their lowest branches touch, forming caves. The cedar bark and shredded wood and fluffy snow spread across the ground beneath looks so inviting that I decide, *why not?* I could choose a wooden bench beside the frozen pool. No one would bother me. Why not the little shadow, the cave underneath a tree? I step carefully around the wires for Christmas lights and I stretch out right there. And it *is* comfortable. Outside the greenery, it doesn't seem there is a breeze. Under the tree, though, I feel the sigh of needles, hear the singing of some tiny unfamiliar creature, native to Detroit I guess. There could be a bird, a sparrow or something. It sings. Then mutters. There is the smell of fresh snow, the thick white odor of winter air. I close my eyes.

In my bones, as I lay there, I feel the traffic beyond the strip, the shudder of life. Voices pass, but I feel safe. All around me, needles tick and branches hum and take in the cold light. The world is drunk with light, but I am sliding deep into the dark. Underneath the snow, the chipped bark, below the plastic set down so the weeds cannot poke through, under the layer of broken glass and topsoil and clay gumbo, I picture a darkness so total it is a fabric of air.

That is when I know I am going to have a baby. It comes to me, the end result of many small signs.

I'm pregnant, I think, and am at once knocked out by sleep. I am dressed very warm and I do not wake up until the Christmas lights all around me blink on and off in dazzling and starry novas. Then, as I stumble back into normal life, I realize that Jack would be furious if he saw me. It occurs to me how weird it is that I am sleeping outdoors, while inside the motel my husband has two queen-sized beds to himself, with royal-blue velveteen spreads.

Yet, it has become normal for me to guard Jack. I make him human, protect the old fuck, make sure that he sleeps.

The facts only begin to clarify in Minneapolis–St. Paul, at Big Sioux Lodge. I do believe that motel is cursed by Indians. A thirty-foot chief constructed out of fiberglass waves How. Right out front. That's for starters. Inside, the place is littered with designs. The rubber mats to wipe your feet on, the carpets, the cocktail napkins, all full of squares and diamonds, beadwork-looking. Strange. There are a bunch of tired-looking plaster Indians dressed up, enclosed in glass. The animals these people lived off of are stuffed and hiding in the rafters, poised to leap down and attack. Foxes, wolves, raccoons, squirrels, and wild goats. It's freezing cold the night we play at the Big Sioux. Furnace is set too low. The lounge is full of families bumped off a canceled Northwest flight to Billings. Montanans, stuck in worse weather than their own. You can imagine the mood they are in already. Our show does nothing but give them a target to concentrate their irritations.

It is wild, though, the things Jack tries. He has always told me that patter with the audience is his strong suit, but he's deluded. He starts out with a few remarks, making up his family. "My uncle was a deep-sea diver, but he was too polite to last. Met a mermaid and tipped his hat to her. I had an aunt, too, an old maid. She let the dust accumulate beneath the bed. How come? She heard man is made of dust." He gets to me, his wife. "She wouldn't kiss me last night. Said, 'Honey, my lips are chapped.' 'Well,' I said, 'one more chap won't hurt 'em!

"You people come here in an airplane? I hate 'em. I stay on terra firma. The firma the ground the lessa the terra."

Stale laughter. Unbelieving. Where did he dig 'em up? Soon after that, we swing into "Raindrops Keep Fallin' on My Head," "Let's Fall in Love," "I Fall to Pieces." Then Jack asks the crowd if there are any requests.

"Harmonize," a voice calls from a back booth. Jack shoots me a foul look and then it is like we have started some kind of trend, or maybe our airlines passengers have got a fright that day and, you know, the way you wake up in the morning and a song is going in your head and you realize it is a comment on your life, they ask for "Listen to the Falling Rain," "When Autumn Leaves Start to Fall." We keep singing for them, taking requests. I think the emphasis on falling sets some kind of tone. Morbid. And when we sit down to take our break a weird thing happens. Of course, Jack hasn't slept well and I am walking on pins anyway, but he looks at me, all critical.

"Your lipstick's off center," he says.

I have my purse. When his back is turned, I take out a little lipstick tube with a mirror attached. I look at my lips, apply a touch-up.

"Straight now?" I ask, my voice sarcastic.

He looks over my head, studying a stuffed hawk, and speaks in a dreamy voice. "It's your mouth, to be honest, your mouth is set crooked on your face."

That gets to me, I mean, I've worked so hard on my damn

face, spent so much money getting the right makeup and studying instructions. Just to have him say I'm still put together crooked. What does he know! Jack tips the strong line of his jaw away from me.

"Goes with the rest." He grabs my arm, hauls me up. I have no time to react, or maybe I am numb. Before I even take in his remark properly, I am in front of the crowd drawing out the opening to "Snowbird." And then, that night, after we play until the lounge closes, we go upstairs to bed. I hang our clothes up, turn the covers down, and loosen the tight, clean, sheets.

"I've figured things out," Jack says. "It's you. It's you all along. You took the check, somehow cashed it. Put it who knows where."

"What do you mean?" Tears swell in my eyes. Never mind that I did it. That he would *suspect* me. That's what hurts. "What check. Are you crazy?"

"There's a record. There's a canceled check, Marlis. I've got friends in the bank. Either you give me the cash, or I'll prosecute."

Jack closes his eyes to block out my face. I turn off the lights. The night, the air, all are still and very black around us. The room's drapes shut out the lights from the parking lot. From time to time, we hear other people in the hallway. Doors close with hollow watery booms. Voices drop like stones.

"They told you wrong," I say, "whoever they are. Mistakes are made. I love you. I love you so deep."

I touch Jack's chest and rear over him and scissor him between my legs. Maybe I can seduce him, make him want me the same desperate way he seemed to want me at first. My old methods don't work very well though, not anymore.

"A bank check will be just fine," he says, turning from me.

We're awkward sexually. Ever since Jack banged his head, he's gotten wary. We chip our teeth, knock elbows, make popping noises when he slides his chest against mine. I wish it was easier to be his lover, but it's hard work and I get famished. I eat big meals, do sit-ups every night, but things get worse. I lose the energy to make him love me and I roll off him, bored. A wish creeps over me. If only Jack was made of cardboard, an actor, a TV personality! I could deal with him so much better. But there he is, real, lying next to me. I hold my breath as he turns to meet slumber. I don't dare touch him, or speak, or make any noise at all. Even the sound of my breathing, the ragged need of it, even the rustle of the bedsheets, seems much too loud.

"Please," I say. "Love me back. Until death."

Underneath the pine, back in Detroit, something happened. I felt the movement beneath the snowy bark mulch, the grab of the earth. His baby's in me, I know it, and I think he'd better love me soon or I will start to think of him as cardboard, as ions. I hold my breath as he shifts, his body rasping at the sheets. The way I do with my fantasy men, I imagine his arms reaching, unfolding, his presence blooming toward me in the rich, heavy air. I lay still. Jack often draws away or suddenly goes cold when he senses me wanting him. To get him I freeze, a rabbit, allow his hands to cross me in rough circles until the rush of tension that fills him runs over and I am set free. But nothing I do attracts him that night. At last, because my heart finally aches like a hand squeezed it, I touch his arm. He shrugs away from me and curls around his treasure. I think of his penis. His best part. His worst. I get mad. I decide that he can have it, all to himself. I turn too, lie on my back staring into the rushing dark.

The room deepens. I don't dare speak or make any noise at all. I begin to touch the well between my hips, encourage myself, to make myself rounder and wetter with my own hands, and as I do I feel the black joy that was spread evenly inside of me gather heavily until it presses like oiled water against my skin. When it finally is too much, I take my hands away and then I am floating on a comfortable raft. Jack is sleeping, or else he is listening. I don't care. I do the same, again, again, until my legs hinge with a sudden cramp. The dim water folds over on itself, becomes a wave of pure lonesomeness. I never saw the ocean, but I know its sound. A roaring emptiness. I curl around a pillow and let the waves crash.

For the first time, though, instead of going to sleep feeling sorry for myself, something happens. I get a witness, a voice, a simple feeling of companionship from right inside. *The baby,* I think at first. But no, it is different. It is me who calms me down. Me who says, *You are something. You are a protector. You are a mother. Giving life is sexier than fucking Jack. Live it, baby, live it!* I'm so happy that I sleep like a garden and my child my secret. Sleep like an aquarium bubbling in stillness holding safe my little fish.

Since the day I turned thirteen, I never begin my morning without the ritual of eyeliner, mascara, blush, and lipstick. The next morning is the first. I forget about it because good feelings still are soaking into me. New ones, big ones. I'm so important now with life that I don't even need to check my face and hair in the mirror. Jack is downstairs, eating breakfast. He must have slept real well, that means. After long sleeps he always orders the specials that include minute steaks, hash browns, three eggs instead of two.

Usually after a good night's sleep, once in a blue moon, after making love, I go downstairs fresh and put together, perfect as I can make myself. Jack and I sit across the table from each other. Everything around us seems interesting and intense. We read our place mats out loud, flip through the packets of sugar. Even the words on the menu make us laugh. But that morning, as I stand in the doorway by the Please Wait to Be Seated sign, I catch sight of Jack from behind. He sits alone at the counter. Clearly, he does not want company. His back is hunched over his food and his elbows are moving, up and down, up and down, pumping at his work. He eats like a mechanical horse, everything about him given over to the one task.

I turn and walk out. Drumbeats, a wailing kind of faraway sound, Indian theme music comes from the loudspeakers. It is a music so foreign to me that I cannot tell whether it is meant to be sad, happy, or something more complicated. I sit down in the lobby, next to a shallow pool laid with blue tiles. Under the ripple of the spotlighted water, coins glint, a hundred of them, two hundred, each one marking a person's wish. Glass cases line the wall, floodlit and labeled with names and dates. It is just me, and a hundred dollars worth of small desires. I take out a quarter. I want to get my desires all right.

"I hope lightning strikes and burns this place down," I decide, but I'm kidding around. I've got ahold of something. For the first time, I have the words for what I want. This baby, I say. You. I'm talking to a tiny being. So formless it can't yet dream. Real love, I ask for, true love given and returned. Wherever it comes from, I say, wherever it goes.

It occurs to me that I should move that money back in Fargo to a different account, or get cash. This baby needs support. When I throw in my next coin the ripples from the little splash spread and continue, moving outward, widening all day.

Billings is our next engagement. A Best Western there. If any of those Montana passengers happen in by chance I think they'll take out two ropes and hang us. We practice. Play tapes in the car. Jack's ferocious. Eventually, we stop and park at a small wayside rest stop. Rattlesnakes Have Been Sighted Here, a sign says, but surely they are hibernating now in a frozen heap. I look over at Jack. He feels me watching him, but he doesn't react.

A few Russian olive trees, their branches spiky and silver, gleam beside the winter picnic tables. I have bought the makings for lunch in a paper bag that now I take out of the backseat. It is a warm winter day and people are wandering in sun. I brush off the table and begin to make a sandwich, the way Jack especially likes it. Three kinds of lunch meat, two kinds of cheese, and the fat white bread used for Texas Toast. I am cutting the sandwich in half with this little paring knife I bought, when Jack comes up behind me and grabs my arm.

"What are you doing?" he demands.

"I'm making you a sandwich," I answer, pulling away my arm.

"You're putting mayo on it."

I decide to tell him. Maybe not the best way, but right then and there.

"I'm pregnant, I need the calories, Jack."

"I like mustard."

That is his answer. I wait for him to say he's glad, then when he doesn't, to say he's scared, even to say he's sorry. Pregnant! I'm pregnant, asshole! Suddenly I scream it in his face.

Stubborn, he won't deal with this at all. He totally ignores my shriek.

"Only in diners. I eat mayo in diners," he mumbles, incredulous, as though I've done something evil.

"I could care less. I'm pregnant," I say in a tiny voice now, for the last time. My words shake and I can feel the anger coming in through steam vents, way down.

"What kind of game are you playing?" Jack's voice goes ragged. Then he twists my arm, sharp, and the knife goes springing across the table, cartwheels off onto its point into a clump of snow. I hear myself yell and I watch the knife as it falls. I watch very closely because the pain in my arm, the wrench, electrifies me. The wooden boards stand out in focus. The texture of the risen bread.

"Why are you doing this to me?" says Jack, letting go.

I turn, cradling my elbow. The anger squeezes to a little place in the closet of my fear. I knew I'd touch the live wire like I did, so many times, with my father. You never knew where it was exposed, when it would shock you.

"Doing to you?"

I'm like a baby myself, bewildered. I used to pee myself listening to my dad walk through the house, looking for me, searching where I hid. I'm back there suddenly. I can't speak, my tongue has stuck to the dry inside of my mouth and my brain does not connect with it anyway. I raise my head and meet the eyes of a woman walking her dog in a little knitted sweater just a few feet away. The woman's mouth opens, so I shrug at her and shake my head. I am embarrassed for Jack, believe it or not, afraid that the woman will think badly of him. Think he's a wife beater. Something. I hope he will act upset too, but he just bites into his sandwich, chews, and then that big clean football-captain smile spreads across his face, all white keys. I hold my arm and look into his eyes. Clear, deep, brown. Fixed as a bird's. The little muscles around his mouth freeze solid.

I'm hurt bad, inside. Yet I feel myself smile back into his face. My lips tremble. I've never been pregnant before. He doesn't believe me. I don't know what else to do.

What the hell do you know? I think, looking away from his comfortless, chewing jaws, into the twigs, so thin, so silver, so calm. There is a sorrow in them deeper than me. Their silence chills me. *What the hell do you know about being a woman?*

That's when anger comes back, welcome and filling.

That's when I decide I'll teach him.

I keep smiling as we get into the car, as we drive. The smile is easy to hold now because I've got my lesson plan in place. I'm figuring. The grin is painted on me, perfect, as though I have been skinned, dried, and stuffed. Just before Billings, in one of those big gas station stores that sell everything, we stop and get out of the car. Jack leans over and hits the lever on the gas pump, then the cash button. He thrusts the metal tube angrily into the mouth of the tank and sets the flow. Then he throws himself against the door and leans there, frowning absently at his boots. I look at him for a minute. Detached. I walk away. I go into the ladies room, take off my coat, examine the back of my arm in the mirror, and can see nothing. It feels looser though, the joint unhinged a little, though it doesn't hurt. I pick up the phone and dial the number of the bank in Fargo. They've got passwords they use. My mother's maiden name. Which was Cook, the name I use now. I make certain that the money's all still there and then I hang up the telephone.

I could almost have imagined that Jack's punishment hadn't happened, not really, not so bad it took my breath away. When I come out of the stall, I stand before a padlocked dispenser of condoms. Placed in This Establishment for Your Convenience, says the lettering on its front. Fifty cents. Two quarters only.

I gaze into the metal side, into the slick finish of my own reflection. I pluck two quarters out of my pocket and put them into the machine. I turn the handle and a little square box drops into my hand. Savage Bliss. Arouse Her Animal Passions, the package says. I get cold inside when I look at it—it's like, *I want my animal passions*, why not? I want savage bliss! I put the box in my purse, go out the door, and stand beside Jack, thinking I will give him one last chance. This is it. He is sliding money into the slot of a plastic box full of small soft animals, plush rhinos and pink elephants and candy-striped bears. Over them a little tin crane's arm swings loose. Jack works it from a lever.

"Which one do you want?" he says.

"None of them."

"Come on, I want to get you one," says Jack. He is in a cajoling mood, charming, his voice light and oblivious.

"That's not what I want," I say.

"Well, you're going to get one anyway."

"Why don't you ask me what I do want?"

"What do you want?"

Jack gives this embarrassed laugh because I tell him that I want my animal passions. He shrugs, turns all of his attention to the box. The tin claw hovers, touching down. He is going for an elephant with slit black eyes and a long blind trunk that pushes from blue plush. Jack is trying to grab the trunk. The back of the box is mirrored, reflecting the scene somehow from another mirror, one of the infinite-dimension tricks from movies. The pointed tips of the pincers touch the trunk and close. Jack has good small-motor coordination, wins prizes at the carnival stands, pitching softballs at wooden milk bottles, shooting lead ducks. Part of me admires his delicate touch with the loaded controls, and part of me watches this all happen in the mirror.

I grab his arm, as if in excitement. The crane swings and

clinks against the side of the box, the claw bounces, and Jack goes dark with anger. For the second time he does it. He shoves me. He just hits me out of his way.

"What the hell did you do that for?" he says.

"What do you think?"

I'm holding my arm. I'm scared of him, but now I know that if I show him weakness he'll bully. I stand up to him and look him straight in the eye. "You. Jack. You listen to me. I want you to say you love me. You're glad. The baby's yours."

He regards me for a moment, and then his hands drop foolishly to his sides. He bites his lips, runs his hand through his hair and makes it into a forlorn mess.

"Are you, really?" he asks in a small, false voice. He opens his arms, tries to hold my shoulders, moves me close to him, shuts me up.

I pull away.

"Say you're sorry, too."

My words rasp out louder than I mean them to and an elderly woman prodding bags of popcorn, choosing the freshest, looks around at us and stares, her eyes bland and dead. Jack strides off, so I address her and an old rancher who has walked in, just then, with his wallet open in his hands.

"Can you believe it," I say, pointing at Jack's retreating back. "He twisted my arm when he found out I was pregnant. Shoved me. Hit me. I'm through with him, so he won't need this."

I take the packaged condom from my purse, walk over to the rancher. Beside him, the woman comes to sudden life. Plump and tiny, she backs away from me. Her big eyes are wet and mystified behind their lenses, and she holds the shiny black bag of popcorn between us, pushes it in panic at the air. I sidestep her and grab the rancher's dry, tough hand before he can jerk it away. He is hairless, work-hard and slim. He wears a denim storm-coat and his hips are still proud in his jeans. I close his fingers like leather gloves around the tiny package.

"Mister, you just got lucky," I say to him.

He smiles, looking at the packaged condom, then meets my

eyes and nods. As he and I walk out the door together and then on, across the parking lot, toward his pickup, something rises from underneath me, dark, powerful, a wind, a water. I rush, the black noise surrounding me. My head's a buzzing hive. The stones in the asphalt, the bits of glittering mica, the aluminum pop rings pressed into the tar stand out in flat focus as if my eyes are an expensive microscope. I have no plan in mind except maybe, I think, I'll spend two hours with this guy and have him drop me off in time for the evening show. Something is happening. Jack's wrench of my arm is like the first yank on a pump handle and all day the emotion that has poured into the underground basin is leaking steadily into the world.

As we drive off, the pickup fills with the humming tension of it, the space around the man and me. Riding along, I tell him to stop at the first motel and get us a room. So he parks the pickup carefully steering into the farthest spot. He cuts the engine, turns to me, and I think, *Oh god he wants it here, right here.* But he only looks at me with a quiet in his eyes, something I don't recognize. Like he feels sorry for me. He unsnaps his shirt pocket and takes out the condom. He holds it at arm's length to read it, then puts it back in his shirt pocket.

"Let's go use that," I say in my most throaty voice, looking up at him through my eyelashes.

He shakes his head though, reaches across the front seat, and tucks a strand of hair behind my ears.

"Still wet back there," he gently says. "Let me take you home."

That man's kind act both puts me together and really hurts. It shows me what heartwood a real man is made out of and that little revelation keeps my fury slowly pouring out so that the motel room Jack and I inhabit at the Billings Best Western is knee-deep before I even enter, and it's filling deeper, the oily water sloshing black.

That night, I take a long time getting my hair perfect, setting it to ripple down my shoulders in a frosted mane. I choose a red V-neck chiffon and a piece of jewelry with real drama—a large filigreed arrowhead hanging from a wire neck band. I stay in the little tile bathroom, at the vanity sink, surrounded by my beauty equipment. Blow dryer. Electric rollers. Sprays. A pronged curling iron. These things are like defensive weaponry. They bristle, hot and female.

Jack does not come near me. He sits right inside the door, in a chair by the window. He sips from a clear cup and contemplates what is happening below him in the courtyard. It is well after lunch and the sun's rays are long and blue, snowmobilers stand on the deck, sit in the white chairs, also drinking out of cups. I hear one of them shout, "You wanna party?"

"No thanks," I hear Jack answer. I know that as he watches them he worries that later on this evening, maybe as late as after the show, the party will still be going on underneath our room. I know it too. I can hear it—their voices rising, their laughter, loud and drunken. He never wanted to get stuck here. I was never his intent. I am a stopping place, a way station on the road to somewhere else, a temporary residence where he can wait while his luck changes and the damage collects out behind him.

It has taken me a long time to get to this, but now things will change.

Rain fills his tracks. Luck runs out the holes. He leaves his wallet with our money in his pants while he showers and I pluck it out, car keys too, grab my suitcase. When I do not return from fetching ice for his drink, he looks around. No me. Jack finds himself stranded at the Billings Best Western with ten dollars, a suitcase, and no ice bucket, even.

He does not believe the truth at first. He continues sitting in the same spot. The patch of trampled snow goes darker below, reflecting nothing. Voices bounce off the packed flakes. Engines rev and whine as moon-booted folks dance to a portable tape deck. A woman passes, bringing ice, and she isn't me. The night deepens all around Jack Mauser. He does the show solo, returns, watches the closing of many numbered doors, and finally goes inside our room, crams the pillow to his head.

He is thinking of me, how I'm supposed to take care of him, like a daughter, like a wife, like a nothing, like a manic-depressive, which I am. He is planning how he'll throw me down when I come back. He thinks I will come back, but then maybe he sees in his mind a cracked wedding bell, blondy brown hair, a bunch of tin cans tied to a fender, bouncing, rattling, behind a hot red car that speeds away and disappears.

I don't really leave. I slip back into the motel without him knowing, and I take another room across the court from Jack. One day goes by, then another. Morning number three. All day long, I nap, watch television, file and polish my nails, read a bunch of magazines and western books. I order dinner from room service, watch him go out alone to our gig, dressed in the ruffled tux and mentally rehearsing worried jokes. I am sitting behind the curtains, playing solitaire, when he returns after the show. I watch him slump, wearily jiggling the key in the lock. He looks worn-out. I doze for an hour, watch a talk show the second, then walk over to his room, and let myself in with the key I've kept.

You might wonder if I have a plan at this point. Well, I do have a plan. It involves several things I bought this morning at a hardware store—clothesline, duct tape. It involves a curling iron, too. There he is on the bed, truly sleeping. Once he is out, he is out. I know that. Getting there is what is so troubling to Jack Mauser.

I take a long piece of cut tape in my hands. I slip it around one of Jack's wrists, quickly, then the other, while he is lost in a dream.

"Wake up," I say, "I'm here, honey."

He kicks his legs back and I loop and tie him like a rodeo calf. Then he is lying on the bed, on the nice wide white sheets, all four pillows stuffed around him, the quilted polyester spread folded neatly at the base.

I turn on the lamp.

He is confused at first. He is very surprised, I'll tell you that. His eyes are huge, the pupils surrounded by white.

"What the fuck!" He opens his mouth to yell louder and I flex a piece of duct tape before him.

"Okay," he says, "I'll be quiet. I'll shut up. Just tell me what's going on."

In answer, I sit down on a chair, next to the bed. I put my bag of beauty equipment down at my feet. First I take out my curling iron, show it to him. I plug it into the socket to heat. I remove a pair of tweezers from a leather case, and test the end to see how neatly they clasp.

"It hurts to be a girl," I tell Jack, looking deep into his face.

His eyes widen.

"So?" he says.

"So, feel."

I hold the tweezers out. His eyes follow the gleaming instrument up, up over his nose, until he can't see what I am doing. What do you think? I pluck one hair, another, from his eyebrows.

"Ow," he says. "Cut it out. Come on, Marlis. Please."

"I'm waiting for the magic words, Jack."

He shuts his mouth in a firm straight line, so I spend half an hour evening and straightening the line, making him look half glowering and half shocked. The mustache after that, I decide. It has to go. And the leg hair. Lucky I have just bought a hot wax kit.

"Did you think of the words yet?" I ask him.

"Sure," he says. "I know what you want to hear, but you can't break me, Marlis."

He's stubborn. I put a pot of in-room coffee water on to boil and heat the little pan with its chunk of leathery wax. I apply it to Jack's legs with the tongue depressor that's included, spread the little muslin strips over, rub and rip. Towels. Tissue.

"Shit! Holy hell. That hurts!"

"I know," I sympathize. "I do it every four weeks just to make myself all smooth for you, Jack. Now will you say it?"

"Under duress? Under torture? Would that really satisfy you?"

"Yes."

But he frowns in outrage, falls silent.

I decide that Jack's ears look nude.

"You need something," I say critically, tapping each side of my neck, "dangly. Right about to here."

I have a big silver bird brooch with a long sharp needle. I take that from my jewelry case and cauterize it. He hates shots. I know it. I remember. I wipe his earlobes with alcohol, and punch the holes through, just perfect. I have a smaller needle, just a sewing needle, which I poke through after that, leaving a loop of thread. His face is fierce, his eyes are rolling back. My hand shakes and I get tears in my eyes.

"Hey, you're a guy, right?" I've got gravel in my throat, can't take it. "You're tough enough to Dutch-rub my face. Tough enough to twist a pregnant woman's arm. Tough."

I prop him up on his pillows and spread the towels beneath his legs to finish the wax job.

"I can't get to your armpits," I apologize, "or else I'd wax them for you too."

I cut his pajamas off, thinking "bikini line," but his legs are trembling, jerking away from my touch. It is that involuntary flinch that gets me. I can't go on, I think, can't keep doing this. I put the scissors down.

"Say it?" I ask. But he has regressed. He glares at me like a two-year-old and screws his lips shut.

"How about curlers, sweetie?" I feel ferocious!

Brush rollers. Pins. I do Jack's bangs with my hot iron, and then I spread a couple teaspoons of pink styling gel into his manly hair and set it with the stiff little mesh and wire contraptions. Lay him down. There. Let him sleep on those prickles.

"You should have breast implants, here." I touch his chest with one light finger. He shudders. "But forget that. There are worse things."

Slowly, I show him the high heels.

I draw from my handbag a huge pair, red and spiked. I hit

a sale at a consignment store. $12.95. The toes are narrow wedges into which I tease globs of the Super Glue I normally use to repair cracks in my fingernails.

"You don't even have to walk in these, I promise," I tell Jack. "Just wear them. They make your ankles look so slim."

I give him one last chance. I stand there, holding the shoes and the duct tape in my hand.

"Say it, say it, asshole," I beg softly. "Say you love me, you adore me. You're crazy about me, really. Say you couldn't be happier. Say you're glad about the baby."

He just looks at me, helpless, and he opens his mouth, I'll give him that. A sound comes out of him, but it's just a moan, a cry, no kind of word.

So I fit the shoes on. His feet tuck right into them, a tight fit, just gorgeous. I double tape his ankles to the end of the bed. Then, before leaving, I kiss each red toe, tap the point, and stand at the end of the bed.

"What's wrong with you?" I say.

"I don't know," he whispers back.

"We're both sick then."

"Don't leave me here like this."

"You don't want this baby."

He's silent, but I see that he can't lie to me at least. There's that, anyway. Even after torture he won't deceive me about his true feelings.

"Okay, Jack. You give me no choice."

I cut a piece of tape and smooth it across his mouth. I turn away. Leaving the room and leaving Jack and all I hoped behind, a washing, tearing, pitiless sadness comes down. Why do we wander? Why do we long so hard? Why do we ever let our hearts fall open?

§

Baptism River

Candice and Marlis

*A*lthough the women found the picture of Jack in spike heels irresistible, their own feet, half frozen, thawing and unthawing, stung with such fierce poignancy that their humor was invaded by sympathy, and nobody laughed.

"Here I was, broke," Marlis went on. "Knocked up. Which I did not expect, but which I halfway treasured and half resented. Then Candice calls me. She asks me if I want to travel up north, to Superior. I go, *what*? You're his former wife! But she means it, and after all, I'm a former too, now. Plus, I gave the money back, or half of it anyway. Jack figured it would cost more to prosecute me and get the rest of it—after all, I cashed the check when we were married. Legally, it was half mine. He's so furious that he never answers my letters. My phone calls. I'm hardly in a mood to sit around and think what to do with myself next. I can't support a baby all its life, even on Jack's check, which I think now he owed me, don't you? I don't know what my next move is and I need space. So I say

I'll go with Candice and we take off to visit this really nice resort which we never *get* to of course. Never do."

Marlis's voice trailed off and Candice took over.

"Here's how I saw it. I was the one who wanted a baby all those years." Candice, huddled close to Marlis, ached with cold but gathered her voice. Even now, her resentment warmed her. "Why did Marlis get pregnant, just like that? I found out when she mailed this letter to Jack's box, not knowing we still shared a key. I read the letter. I decided. That baby was supposed to have been mine—I deserved it! You don't understand, I suppose. You think that I should have sat back and felt sorry for myself and taken out my rage and disappointment on myself by drinking, binge-eating, crying, whatever. Self-pity isn't in my repertoire. I am a professional with professional commitments, with patients. I had been cheated out of a child and Marlis had what I wanted.

"I had to stay close—you know that old saying, *Keep your friends close and your enemies closer?* That's what I did. I showed no anger at all toward Jack or toward Marlis after I learned of her condition. In fact, as soon as I understood from reading Jack's mail that Marlis wasn't even certain that she wanted to bear the child at all, I asked Marlis to come along on a trip to the north woods."

"I knew it was a setup, too," said Marlis.

"I had to get you alone."

"Fine. You got me."

"Times are better now in Silver Bay, Minnesota," Candice went on, "but when I had last been there, real estate was going for nothing. The town sits like a wedge along Lake Superior. A mining company had just pulled out, leaving a bed of asbestos sunk along the western shore. An executive home could be had for the price of a cottage, a ranch style on the faith of a promise. They had to drive down to Duluth for any dental work. Imagine! I went up there with Marlis pregnant. By the time we got that far north, the sun was setting and the loading ramps along the highway, where barges stopped for taconite, stood abandoned. They loomed out of the dusk, huge, their edges washed over by waves.

"Out from the shadow of the wooded cliffs, the last of the sun flared. Its radiance was like a burnish on Marlis's face, dramatic. Pretty. *The baby will be pretty*, I thought. Marlis wasn't sleeping, she never sleeps! She was just not talking. Slumped against the door, frowning, hands pressed between her thighs, she guarded herself against me."

"I knew," said Marlis, "I knew!"

"Knew what?" asked Dot.

"It was weird, her inviting me along. Lake Superior never gives up its dead. That phrase kept running through my mind."

"What made you . . . " Dot began, then remembered what Marlis had done, the spiked heels, the duct tape. Perhaps she wanted an ally, another woman in case Jack flared up. But, it seemed, Marlis wasn't thinking of Jack.

"What made you go with her?" Eleanor asked this, curious, but then she saw Marlis turn toward Candice, her face glimmering very faintly, softly, within its own shadow, and she knew. For a few moments, as they held each other's gaze, the air between the two women perceptibly warmed.

Candice went on.

We turned off for town, the light of the sky midnight blue. I saw the Mariner Motel, its coiled neon rope. I pointed it out. She didn't answer, made no remark at all even though the Mariner was obviously not this luxury resort I promised—fireplace, fancy dining, heated pools, a workout room. There was supposed to be exquisite scenery, rocks jutting into the crashing waves and so on.

"Tomorrow," I told her, "we'll get to the Blue Dolphin. It has tennis courts, the works. It's a little farther up the shore."

Marlis got out and stretched as soon as I stopped beneath the carport—she didn't seem all that disappointed, she combed her ponytail into a thick blue band with her fingers, hopped up and down to warm herself. It was a raw spring night, the air wet with unshed rain, clouds and wind rolling in from the northwest. I collected my purse and straightened the car—my fancy car, littered with bags, soda cans, newspapers, sweaters, and shoes.

Anyway, I had made an unnecessary reservation for our room, a large double, away from the road and the turnoff, which I remembered as full of traffic and gasping semis. Now everything was quiet and from the motel I could even hear the pounding and breaking of waves on the other side of the highway.

I had this fateful feeling, as though everything was supernatural, important in a larger sense. I tuned in every detail of what we saw and did that night. Inside the office, the air was warm with the odor of browned onions, meat, lemon cream, wood polish. The woman who answered the bell tied to the door had stepped out of her bath and her head was wrapped in a towel. Her face shone, her skin was soft and porous-looking, very white. She wet her finger on her tongue before turning the pages of the record book until she found us, handed over our key with the slip for me to sign.

"Take a brochure," she urged as we left. There was a small wooden rack beside the door, full of advertised attractions. I collected a free newspaper, Marlis chose several bright maps. Soon we were sitting on chairs in our room, warming our feet by the coils of a small, dangerous-looking electric heater.

"Hey," said Marlis, "there's one bed in here. It's big, but I'm not sleeping with you."

Of course, the lady at the desk had asked me if it was all right, given me a special rate and everything. We'd already worked out the details. Marlis seemed to notice all of a sudden, and threw the maps on the floor. She opened her suitcase and pulled out a paperback with foil letters bold on the cover.

When I put my hand on her shoulder, she shrugged it off and settled deeper into her reading.

"I'll sleep in the bathtub," she decided.

She got up in her stocking feet and took her book into the bathroom, shut and locked the door. She lounged back—I pictured it—in the tub and continued to read.

I put the paper aside and lay back in my bed, still in my good tan trench coat. A tension headache was starting to come on. I needed to say the words first, to say them right. All the way here I had imagined the proper moment, the way I would present this. But the blood beat so hard in my throat that I thought my voice would catch.

I breathed deeply and I formed my sentence.

I kept it there, round, whole, and ready for a good half an hour. When the bathroom door opened and she appeared, I let it out.

"You're pregnant."

I didn't expect an answer, but there was no movement either. She stood without speaking until I finally sat up. Then I found that Marlis had vanished, stolen out the door of the room, silent as a deer.

There was nowhere for her to go but the motel coffee shop, that or the cold shell of the car. I stepped into the bathroom and washed my face, put on fresh makeup, and brushed my hair. Then I went outside, across the parking lot, and found the back door of the café, which was quiet and empty. The same woman who checked us in at the desk followed me into the large room. Her wet hair was combed out now and nearly dry, a fluffy, frizzed gray. She threaded among the carefully set tables, handed me a menu as I took a chair across from Marlis. There was a cup of black coffee before her. The menu was at her elbow, closed.

"What are you having?" I shrugged from my coat, pulled off the long scarf, the red silk one Jack had given me, and folded it into the sleeve.

"That's nice," said Marlis, noticing.

"You want it?" I offered.

She looked surprised. I could tell she did, but she wouldn't say so. I opened the menu.

Marlis stared at me, hard. I felt her glare on my forehead and kept my eyes centered on the food descriptions. Homey, with a soup of the day. Split pea. When I glanced at her, she was taking little tiny sips of coffee. Then the woman came back.

"Taco salad," Marlis said.

I ordered the same, and wanted to order milk, for both of us, but I didn't dare, not yet. Marlis folded her hands in her lap and looked steadily past me, at the fireplace set into the wall. No fire had ever been lit there. I let my eyes rest upon her face—kept thinking how nice the baby would look. Marlis's hard, slightly jutting cheekbones. The long flat fall of her hair, vivid, shot through with honey-colored highlights.

"Did you bug my phone calls? Or what?"

"You wrote it to Jack." I would not take guilt on, none whatsoever. "I took it from his mailbox when I went to pick up my own letters."

I pushed the slit envelope and its contents across the table. She kept herself from snatching it up, just looked at it, her face slowly reddening. The script of the address was large, messy, full of loops. Self-important, I thought. Childish. She passed her fingers over, as if the paper gave off heat.

I had made up my mind not to apologize, to keep her on the defensive, so I didn't say a word and tried not to move my hands too much, not to appear nervous. She would pick up on that immediately. I placed one hand on the handle of my coffee cup and kept it there, the other was curled in my lap. But Marlis was a tough opponent. She sat across from me the way a chess player sits—motionless, calm, in a state of seeming unawareness. I knew her mind was working and part of me admired her for allowing the letter to lie between us, its white rectangle an accusation and a question. She did not even move to thank or acknowledge the waitress when the woman put down the fluted tortilla shells full of salad before us and fussed a bit with the arrangement of the forks and water glasses. Only when we were alone again did Marlis shift her hands. Carefully, she slid the letter onto her place mat and removed its message, a thin slip of paper scrawled on both sides with heavy black marker.

Dear Jack, it began. *Do you want your baby?*

She didn't read it. She didn't even look at it. She ripped it down the middle, ripped it down the center again, and again, yet again, until she had a tiny pile too thick to tear. She then tore each piece once more until she had a handful of flakes that she sprinkled upon her salad.

"Marlis, you're being . . ." I began, but then I stopped. She proceeded to cover the bits of paper with the contents of three small paper bowls—sour cream, salsa, guacamole. When she had mixed up the salad with the paper and coated each piece evenly, she began to eat, tearing apart the nest that she had just created.

I'm not a bad person, not someone who would normally cause another person to do such a thing. I didn't want to hurt Marlis. It was just that she couldn't know. She couldn't understand, couldn't possibly visualize what a treasure her problem was, that's what she had called it, *your goddamn problem too, Jack.*

"What are you looking at?"

Her voice was hostile, and I guessed I'd been staring at her too closely, reminding her of what I knew was in the letter, and of the question of the baby itself. Or, excuse me, of her pregnancy. I kept quiet, looked away, determined to use the right language when I talked, as if I were filling out forms for an agency that fed each bite of information into some complicated file that would be checked and rechecked. We finished our dinners and I ordered an ice cream. I offered her some. She waved it away. Her eyes were shallow with dull tiredness, her lips pale.

"I decide." She said this suddenly, with an offhand firmness, very adult. I had expected exactly this, what else? Still, the words knocked through me and for several moments I couldn't take a steady breath. Then I forced my chest to fill.

"Of course you decide," I said, slow. "Just so you know, *that* isn't your only option."

She didn't answer, just folded her arms, stared down at her half-empty cup, drummed her fingers across her sleeves.

"*That?*" she mocked. "An abortion, you mean?"

"What I mean . . ." I tried to get some dignity back, "I'll take care of you. I'll get you through the birth, you know, and afterward I'll take the baby."

She raised her eyes to mine. "You'll what?"

"Adopt it."

She hugged herself tighter and I could tell that tears were pushing behind her eyes. She blinked, put a fist to her cheek. She sat that way a long while without moving, then slowly looked up at me, her eyes puffed and red, her voice ragged.

"You arrogant bitch," she said. "Like I'd give you *my* baby, *mine*?"

The words hung in the air between us, the rectangle of blurred space dividing the sides of the bed where we lay, both awake, staring into the sky of ceiling tiles.

"You don't understand, not yet," I said.

"Yes, I do." Her tone was calm, matter-of-fact. Her self-possession, her lack of fear, her confidence was a wall.

For a while, it stopped me.

"You'd always wonder." I knew where to hit that wall, how to get to her. I kept talking. The sentences tumbled out, solid as stones. "Was it a boy or girl? What sort of personality, what color hair? When was its birthday? You'll find yourself crying, for no reason, on the anniversary of the day you got rid of your baby. You'll hate yourself somewhere, deep inside, nowhere you can reach. You'll have another child, someday, and then you'll know this child was real. Or you won't, like me."

She switched the side lamp on and sat behind the harsh pool of brilliance, where I couldn't see her. I must have dozed off. Next, I heard Marlis putting on her clothes, bottles clinking in the bathroom. The suitcase fell off of its little stand, but I knew she wouldn't go. I counted on my words sinking in. And I was right. The bathroom door shut and locked and soon after I heard her crying. Her weeping sounded like rain beating on the wall in sheets, waves on cold rocks. Her sorrowful voice was someone drowning in it all. Time after time, when the noise receded, I thought of tapping on the door. Then just as I rose a new storm of weeping would start, and I fell back beneath the covers. I must have slept for hours, sunk in the blankness that comes after strong emotion, the distance driving, watching the tar move, the yellow line.

Noise outside our window wakened me. The light in the bathroom was still on. In the parking lot more car doors slammed. A trunk opened. Cans rattled in an ice cooler. A key jiggled in a lock. The door of the room next to ours opened and shut.

A chair fell over. Water poured into the drain. I sat up. I was sleeping in a full-length slip. I put on my trench coat as I got out of bed, pulled the belt tight around me, and stepped into my shoes. I grabbed my purse, opened my door, walked out onto the thin band of sidewalk that ran around the motel courtyard. The wind was cool, fresh with mist, rattling the gutters along the roof. I stood before the door of the next room listening to the blare of the television for several minutes, pushing sleep away. A woman laughed as my hand fell in a sharp knock. At once, the sound lowered, the door opened. I was looking into a shadowed bar of space, and couldn't make out her features.

"Could you please keep the noise down?"

"Fuck no." Her voice rough, good-natured. "I'm partying."

"I'm trying to sleep next door," I said. "I have my sister with me."

"Sister?" There was Marlis, beside her, a drink in her hand. Her knees were locked so she'd stay up. "Your fucking sister? That's what I am?"

The woman completely ignored this.

"You want to party?" she asked me again.

I now expected hostility, even threats, so her pleasant invitation took me by surprise.

"Come on. I only do this every twenty-four years. They dropped me off here, got rid of me. I'm all alone except for your sister, or whatever. She's partying with me."

She stepped back, turned on the lights. Marlis went into the bathroom again. I heard her in there, trying to pretend that she wasn't sick. *Good*, I thought. The woman and I regarded each other. Her yellow-brown hair was permanented, cut in a kinky shag, and her long plain face was young and raw-looking, the makeup smudged off in shiny patches. She waved at a brown plastic motel chair and settled herself, loose limbed. Her feet were bare and she wore a modest purple-brown blouse and tight new jeans.

"I'm out of work," she informed me. "Shit. Can I fix you a screwdriver?" She pulled a jug of orange juice from an ice bucket, poured a glass half full. I watched her tip in the vodka, add a dollop more. I took the glass.

"Actually," I said, staring at the surface. "I don't drink."

"Me neither." She took out a package of cigarettes and began to shake them until one popped free. "Or smoke." She clamped her mouth down and drew one out from the others. The drink tasted greasy and metallic and only slightly cold. I put down the cup. Then I picked it up and drank some more.

"So why is it you only do this every twenty-four years?"

"I'm twenty-four. It's my birthday. What about yours? What do you like to do on your birthday?"

"My husband used to take me out to dinner."

I was beginning to feel ridiculous and yet I had lost my advantage. I was wide awake, too, and listening through the bathroom door for Marlis. I put the glass on the bedside table, and stood up. My coat fell open.

"Nice slip," said the woman. "Where'd your sister go?"

"She's in the bathroom."

Standing up so quickly made me dizzy and I sat back down, held the edge of my chair. "She's pregnant."

"You're kidding."

"Maybe I should get her."

"Yeah."

We sat there, I don't know how long, and then I stood again. The woman got up with me and stood alongside me, looking at the shut door to the bathroom, at the thin frame of light all along the sides.

"Hey," she called, knocking on the hollow wood. "Hey you, in there. Come on out."

There was no answer.

"Maybe we should get the manager," I said. I went hollow inside, weak, fearing suddenly that Marlis had passed out, or worse, fallen, hit her head, slit her wrists, anything that would put my baby in danger. The woman tried the door. It was locked, but the handle was cheap and loose.

"Where's your purse?" she asked, then saw it on the chair and picked it up, took out my wallet.

"Don't worry," she said. "I'm not ripping you off. I just want some form of ID."

She took one of my credit cards and carefully inserted it between the door and the jamb and pulled it up until the latch caught.

I pushed forward, tried to shove her aside, but she just shrugged me off and bent over. Marlis shifted, looked up at us, frowned. She was curled on the floor with all of the towels spread over her. She had used a rolled-up towel for a pillow.

"What do you want?" She looked into the woman's face.

"Are you okay?" said the woman.

"I'm fine," said Marlis. She stood up, shed the towels in a heap. "I was sleeping. I'm pregnant."

The woman nodded, frowning, as if she'd finally taken in the serious information, the pertinent fact. She looked back and forth between the two of us. She said nothing, just walked past me, pulling down her shirt, straightening her hair.

"You two, whatevers, I get it now," she said. "I've heard about these things—women. She's not your sister," the woman pointed at me. "You inseminated her. I've read about this stuff," she paused, looked darkly into the new drink she'd fixed. "You've got to be from down in the Cities. That's where this stuff's happening. Up here we don't have the right equipment. Now you get out of here. Just go do your thing in some other motel room. All by yourself. Let me party in peace, okay?"

Marlis and I went calmly out the door, walking carefully, all of a sudden trying to keep our faces straight. Not to laugh. The woman's assumptions, so hilarious! Unbearable! We got into our room. I heard her door shut, and then the motel and courtyard were quiet again except for us—laughing like we couldn't quit.

Marlis pushed past me, pulled the spread down, jumped into bed still laughing and turned out the light.

"Can you believe it? Oh, God!"

We were overcome. Every time one of us would manage some control the other would say something, low, 'down in the Cities,' or 'You two, whatevers,' and we'd have a fit again.

I was still wearing my trench coat and my shoes. I lay there on top of the covers, shuddering, trying to stop, unable to stop laughing entirely—although after a time we wound down, very slowly, into a state where the laughter bubbled out slower, slower. Maybe an hour passed, maybe it was two. I didn't drift off, even once. I don't think my eyes closed. I listened to Marlis's slow breathing, to the sounds next door, the muted television, then the roaming and the pacing of the woman's stockinged footsteps. A few times, she softly called out. Once, the phone rang. She talked and talked, but her voice wasn't loud enough to make out any words. Morning came on more gradually than I realized it could—dawn seemed to go on for hours. The light in the room was slightly less black and then it was almost gray. Then it was grainy, like a mist, and outlines of the furniture stood clear. When I could see the details of the drawer handles, and the pattern in the paper on the wall, I spoke.

"I'm sorry about last night."

There was no answer, but she stirred.

"It's not that I didn't mean it," I went on. "I'm serious, I've thought it all out. I respect how you feel, too, it's just that, you know, there won't be opportunities like this. I'm here for you. I'll do anything, Marlis, anything for the baby. You don't know how much I wanted one. See, I can't conceive. That's the thing. It won't have to ever know. You can be a secret, or not. Whatever. Marlis?"

"What?" She was groggy, put upon. "What now?"

"I want . . ."

She could hear me.

"I want to hold this baby . . . answer its cry in the middle of the night. I want to name it."

"Don't you ever quit?" She turned, put the pillow over her head. Her voice was muffled, begging, ragged paper.

"Listen to me. This is a chance for both of us. You too. You won't have this on your conscience."

I could feel her working, waking up, her mind gathering. She removed the pillow, which I took as a positive sign.

"Whose goddamn conscience are you talking about?"

She didn't give me a chance to answer. She leaped up, looked down at me where I was lying in my coat and shoes.

"What do you know?"

She lifted her white sweatshirt, punched her own flat-muscled stomach.

"I'm supposed to carry your baby for you? Have it? Have it hate me all its life?"

I shrank away from the strength of her, the anger.

"You're not the one who's scared."

"Yes, I'm scared," I cried, full of emotion, rising.

"You're bullshit!"

"Your mother gave you up," I guessed, on sheer instinct. "You're here because she gave you up. You're the baby. You."

Marlis looked at me, her face whitening and whitening until she was a bloodless vampire grown old, hungry, vulnerable with wanting.

"How would you know anything about anything," she said, soft and weary.

Marlis went down then. She cried, spent herself, cried all through the hours of the early morning, only this time she couldn't move or lock herself away. I was able to grab her, comfort her, press my fingers into her shoulders as she rocked back and forth. I didn't take my hands from her. Her skin grew cold, harsh to the touch. But I didn't move away, not a fraction of an inch, not even when she tried to push me. Not even when the woman next door, now trying to sleep, pounded on the thin wall. I held her down on the floor and kept her arms from thrashing. I stroked her hair and pushed her head back to the carpet when she tried to lift it. As her cries grew in depth and length, harder, softer, shaking her from farther inside, I felt, helplessly, the slow beginning of my joy. I could feel it happen to me the same way that it would happen to Marlis. I could feel it moving, like a sparrow, like a tiny fish, brushing against the inside of my skin. I could feel its hair, soft as the down on Marlis's cheek, and I could feel the numb little starfish hands, the blind fingertips, reaching mine.

§

Candice

*S*o let me tell you. I have to make a kind of admission. That woman's conclusion about us—you know, *lesbians*—it haunted me. I kept on thinking it over and returning to it. First, it was the very idea! Laughable. Then it was upsetting, faintly painful, like an inner mental bruise. I kept avoiding the thought until I realized that I was avoiding it deliberately and the very act of not wanting to get near the topic might mean that it threatened me. Could the whole idea have some weird attraction? Was it weird? I'm from a normal family, whatever that means, but the whole idea, somehow that felt normal too.

Once I thought that way, I started purposefully thinking about the subject as much as I could, whenever it touched my mind, just to see. All at once the question was there so often that I could not avoid it. I became hyper-aware of women, their breasts in their clothing only inches from me, walking by. I thought of their feet, stiff and tortured in pointed shoes or narrow, sensitive, monkeylike feet with long fey toes. Eyes. I wondered what it would be like to look into a woman's eyes, to have her look back at me the same way she would look at a man. It gave me a chill to imagine a woman touching me the way I'd touched Jack, but worse, or better. I could see myself standing before a woman, her face held up to my face. Searching. I could see myself folding my hands beneath her hair as I drew her forward, as my lips traced hers, as our nipples grazed inside our shirts.

I had to stop myself or I'd go further and set a bedroom in focus, a scenario, take off our clothes and then I would be lost as in the depth of my own reflection, on a set of side-by-side infinity mirrors. I thought about women. I thought about Marlis. Not in that way at first, just in a protective way. Possessive maybe. I thought of her as having the baby for both of us. I thought of her somehow as me, as though our bodies had merged already, and I had all of her feelings—morning sickness. I had that! I gained weight. My hair thickened. I felt marvelous, surging hormones. Sympathetic pregnancy. Of course, Marlis wasn't exactly crazy about me getting anywhere near her. I had to pretend to meet her accidentally at her prenatal appointments.

§

The Waiting Room

Candice and Marlis

*C*andice and Marlis recall everything about the maternity waiting room. Hateful—soothing, depressingly familiar, a purgatory of mauve paint and stacks of toy ads and magazines. Bright-eyed infants drooled on glossy covers, stylish blimps posed in maternity getups, quick cooking suggestions blared out, bold, and vague cross-eyed celebrities made calculating confessions. *I don't belong here,* screamed Marlis's inner voice, *no, no, no!* She glared grimly at the other pregnant women, their foolish, floppy-bowed collars and ratty hair, their clownish businesslike waddles and expressionless suspension in time. *No, no, no! I'm not one of you!* But her name would be called, in sequence, just as theirs, and she would push herself out of the padded plastic chair and toddle in to see Doctor Boiseart, who would squeeze a blob of clear jelly onto the violet skin next to her navel, set his microphone on that blob, and move it around until it picked up the ecstatic triple-time thrump of the baby's heart.

Marlis was staring at the pattern of print in a page of her book, and she was trying to deny and ignore the panic and the boredom, when through the waiting room doors walked Candice, whom she'd told to stay away from her.

Marlis's mouth opened, but she didn't tell Candice to go to hell. Candice stopped before her and waited.

"You look good," said Candice.

"Oh, just *blooming*."

Marlis was furious at Candice's black skintight sweater outfit. She would take a little of her stash of Jack's money out of her sock drawer and buy herself an outfit. No, a stroller. She definitely would need a stroller. Confused, she wished for new shoes and envied Candice's accessories. Candice was holding a huge suitcase-square purse that looked chic and official. Probably, thought Marlis miserably, the case was packed with stupid dental records.

Candice sat down across from Marlis and stared calmly into the bumpy weave of the carpet. She kept her eyes fixed for such a long time that Marlis's gaze inevitably followed the invisible beam to the patch—mauve also, like the walls—and took root. Marlis's feet grew hot. At first it was just the callused edges, the hard skin from going barefooted in her childhood, the edges that burned. But then the sinew of her strong arches, the sensitive wells between her toes, the pinched toes themselves, began to throb.

"You," Marlis's voice was low. She scraped the heavy rubber soles of her shoes on the carpet, trying to put out the flames, the sting. "You."

She did not know what else to say, how to put it. Both women looked back at the undistinguished patch of carpet and then, as if their thoughts had woven subtly and invisibly into shared strands, they both rose and regarded each other when the name Marlis Mauser was called.

A bolt of intense nausea shot through Candice and she reached for Marlis's hands, but Marlis quickly hid them in her pockets. She stared at Candice, tired, her face eager, too thin in the cheeks but clear. Her features were worn and her eyebrows, black and emphatic. Her eyes were quiet. She was so lovely, thought Candice, so quietly and definitively *lovely*, although there were dark smudges underneath her eyes and her lips were carved thin, very pale. Marlis shook her shoulders in a careless shrug, accepting Candice's presence. The two walked across the floor of the waiting room together and then vanished, with a nurse, into a little door at the end of the hall.

The perineum irons out and then the baby's head shows, you puuuuuush, you puuuuuush, and then the crown appears, just like through a little turtleneck. See here?

The Lamaze instructor was pushing the large head of a realistic plastic baby doll through a tight little garment, pulling the turtleneck down evenly around it. Marlis sat cross-legged on a square pillow, vast in men's sixty-inch waisted overalls. Man Mountain, the all-star wrestler, wore them once, she was sure. She'd found them in a Goodwill bin. She had persuaded Jack to pay her tuition to night casino school. *It's either that or alimony*, she threatened. Dealing cards was something that she could do, even big as she was. Her hands were already quick and limber from the piano. Her hands were marvelous. Good with cards. Candice admired her hands, gave her a topaz ring. Jack visited her every morning now. He stopped in on his way to work, and looked stricken at her growing size. She lived right near Island Park. Her thoughts veered off—wouldn't it be perfect, she could let the baby swim in the wading pool there. But wait, Candice wanted to keep the baby—that's how it was supposed to work! During those last few weeks, Marlis moved in a dream occasionally turned nightmare—she was holding someone infinitely dear in her arms. The doll melted. She watched her baby strut into the shallow blue of the park pool. He vanished. If only she could lose consciousness for a month or so, have the baby and be done with it. Not go through labor, not hear its first cry—the thing she dreaded more than anything else.

Candice leaned over, supported Marlis, helping her practice her squatting. The muscles in Marlis's back strained. Her legs had weakened, her hip joints loosened. She was monumental, grand, an overstated statue, still her hair was combed and sprayed into a pretty French twist, her face was delicate, smooth, the dark eyebrows plucked to a perfect shape, and angry.

The two women are sitting at the secondhand table in Marlis's apartment, eating bread. They have a new-baked loaf between them. They tear apart the rye with dreamy fingers, wiping the soft interior, the magic crust, each scrap across a thick roll of whitish, warm, unsalted sweet butter. The oil spreads up their fingers, cuffed wrists, the corners of their mouths, their gleaming lips, their faces, shining. Marlis's stark-boned and pleasant, her neck muscular, hair an impatient loop. She eats efficiently, but stops, toppling sideways in laughter.

Marlis groans, her voice choking.

"Stop!"

They are talking about how this mood disorder thing was supposed to be Marlis's problem, but she feels good now. She doesn't have that fury that just takes over. She is so cheerful, thinks it's the soothing effect of hormones. They talk about the father of the baby. How Jack is acting shattered and pleased, all at once, working his crews double overtime and every weekend. With each wipe of butter life seems more hilarious and shocking and their unhappiness together seems warm, cozy, complete.

"Oh God!" Marlis screams. "Oh God! I'm tearing!"

Marlis is in pain, terrible and surprising pain. They told her about hard work. Discomfort. This is not discomfort! She is so confounded at this that when the contractions stop she is overcome with hysterical fits of laughter. For the first two hours, half a lifetime ago, she was bored and told the nurses she wanted Pitocin to speed things up. Now things are going a thousand miles a minute and she's dazzled. She's going deeper, trying not to fall apart before the next round.

"No, no, no!" she bellows. Then there is an inchoate scream that turns in her ears to yodeling trills and makes weird melody of what the stiff black pinchers are doing to her.

Candice tries to maintain her professional demeanor, but the sight of Marlis in pain shakes her. Candice roughly pushes a nurse aside and holds her own hands firm on Marlis's shoulders.

A nervous smear of a grin wipes itself across the nurse's face, and as she leaves, as Doctor Boiseart arrives, the nurse shrugs and lifts her brows. Marlis is making dog sounds, woofing earnestly with Candice. They are staring at each other, looking down deep into each other's eyes, barking. Woof! Woof! Woof! The doctor checks Marlis, trying to be gentle. Marlis plants her foot in his face, cracks her heel into his jaw sideways. Woof! He staggers against a different nurse, just entering her shift, and catches at her hands. This competent and quiet woman leads him out the door.

"Drugs!" Candice shrieks after him.

"Where are they?" She glares at Doctor Boiseart when he returns, two contractions later. Marlis's face gleams with sweat, her eye makeup is smeared, her lips raw, dangerous.

"Not to worry," says the doctor in his most soothing voice. "She's well along, it won't take long now. I like to follow the patient's instructions and Marlis here"—he smiles at Marlis, straining, face deepening to maroon, veins popping in her neck, teeth gnashing—"Marlis here stated she wanted natural childbirth—"

"Waaaow! WaaaOW!"

"I'm here."

Candice has Marlis's hands in hers. She is holding her shoulders, her head in a headlock, she is breathing with her, puffing madly. Steam engine screaming, then puffing again, they make it all the way to the top and then slide down. Limp as a fish, eyes rolled back in her skull, Marlis rests.

"Okay."

Candice grabs the front of Doctor Boiseart's hospital scrubs. Her arms are skinny, but the muscles are hard as looped wires. "Okay, you jerk-off." She pushes her face into his bland, concerned, surprised face. "You get the *epidural now or I'll kill you with my bare hands.*"

"Calm down. You're very very upset," says Doctor Boiseart. "Let me talk to Marlis. Let me hear what she says. Let me go. Please."

Candice releases the doctor, dusts off her hands, and they both bend down to Marlis, looking full into her face. The doctor has her wrist in his hand, his finger on her pulse, his voice is very quiet. The baby's heart monitor is fine, normal, spewing out a computerlike machine beside them.

"Marlis, Marlis?"

Marlis's eyes open. She licks her chapped lips. Her gaze will not focus.

"Marlis, you appear to be somewhat —"

Marlis surges, whipping free of the doctor, and then she's banging up and down as if a giant hand has tossed her. Side to side. Her fist jabs, an undercut, and her muscled arms whirl. For the space of this contraction there is chaos in the room. Stainless-steel basins fly, rubber tubing, carts bang against the walls, as though a poltergeist has taken over. Candice hops back and forth like a cricket, close but out of range. Doctor Boiseart, flung aside like a rag doll, bounds back to support Marlis.

When the contraction is over, he gestures to the nurse, to Marlis. He walks out the door.

"Oh, no you don't!"

Candice shrieks, leaps across the spilled water pitcher, ice bucket, receiving towels. She slips, falls full across him, and then, in the sudden cessation of space between Marlis's contractions, she speaks violently and critically as she presses a small yellow card into his hand.

"My attorney's card."

Doctor Boiseart waves the card off and backs firmly out of the door. Just outside, his instructions can be heard — tense, rapid, calm.

Marlis has been crying for weeks. It doesn't seem possible to Candice that a human body is capable of manufacturing such a vast supply of tears. Marlis won't see Jack. She won't sign papers to give up the baby. She won't do anything she was supposed to do, of course. Candice has moved into the apartment to take care of Marlis and the baby. She has canceled her appointments and taken a week's vacation in order to watch over Marlis, who stays in her room or wanders, simpleminded, clunking, still soft with pregnancy, up and down the short hallway, up and down, back and forth, hair matted in strings, face savage and bewildered, rocking the baby. From time to time, she pauses at a wall and shakes herself like a big mastiff shedding rain. She starts moving again, tears streaming, makes her way to the kitchen.

"It is just postpartum blues," says Candice, but she's brought Marlis back to her psychiatrist. Candice keeps the baby in her arms, close, rocking him softly until he relaxes in sleep and she can put him down, moving her hands away stealthily, as if he's a hair-trigger bomb.

It is night. Candice hears the thump of Marlis's feet hitting the floor in the next room. She hears the drag of her steps, like Frankenstein, and Marlis's exhausted sighs. Her sighs are steam pipes in the old third-floor ballroom apartment. Her sighs seem to move through the walls, streaming and evaporating, shedding heat. In a bank of the full moon's light, Marlis ambles the hall and pauses in the kitchen, to cough, to groan, to wipe the tears back over her face into her hair. Her hair has been washed over and over in her own tears. Her face, too, is shiny and bathed. Her skin glistens as she opens the refrigerator, its yellow glow startling and false. She bends into the humming interior and pokes at a carton of yogurt, a block of cheese. She draws back her hand and turns. The refrigerator door drifts shut and she stands barefoot in men's pajamas, looking at the mopboards.

Candice steps slowly closer to Marlis and holds her arm with both hands. She remembers her grandmother's admonition. She's heard that when people sleepwalk they are searching for their souls. It is dangerous to wake a sleepwalker. With extreme gentleness, Candice leads Marlis down the dim corridor and back into her room with the green-and-rose-flowered wallpaper. With a formal movement, restrained and decisive, as if they were about to waltz, Candice turns Marlis around at the side of her bed and helps her sit, eases the exhausted woman backward, onto the pillows. In the room, there is a golden-shaded lamp and it is on, left burning all night, and in the light Marlis's high-boned face is serene and full, her lips curving in a sleep smile. Looking straight at Candice, her eyes slightly unfocused, she unbuttons her pajama top and lets the shirt glide away, crumpling around her waist. Her breasts are ivory and pink, firm as marble. Blue veined. Candice looks away, but then she looks back, her gaze drawn up and around the curve of her breasts to Marlis's face. The two regard each other in the comforting light.

Neither dares speak — Candice to ask if Marlis is awake, Marlis to ask if this is wrong. So they say nothing and between them the light falls, like a spell, so warm although the room is cold. Candice, in her silk bathrobe, feels weightless, uncanny, as though she is now reading the end of a mystery. She knew the clues and she felt them, there all along, hints and outlines, but each separate emotional step had to be taken before this moment could arrive. It is worked out in advance, then, and it is completely right for her to lean forward and hold Marlis's face and bend into the tangle and swoop of both of their hair.

The first kiss tells everything. If you are lost in that moment, then you will not find yourself again for many years. If you are unshocked, if your mind keeps clicking, if you can think what to do with your teeth, your tongue, then you'll be fine. It won't hurt, not really, whatever happens. This was not the case with either of them: from the first touch it seemed to them that they had crossed and were held within that electrical field — a strip of bronze grass — that exists between the bodies of women. They were suspended in the fascination of their own likenesses at first — how soft their faces were, unbearded, unshaved, how when their breasts touched Marlis's slowly streamed. When Candice lowered her hips onto Marlis's they began to laugh together for no reason except surprise at what violent pleasure this gave them. They rolled over, began to touch each other quickly, slowly, curiously.

While making love, it did not occur to Marlis, at least, that they were doing anything that fit a category, anything that had a name. Her body seemed so powerful it was like a physical shock to her. It was for both of them as though they were inventing each gesture and act, out of nothing and as they went along. But as they went into it, and they did not stop to eat or sleep or do the dishes or answer the phone or go to work, as they stayed in the metal grasses and occasionally bathed or dressed each other, took care of the baby, settled into bed only to begin touching once more, they sometimes talked dreamily of what all of this might mean. Implications drifted over Candice and disappeared—she remembered vaguely that she had once regarded what seemed entirely normal, now, as absurd, foreign, freakish. The baby lay between the two of them—he was a lovely little baby, with fine long fingers and dark coppery hair.

The afternoons came on slow as honey and the last fierce beams of light struck their bodies with uncapped radiance. Sometimes they slept molded together in a liquid shape and sometimes they lay carefully on either side of the bed, hands gravely clasped, their individual thoughts latticing up the walls.

§

Rotating Wild

JANUARY 6, 5:52 A.M.

Eleanor

"*S*o!" Eleanor spoke in a piercing clinical tone. "You took control of Marlis. Put her under your wing. Likely. Likely." She drummed her gloved fingers together. "I think not. Rather, it was for *you*, Candice."

"Who cares," said Candice, her voice tired with cold, slurring with confusion.

"Surely," said Eleanor sharply. The dangerous exhaustion in Candice's tone decided Eleanor. She would use the bond she had sensed between the two women in the backseat to goad them both to consciousness.

"I detest sexual hypocrisy! You were gay all along, Candice. Frigid with Jack—don't ask me how I know. And now you pretend your love affair is all about the baby, when it's about *you*.

"You're crazy about Marlis. You love her," said Eleanor, her voice triumphant and malicious. Candice did not respond.

"Say it!"

"I'm crazy about Marlis," said Candice with a quiet, sub-dued definition. "I love her very much."

"For herself," said Eleanor.

"For herself."

Marlis began to laugh in a dangerous, abrupt way.

"You better shut up, Eleanor."

"And you," Eleanor turned on her, "so passive in all of this. Manipulated? Not exactly. Parasitic, that's more accurate. You're a sort of nematode."

Eleanor's voice became detached, as though she were observing microscopic activity. "A nematode gets inside of its host and reproduces with itself, grows two sets of sexual organs. It could be called the most self-absorbed creature on earth. That's you, basically, crawling into the warm space of a relationship and stealing the potential between two humans to reproduce."

At first Marlis said nothing. The silence lasted so long that it became a tension. However, when she finally spoke it was in a normal voice. "I suppose you're right, Eleanor, being as you're this big intellect. It's time to clean the tailpipe out, though, your turn."

"I did already." Eleanor would have pressed the point but her righteousness had turned to stark jealousy. She understood that she had gone too far. The women prepared, formed a link of their hands. Eleanor was already warmly dressed, but in addition, she now put on every extra piece of Jack's discarded clothing and stuffed her boots with old socks, greasy rags, and newspapers. She wound the space blanket over her head and edged out into the press and bite of the wind, holding on to Marlis, feeling her way along the edge of the hood. The snow had drifted smoothly over the front of the car, providing insu-lation, and a well had formed just behind the back fender so that the exhaust pipe was left in a natural empty spot that only periodically had drifted in and then blown clear. They would most certainly have suffocated, otherwise. Still, it was a good thing that Marlis made her suggestion, for as it turned out snow had once again been driven into the opening of the pipe and the carbon monoxide might have killed them when the engine was next turned on. Eleanor managed to dislodge the snow, and then, still gripping Marlis's mitted palm, she yanked to indicate that they should all collapse themselves, holding fast, back through the window.

Up until that moment the wind had blown with steady but unparticular force against them all, but suddenly, and with one savage gust, it seemed to seize on Eleanor. She wrestled herself toward Marlis and held on tighter, but the air tore at them from unpredictable directions. Marlis's arm was wrenched, for Dot's grip on her other hand was stubborn, and she was trapped on that side, held absolutely fast, while she tried to keep her twisting purchase. The tremulous hatred that had gripped her heart now burst through her in radiating bands. She opened her mouth to call but the air was solid with sheer blowing snow. A mouthful of ice stopped her tongue, her voice was lost. She braced herself and pulled as hard as she could, but almost tenderly, with sudden joy, she felt a wickedness assail the muscles in the arm that worked the hand that held Eleanor's.

Marlis held her ground, clenched her eyes shut, ordered strength to her hands, attempted to grip harder, but, in clenching down, the force of her own goodness ebbed entirely. Marlis realized that instead of holding tighter, she was letting go. She willed herself not to. Impossible that she could do this, she would not, she couldn't, she must not . . . but the pleasurable image of their unclasping fingers formed in her head. Marlis's hand arched open, a sudden spring, and Eleanor Mauser whirled into the white night.

Momentous freedom. In spite of what she knew had happened to her, Eleanor at first felt the numb bliss of a dream flyer. She zipped end over end. Headfirst. She spun like a top and tumbled along the pointed tips of drifts, light as a balled dry weed, a Russian thistle. In her layers of down, her jackets and shirts and socks, she bounced harmlessly off solid gusts. It was a funhouse ride, nothing to fear, no obstacle now. She traveled in the second circle of complete white darkness and she was not afraid. Not cold even. Her attempts to steer herself, movements that were dancelike, repetitive, kept her warm enough, and her collection of clothing preserved whatever heat she generated, so that truly, through the nothingness, she felt certain that she would outlast the storm and calmed herself still further with the surprising comforts of her situation.

Bouncing, tumbling, she sped on frozen ground, drift-tip to tip. This could go on, and on, and on, she oddly thought. She might fly indefinitely, until dawn, the end of the blizzard. Surely then she would right herself and walk across the glittering new landscape to the nearest marker. A comfortable weariness held her, but the exhaustion slowly became a familiar state of being and she didn't stop moving. She continued, warming to a trance.

Death may be near, she thought, rousing herself to go on, to walk, to keep moving on and on through the night. Perhaps, in fact, here was the beginning of her life, events unreeling, flooding, in such colors, under such strong lights. Perhaps this was the actual substance of her existence and all that she had lived up until that moment was the dream that the woman dreamed, the one who now rose and settled with such fervor in the wind, curled like a shell inside a shell, still warm in the roaring blackness, safe, rotating wild in the blank new elements.

The two other women strained to drag Marlis back into the car. Several times, she broke away and tried to bound back into the wind, but the air was springy as a rubber wall and tore the breath from her mouth.

"I've got to get her!" Marlis gasped out.

Dot held her fast, straddling her to keep her down.

"You'd never find her."

Marlis gave up with such easy satisfaction that Dot felt her own heart sag with responsibility. She pushed open the car door, and they ventured out again into the stinging blur. She groped around and around the sides of the car, hoping Eleanor had fallen close to the automobile or been driven against it. But nothing. Pushing back into the car, finally, Dot huddled in the front seat and tried to block out Marlis. But Marlis continued to talk faster, louder, in an alternately pitiful and furious voice, blaming and congratulating herself, uttering incoherent explanations.

"You didn't let her go on purpose," Dot said at last, trying to calm her and shut her up.

"Nematode, my ass!" said Marlis, indignant. "Of course I did."

PART FOUR

Balancing Tricks

§

A Conversation

Eleanor

*E*leanor stumbled, fell, picked herself up, ran smack into something. She saw stars, bursting planets. An array of fiery atoms shot full speed across her vision and then an arresting light shone out. She blinked, shuddered her way out of a black, lightless well, groundwater draining. Once again she was a blown bubble, comfortable and free, bobbing to the surface. The snow parted. Sunlight glittered on her eyelids. Warmth broke across her throat. The light intensified into white shock, emanated from an indefinite source. It vibrated all around Eleanor, and then it seemed to shrink away, to withdraw into the white shadows. Following it, dazzled, she saw that the light had spread from beneath the folds of a cloak that now recast itself with quiet seams across that radiance. The brilliance was contained, but still leaked in small beams from the little rents and openings in the hood and the habit of the uninvited presence.

It's the hitchhiker, thought Eleanor, remembering the person who had slept behind the tire, with the unused jack, in silence. She got out and followed me, to save me!

Now Eleanor watched the personage yawn, stretch bent arms out in incremental creaks. The stranger raised herself and fell into step beside Eleanor. Gripping the taller woman's shoulder, she spoke in a thin whine.

"Beautiful and blessed child," she rebuked. "It is hard to be so old, hard to be so weak. At one time, I would have taken up the paddle to the butter churn and given you a whack."

Eleanor's mouth went stone dry, her throat hurt, she coughed and shuddered, aching with shock. *Could it be?* She leaned closer and took the nun's arm. The wind grabbed them and they spun and sped along the frozen ground.

"I have been traveling, dear Eleanor," said the nun in the shifting light. "I have been on a long and interesting journey. It was not, as you might think, a pilgrimage, for I had no destination in mind when I began and none presented itself en route. It is enough to say, I hope, that I find myself possessed of the holy fire and must go wherever it burns."

Where's my notebook? thought Eleanor. *You don't have it! Memorize each word!*

"You have spoken of love, I have heard it all," the nun went on. "You and your sisters are blind women touching the vast body of the elephant, each describing the oddness beneath the surface of her hands. Love is brutalizing, a raw force, frail as blossoms, tough as catgut wire. Lost, found, sprinkled with the wild sweet oils, love changes and is immutable. You have all been students of habitual, everyday contentment. You have all known the deep and twisting nights, the scarves of the magician threaded through the body, changing colors, knotted and then separate. And, too, you know and understand the love a child bears its mother, its father, a parent bears its child. It is a love that is no other thing but pure salvation, and by it, Christ's balancing trick was inspired and foretold."

"What balancing trick?" cried Eleanor, shaking harder.

In this dangerous cold the brain worked feverishly, she told herself. People saw things, apparitions—this was one. She feared her mind had flipped open like a lurid jewel box and shown her the false, brilliant colors of the first inviting hallucinations that signaled an ornate mind-death. Eleanor attempted to right herself, to seize her thoughts from wandering, for she could feel sense dissipating and unrealities replacing all she trusted in her perceptions.

"Sister . . ." Eleanor stuttered, lapsing to incoherence. In her dulled limbs and brain, in her frightened mystery, she was now beginning to understand that the presence of the nun—vaporized last summer practically before her own eyes, after all—signaled that she herself was frozen dead. The vision flooded Eleanor with fear and yet, since she possessed a steely, rational aspect as well, she attempted to control her terror and to seize upon the moment that was hers alone. If by any chance this was an actual saintly appearance, then she, after all, was surely the reason that Sister Leopolda had elected to pay a visit—if this was a visit—if this was no hallucination—and so for the purposes of her own study she made a supreme effort and addressed the nun in a voice only slightly numbed with shock.

"What balancing trick, did you say, of Christ?"

Leopolda's answer, glass shards, cracked through the driving snow.

"Why, his trick on the cross!"

Her laughter trembled in a howl of wind and stilled Eleanor's heart. It seemed that she herself was hovering in space—her body light, her senses far-reaching, her thoughts huge. Her attention was entirely fixed on the presence, on Leopolda. And now, as the old woman stilled her laughter and regarded the younger with an enveloping look, peace descended. It was as though the two of them were locked together in a vault of serenity and warmth. The blackness outside their cave deepened. Within, pale light leaked from the folds of Leopolda's habit, glowing up into her starved features from beneath, but gently, so that the old woman seemed weighted with a sad mirth. The sudden odor of mock orange, an elusive spring drift of fragrance rose, as from a crushed handful of flowers, and Eleanor leaned nearer.

"Balancing tricks," Sister Leopolda wheezed meditatively. "We have no need of tricks. We are held upon the cross by our own desires."

"What do I do?" Eleanor mumbled, her lips, her whole face stiffening. She was losing consciousness, but she was not alarmed anymore. "What do I do?"

"Pull forth the nails," the nun said with slow kindness to Eleanor, ". . . *only pull forth the nails*."

It seemed until that moment Eleanor's hands tightened around their desperation, their fever to hold, their grasping sorrow. Now her fingers opened and a sensual relaxation loosened her entire body so she drifted in the old nun's presence on a wholly delicious wave. Drifted forward. She was still moving through the crisis, through the blizzard. There was a question in her mind whether she was dead now, and she knew if so that death itself was an orgasmic cessation, a deliverance. In another way, she observed with stoical sharpness, her physical limitations were in themselves a form of undisclosed suffering, and always had been. Once out of her body, she understood how narrow was her lifelong confinement. And yet, it had been good, her body, a shelter. This was quite another marvel entirely, though, this freedom combined of flying, swimming, floating—all weightless actions.

"Isn't it interesting," she remarked to the nun, maneuvering in liquid space, "that all along we actually know in our bones how to fly?"

"It isn't floating that we do in the womb," the other woman answered. "We are flying those first five months, swooping and diving. It is during the last months that we learn what it is to be held too close, imprisoned, confined. And then comes the frightful journey of our birth. Oh, what this teaches us—do you suppose any child is ever born unmarked?"

"Desire," Eleanor meditated. "The mark we are born with? Love?"

"The stigma, the blessing."

"Lace hearts, black roses. Chopin!" Eleanor cried out rebelliously into the night.

"You want nothing of the sort," the nun admonished her. "You want abiding rightness, an assurance of your course. You will *not* find all that in a man. No, that imaginary conviction is a cross that will break his back."

"Abiding rightness," Eleanor repeated.

"Just as his belief will break yours," the nun replied. "Now hold on to this low branch."

Trees donated by the Lion's Club International, Fargo Chapter, saved Eleanor. The first one she clung to she never wanted to leave. She thought it was a shrub, a windbreak shrub, for it was young and covered up to just below the crown. The next she was blown toward, in a line. Just the same. And then the next, when she got to that, the air howling in her ears like a thousand jets. Holding on, Eleanor realized that she was following a row of trees and that these were spaced too far apart to be a windbreak. She remembered that the trees led down the brand-new concrete gutters and curbs in one long swoop to Hector International Airport itself—warm, cozy, bold, the doors a salvation of glass and polished steel. She touched the next tree, blew past the fifth, but then made a half dozen more and eventually, stepping easily over the arm of the short-term parking gate, lunged toward the temporary loading zone.

She blasted forward over the remaining drifts and landed in a swoop of snowless concrete at the doorway. She threw herself at the transparent sheet, pounding, and shouted though she had no voice, until she fell through one automatic door left to open suddenly as if she'd screamed sesame. There was a sudden quiet into which her voice struck like a bell, drawing, from within the airport carcass, a flashlight beam and a watchman and a stranded rental car agent in a green vest who rushed, questioning the odd sound, still carrying hot coffee and magazines.

§

The Tale of the Unknown Passenger

JANUARY 6, 6:37 A.M.

*T*he hitchhiker crept from the back of the car with stealthy agility and crouched in the passenger's seat cradling Dot's hunched form. He opened the car window, tested her breathing, realized she was in jeopardy. Pinching her nose shut and cupping her jaw, he sealed her mouth with his and blew slowly to resuscitate her, heavily, twice. He blew again, again. At last, Dot started, stirred as though in a dream and then took a deep sickening breath that restored her.

The other two women — Candice and Marlis — were bound close and breathing normally beside a drafty window in the backseat. Once slightly roused, they stirred, but then plunged back into an exhausted, healing sleep. With a thick, tensile thumb, the stranger flicked the metal catch of a disposable lighter and peered into Dot's eyes. The flame caught in the fathomless iris, frail and stiff, and the hitchhiker snapped the light out, then settled back. Still holding Dot, he spoke.

"You're okay, I think. There was a funnel in the snow, that happens. The stuff must be coming into the driver's seat from under the car."

Opening the door, he disappeared for a long five minutes, digging snow away from the tailpipe once more. When he dove back into the car, gasping, Dot slid her quilted body, heavy and cold with longing, against Gerry's. He was still dressed in the same thick blanketlike rags and cowl he'd worn when Dot bought a whole pizza for him back in the bar. As he warmed, slowly, Gerry shifted closer, smelling of snow, wool, fried onions, heat. In spite of their endless separations and sorrows, life surged up, between their hands, then, amazing them both. They drew closer, hope rising between them. Here was one time, out of time. Before and after this moment days and weeks would pass. She would be without Gerry once more. But she saw that if he managed to stay hidden, there would always be these times where nothing else existed—no mistakes, no laws, no possible guilt or innocence.

Out of nowhere, your love arrives. His eyes are on you from the moment he enters your body, though it is dark, so dark you can't see but only breathe each other's breath. It is like it always was and was always supposed to be. Together, you are singing a very personal interior silent song. Moving. And he is alive, so alive in the wrecked cold. And you also, in the tension. Whatever happens. However long it lasts. A plate. A silver fork. Here is another piece of wedding cake you never got. A white wedge of happiness.

"Plan worked too good, really," Gerry said afterward, holding Dot close. "The damn snow was supposed to let up out there by now."

"I hope you made me pregnant," she whispered. "I love you."

Gerry lowered his forehead to hers, closed his eyes. They sat in the red Explorer mind to mind. Into Gerry's heart came the melancholy and extravagant wish that the half inch of bone between them would conduct their thoughts so that he wouldn't really be alone in the cage of his body. Though he'd long since come to terms with his own mind in solitary, this closeness with Dot could still panic him with hope. That in spite of everything they'd make love more often than once every ten years. That he'd smell the old smells and walk the old earth. That he'd hold their daughter, touch her hair before she grew up entirely. Ask forgiveness of his mother. Drink an ice-cold beer. Ride a horse. Swim.

"I feel like I'm swimming," he said.

Cold stabbed wherever their two bodies were not touching and although they huddled close their feet and hands were losing sensation. Gerry kicked to circulate his blood and Dot rubbed her fingers against his, hard, as if to strike more sparks. They were shivering.

"Those painkillers work?" she said.

"I was high back there, sleeping. Good thing because I was bent double, size of a tire. Every so often I tuned in to see if you'd say anything about me, but mostly I was out of it. I was worrying, too. I mean, I know Lyman went back out with the car for Lipsha, and that little kid, but . . . "

"Baby," said Dot.

"Okay, baby." Gerry's voice shook. "I'm sure he did. He was going to. But I still wish I knew for sure what happened."

"I know he did," said Dot, with too much conviction. "I know he did."

"Of course he did," said Gerry.

The two did not speak now, because they really weren't sure what had happened and the prospect of something going wrong was too much to fully take in, the uncertainty. After a while, Dot pulled her parka tight around her, licked her dry lips. Burning. Tears ached. She slid her arm past Gerry and started the car and the heater again. There was so much despair in her that she almost preferred to freeze and go numb. As the engine rumbled and the warm air revived them, she worked at a beaded orange and white ring and finally pressed the key to her apartment into Gerry's palm.

Blizzard Night

Jack

*J*ack unwedged the invoice crammed against the hasp of the garage door's lock, and slipped back into the failing gray light of his hideout. His breath cracked into the shell, the empty icebox of his chest. He paused, breathing painfully, and drew energy from his plan. During his frantic escape from helping hands in the Amtrak parking lot and the street beyond—where the car had shrugged him off into the arms of stupefied strangers—his brain kept figuring.

Jack's mental index placed the older of the two men who stole Candice's car with the baby strapped into the backseat. Jack had seen the driver's face flashing by in profile, his blunt nose and famous eyes. Gerry Nanapush and no mistake. Jack knew enough about the whole situation to understand the direction the car would ultimately head. Right where he would. Toward the home reservation and beyond, to Canada. Due north.

Jack would be well along on the tail of the car, he hoped,

before the police. His plan connected. In this gathering colli-
sion of weathers, there was only one way to get through on the
roads. Snowplow. Jack grabbed the sleeping bag from his
office, strode directly to the helm of the company's biggest
machine. It was huge, scarred, yellow-blue with an angled
blade before and a flare orange triangle on its blunt tail. He
hoisted himself into the cab and punched the starter, then set
his fingers on the bar of the garage door opener clipped to the
visor. He let the engine warm as the door opened, but the cold
inside the building wasn't bad. The engine didn't kill or even
miss. Outside, the sky looked pre-storm low. The wind was
moody and a shade too warm to hold back moisture. Jack put
the plow in gear, lifted the blade, slowly pulled out, shut the
garage door behind him, and took the street with a hollow clatter and bounce.

The wind was choppier now and fistfuls of ice struck the
windshield—the sidewalks were nearly empty. Halogen streetlights stuttered on as he reached each corner, shedding a
ghostly comfort. In the deep blue-white suspension of the
stormy dusk the situation seemed almost simple—there was
just Jack, the snowplow, and then the car outside somewhere
traveling fast, before him like a star. The hidden will be drawn
to the hidden, the secret the secret, the one the one. He was
sure he'd find them even though the how of finding was a long
shot.

One harm, one fear, another and another, piled on the next
in a tangle of his thoughts. Still, with placid authority, he
began to shovel his way through the streets of Fargo, toward
the interstate, toward the fastest route north. Once, the blade
slammed down and wouldn't move, soldered by a frozen mor-
tise of mud. Jack got out and carefully de-iced and chipped at
the mechanism with a chisel and then loosened it with blobs of
cold oil. He hoisted himself back into the cab and started out
again, into the gleaming vortex. The side streets were blue
holes of underwater calm. Where the pavement was cleared
his blade struck a fierce spume of sparks as he scraped along
into the night. Taking action in itself lifted some of Jack's anx-

iety, and he gathered and hardened his determinations about him.

The cab warmed, bringing out the odor of sweat and grease and clean dirt—that and the acrid smoke of oil burning off the engine filled Jack with familiar comfort. *You fuck up everything you touch*, Candice had once said to him, in fury, *You're, like, Anti Midas. Everything you touch turns to shit!* She had been brokenhearted when he accidentally killed her dog, but it was a goddamn freak occurrence! And the three of them had been careless anyway, Jack, Candy, and the dog. Really, it was the dog's fault! It was all situational, uncanny, how he got himself into these messes. Jumping in with both feet and suddenly over his head. One thing led to the next—for instance, this was where he found himself, logically, after letting his house burn down around him: he had hidden out, hog-tied a nanny, lost his son. Now he was out in the middle of a blizzard. Heading north. Trying to save a baby he'd been too stubborn and blind to claim when that could have made a big difference in all of their lives.

He thought of the bedroom, the revelation about his two former wives. Sleeping together in the house he had once shared with Candice! Somewhere inside he'd known it all along but hadn't had the guts to acknowledge truth. Now truth seemed easier than the results of self-deception.

You want to be together? Why the hell not?

He could see himself saying that to Marlis and Candy and even meaning it. He hadn't wanted to consider the obvious—that his two wives had given up on him, and on men in general, preferring each other. That had been his secret fear. Them together. A direct hit! And yet, how could he blame them? He hadn't managed to treat either of the two women right. Why shouldn't he let them just exist, have a little goddamn joy? Once you got used to the idea. He tried to think like a big man, generous, although it hurt his brain. So his son would grow up around a double set of gorgeous breasts— once precious to Jack, now breasts that lived proudly, on their own terms, with other breasts. *Fine, okay, and if I'm not an asshole when he's little and cute and if he's really my son, which he is, he'll give them such hell once he's a teenager that they'll beg me to take him off their hands.*

Find him, first. Jack nodded into the blurred side mirror. Projecting crazily past the moment was a common failing of his, yes, a feature of his own personality he'd become too familiar with since his troubles. The fact that he himself had put the baby in jeopardy was hard to accept. Next, he might be wrong. Heading north might be the wrong idea, the wrong direction. Still, where else could Gerry go?

Jack was now beginning to see, just catching at the design of his life. Bits and pieces of understanding he had carefully collected and hidden from himself were magically assembling. At last, he understood the shape of what other humans felt about their children. Protective love—it rose up in him like a clear storm. It felt like bubbles, choking him from the inside out. In the grip of frustrated panic, he pounded the seat beside him with a fist, hugged the wheel, promised not to rest, not to cease.

The snow fell, the snow sifted down. Upon a hidden shelf underneath his deepest heart a tiny vial of hope. Jack turned onto the interstate, the gears in amazed complaint, bounced the margin, and then edged out to plow a path for himself as the snow came on and came on. Even with all of his lights blazing he had trouble seeing the road, yet he kept on. Calmly, he paced the big machine north, waiting for the car to appear. Candice's car had snow tires, front wheel drive, and Jack thought that Gerry Nanapush could make it through the weather he was encountering so far, though slowly and with some difficulty. He watched the breakdown lane, just in case they decided to pull over and wait it out. But no car was stuck there, yet, and only dolphin swoops of drifts had collected, ridges, ribbons that his blade divided.

Behind him, headlights showed. Way far back but speeding to his wake. Not bad, he thought. Somebody balanced on his cleared path, on his trail. He could, of course, make out only the glare. It blinded him when he moved his head toward the mirror. Not the police, not probably. Not a big car either. Midsize, like Candy's. A little rowboat bobbing in the wake of a massive tug. It occurred to Jack that if they'd been slowed, if Gerry had done something to evade the police, if there was some reason they got hung up, then the car behind him could be the car he was looking for. He peered back, wondered. If he stopped, would the small car stupidly pass him? What then? He might put them in danger. If only he could get a closer look, identify the car. Both vehicles surged forward, forward, but in slow motion now. Jack ground nearly to a halt as the plow slammed through a harder course of blown snow. Wall after wall. The car rode behind, unswerving, a little minnow. Jack felt tender toward it, anxious.

After that sudden Easter blizzard more than a decade ago this rough winter weather always filled him with a low ache. He felt it now, the bloom of loss. With the odd jab of pity for the car and fear for his son came the memory of that old blizzard night with thoughts like whispered asides. He'd forgotten so much about June—everything, he hoped sometimes. And then, out of nowhere, one detail would surface. Menthol smoke. Her hair like a wave drifting over the back of his hand. A physical intelligence in the way she moved, her hips. Once, he recalled her oval fingernails, the pink polish on them, chipped. She had a doorknob in her purse, gave it to him, laughing. Another time he remembered her eyes following his fingers, counting his money. And the first kiss—bleary, in front of a bar full of strangers, the sweetness of a cream dessert on her careful blotted lips. By now, he had probably remembered everything, every stored detail, and still it was not enough. Not enough to change her mind, her direction, to blow her off course.

Get off my tail, he wanted to say to her, *quit following me*. But her ghost was sad and calm, hanging on with long fingernails like silver hooks. In spite of all of his other wives, he'd stayed married to a ghost. Her haunting was simple. Repressed hunger in the way she cut the steak. Jack remembered whenever he cut his. Her smile, girlish and desperate, gleamed out when another woman tipped her face back, dancing through the scarves of smoke. If he had gone after her and brought her home, turned her around, if he had not been so surprised and ashamed at himself to find that he was weeping, that he couldn't get it up. Young then, he was horrified, as though a limp dick meant something. Now, nobody wanted it. Up or down. It didn't matter. If he hadn't had a toothache, or been less drunk. If he hadn't lost his feelings and his way, if he hadn't driven Eleanor so far, so fast from him, at such a young age. So many ways to live things right. He lived that one-night marriage every night. He thought about June Morrissey now, in this immensity of snow, and he smiled with a dreamy puzzlement recalling her crooked front tooth.

Oh yes, his hand moved on the wheel, if only she'd stop on that hidden rise and look on back, glancing over her shoulder, her mane blown which-ways by scudding wind, if only she had turned around, walked back. She could have done that! The plow banged a deeper drift and Jack downshifted, almost stalled but revved into reverse to plow this tough wave. Worried that the car would skid into the back end of his plow, he glanced into the rearview, pausing.

No car.

Only the red tail glow of his flashing brake lights. No car. No lights. So maybe they had stopped back there, whoever they were, people out on fool errands. Idiots, for sure, thinking there was somewhere they had to go. Jack plowed through the snowbank carefully. He kept on traveling, heading north, even though now something dragged slow in his arms. He kept wondering who the people were. If, by some chance that was *the* car, was his son in it? Or if not, why had the car stopped? Why was the car out on a night like this one?

First he told himself that it couldn't be the car he was looking for. Probably it was useless people—the kind like Marlis Cook, user and loser, who'd hold a good Samaritan liable for any honest accident. Not to mention that they'd give him away, his game, his rationale went. He kept on driving north. Next, he told himself that they wouldn't have ventured out at all, anyway, without a pack of blankets, food, a sleeping bag, emergency flares. All the normal things you kept in your car. Naturally. Even if they had to quit, tough out the night, they'd be found by the time the storm leveled off. In the morning, the car would be iced over with their breath, there might be a touch of frostbite, but they would be fine. He put the picture of his son in his head, the tiny sparrow hands and round calm face that astounded him with a jolt of mystery. His child, his son, that was where his duty lay—but there was no way either car could go forward, he saw that for certain. No way that the car with his son in it wouldn't at some point have stopped ahead, stalled, met a drift it couldn't master. Gerry Nanapush would be there, and he had to get to him. Behind him, the poor assholes that tried to stick to his plow's wake would freeze.

His son *could* be in that car, couldn't he? Not likely? Maybe.

He glanced instinctively into the rearview mirror and for an instant saw not blackness or his own taillights' reflection or even a nothingness of blown snow but June's gaze. She looked frozen and weary, and yet in a way almost hopeful, still expecting something good to happen in her life, though things did not work out that way. A smile worked across his face, thinking of the doorknob. His wedding present. And then the bus that never came, the paint pony, the sky trail, the northern lights. She looked as though she still imagined he might bend over and hold her to his chest and carry her home, that there might be mercy for her yet.

She decided him. In lowest gear, he slowly banked and turned and went back for the car. He traveled in a painstaking search along the ditches and to either side of the road. For several miles he felt ridiculous. Frequent whiteouts made him stop. He held himself poised in the driving snow and waited for the slam of some other vehicle nosing forward, but nothing, and then he angled and edged around, dragging, chains biting down to pavement.

He wouldn't have seen where the car went at all but for the rutted skid he glimpsed during a brief cessation. In that pocket of calm, he saw two dim but deep-cut tracks that swerved off road and across the filled ditch right over into a field. Jack stopped the truck. He left his snowplow idling, zipped his coverall suit and jacket to his chin. Then he jumped from the vehicle onto the margin of road. As he stood there, the engine roaring and trembling behind him, the headlights trained into the flat blackness caught a flatter, bluer, temporary swatch of whiteness, and he thought it was the car. Climbing back into his cab, he rummaged the seat, the tackle box, the storage bin behind the seat, found rope, and tied one end to the shut door handle behind. He tied the other end of the rope to himself. He threw it down. Stupid! However long, the rope wasn't long enough! He opened the door, tossed in the armful of tangle, flipped his parka's hood and walked into the solid air. He saw nothing before him, nothing behind, but counted on that flat doorway in the snow to stop him.

He raised one foot, he dragged the next ahead, kept going although he began to think maybe this was wrong, that if he ran into a fence line he'd be lucky. Then he remembered that this was sugar beet country. There were no fence lines. If he missed the car he was looking for maybe he'd walk forever, on and on. He would go straight west, on into the other world of the Ojibwa dead where skeletons gambled, throwing and concealing human wristbones. He saw their arms rise and toss, but he lunged ahead anyway. He thought of his mother's laugh, her eyes. He remembered her as a shadow, as a protective arm, her face again wild and fascinated. He saw her hand throwing down the cards and heard the roar of her blood. The beat of her heart sounded in his ears, and he missed her like a child. She used to break path for him in winter, all the way to school. Throwing himself forward, he hit against a waist-high wall.

At first he thought it was the car, but could the snow have

drifted so high already? That seemed impossible. One step and he was on top, as on a low drift. He stamped back and forth, but at once felt certain there was only snow beneath his feet. He turned around, around again, and was thoroughly confused. Twinges of anxiety shot through his chest, sinking needlelike pains, and then he moved the way the wind blew him because he couldn't help it, the wind was stronger. He could no longer tell where it was coming from, maybe it had switched directions. He kept on walking, moving forward. Knowing that he'd missed the car, he stretched out his arms as though a woman would walk into them.

He walked, he walked. Even when he fell on all fours to crawl on legs and arms that were stump-wooden, he kept moving. He kept moving after his body seized, finally, and went nerveless. That old body only kept him back for a moment and then he felt himself rise in a new and more enduring shape.

He continued onward. The sun blazed over the rim of the horizon into a sheet of space. Or was that only in his mind, was he seeing things? A black cloud blanket sucked the sun back. He thought he saw it vanish as the night closed again. Once, Jack smiled in amazed pleasure. He caught a glimpse of June, just before him. The wind was blowing her hair straight past, banging her purse on her thigh. She was wearing a wedding dress, a real one this time, white net full and stiff with lace. Confidently, over the brilliant drifts, she stepped forward. Her veil was a billow clouding her face. Jack turned around and focused hard on the way he had come. By that time, he'd walked such a great distance, too far to turn around. He had spent so much time getting where he was going. And it was all right. His tracks were obscured, his trail drifted over, his path back to the living blown clean. He followed her meekly. She was bringing him home.

He walked in a big circle and then a small one and smaller, concentric, following June. It took him all night to get back where he started. But just before dawn fully broke Jack hit the same waist-high wall he'd climbed on first leaving the truck. He staggered, hit the thing again, groped with his numb mitts, slugged at the smooth crust, screamed for a door handle. He found a catch, pulled, and was through and into a dark unsnowed and frigid interior of utter blackness. He slid by feel, encountering a shape, one shape, a human's shape, a someone, a whatever, a head anyway, a body that he shook and shook.

Jack dragged a medium-size but very heavy person from that car—he couldn't tell if the car was Candice's, or whose—there was a car seat in it but the seat was empty and the floors were empty and the shell was black and he was going to die, too, along with this stranger. Shaggy in blankets, through the waning blizzard and up onto the seat in the snowplow's cab, Jack dragged what turned out to be a young man and set him down beside him. The engine had cut but it started up again and Jack drove, drove on north, now on reserve gas, flamed with adrenaline. Saved.

The snow died down and the highway was again visible, snow running back and forth like threads on a mechanical loom weaving whiteness to a sheer drape that covered the flat world from one sky to the next in all directions. Now he welcomed the faint graying of the night and glanced over at the sleeping face of the man he'd rescued—the face was young, just past twenty maybe, familiar like a lot of Chippewa faces were familiar to him. Not bad-looking, could be a cousin. The sun blazed over the rim of the horizon into a sheet of space beneath a black cloud blanket, and rose, a band of hammered brass.

As the dazzling light lifted weightless into the dark suspension of sky, the rescued man next to him awakened, turned, and on seeing Jack smiled in amazed pleasure. One tooth in his grin pushed a little past the other, crooked. Jack turned back and focused hard on the road.

Then the wail. From beside him, the startling sound.

"What the hell . . ." Jack cried, clanking to a halt. "Take it easy . . ." In the confusion of his find he thought he was hallucinating another presence in the car but that strange, awful, cry came again now, again and again, a baby's indignant spoiling squawl of hunger straight from the inside of the young man's jacket, which he unzipped and opened to reveal—tiny, raw, screaming, red—the original of Jack's own face.

§

The Disappearance

*T*he members of the Trollwood snowmobile rescue squad pulled with a whining roar into the emergency lot of the hospital. Night-duty personnel, whose shifts weren't quite over, surged forward with stretchers and warming blankets. Something had gone wrong, however. Only three women. The snowmobiler who'd brought up the rear was astonished and horrified, upon halting near the emergency doors, to find that two empty gloves were tucked into the belt at his waist and that the big woman who'd been attached to them and who'd straddled the seat behind him, was gone. Sucked off into this awful night.

Right out of the gloves!

He held them as though to draw her back into them and purposefully mounted his machine, but a series of wild, terrific gusts belted the hospital and made any thought of backtracking to rescue the poor woman out of the question. The rescuers themselves could barely see out the lighted doors now, and although, once inside, the man who'd lost his rescued party became hysterical and had to be dissuaded from setting out yet again and calmed with an orange drink and Valium, there was at least the celebratory rescue of the others. Quite an arrangement of wives, and one, the driver of the red Explorer evidently, when questioned by the police, had let them know that the unidentified woman who'd fallen off the back of the last rescuer's snowmobile was none other than her own mother.

They'd knocked her out with a sedative, too, Dot Mauser, on learning that sad fact.

§

Two
Front-Page
Articles

WIDOWS NEARLY FREEZE
IN GRIEF-STRUCK SHOCK

They told stories until dawn and subsisted on Halloween candy. That was how four local women described an overnight blizzard ordeal that ended well after sunrise with a daring snowmobile rescue by local volunteers. Candice Pantamounty, Dot Nanapush Mauser, Eleanor Mauser, and Marlis Cook Mauser found themselves trapped together after attending the funeral, earlier that day, of their former husband, Jack Mauser. (See accompanying headline article.) Following a mourners' dinner at a West Fargo steak house and casino, the women decided to drive back to the city.

"Unfortunately," Dot Mauser said, "I was foolhardy, as the driver. You read about these things in the papers and always second-guess blizzard victims. I never should have chanced it."

Others of the rescued women agreed with Mrs. Mauser but also praised her for her coolheadedness, emergency preparations, and for the knowledge that probably saved their lives. The blizzard kit contained high-caloric foods, candles, a space blanket, and other essentials. Conscious of the fact that most people who died trapped in winter-mired automobiles suffocate from a buildup of carbon monoxide, the women were careful to keep the car's tailpipe unclogged.

"Every hour or so, we formed a human chain and the first one out at the end made certain that the job was done," said Candice Pantamounty, a prominent Fargo dentist. "It was during one of these routine cleaning jobs that the wind ripped Eleanor Mauser away."

Eleanor Mauser, however, subsequently found her way through subzero windchill and driving snow to the entryway doors of Hector International Airport, where she was able to attract the attention of the night watchman, who alerted the Fargo police and fire department to the plight of the stranded women. The Trollwood Chapter of the local Snowmobile Volunteers was able to locate the buried automobile, a Ford Explorer, and to carry all but one of the motorists to safety. Rescuers speculate that the missing woman may have fallen from the snowmobile on the way to the hospital, but no reports of her whereabouts have surfaced. Dot Nanapush Mauser remains hospitalized, in good condition. The other women were kept for observation several hours at Merit Care Saint Luke's Hospital, Fargo, and released after treatment for minor frostbite.

FURIOUS NANNY ACCUSES CONTRACTOR OF FAKING OWN DEATH

Mrs. Tillie Kroshus, nanny to John James Mauser Jr., of Fargo, reported to local police a possible kidnapping of her charge by the child's father, John Mauser Sr., head of Mauser and Mauser, Inc., and responsible for the troubled Crest Development. Mauser Sr.'s body had supposedly been discovered January 1 in the basement of his burned dwelling, and he was assumed to have perished in the blaze.

Mrs. Kroshus, however, insists that Mr. Mauser entered the home of his former wife, Candice Panta-mounty, D.D.S., late yesterday afternoon. According to Mrs. Kroshus, a back door was opened by Mr. Mauser with a key, and he surprised her while she was making an emergency phone call. The alleged Jack Mauser Sr. then proceeded to tie Mrs. Kroshus into a chair, and left with the baby in its car seat, she further claims. Local police have issued an all points bulletin for Mr. Mauser, who is believed to have fled the premises in his former wife's car, a white 1993 Honda Civic.

§

Smile of the Wolf

JANUARY 6, 7:40 A.M.

Gerry and Shawn

*E*arly, grainy half-light in an old apartment by the frozen river. Gerry slips into the brown-aired entryway and jiggles the key in the lock, pulling outward the way Dot told him, closing the door after and treading softly up the cat-gray carpeted stairs. There's a shaky little banister at the top and he holds it, shifting on the landing and blinking to let his eyes adjust. The doors to their rooms are open. Two little bedrooms. A kitchen off to the side. The one bedroom he knows is his daughter's. Shawn's breathing in there, calmly in the good oblivion. In this year's school picture, she looked solid, her mother's sharp eyes and a combination of their hair, dark brown and shaded with red lights. Her chin stuck out. Her front teeth with braces off were square and pretty and there was a wrenching little dent of a dimple beside her grin. And her eyes, her eyes, a little sad but surely promising bold actions.

She's awake. Or she is once he sits down on the stool beside her bed and her eyes open. For a space of time she is just looking at him. Then her lips move and he barely makes out her whisper.

Don't be a dream.

That's when he bends to her and Shawn vaults fierce against his chest, and they are holding on and holding on in the dim morning so that he knows how good it feels. Her against him and the way his arms fit around his real, not fantasy child. He presses his face against the whirlwind in the crown of her hair and the two of them rock back and forth. Wordless. His heart on the ground. There is the smell of her hair, sleep on her breath. A musty, eager sweetness. Even then, the slow, long moment vanishes.

Thin light comes up in the window, but there is still so much blowing, drifting snow. Pellets of ice brush the house and there's this sense of promise, a gathering exhilaration as the morning strengthens. Another bout of blizzard weather is set to arrive. The wind will pick up and hide him.

"It'll all come clear, you'll see," says Gerry after a while, he doesn't know why. Then Shawn leans back holding his hands and drinks him in steadily and hungrily with tears collecting just under the starry lids of those molten brown eyes.

"You're out of there. You're gonna stay," she says forcefully, staring through him.

Gerry tips his head to the side but he can't speak. No answer forms. So he puts his palm to the softness of her determined face. He strokes her hair back, wisp by wisp, tucking strands behind her ear, along her temples. There is too much to feel here and he aches in places and hurts garishly in others so that all the incoming messages feel much the same. But he looks down at Shawn and knows that she feels just one clear thing. Shame hits him that he could think to tell her anything at all about clarity. *It'll all come clear. Bullshit.* He's the one who fucked things up so bad. It's clear already, to her, what's going on and she knows of course she can't stop him. Her mother's daughter though, she won't admit this. He can't either.

"Sure I am," he says.

She leans back into the covers, then, smiling at him. All the years. All the bedtime stories he could have but probably wouldn't have told her anyway, and now she's past them, just about. . . . She tunes in, grinning at him.

"So tell me a wake-up story."

Her face rounds magically. Five child-years drop off and she wills herself to be a little girl in sheer suspense.

"I don't think so," says Gerry. "You know me."

She frowns as though saying, *How can he be so dense?* Of course, she doesn't know him. He tries to explain.

"I'm not a storytelling kind of guy."

"Could you be one just this morning?"

She turns over, pulling herself tense in the blanket. Half the curves there are a woman's and half are the eager, awkward angles of a child. Their knees touch. Her face is a radiant cup. Gerry's dazed in its reflected light.

"This story," he says, angling for ideas. "What do you want it to be about?"

Her face is serene and commanding. "Prison."

His hand pauses, then resumes its slow pattern on her brow.

"There are no stories in that place."

"About when you were my age, then," she says. "A time you got in trouble at school. Or your friends dumped you." She moves over, making a spot for him to stretch out on the side of the low bed. Which he does, his legs gratefully extending, his head tipping back, sleep washing over him, a swift torrent.

"When I was around your age," he starts, drifting lower, then snaps awake. "You've got to understand that I was not a good person to begin with, not really good. I could behave if the pressure was on, but it did not come natural to me."

Then he stops. "But you. Tell me a story. Something."

"What?"

Her voice is so gentle and warming. She leans over him, guarding him, watching.

"Something ordinary. Just the usual."

Gerry's floating, his body planing on a raft of pure comfort. It's a poignant overload. In the past twelve hours he's experienced a degree of pleasure so intense there seems no limit to the possibilities of the mind or body. Everything expanding. Traveling as fast as light, as dark. And it's going to snow again. And no one knows Dot and Shawn are living here, yet, because they just moved. He's at least a couple of hours ahead of his pursuers. Having safety and freedom and his daughter all at once unbalances Gerry and the painkillers, too, fizz up gently around his ears. He doesn't want to follow a story line. He just wants to hear the lull of Shawn's voice.

"How about your neighbors?"

Shawn pulls a blanket up and tucks it under his chin, almost motherly. "Okay. There's this woman? She has a tomcat named Uncle Louie."

Shawn's voice falls, describing, rises, telling.

"Mr. Morton. He's, like, obsessive about his snowmobile. It's such a joke. He's always out there in the garage, you know, it's right behind the apartment building. Number 21. He keeps the key above the door frame. He'll like be polishing his helmet. And that moon suit, boots, the works. He keeps that out there in a closet. Once, he went a hundred miles up the river with Mrs. Morton. They made this fire. Drank this bottle of champagne."

"Sounds kind of nice."

"Yeah, I guess."

Gerry's dropping off, over the cliff, consciousness like clear air above and sleep drifting interminably below, a puffy cloud, catching him, buoyant.

"Where's this guy keep the gas can?" he mumbles, sinking.

Shawn's voice continues, light, sometimes childish, other times lower and mature. She's halfway there. Next time she'll be all grown up. She smooths the blanket, lapses, drops the trains of sentences, trails off listening to sifting snow. The forward push of a new storm system shakes the siding of the house. She stares seriously ahead, listening to her father breathe, and does not smile. He breathes nice, low and deep from the bottom of his chest. She decides that she will breathe with him and memorize how to do this.

A pounding on the door like they will break it down and her eyes spring open in the grainy blizzard light. While they give bullhorn warnings and yell downstairs, she steps into jeans crumpled in a pool upon the floor. Kicks a pair of underwear and one stray sock beneath the bed. Pulls on her mother's Bison sweatshirt and stuffs her pajamas under the pillow. While they are breaking down the door she steps out into the hallway. She sits down on the top stair, watches the old wood around the lock splinter. As they leap through and around the corner, like on the TV shows, only louder and no music, she grips her knees tight. The palms of her hands sting. Only when they stampede in and past her with their guns out, with their bullet vests, does she let the heavy tears that she's been saving behind her eyelids pour. She hears them yell, jump into each room. Kick open closets. Something breaks. Her throat clenches shut. Her tears are electric voltage. Hot. Speeding time up. She doesn't stop them, but they don't give her the old relief. They do not cause the men to quit their searching or even pay her one bit of attention. Eventually, she quits.

He's gone. They don't find him. No sign he sat beside her, let her talk to him and talk to him, no sign he stroked her hair. She puts her hand to the side of her face where his hand touched. It's like she's keeping him safe, a secret, that way. Two of the men order her downstairs and sit her at the kitchen table. One's short and uses a soft voice, and the other is tall and says he has no patience. But the shorter man with hair the color of her sandbox sand way back as a baby, in Argus, and sad round greenish eyes says, "We scared the hell out of her. Shut up, Ted, let me talk to her."

The shorter one looks directly at her, crouching to her height, so she has to turn her head to look away from his eyes.

"What's your name, honey?"

She tells him.

"Listen, Shawn. We know your dad was here. He probably wanted to see you, and that's just fine, but you probably know he escaped and we have to take him back in. Now we don't want to hurt him, but we do need your help. Did he tell you where he was going next?"

The man smiles a serious smile, his pleasant eyes caring for her, calm. She nearly nods but something freezes along her neck. A chill from the other officer, his hand along his hip.

"Please tell us," the man with the light brown hair says, "Shawn, we really need to find him before some of the others. They're . . . I guess you'd say trigger-happy. Shawn, this is a way to help your dad."

Tears mist her eyes again. She hides in the fog and waits, thinking. At last she speaks, her voice as tiny as she can make it.

"He's out? Escaped? Where's my mom?"

The smaller man looks up at the bigger man. His lips move.

"Let's stick to your dad for the moment."

Shawn nods, finds that he has allowed her gaze to drop so that she can now study her hands folded in her lap. She thinks some more.

"Look, Shawn," the man says, "you're obviously smart. You have a good mother. You're damn lucky to have a mother like her. We don't want to implicate *her* in anything. Right? Does she ever give you advice?" He waits, his voice sharpens. "Does she?"

"Yes," says Shawn.

"Has she ever told you to tell the truth?"

"Yes." Shawn rearranges her hands. Her mouth is dry. She has to go to the bathroom, presses her knees together. The man's words are winding all around her, strings. Soft thin ropes. She tries to breathe normally and not jiggle her feet. She knows all the old ploys—crying, falling silent, screaming—no stubbornness will get her out of this.

"So you wouldn't want to let your mom down," says the man. His voice drops a pitch, gentles. "Shawn, was your daddy here?"

His question sinks into her understanding. *He said they knew but they don't know.*

Shawn lets the man's lie into her mind. There is something she has to do now, the right thing. The ropes are flying, snaking out swift and hungry, and she can't cast them off. They loop around and around her arms like yarn. If she says the right thing somehow they will all unravel. The other man breathes out explosively and swears. She feels the scissors drop into her hands.

"My dad's an asshole," she says, her voice flat and cold. Looking one man and then the other in the eye, she cuts the strings. "I'm scared to death of him and so's my mom. If he ever came around I'd call 911."

The shorter man drops back on his heels, elbow on his bent knee.

"Huh," he says, not like a question but as though something is explained to him. Inside of her, while the two men are looking at each other over her head and exchanging words back and forth with no sound, a version of herself is saying *Sorry, sorry, sorry,* to her father, and *You know I didn't mean it,* and to her mom and dad both, *Where are you?* And all the while the strings of the man's words are falling, little scraps on the ground, littering the floor.

"Okay," he gets up. "That's enough. Now listen, Shawn, you mother's okay. I know you're worried about her. She got stuck in the winter storm and she might have a few complications. They're making sure she's all right at the hospital. We're going to take you there. Get your coat."

Shawn goes straight to the closet, bends over tying boots on her feet, then straightens and puts on her parka with the fake-fur ruff that bristles around her face.

All of the other men have left except for the two officers, who are waiting for her at the door. The one who spoke to her, the brown-haired one, is putting on his gloves and adjusting his hat. The other, the one named Ted without any patience, is staring out the window at the closed garages just half-visible in blowing snow. The white moves faster and springs up suddenly, a curtain. He shakes his head and his shoulder itches. Something's wrong but he's too edgy to sit still any longer and attempt to figure out how they should have interviewed the girl, let alone the mother, who was too hypothermic to say much at all. He turns to ask the daughter if she's ready. She's staring. That's what itched his shoulder. He catches just a glimpse, then, in the shadowy hallway, of her grin. *Like a wolf pup*, he thinks, narrowing his eyes, stepping toward her. He peers closer to try and figure out what she is thinking. But her face now, dangerous and bland, is the mask of a woman.

§

Mauser and Mauser

JANUARY 7, 1995

Jack, Jack Junior, Lyman Lamartine

*A*s he got closer, Jack could breathe the difference even in the warmed dry air the blower threw across them. He could always breathe the difference coming back onto the reservation. The trees and the snowy lakes. Even though the old people, his mother, called the land leftovers, scraps the whites didn't want, she loved the place. Now Jack was hit by feeling for it. Memories came to him in his weariness, pure and strange. Plump little eider ducks through clattering reeds. The hiss of ice forming in bands on the October lake. Old days and times were clouds in his mind. Crescent of soft grass alongside a hill where he'd once hidden all day while his mother howled in a rhythmical sequence. A bell ringing full over winter fields. A rosary in someone's cracked hands.

He opened the window. There was a taste of woodsmoke to the wind in his mouth. The farms were fewer, then bigger, then

smaller, then a herd of pickups by a certain door announced a
wake or a wedding. Each house with someone in it or some
memory, long ago. Sometimes through the filter of his mother's
crazy silence. Birch trees in white abandoned pastures and
their blue shadows reflecting whiteness against the white
snow. The sunlight opened and shut and dizzied him. The kid
who had stayed with his son slept long with his mouth a troubled line, weary. The baby, having drunk a thawed bottle, was
passed out, still zipped against his rescuer.

Candice was hysterical on the receiving end of the telephone
call and Marlis, in the background, kept shouting that her
breasts hurt and to give her the phone. Candice's lips were
pressed tight to the mouthpiece. Jack held the baby close to
the phone until he made a small gurgling noise.
    "See?"
    "That's him!" Candice shrieked once again, gave up the
phone to Marlis.
    "She's kind of heated up," said Marlis. "Bring him down
here."
    Jack hesitated. "Could you get up here, somehow?"
    "Scared of the police?"
    "I don't know what my situation is, whether the bank —"
    "Look," said Marlis. "We'd be up there by now but she's
down with some damn kind of virus. I mean, it was fucking
cold in that car, Jack. Get your ass down here!"
    Jack paused. Marlis took a deep, crazed breath.
    "I'm our baby's legal mother, you're the dad. I could haul
your ass to jail for life for kidnapping."
    "Oh, Jesus, Marlis . . ."
    "But you did save him."
    "Yes," said Jack, meek.
    "So Hegelstead?" Marlis went on, more evenly. "He issued
this statement. According to him, you'd gone on a vacation and
your house just, boom, went. With your teeth in it and all. Like
anyone believes that! Candice is still pissed about that bridgework."

"I'm . . . well, can I say it enough? Sorry! Truly sorry."

"Shove it, Jack. Like I said, I'm not pressing charges or anything, against anyone, even that guy you found. He saved John's life anyway, I mean, just think."

Jack just thought.

"I suppose," said Marlis, "you thought I'd screw you the way I tried the time you saved me in that store. Mouth to mouth."

"Maybe," Jack said.

"Well, give me credit."

Marlis paused.

"Did they catch his father, that escaped convict?" she asked.

"Not yet. I was stupid to leave the car running."

"What's new? Just drive him back down here. Like now. Strap him in good though."

"In the snowplow?"

"Rent something."

"This is the reservation."

"Steal something."

"Real funny, Marlis. I'll start as soon as I call Hegelstead. Take care of Candy?"

"Like you care." Marlis suddenly dropped her voice, low. "She'll be fine once she starts drilling people's teeth again, I mean, she's kind of an artist, don't you think, Jack? It's hard for her to be without her work. We're booking appointments straight through March—this relieved look came over Candy's face when she heard that, so I know she'll be herself real soon. There's some emergencies. A broken bicuspid tomorrow. She'll be okay as soon as she's working with a patient."

"Until then, give her some Novocain."

"Straight to the head."

"How are you?" Jack paused. "Cleaned up, sober?"

"You should ask."

"Right." Jack stopped. "As of New Year's, for me. It's been since New Year's."

"Since your resurrection." Marlis's voice dragged sarcastically. "Quit congratulating yourself and get the baby down here, quick."

Jack went out to the homey motel lobby, found the *Forum*, and read the article describing his four wives' ordeal—it somehow gave him a comfortable feeling, to think of them all together like that, talking through the night. It was as though his whole life had come together without his knowing it or having to feel responsible, though he was. It was his funeral that they had bothered to attend, after all. A pang of nostalgia shot through him, a momentary bolt of weakness. He braced himself. Then he really imagined what they might have talked about and he was glad he wouldn't know. He was tired, but the baby had allowed him to sleep four hours that morning. They had stretched out on the bed side by side.

Mauser and Mauser, he had thought.

It had been five years since Jack talked to Lyman Lamartine. In that time Lyman had not so much changed as consolidated. He was who he always was, but now more so. Professionally so. Pieces of energy, scattered plans, excited plots—now these had evolved into the serious development schemes of a man who had the local clout and federal money to do as he wished. Lyman never walked through doors, he barged, looking eagerly ahead to zero in and apply instant leverage. Spotting Jack, Lyman's tough body widened, bristling like a muscular dog. As he approached, he stared at Jack and assessed him with shrewd green-brown eyes. He smiled at Jack Mauser's getup, at the baby in his arms. Something in his manner told Jack there was a hidden level of feeling in his greeting. He stared keenly at the baby, regarded the two of them with something the situation, as far as Jack knew, did not warrant. Gratitude. Relief. Shaking Jack's hand, Lyman looked genuinely glad to see him. His eyes gleamed behind gradient tinted lenses shading his sharp eyes.

The two sat across from each other in the padded booth of the motel coffee shop.

"Eggs over easy, no butter on the toast," said Lyman to the waitress, then to Jack, "You've got an armful."

"Soup," said Jack. "Two bowls."

He jiggled his son lightly. He was still deeply cold inside, as though an icicle was lodged in his stomach, as though his core hadn't warmed from the night before. Soup would do it. Hot. John Jr. was drinking from a bottle Jack had bought from a drugstore, sucking formula painstakingly mixed from the directions.

"He likes this stuff—not the real thing, but not bad, huh?"

"When's Mom showing up?"

"I'm driving him down to her." Jack paused, shifting the baby. "Hegelstead call you?"

"I talked to him yesterday, Jack." Lyman spoke deliberately, stirring his coffee, meditating. "Of course, we never thought you'd surface so quick up here. Like this. Pretty dramatic."

"All the world's a stage," said Jack.

"Still spouting rhymes."

Jack shrugged. "My second wife was a brain, is a brain. She studied with nuns."

"Let's see, that makes one dead, one to the convent—"

"Two gone lesbian, one doing okay, and they all hate me," Jack finished.

Lyman dropped it. He knew all about June, his deceased sister-in-law. He remembered everything about everybody, and Jack understood that the only way to counter Lyman's shrewd self-serving honesty was to admit all and do Lyman one better. Their booth was built against a back window. They both gazed through the glass, silent, thinking about the snow as they looked over the blowing fields where the stuff lay dense and solid. For days after this weather system moved through, people would be shoveling out. There would be more cars found within suave tapered drifts. More old men and children lost in their backyards. Every so often, whiteness blew up in a scarf, shedding particles of diamond dust that hung glittering in the air.

Jack drank the soup. Poured it down himself. Held the baby close. As the heat reached his center, he felt the inside of himself come to life. As though he were melting. The thought of them all, his wives, the ridiculous miserable entrapment, their survival. Slowly, absurdly, he felt the warmth spread in him and build like freedom through his whole body until his hands shook repressing it, his legs, his feet. He burst out with one or two helpless shudders and the intelligent little baby watched him, alert with fascination. Lyman watched Jack, too, as though calculating the man's sanity in terms of dollars. How much. How little. What could Lyman Lamartine get out of it?

Half an hour later, the baby in his lap drinking from another bottle, this one full of apple juice, Jack ate more lunch. A club sandwich was half gone on his plate. Lyman described his latest project, and Jack managed to keep his jaw shut firmly enough and to look serious and considering as he took in the general shape of Lyman's plans and ideas. Lyman had brought charts and proposals. And maps. There was a detailed map drawn up of the proposed casino location and listing the present, enrolled owners of that land. Relatives. Jack knew the names. He said nothing. The baby slept in his arms, slumped weightlessly against him, a tiny bean sack. Jack was still wearing the old one-piece workman's overalls. Lyman wore a light wool three-piece suit, tailored perfectly. His precise haircut flared, his lapels lay perfectly flat. His feet were hugged by soft elkhide cowboy boots.

"And here" — Lyman's square hand paused lovingly over a sickle-moon-shaped building that looked out on a squiggly circle of blueprint water — "we're planning for the casino. We've got the drawings, not the contractors yet. We need a head of operations, a project manager. Someone people can accept."

Jack nodded vacantly.

"You're enrolled here," Lyman said pointedly.

Jack stroked his son's head. "Look, Lyman, as you know I got into some trouble, of the monetary sort. Big development that didn't pan out, too much credit for me to handle, subcontractors on my tail." Jack looked tired, gazing into the baby's eyes.

"I talked to Hegelstead," said Lyman.

"He has this idea. To put it simply, I faked my own death." Jack gave an abrupt laugh, took a swig of coffee with his free hand. "Didn't preplan it that way—it just seemed convenient at the time."

"Sure," said Lyman, as though it were the most predictable act in the world. "But you're not catching my drift."

Jack's head inclined, his vision slowly forming.

"Your drift?"

Lyman waved both hands, ducked his head deprecatingly. "So far, no charges have been pressed. I may even be able to offer you a role in this project, provided you can help us come up with a few investors."

Jack's laugh sounded over the other tables.

"Me? Why would . . . I'm sorry, I've got no credibility at all at this point. Hegelstead, the signator on my line of credit, he can haul my ass up. So far, I've dodged, got my court dates extended. But now that I'm alive—"

"You still don't see it."

Lyman sat quietly, studying his folded hands, frowning into the black tedium of his coffee. He had aged carefully, not to wisdom but to power, and the care of his hands and expertly trimmed long hair and the fine shave of what there was of his beard told the story. He was impervious, impeccable. He reached the heart of what he had to say to Jack.

"The only way your banker can possibly recoup his losses is to *loan you more money.* I know you see that too. Don't be coy, Jack. You're finally onto something big, a guaranteed lucrative project, a long-term money-making property, an on-site funding source. Jack, it's the only way they'll get back their investment. Throw good money after, excuse me, bad. I've got a Reno family—a company really—interested, but I need some matching funds to present a more attractive profile to the state commissioner. That's where you come in, Jack, part of the profile. Tribally operated, tribal employers, tribal management—

that is, once management is trained in. And in the first place, first of all, listen to this: built by a tribally enrolled contractor."

"Looks good on paper," said Jack. "How much am I worth?"

Lyman smiled. "How much? For me paying off your subcontractors, saving your neck?"

The two locked gazes. Jack dropped his. His voice was sorrowful.

"I'd be in hock to you, say, for the rest of my life."

"I doubt you'll live long enough to pay me off," said Lyman, his eyes measuring but not cruel. "Once you're back, you're back for good. You're my man."

"Better yours than Hegelstead's."

"That so?" Lyman frowned at his fingertips.

Jack rocked the baby, half dreamily, his heart both lifting and sinking. He was a hostage of his past and his life of temporary fixes. Now he would be part of the biggest temporary concept yet — the thrill of instant money. The power of house odds. The security of eventual small-time petty loss. Nothing new. There was no way he could turn this down or back out. He hadn't the faintest prospect of any other solution to his life. Still, it was so sudden, this return, this rescue. He had the sense of a swift undertow, pulling from beneath the glazed Formica table, tugging. Home. An old anxiety formed. He had thought he might come back here if he failed. But never that he'd come here needing to save his skin. Save himself in a big way, that is, with a project he would have underbid to get and have fought for. A little fractured excitement struck. The tinge of anticipation, the idea of the buildings, the complex itself set down on paper for now, real foundation tomorrow. Beams, boards, steel, stone, and below him the earth his same childhood dirt — rising around his ankles.

§

February Thaw

Dot

*T*he first day in the hospital, I see and hear nothing. On the second day, millions of holes in the tile-foam ceiling. I squeeze my eyes shut. I hate those tiles, the urge to count. My mother and my aunt take turns sitting beside me, reading silently from huge library books, romantic novels splayed open on their knees. *He sidled toward her with casual insouciance refusing to hide the obvious challenge of his love wand.* Did I really hear that? I open my eyes once more, later on. Shawn is there, staring out the window. She turns to look at me, sad, chewing gum. Lights whirl. I shut my eyes again. Shawn's voice rises. Ma? Ma? Ma? Every time I wake, try to rise, something fells me with a soft interior blow. I sleep and sleep.

"Is she sleeping too much?" I hear my mother ask the doctor.

"She's been through trauma. Sleep is a great repair shop."

He has a kind voice, quiet and neutral.

"We'd like to see her just a bit more active, though," he says.

I feel Aunt Mary's hands. I know her grip. She's shaking

me back and forth but dark engulfs me. Sleep foams up in a comfortable helmet around my ears and, easily, I slip away. I am starting to remember in distinct and unwanted, beautiful pictures, that I was with Gerry. Details. Depth of his kiss and hunger. Mine. They try to keep me awake, but I want to sink into the buzzing sigh of dreams where he's still there and real. My mother talks to me, but I know her voice so well that even its distress and loud pitch make me cozy, warm, tired, like a child who's been out in the snow. That's what I am. They put ice on my eyelids. They sing to me, grating songs, and rub my arms and feet. But I am sliding down the pole, the long, greased pole, into warm feathers.

"Wake up! Smell the toast!" Aunt Mary shouts.

I smile at her rough worry. Then I go down, down into the feathers, into the dream, back to Gerry. It is days before I wake.

When I do, though, I panic. I remember it all in detail then, especially the part where I was questioned by the police emergency squad about the hitchhiker. I remember I told them she was my mother. Celestine!

The nurse appears, not very friendly. I feel like I'm in a movie where a two-way mirror could be watching for clues about Gerry, a camera, people taking notes behind the false surface. My first conscious words could be taped, the juice pitcher or the IV stand wired. Still, I can't help but say the same words I'd say if I were five years old.

"I want my mother!"

The nurse gives me a pinched, dry look. Perhaps she's FBI or maybe I have just been a boring patient. Then it occurs to me, Hey, if they were trying to fool me they'd put a sympathetic nurse in here to gain my trust. This one has no interest in me, none. I relax, smile at her gratefully. She points at the phone, but apparently she doesn't know my mom's right around the corner because before I can decide what to say into the receiver in case the line is tapped, Mom walks into the room bearing a turkey pita pocket on a red plastic tray. She's never looked so much herself or so good.

"Mom!" I try to make my eyes stare volumes.

She puts the tray down and comes to me, her face all filled with the same relief she would register if I really were five years old. There is a one-piece molded chair next to the bed. She sits down in it, peers quickly over her shoulder, and then leans to my ear and whispers.

"They're okay. Both of them."

"Shawn?" I say. "Gerry?"

She nods. "Jack too." Then can't help herself, a wicked glance. "Both of your husbands. Shawn was here, remember?"

I prop myself up enough to glance across her shoulder. She is telling me how Jack got out of the burning house and where he turned up. No sign of doctor, police, anyone official whatsoever. Still, I'm nervous and try to talk in a code of shorthand.

"So you're okay," I say casually, nodding encouragement. "*No frostbite?*"

Mom lowers her chin and her brown eyes hold mine, steady, as she considers her answer. I am in suspense. She knows it, but knows too that my suspense is small payment she's exacting for what she has done for me.

"Aunt Mary was over for breakfast and she took the call. When they explained to her what had happened, she just said . . ." Here Mom's eyes light and I see that she's taken on a reflection of Aunt Mary's pleasure in the intrigue.

"Aunt Mary said . . ." I prompt.

"She said, 'Oh don't worry about Celestine. She probably jumped off the machine to grab herself a cup of coffee. She'll be all right.'"

I take this in. They must have thought they had a nutcase on the phone, but no matter.

"I drove here. Showed up at the hospital," she goes on. "They examined me. Pronounced me fit. I've been here ever since."

I close my fingers over her big knuckled fist and then for some reason, since we can't, just can't, look directly at each other for too long, I examine our hands. Mine are raw, swollen, red. But no frozen fingers chopped off in my sleep. I remember I had a nightmare about that. Happened to some man that Mom knew on the reservation, many years ago. I flex my fingers over hers, glad to have ten although they throb, and then, to my surprise, Mom reaches her other hand over and puts that hand on top of mine so she is holding my hand in both of hers. I glance up at her and then it seems natural, it seems easy, it seems just right to tell her to her face that I love her.

It doesn't happen all that often we get the nerve to say it to each other in person. Usually, it comes more easy on the phone. And we're not always too reliable with it, neither one of us—sometimes the timing's off and one of us is just going out the door and the door slams, or it comes by surprise and one of us will get choked up and try to hide our sudden reaction and it becomes a big production. It's just not predictable, that's all, to say those words and take the awkward chance. But this time everything fits.

Mom says, "I love you, too." Right out, like that, and then it's over and the nurse comes in so there is no uncomfortable moment where we struggle with the understatement.

I used to want to be with her every minute of the day. My feelings were her feelings. I lived in the circle of her. Fear came over me at night when I imagined all the dangers and to ward them off I crossed my fingers, my legs underneath the blankets, my eyes, went to sleep with my hair knotted under my chin so that no harm would come to my Celestine. For I sometimes called her Celestine because I liked her name—it set her off. And she was set off, too, by size and her independent life. By her clothes, which she didn't care if they were man's or woman's, and by a laugh that developed in her over the years of my childhood. Though rare, it was like a great fountain springing up out of the ground unexpectedly so that, amazed, you laughed along with her at nothing.

Which is what we do, gaining such a look from the nurse that it sends us off even worse, makes us helpless with the bubbling humor that is our way, I guess, of dealing with the lucky fact that I'm not dead.

❀   ❀   ❀

"So you're back," Aunt Mary states in a flat voice, unimpressed.

"What?"

I stop inside the shop door, the bell still jingling, spread out my arms, and drop my mouth open. I haven't seen her since I was half conscious. I can't believe her.

"Let's examine this scene, Aunt Mary," I say. "I nearly freeze to death, stuck in a car all night with Jack's former wives, none of which I knew about when we got married. I survive their endless jabber. Half starved, half frozen, I return to my aunt's place. My aunt says, 'So you're back.'"

"Come!" Aunt Mary orders, holding her arms in a V. She is wearing a gaily flowered calico apron over a sagging denim dress. Her brown stockings are rolled in a padded ring around her ankles. Her feet are small, chubby, light, in a pair of soft Hush Puppies.

I approach and step warily near, as though her arms might snap shut. Standing close to Aunt Mary, holding her, I am aware how much she's shrunken, hardened, and dried on her tough bones. She even smells like clean sinew, leathery oak leaves.

Aunt Mary ceremoniously folds her arms at the elbows, clasps them around me, and with her hands proceeds to pat, pat, pat. Her pats are carefully administered, timed as though she's filling a prescription, but when she releases me her yellow eyes gleam with a hint of tenderness. It is an unwilled inner response. I feel no relief, though. In fact, I am annoyed at how I always must coax affection out of her. What do I have to do? The slightest gesture with either of them will not come easy.

"Celestine's cooking," she says now. "We're making you a big surprise dinner."

In the kitchen, Shawn is arguing with Mom. Now we can hear the reassuring rise and fall of their voices. *Your finger did not just happen to go into the frosting. It was your whole damn hand anyway! . . . Well, sorry! Like, I didn't mean it. . . . Here, smooth it over. . . . Not your finger, use a spatula! . . . Treat me like a leper,*

Grandma! . . . I wasn't. Germs are germs. You might have some kind of cold. You don't want to get your mother sick again.

There is silence, then, as Shawn presumably repairs the damage.

"What are they making?" I ask Aunt Mary.

"Go find out," says my aunt, turning away from me now in the strength of her feeling.

Later, working in the kitchen, dunking tomatoes into boiling water, lifting them out and running them under cold to raise the skins, I have this wave of a nameless emotion. I don't know what to call it, is what I mean. Regret? Love? Nostalgia? Weary contentment? I'm tired of trying so hard. It starts, anyway, when my mother asks point-blank about my marital status. Whether I am divorced from my second husband yet, whether I haven't finally decided to cut my ties to my first. The parboiled tomatoes are steaming hot for a moment in my hands, then the cold water curls the skin back like parchment and the flesh is exposed—slippery, firm, red, like the inside of a human mouth.

I say something noncommittal, for I've ditched Gerry's papers at the last minute. Jack's not valid anyway. I don't want to explain all the complexity. I pull off the skins whole, remove the cone of each tomato's navel with a paring knife, and set them in a baking dish. As I work, I began to feel too big for myself, as though my own skin is too tight.

Happy to be alive, is my next conclusion. *I must be feeling happy to be alive.*

Still, that seems too simply drawn for the crosshatched, messy, unsettled feeling that fills me. *Happy that I'm free of Jack, his net of complications? Glad I got to be with Gerry, just that once?* I slice a sliver of yellow butter into the middle of each tomato, salt and pepper them and sprinkle a lavish fistful of herbed bread crumbs over their plump tops. I put the cover on the baking dish and slide it into the oven.

The telephone rings. Aunt Mary talks for a few minutes, then calls me into the next room, mouthing the word "Jack" as she hands the receiver to me.

"What do you want?" My voice is rough.

"I'm in town," he answers. "Finishing up the road past the convent. Guess who's working for me again? Your old boyfriend, Moon."

"You're kidding."

"I wish. I owe him and his dad worse than ever. I owe everybody," says Jack. "I owe you."

"You don't owe me."

"I thought maybe I could come by, see you."

"For what?"

There's silence, hurt. *What's he got to feel hurt about? He does owe me — to leave me alone!*

"You don't owe me. I don't want anything."

I can see it. Or imagine it. I know him well enough. On the other end of the phone, in the nearly dismantled company office trailer, Jack makes a pained, sarcastic face, yet speaks in a reasonable tone.

"Okay then. Your stuff." His voice is forced neutral, helpful. "All of your stuff that wasn't burned up is still here, in my car. Your jacket, nail polish, bits of jewelry."

"Put my things in a paper sack. Put the sack in your car. Drive over here to Aunt Mary's. Take out the sack. Leave it on the steps."

"That's all?"

"I cried for you, Jack."

"I know. . . . I mean, you did?"

"When I found out, I cried like a baby. Once a woman cries over you like that, there's nothing left."

"Even when the guy comes back to life?"

"Especially then. I don't want to see you, Jack. Get it?"

"Yeah. Well, how about Shawn?"

"I'm going out. Say hi to her when you drop off my stuff. And Jack?"

"Yes?"

"Go back to Eleanor. I mean this in all sincerity. You two deserve each other."

"Thank you, Dot."

I can't help it. This surprises me, but tears spin hot behind my eyes and I hang up the phone. I move quickly, trying to outdistance the sentiment. That's all it is. Not love. Love is what I feel for Gerry Nanapush. A lost cause. Burnt hope. But it's something. It's all I've got. I grab an old coat and walk outside. There is a small yard behind Aunt Mary's shop— sometimes gardened, sometimes piled with junk, sometimes holding Aunt Mary's dogs. At present, there is only one dog there, chained to his house. He's a golden retriever–shepherd–lab mixture with some beagle tossed in on the side. I unhook him and start walking with him, the chain dragging on the ground between us, the old dog leading me whatever way he wants to go.

First he seems intent on tasting the limits of his freedom, and pulls at the chain as I follow him in weaving circles. Then he stops, his wet black nose testing the air, his dark eyes fixed upon the tiny figure of a man and dog retreating around a corner, in the distance. Aunt Mary's dog's face quivers delicately and he leaps against the end of the chain, his whole body filled with tension. Even after the two figures are out of sight, the dog holds his alert stance, fixed on the vanished ones in a fugue of longing interest. I stand behind, watching, and I know that he can still smell and see the other dog even though it is gone. Aunt Mary's dog is watching the other dog in its mind's eye. At the moment, with its whole being, it wants no other thing but to get near that dog.

At last, diverted, Aunt Mary's dog begins to trot evenly through the snow toward the bases of trees that bear intricate messages. We pass into a strip of full-grown shelter belt that once shielded a precious acre of hard winter wheat and now surrounds the high school football practice field on three sides. The trees are box elder, scrubby and quick growing, not long-lived, but generous in their willingness to reproduce. Between the two rows a walking path is trodden down, and the trees are tall enough to mesh overhead. The dog and I do laps, walking down the soothing tunnel, making a right turn, following that tunnel to the end, turning once more. Every time we pass along the one corner that is not bounded by trees we step into a field of dazzling light, blink until our eyes adjust. Each time, I feel my brain contract in pleasure, my face tip, my whole self open out underneath the sky.

The last time around, I glance out the shelter of trees before stepping into the clear, and see Jack's red Explorer with the Mauser and Mauser sign on the side door. He is cruising by, slow and steady, as though he is inspecting the streets. I stop, watch Jack and the car—*I could have died in that car*—from just outside the bower of low branches. I make the dog sit, pushing down his rear end every time it bounces up, and stand where my former husband can plainly see me.

Jack parks the car and gets out, as though he knows that this field is logically the place I'll walk, as though he has sensed I am here. He stretches his arms, cups his hands to his mouth, and calls me. I nearly go to him, but then notice that he is facing in slightly the wrong direction. He calls again, turns his back, turns around again, full circle. He yells directly at me without seeing me. My mittens are bright orange. He'll catch them if I raise my hands. He calls again. I decide not to wave.

Jack shrugs, jams his hands in his pocket, saunters around the back of his car, and hops into the driver's seat once more. Drives off.

I keep walking.

I try to tell myself this: All in all, having a man by my side a few hours every few years is about as much as I can stand of a marriage. Hey, it works! I have this guy I love, he is just . . . well, *not available*. Some people meet the way the sky meets earth, inevitably, and there is no stopping or holding back their love. It exists in a finished world, beyond the reach of common sense. That's how I love Gerry, and that is that, that is all. The last night I saw him, I couldn't follow him, not with our daughter, not live on the run, beyond all kindness or the law. I have to raise our Shawn, my part of the deal. And now I don't know where he is. Nobody does.

I try to imagine him underwater, safe, suspended warm below ice, breathing the tiny pockets of air as he floats the river. Or in the north woods of Minnesota, leaving no tracks, building no fires. Farther north than that, maybe, where the rocks jut from shore in pink embattlements. In the lakes, on the pure islands, there is no telling. Abandoned churches, abandoned towns might harbor him. There is more lonely space out here than people could imagine or see, for it opens in the human heart, I think, horrified at how it yawns, *in my human heart.*

Longing for Gerry grabs me.

I am seized with the thing I can't wrestle down. It gets me, throws me to the ice stubble on the earth. All I can do is let it pin me down and hold me, scared. Beside me, the dog mysterious and unworried. I breathe the comfort of the ground because I can't breathe otherwise for all the sorrow. All the sorrow is filling me and spilling out of me. Longing, and more longing, until I'm more hollow than I knew. I go far back, sinking through the years. He's everything I miss and all I'll never have. But more than even that, he is himself. He is the comfort of the happiness that lives between our separate bodies. My eyes are open. My eyes are seeing him. If I've got to lie here, stunned, I want to look out on the same world as he is looking at now. Somewhere. Surely, we'll be together.

Icicles, at eye level. Raw wet dirt. Ice ground into snow. Crystals. I don't just ache, it is more a sickness. *There's something wrong with me,* I think in fear, as the tears rake through me.

But it goes. It goes through like a storm of weather. Strikes me, shakes me, passes. I'm almost sorry. I always think that I'll be lost forever when I'm going through it. But when I come out the other side, I am more intact than before. It is almost worse, I think, that the sorrow doesn't kill you. The longing for someone. I'll probably have to suffer it again, and again, there's no choice about it, just suffer.

As always, a *what the hell* moment comes into my mind. I get up. My face is swollen, charged, heated. My sinuses feel as though they are filled with plaster. I start walking.

I walk a lap. I walk two.

People are always bothering me to go into business with them, I think now, trying to get my mind stuck on something new. My aunt. My mother. They are all excited about opening up a gas station like the Super Pumper.

"Oh, why the hell not," I say, loud and angry. I shout it again right across the football field. "Why not?"

The question hangs frozen in the air. My feelings change slowly, as I pace forward. I start to plot. There is this combination of irritation and pleasure at the prospect of our business. It could be good! Aunt Mary's shop is in the perfect location, and we could get a franchise. Once my mother learned that ice could be sold for ninety cents a bag she was both disgusted and intrigued. Ice, we'll have that, and lots of it. We'll have sodas. We'll have a video section, ready-made lunches, espresso, fancy breakfast rolls, Harley T-shirts.

I call the dog to me, feed him the half a granola bar I am carrying in my pocket. A free bag of popcorn with every fill-up. Other incentives, too. The only thing to do when you are faced with loss is bow down and accept it. Bend to the driving wind, I think, *but that's not me.* The dog walks cheerfully beside me. Happy to know the route. I keep walking around and around the field, growing calmer with each rotation, smelling the clean dirt in the snow, breaking off an occasional frozen twig to chew, crushing in my gloves the wild balsam that volunteers its fragrance where it sprouts up between the orderly rows.

§

Spring Morning

MARCH 1995

Marlis

*T*he red tractor and planter evenly spanned rows, traveling east west, west east, in straight unvaried lines from the ditch boundary of the interstate to the edge of the Crest development. Chuck Mauser had just leased his land back from Jack. The legal papers specified a decade's lease and an option on another ten years after. Plus, he had bought that big house at the end of the cul-de-sac. And his wife returned. Big losses always make big winners, and Chuck was taking his ease. He was planting. He was sure that he would have a bumper year. Fields of sunflowers. Fat, frowsy, golden, spurting light. Confection seed. He looked forward to the sight of it.

So if the dust rose slightly in his wake, it was his dust and if the fertilizer wasn't top grade it wasn't his top grade but if he did everything right and came out ahead this year it would be his coming out ahead. His fields. His flowers. The planter turned in a wide arc.

❀   ❀   ❀

Candice Pantamounty and Marlis Cook had also bought one of the houses in Jack's development, at a ridiculously low price. Saturday morning and Jack was visiting. On the kitchen table, a big box of assorted chocolates, Marlis's favorite kind. The windows of the house looked out on plowed fields, still black, Chuck's fields. Jack watched the red equipment as it moved up and down the rows with an irritating, sober patience. He was gripped for a moment, mesmerized by the silence of the sky, the field, the peace of the scene. All of this erased his annoyance and he took a deep breath as he turned away. There was no golden life out there. Only the uncertain ripening of fields. Inside the house, sunlight blared across the polished wood and John Jr. clumped through its glow.

John Mauser Jr. refused to stop nursing even at the age when most babies are more interested in stepping off the tops of staircases and swallowing pennies. He was big and chubby and healthy with a round-fisted walk and a square-jawed face. His hair was medium brown, and stuck out in a static thatch. He could eat with a spoon, but preferred to use it as a catapult to lob strings of puréed beans and spaghetti and squash and apricot around the room, or at his mother.

Marlis curled on the couch. Her soft, thin legs were cased in tight maroon leggings, and her sweater, of something new like woven velvet, fastened down the front with tiny glimmering buttons of sea abalone. John Jr. leaned into his mother's lap and carefully, like a kitten that has been reprimanded for clawing, tapped with curled fingers at her left breast.

"That one's his favorite," said Marlis, hauling the boy into her lap. "I don't know why. Maybe it tastes better or something."

Jack opened his mouth, closed it, found his mouth was watering, swallowed. There was a lump in his throat. He coughed.

"You okay?"

John Jr. soldered himself to Marlis and drew passionately at her nipple. Clutching the top of her sweater in his fist, he rhythmically flexed his fingers on the loose knitting. Jack wiped a hand across his face, shook his head to blur his vision, tried to focus elsewhere.

The corners of Marlis's lips slowly drew up into the tiny creases that surrounded her mouth, not wrinkles, not dimples either, but apostrophes, Jack thought, as though her smile was in quotes. *No wonder I got into trouble with her. She is trouble. Look at that.* He happened to glance at his own hands and suddenly couldn't look at them, couldn't stand to see them lying on his lap. They were not regular hands that never had hit a woman. He'd hurt her, twisted her arm and now she was the woman nursing his baby. His hands scuttled underneath the pillow like frightened crabs.

"Hey," said Marlis lightly, casually, blatantly changing John Jr. from one breast to the next. "You ever think about . . . you know, about us?"

Her nipples had darkened to the same shade of deepened pink as her sweater, a cross between fuchsia, mauve, and poppy. Deep poppy orange. Blood orange. John Jr. sank toward her with a rough sigh of greed and Jack's eyes burned. He snapped his fingers against his knees, shook his hands. There was a little nerve damage from the frostbite, but no lasting problems. A twinge of old pain shot from the corner of his jaw straight upward, into his brain. Candice was booked solid with dental appointments for the morning, but she was going to work him into her schedule that afternoon. Give up half of her free afternoon to fix an old filling for Jack and take casts for new bridgework.

"No, I never do." Jack straightened in the chair, then jumped up, began to pace. "Too much else to think about, Marlis."

"Right. Mellowing out on us, Jack?"

"No! I mean, let him nurse and all." Jack nodded, indicating John Jr. "Let him fall asleep. I'll get some water, sit here, talk."

"Sure, get some water, get me those chocolates, too," Marlis called. Her hair was different now—longer, straighter, it fell in shining feathers all around her face. There was some earth red in it, a hint, an undertone, maybe her real color. She gazed up at Jack through strands of hair when he opened the box before her.

"You pick for me," she said.

Jack plucked out a heavy piece of candy shaped like a leaf and Marlis opened her mouth. He laid the chocolate on her tongue and her lips closed swift and dry on his finger. She was still looking at him.

"I think about us," Marlis said simply, without dropping her eyes.

Jack turned away and sat down across from her in the chair, where he was safer and could disguise his hard-on. She was so pretty just sitting there with the baby in her arms, the little bruiser. Eating her chocolate. She was so different than the Marlis who had gotten drunk with him and gone on a long bender and ended up— He wouldn't think about that. Very different, or was he just projecting this picture onto her? What did it matter, to him anyway? She pressed the tip of her tongue against her upper lip and very gently eased John Jr. away from her wet nipple. The baby was entirely limp. His mouth clamped down stubbornly, on nothing.

"Take him, Jack," she whispered.

Jack put down his glass of water. He bent over the two— John Jr.'s mouth dropped open in sleep and he sucked softly and reflexively. He still had a tiny nursing callus on his upper lip. He had teeth.

"He ever bite?" Jack whispered.

"Yeah, once. I yelled. He started to cry, sobbed and sobbed."

"I would too."

John Jr.'s clear forehead was damp with fervor, his breath was sweet and hot. Jack carried him into his bedroom and laid him down, arms outflung, legs spread, toes stuck straight upward in stubborn bliss. Marlis came into the room behind

Jack and slowly slid her arms around his waist. Jack circled her wrists with his hands. Her fingers brushed down his stomach. He pulled her wrists up. She slid her fingers down again. He pulled up her wrists and then he stood looking down at John Jr. with his hand clasped around Marlis's wrists and her breasts pressing, one on either side of his spine, her soft breasts growing harder, filling with weak, sweet milk. He was pretending it was for real. Him there, her, the baby. Her breasts grazing the small of his back. His heart jumped. He let go of her wrists. She took his hand like a simple friend and pleasantly drew him into the next room, a little sitting type of room with closets on one side and a sunny window studded with patchwork pillows.

From the house plans, Jack remembered nodding at the tiny blue square—this was called the guest bedroom.

Marlis pulled the shade down and unbuckled his belt.

"Lay down," she ordered.

"You sound like Candice."

Marlis started to laugh and then she stopped, crouched over him, and began to move, but very differently than before, in the old days. She was gentle as rain with him, light and careful.

"Wait," he was naked, uncomfortable. "I feel bad, I feel like I'm using—"

"Shut up, Jack," said Marlis. "*I'm* using *you*."

"Oh, well then," Jack mumbled.

"Don't fall down on the job," Marlis whispered, moving faster and faster.

She still wore her reddish sweater, and when it was over Jack stroked the uneven knitting compulsively, gathering and releasing the weave in his fingers. Marlis sprawled on top of him, rich and heavy, wordless. Confusion. He wanted to go to sleep there, open the shades and let the sun fall upon them both, breathing deeply, at peace. The room smelled of clean wood and new paint, aromatic, sharp, of window cleansers and polyurethane floor finish. He let the air fill him, the new carpet fragrance, the undertone of mortar and ceramic dust from the bathroom tiles across the hall. She stirred, as though to leave. He tested the end of her hair in his mouth. A faint gloom invaded him at the soapy red cilantro taste.

§

Spring Afternoon

MARCH 1995

Candice

*C*andice was sitting at the beige front desk making neat check marks in tiny black squares when he arrived in her office. She had slipped down her goggles and face mask and her eyes were bare, prim, blue, like some sort of flower he'd asked the name of once—bachelor's buttons. Or those roadside flowers, chicory. Distracted by her paperwork, she smiled at him and gestured him back, into her dentist's chair.

She was pondering some mix-up, bent compulsively over her big appointment calendar. Her hair was frosted blond, sun-shot, straight, childishly sticking up behind the strap of her face mask, touchingly carefree in its simple bowl cut. Jack grinned weakly at the top of her head as he passed behind the desk into her treatment room.

He eased into the padded chair.

Still the forest green Naugahyde, still the same posters— birch tree stand in winter, very pristine, very soothing, right up there on the ceiling. The swamp oak on the wall, he'd always liked that one. Hung with lime green mosses. And the autumn prairie poster was also in place on the far wall, the ash-colored tallgrass, gnarled oak. There was the same polar bear in the corner with its morose cub posed between fur-block front paws. Jack breathed deeply, his jaw throbbing, and he tried to relax his neck against the firm headrest.

"Let's take a look."

Candice, treading in on white rubber soles. Jack obediently opened his mouth and she switched on the oval light above them both. With her stiff pink-white mask covering the lower half of her face, she was a mysterious priestess. She tested his sore tooth with probing gentility, then cradled his jaw soothingly in her gloved hand.

"Let me take an X ray," she said. "I'll do it myself."

She draped him with a lead-lined body-shield and made him close his jaw on a plastic-coated film. Buzzing the picture, she warned, "Don't move." He froze.

She developed the piece of film and returned.

"There's decay all around that filling, just as I suspected, Jack. I'll have to take out the old one and refill the tooth. Lucky you came in now—this was going to invade the nerve. You don't need a root canal, but just barely. Marlis called. This may take longer than I thought."

"Marlis called?" Jack's voice was faint.

"Just before you got here," said Candice.

She swabbed the lower inside corner of his mouth with a gauze pad and laid a Q-tip full of topical anesthetic against the inside hinge of his jaw. He bit down delicately on the wooden stick. Her assistant had gone home, so Candice prepared everything that she would need all by herself, working next to him.

"So you were over at the house, saw John?"

"Yesh." Jack clenched his teeth, looked deeply into the birch forest.

Candice smiled to herself, he could hear it in her voice, "That's nice. He's getting big, huh?"

She wheeled herself around the back of his head on her

padded rolling stool and soon, he knew, because he saw the tops of her knuckles closed around the plunger, she held the Novocain just under the line of his jaw where he could not see the needle's gleaming length. His eyes flicked into hers, blue flowers, wide from underneath. With her other hand she drew the swab from his open mouth.

"And Marlis?"

Candice spoke pleasantly, lifting the needle just under his nose, where he still couldn't see it. "How was she?"

The tip of the needle touched his gum line, but paused as she waited for him to answer.

"Uhnn." He made a doglike, questioning sound of panic deep in his throat.

"Relax. Breathe deeply from your lower middle, Jack."

The needle went in.

"So you think she's doing all right?"

Jack concentrated on his breathing, tried not to pant too hard against the side of her hand. She had a steadfast grip, great patience and strength in her small fingers—she exercised at night with a green ball of clay. That was why she could administer a shot of Novocain so slowly that—oh god—to his relief it didn't hurt, not at all, not one bit. Jack's eyes rolled up into hers once again and his heart quickened. Her irises were the color of a stormy lake, suddenly, a wind-whipped gray. What? Did she expect him to answer? She had to know!

There was a dull pressure from the needle. His heart raced faster and he tried not to choke.

"Actually," Candice spoke soothingly, as though to herself. "It's nice being over forty. Means a certain amount of bullshit is behind you. Of course Marlis, being younger, has a lot still in front of her. Still, I love her so much, Jack, and she's a wonderful mother."

Jack looked up again and realized that he had seen Candy's eyes turn that color before—when she was lost, passionately in love with him, and his heart sank to a low, shamed thudding as he grasped the depth of her feeling for Marlis. She briskly retracted the needle, as relieved as he that it was over.

With efficient dispatch she whipped it behind her and set it into a tray. Jack realized that she had been infinitely tender with him, anxious not to cause him pain. As his jaw numbed, growing tingly, quiet, then puffing out, love for both of his former wives came over him with a depressing intensity. He wanted them both so much, so uselessly, and he was at the same time hugely relieved that his lapse with Marlis wasn't yet discovered. He had the sudden, odd sensation that he was stuffed with straw, thrown down in the chair. He saw himself propped up, boneless, laughing crazily like the scarecrow in the movie, then flopping down again, nerveless and still.

"Comfortable?"

He was, completely. They smiled and exchanged their impressions of John Jr. until Jack's jaw numbed, his words slurred. Candice truly didn't know what had just happened with Marlis, did she, wondered Jack. Wait. *Did she?* Swooning with apprehension, Jack stretched his jaws open, and Candice leaned forward with her precise little drill.

§

A Light from
the West

AUGUST 1995

Anna and Lawrence

*Y*ou *just missed dying in your sleep*, was her first waking thought, and because she always consulted her first thoughts for truths or insights, Anna Schlick remained quiet and wary. For weeks now, she had been waiting for the drumroll, for her death. But death was getting even with her now. In return for her two bold rescues, death required of Anna perfect precision and timing. She was tired of practicing. She was impatient, but it seemed that for all of her determination she couldn't get the trick right. She held on too long. Let go too fast. Struggled too hard or not hard enough. There was an art to the feat, of course, but she'd never known that. She was tired.

And every day the room where she waited for death became more beautiful to her, luring her back to life from the sheer space behind her eyelids. The walls were painted bone, the woodwork a paler ivory. There was a graceful little fig tree in a brown clay pot. Curtains of an ethereal sheer stuff diffused raw sunlight as the sun passed over, east to west. For years, the sun had risen at her feet and set behind her head, passing over her entirely, and she had never noticed, of course, until she stayed and watched the change of light. Blue, also. There was a powerful shade of blue in the vase of flowers Lawrence changed every other day. No blue is ordinary. Blue is the stuff of the soul. But this blue, Anna had decided, watching it, was the blueness of life. The blue of this particular vase held within it a stark depth reflecting slashes of brilliance. Czech glass, bought at a Fargo antique store, probably carried overland a hundred years ago, made with an old art in an old land. By an old man too! For an old woman! She laughed. The vase was sometimes filled with a secret humor.

July blue of glacial silt in a lake reflecting an impassive blaze of sky. The leafy blueness of childhood's solitudes. A three A.M. midsummer blue when there's a cool swash of air to drink and the birds fall silent just half an hour, that blue hour, before starting to sing again. And the sex blue of a man's faded cotton shirt soaking up the darker hay blue of his clean sweat. And the blue of twilight and dusk which was the color that washed up from the center of her body when she opened herself entirely to a man.

She had to take a breath.

She had to take a breath.

There was an oxygen tank fixed in a stand next to her bed, and a brilliant mask of orange-gold plastic dangled, hooked to the carved headboard. Her hand was heavy, though, filled with buckshot. Too heavy to lift all the way to the mask. The mask the color of yolks of eggs her favorite chicken laid, back there, in Hungry Horse, where chickens laid real eggs. She, who once had such a quick, sure grip on the trapeze bar, now couldn't lift her own hand. Her hand would not move at all. Her breath would not enter and the need was piercing, a jolt of agony, and then she was standing high in glittery warm air.

Circus air. The roar of turbine fans.

She stared at nothing. A light pump of her knees and she

was swinging through the pain, an eerie syrup that slowed her rush until her body burst past need. The snap of cables shuddered through her. There were four or six great rips of sound, and she was falling. The sheer tent buckled. A silver bar swung beyond her grasp.

There was time to think.

Her mother and father were fishing off a dock. Sails on an ethereal reservoir, blue-green and blue-topaz. Fireweed burned its purple and magenta flowers from base to tip. The air rushed into her at last and it was like breathing sheer light. A hand caught at her hand, desperate in its grip. She knew it was her first husband's hand, and she was annoyed, because that meant they were going down, down together, and all because he was afraid to die alone. She, however, preferred it! One by one she pried his fingers off, and then she was free. Far below, her legs drummed the mattress, kicking for oxygen. Water that her heart couldn't pump off filled her lungs. She fell at an increasing speed. Past the blue vase and the swirl in its curved side, past the vague roses, the gold threads in the lamp shade, past Eleanor's face at one minute old, at two months, two years and then a flash of years and expressions that blended to her mature face as Anna fell past her daughter, longingly, sweeping her hands across her lovely cheekbones, touching her lips to her girl's forehead as though to check for fever. Falling past. Just missing Lawrence, who stood a hands-breadth away with his arms out to catch her. She looked into his startled blue eyes. A glare of silence.

The white-throated sparrow sang. Five clear notes.

Light rained in. A vibrating eastern light. The fig tree leaves spread, sharp and motionless.

Up the stairs walked Lawrence Schlick, already dressed in a casual brown shirt and old gardening pants. Unshaven. He was bringing coffee up the stairs, a mug in each hand, one black and one with cream. He tapped the door open with the ball of his bare foot and knew death had entered first. He walked over to Anna's side, carefully set down the cups on the bedside table, resting them on a thick magazine. He took her wrist in both hands. The pulse in his thumb was so strong he pretended it was hers. But from the first glance at her face, he had known. Her eyes were open. Gently, he touched them down and composed her arms and legs, removed the pillow behind her head and laid her flat. He drew a chair up to the bed and then he sat.

Lawrence Schlick drank his coffee and milk sip by sip. When he finished his cup, he put it down and absently picked up hers. Black. He lifted the cup and put it to his lips. For half an hour, at least, his gaze upon Anna blurred and distant, he lifted the cup and inhaled its bitterness, then set it down. Occasionally, he swallowed a mouthful. Finally, when it was all gone he sighed and put down the cup. He walked into the bathroom next to the bedroom and intently, with his usual care, he ran water into the sink and soaped his face. He shaved, the razor lightly held, pulling his skin tight. Then rinsed the blade and ran his palms over his cheeks and chin. White shirt, crisp and starched. His best slacks. A pair of expensive, sober, comfortable black leather shoes.

He returned to the bedroom and bent over Anna, smoothed her white nightgown around her limbs, and lifted her into his arms. She was too light. His eyes burned. He carried her downstairs, then to the mortuary renovated into the mansion. He could hold her in one arm, supporting her with a knee, when he opened the door. Setting her carefully upon his worktable, he looked deeply into her face, brushed a lock of hair from her eyes. He smiled musingly at her. Anna's features still seemed suffused with life. He wouldn't need his box of creams or powders. A basin of lukewarm water. Her favorite almond soap. A pair of scissors which he used to clip off her nightgown. No one else should ever wear it.

He tore the nightgown into wide strips, then squares. He wet and wrung out the cloth and wiped along her face first. Ears. The valve and whorl. He wiped down the sleek curve of her neck, the small notch at the base of her throat and then across each curved collarbone and the polished, small, rounded knobs at the tops of her shoulders. He fanned the fingers of her right hand out upon his own hand and washed each finger, pulling gently with the wet cloth. Then the other hand, each palm thick with moon-shaped scars. He used a small diamond file on the sides and tips of each fingernail. Her two fifth fingers stopped him. He compared them, frowned—one was slightly crooked. It bothered him that he had never truly noticed this before. He rubbed the finger, set it down, wiped up the underside of her arm and down her torso, crossing her waist, and then her heavy breasts. Carefully, he smoothed them with both hands, then cupped them hard and bent, almost fainting against her.

He breathed against her skin, a hollow languishing smell, and her perfume, and the harrowing smell of death, and the smell of his own touch there, too, and the bergamot scent of ironing and the bleach and boron of his laundering. That revived him. The rest of her he washed quickly and then he dressed her in the same dress she'd worn on their wedding day, a pale chiffon just between the colors pink and ivory, a dress he'd adored on her. He smoothed the folds down, brushed her hair with critical dispatch, fluffing its curve around her face. He used no hair spray. Last, he fit a pair of white pumps onto her feet. He stepped back, as he always did, composed himself to regard his work. Bent forward again, took the shoes off. Better. He stroked the arch of one of her feet. Brooding, he slowly wiped a bit of dust from her face, his fingerprint.

He carried her across the room, then, and placed her body on a long rolling tray upon a tracked table that was fitted against a door in the wall. He laid her there carefully and then he turned two white dials on a metal panel in the inset cabinet and sat down next to her on the edge of the flat low counter. He studied his shoes, slowly worked at the toe of one with a bit of the same cloth, and then sat up and looked around the room as though he were seeing it for the first time. He examined each piece of equipment intently—the shelves, the neat instruments, the chemicals, the round high-powered lights. He patted his hands on both sides of his head, smoothed his fine hair along his skull. His face was shiny and broad, the light fell evenly on it—a placid face that did not express suffering gracefully. The raw shock made his mouth rubbery and loose. Yet every so often he exerted a steel control. Hardened his eyes. Flexed his fingers. Tightened his lips to a line as he opened the waist-high ceramic doors set into the wall.

Now the low table where Anna lay slid forward into his hands and he pushed it carefully, tucking her dress close, through the opening into the black interior. He drew a breath from deep in his heart and his throat chilled, his pulse throbbed so violently he almost choked. He had to steady himself on the trolley sides as he climbed in behind her. He lay beside his wife for a moment as though to take the fit of the narrow space. One sound, the shuddering whine of a woman deep in labor, escaped him. He panted hard to overcome his dizzy faint. Then, businesslike, he leaned forward and pulled the doors shut from the inside on weighted springs. They clasped perfectly, locked. In vibrating blackness, he held on to Anna as tightly as he could. Tighter, closer, until the timers clicked over in the wall and there was a thick roar of consuming fire.

§

The Stone Virgin

APRIL 1995

Jack

*O*n the same road by which all else arrived and departed
from Argus, a truck approached, downshifting slowly, coasting
toward the first stoplight, where the driver looked from side to
side. The man was eager to unload and finish his job, to turn
around and go home. The delivery was unusual, the address a
convent. His load was a remarkable statue of specially quar-
ried stone—a seamless porphyry from Carrara, Italy. The
statue had been paid for by an anonymous benefactor, trans-
lated in the rough by an equally anonymous stonecutter, who
then passed the form on to a finish artisan.

In the mind of this Italian sculptor, whose wife had
recently lost their long awaited child, a son, there reposed a set
of lovely features caught in an impenetrable derangement of
sorrow. The sculptor was able to exorcise his grief and his
wife's only through the work of his carving tools. However,
when the statue was at last completed, he turned away, disturbed, for he had brought to being an image that failed in any

way to convey either his wife's bereavement or his own but
registered, instead, a repressed passion of rage and ardor. He
wrapped and crated the statue himself, showed her to no one.
She was not meek in her suffering, but unquantifiably wild,
like a woman from the southern hills. Pulling down over his
Virgin's face the padded hood of wool and muslin, the maker
felt the singe of her gaze on his fingers. He dropped the cloth
and twine as though stung, crossed his breast and forehead
lightly, once, twice, kissed the tips of his knuckles, and hurried
home to feed his motionless wife a cup of blood soup.

Two months later, a trucking company out of Duluth-
Superior unloaded the statue from a Great Lakes freighter,
and she was then brought overland to Argus. Once the truck
entered the area of the convent, there was some difficulty
about the method of delivery, for work on the connecting road
near the stone residence had been abandoned when Mauser's
company went under, revived again now that he was halfway
on his feet, but things were still a mess. The entire area was a
welter of gaping spring culverts and half-dug ditches, inse-
curely graded roads and meridians blasted and hammered
clear of asphalt, waiting for new paving.

The construction had gone beyond a source of exasperation to the nuns. It had become a penance, a cross, a hair shirt
continually chafing. Just beyond the walls, the whine and roar
of machinery had been unpredictable, stopping and starting on
its own schedule, not God's. The swish of air brakes, gears
grinding, the shouts of men grated on the women's nerves.
Jackhammers rode their spines and their prayers were blipped
through by back-up beepers. Backhoes chugged, ripped out
inconclusive pathways from which the odor of sewer gas
wafted—a dark dankness, an assault. Flashers tripped their
dreams. The noise started with the sun. No repose was possible. The air turned dry and gray. Dirt rose, sifted into the
linen, feathered over the walls in plumes and spurts. Grit fil-
tered into the rising bread dough and as the sisters bit down on
tiny particles they closed their eyes and said a quick prayer to
keep their tempers.

And yet the presence of the crews proved beneficial once the statue arrived. The truck halted, and the driver and a representative of the Mother Superior persuaded a road crew to assist in lifting the stone statue from the back of the truck. With the use of a Mauser and Mauser bucket loader and a crane, she would be transported along the unstable roadbed to the convent, where her pedestal had long waited, centered and installed. The workers gathered, on a lunch break. The driver unlocked the back doors of the truck. The statue had already been uncrated at customs, searched for contraband drugs, and was at this point swathed in sheets of packing foam and muslin, which the two men ripped down from her sides, leaving her to stand unprotected in the gloom of the truck. As they harnessed her with chains, they glanced uneasily at her face, the demure features placid and uncontorted, yet bearing in some fundamental increment of detail the shadow of unnamed emotion.

She stood simply, bearing a sheaf of stiff marble wheat that seemed to tremble slightly in her arms. Her face was bare, cool, and white, chill and pure—she bore no veins or mars of mineral spots. As she was drawn on a dolly from the gloom of the truck, she caught the flat radiance of noon with a passive electricity. The men fell silent, wrestled her forward, redraped her and hung her cautiously in a web of steel-linked chains. Drawn up and up on the crane's arm, she then glided slowly toward the entrance to the convent garden.

She would have reached her new placement easily, had not the road on one side beneath the crane's treads begun to give way in small seeps of sand, mud, aggregate, tipping the machine, stopping it, setting it off balance even farther. Directly into this precarious situation walked Jack Mauser.

He arrived at the convent with his thoughts in a depressive snarl. The morning hadn't gone so well. He was severely put out over the agreement he had once again been forced to make with his attorney, Maynard Moon, over the eternally unemployed and falsely suave Caryl. Jack's nemesis. Maynard Moon prevailed on Jack to keep his failure of a son working and out of greater Fargo. Caryl Moon! What was he, Jack, a social service agency? The guy was certifiable. Jack should have him up on assault charges, maybe attempted murder. Instead, Moon was operating heavy equipment. Hundreds of thousands of dollars worth of Tonka toys. Jack's toys! The bank's. Just the sight of Caryl Moon brought on heart pains.

Jack dreaded Caryl's shit-eating grin all the way to the construction site. When he saw the tilting crane, the statue swinging perilously from the cable, the men in conversation all around, the driver gesturing, still in the cab, Jack's blood surged into his temples.

As he strode into the problem, Jack could feel the pump of anger going solid, and he paused. His mood collected, he lowered his head, one vein beat across his brow. It was surprising both how much and little Jack had changed. He was used to giving orders, used to being obeyed. It was his nature. He was still a hard man with a black stare of command that drew his crew's attention. He gazed up at the statue from below, threw out his arm and circled his hand toward himself, nodding at the driver, *Caryl Moon, of all the dumb shits. Of course it would be Moon,* to come forward, just a little, a little farther. He was sure he could see from the color of the underlay that there were only inches to travel between the machine's faltering tread and secure passage, and so he waved Moon on, and on yet again, even though the statue began a pendulum lurch and swing.

Jack walked backward, gesturing calmly, emphatic. Moon grinned nervously but didn't dare disobey him. It was obvious that the treads were losing ground, that the load was at an awkward angle that strained the chains to the breaking point, but Caryl Moon had followed Jack's unlikely orders successfully before. He calmly did exactly as he was told. Suddenly, a fist of mud gave way, a slab of broken tar buckled, and the cable jerked backward. Jack rolled his arms explosively and roared to Moon, who attempted to gain ground but lost purchase. Trying to stop the statue's swing, he jerked the elbow of the machine at the wrong moment.

The chains snapped. The statue's wrappings tore away in a

rip of sound that stretched Moon's grin tighter and sent everyone scrambling. Then she plunged, falling at an angle. Jack,
twisting in flight, stumbled in the insecure ground, and in his
panic flipped over on his back to receive her.

It all happened in a bolt of sound—the statue fell full
length and sank Jack Mauser with one blow. Her hands and
shoulders crushed his chest, her kiss bent his neck, her impenetrable skirts nearly unmanned him. His blood would stain her
robes, throat, and shoulders. The print of her would never
leave his bones.

They called an ambulance on the truck phone before they
even knew whether Jack, under the stone woman, was dead or
alive. He tried to yell for help, but his mouth filled instantly
with sand. He thought that he would smother even though he
didn't feel hurt, didn't feel dead, and in fact knew in a flash
that his wounds were surface only, already healing. Then a
pocket cleared around his nose, air entered and filled Jack's
chest explosively. Jack could feel his lungs expand as they
hoisted off the statue. Borne out of the hole he'd jammed into
the earth, in a sling, drawn upward by the arms of men, he felt
wonderful. Tucked in the gurney, cozy, covered with blood, his
body felt exquisite, light and powerful. He should have been
one of the worst emergency cases ever seen, too fragile of condition even to helicopter up to the better-equipped hospitals in
Fargo. Inside the ambulance they ran an IV, took his vitals,
disbelieved, shot him full of morphine. At the emergency room,
behind draped curtains, the wide-eyed Filipino doctor wiped
the blood away, laughed amazedly, had the nurse clean Jack's
cuts and cover him with thin gauze bandages while Jack told
her how beautiful and gentle she was and, swooningly, what
lovely collarbones and fingernails and eyelashes she possessed.
In his drugged sleep, they X-rayed Jack. None of his bones
were fractured.

In the morning, he was cheerful, lucid. He woke thinking
*Fuck, not dead! I didn't die in a hospital! I didn't die in a hospital! Not
yet!* He phoned the local men's clothing store and got them to
deliver five hundred dollars worth of slacks and shirts. His

luck had changed, he could feel it. He'd been granted mercy by the woman that the old nun said would kill him. Yes, he was pitied by a woman, and she was even made of stone! The store clerk arrived in an hour, Jack put on new clothes, filled out the discharge forms, met a reporter from the local paper in the lobby, and gave an interview. His account of the accident was richly enthusiastic. He was fully aware of his death as the statue hove out of the sky. It was true, what they said, he modestly asserted. His life had flashed before him, just as you dread it might.

"Then I recognized her," he told the reporter. "I knew her, the statue. I'd seen her before and I knew I wouldn't be hurt."

"You saw her before?" the reporter asked. "Who was she?"

But Jack couldn't quite see her, couldn't answer. She looked like his mother. She looked like June. Like Eleanor. All of his wives. All the women he'd ever loved. He laughed shortly, then fell silent, gazed into the oily dark circle of the coffee in his white foam cup. Smiled. As the statue came toward him, Jack Mauser had felt an unbearable heat of emotion, a jet of fear and joy. The impact had happened slowly, it seemed to him. The face approaching his was so familiar. He was jolted back into an infant's wondering terror as its mother bends over, as it is swooped into her arms. Her size, her body! A blizzard of panic, and then a split second of awareness — replenishing, unending, larger than anything he'd ever built. Wider yet, stranger, fuller in its pour, was the shock of contrition. Then piercing love. He was filled with it so completely that he sank into the soft sand beneath the statue with profound ease, and lived.

§

A Letter to
the Bishop

JULY 6, 1995

Dear Bishop Retzlaff:

Recent events attaching to the statue of the Blessed Virgin
donated to Our Lady of the Wheat Priory by an anonymous
benefactor cause me to write to you. I think you should be aware
that from the first day of its arrival the statue has caused some
unusual concern in this part of your diocese.

   As you may already know, the statue fell from snapped
chains in the process of installation. It landed directly on the
owner of a construction company, who was directing the project
and had stumbled beneath. Though driven into the earth by the
force of the fall, he was unharmed except for a few scratches and
abrasions, and reportedly remains healthy several months later.
All who witnessed the accident term this a very surprising and
unlikely outcome.

   Next, the statue, once properly positioned on the pedestal
provided for it in the garden, developed unusual mottled stains.
The marks were at once perceived to resemble blood, and it was

assumed that they were the result of the wounds suffered by the man, who lay beneath the statue for a short time before the stone could be lifted away. This guess was corroborated as a probable truth once the cleaning company hired to restore the statue was able to remove the spots with a very powerful solvent used specifically for organic matter.

The problem I wish to inform you of now is the return of those stains, *though not in the specific places where they previously marred the statue*. The members of the janitorial company who cleaned the statue swear that the stains are wholly new and cannot be the result of the accident. It is, and I quote directly from the manager of the company, a Lutheran, "as though the stone itself were sweating blood."

The statue is now placed in the garden of Our Lady of the Wheat, and will remain under our close observation. It has been my contention for the past several years—and the presence of this statue only confirms my feeling—that there is something well worth investigating in the entire design and history of persons, places, and even objects surrounding the now deceased Sister Leopolda, who, as you are no doubt aware, spent her final, somewhat difficult years at our convent here in Argus, North Dakota.

Yours in Christ,
Father Jude Miller

§

A Last Chapter

Eleanor and Jack

*T*he winter snow that had seemed so killing and relentless
was in fact a kindness that showed in spring with a heavy
melting runoff that seeped into the earth. A final unseasonable
snow fell overnight, like manna, and lay one brief day on soil
to fix good nitrogen. Farmers seeded with the kind of hope
they hadn't dared possess in years, and soon after planting
time the sun blasted two days of hot, heavy, germinating light
down upon the world. The crops strengthened under the gentle, soaking rains. The weather caused many men and women
to engage hidden optimisms, not only the twice-mortgaged, but
those, too, who hadn't a stake in the sugar beet or sunflower
outcome or soybean or grain futures but merely looked at the
weather as a passing comment, a marker of kindliness or rarity
or pleasant fortune. Rounding the corner through August, the
mild days held, long and sunny. The nights were brief and
quiet. No rain fell the final week.

The harvest would be record breaking.

For months after her encounter with Leopolda's other-
worldly testiness and grace, Eleanor had lived in a state of

unrest. She decided not to resume a job as an academic, at least not at an institution where anybody knew her from before. Her life's work would be a personal research project that would, she hoped, illuminate Sister Leopolda's life and possible sainthood—for already rumors had started to fly, reports of suspect cures and sightings and voices cracking from pots stirred or dishes dropped.

Eleanor had even been approached by a local tribal businessman, Jack's casino partner, Lyman Lamartine, who was eager to prove the truth of the stories and offered to help finance her research and a possible book. He was hoping to cash in, of course, assuming the miracles proved true. Vend statues, postcards of a shrine, holy water, just like the towns of Knock and Lourdes. Religious boomtowns. Kitsch shrines. If nothing else, an actual saint or divine appearance signaled economic salvation.

There was talk of a stigmata at whose appearance the old nun was present. In Argus, photographs that the younger Leopolda had taken of a manifestation of Christ's face in playground ice held Eleanor's long frown. She could easily make out the suffering likeness. And there were other instances— erasures of disease that were thought miraculous, conversions, the way Jack himself had survived the fall of the heavy statue, near the convent where Sister Leopolda was consumed by lightning—a fierce Assumption. It was too eerily compelling.

These phenomena had become a source of gossip, the stories repeated with abandon and no discerning eye for truth. Eleanor maintained that rather than allow the talk to further distort facts, the tales should be tracked down. As far as she knew there existed no substantiated reports, yet, no miracles that held up to scrutiny. There were no perfectly documented cases or cures and no recent sightings at all save her own, witnessed by nobody else.

Eleanor had been frustrated at first, betrayed in every sense when she reached the doors of Hector Airport entirely alone. But as she argued and cajoled and fought with herself she understood, with something like despair, that she didn't know what she believed anymore. *No final truth*, she jotted down, *all is relative, personal, all is subjective and proof is fickle.* Still, though disappointed, she forged ahead into the unknown. *Where all is not known*, she wrote, *there is much to be discovered!* Again in her mind she spoke to the apparition, and received Leopolda's cynical blessing.

Only pull forth the nails.

Eleanor tried, damming up stray thoughts, using strict denial, but time had passed, too much time. She had grown around the nails like living wood, forever anchoring her desires. Finally a thought came to her. If she satisfied her longings they would by definition not be longings anymore. By living out the things she wished, there would be only possible failure. She feared failure even more than continuing to harbor unsatisfied longings. So it seemed quite clear that the only courageous thing to do was to act on her desires. As fully as possible, she decided, as vehemently. As quickly.

Eleanor rented the house of an old farmstead at the edge of the reservation, where she could interview an ancient priest, Father Damien, who'd known Leopolda in her youth. As well, she would find other subjects. She took a part-time job teaching English at the local community college. Days enlarged for her, weeks spread out like blank sheets, and she stepped onto her writing as onto water, buoyed by her decision: *Forget about actually having faith, simply behave as though I possess it!* The appearance of Sister Leopolda, whether wholly real, within her perceptions only, or some of both, sustained her hope and calm. Once, she needed solid proof that another dimension of the spirit existed beyond the material realm, the brain world, the biological deadend of the body. Now she settled gratefully for a possibly invented visitation—one that, however, had saved her life that night.

To her mind, the old nun was a saint. *Saints are humans in a sickness of desire.* Eleanor, meditating on the recalled image of Sister Leopolda's raptor gaze, entered long notes into her computer. *Saints are obsessives. They are focused in their neuroses and dedicated in their instincts. In some ways, they are like other people, only hungrier. Wolves. They tear apart the world with raving teeth to feed their own spiritual longings. Rare, very rare, is the meek little saint who persists in the hardest task of all: being moderate and kind, living low but not obscenely low. Saints have no balance. There is an egoism to their sacrifice.*

A weathered apple tree, thick and patient in the yard, dropped petals of swimming fragrance and grew tiny hard green knobs. The apples ripened. Even the thunder rolled gentler all that summer, in coursing waves, not cracks, and the lightning spun down in finer webs. The clothesline wire sagged between its wooden posts and the wind twanged low. Elm scrub and box elder twisted against the longer view and Eleanor saw everything up close from the tiny, rattling windows over the second-hand wooden table and chair she'd set up in the former living room. On cold days she stoked an ornate stove, a black Glenwood with fancy nickel trim. A swirl of varicolored linoleum covered the creaking floor and everything—the papered walls, uneven handmade cupboards and bookshelves—smelled of clean, serious living. Eleanor was protective of the place. The paint on the inside lintels and doors was so thick that nothing really shut, and the knobs bore paint, too, in the joints and could not be twisted. There was nowhere private in the house, but that did not matter. There was, usually, only Eleanor.

Fed by solitude! she penned triumphantly. *And bags of Fritos!* She was eating strangely. Some days nothing but steamed broccoli and brown rice and other days a wallow of corn chips, ice cream, dark imported beers. She gained back some of the weight she'd lost in the convent and her skin smoothed. Her arms strengthened from furious yard work and her legs grew hard from running to the mailbox, beyond, sometimes an entire six-mile square on ruler-straight roads, along the weathered old T posts bearing glass bells that still carried electrical wires from town. She had a dial telephone, a computer running off a grounded outlet and threatened by dirty lightning-ridden electricity, but functional. She fed a cat gray as drifting ash that came out of the shelter belts, lean and yearning, and at night she was not afraid. The visit from Leopolda had allayed the worst fear, that of extinction, and she felt as though she had been tested, found worthy, on that bitter Little Christmas night back in Fargo.

We're swamped with platitudes, we're swamped with sound bites, we're swamped with tiny chunks of frozen rhetoric, she wrote. *It's time to sit still and listen to the sensible grass.*

Outside her window the yard merged into a small field of hay that leaned and rippled in hypnotic visual speech.

One night, in a moon drift, the late August air billowing and succulent, in the lush scents of turned dirt and growing plants and ancient skunk musk and the sweet pink rugosa roses, the screen door unlatched, Eleanor read in a pool of lamplight by the citronella candle. She was not waiting, but there he came, his truck swerving slightly on the long entrance road, avoiding potholes. Eleanor pressed her palms to her face, smiled absurdly. Dizzy. Dizzy. The sound of his truck struck her like a blow across the thighs. She pushed back her hair, walked to the door to watch the wavering headlights, blinked in amazement at how simple, how exactly as it should be, how normal it was. Her heart knocked with a mixture of contentment and slow wonder. Love—which the young expect, the middle-aged fear or wrestle with or find unbearable or clutch to death—those content in their age, finally, cherish with pained gratitude. She and Jack were visited as Jacob was—by the angel at the bottom of the ladder. Maybe through the years they had grown strong enough to wrestle love, to hold on and not let go.

Though it was different, now, very different. They hadn't tried to live together. That had once driven them to each other's throats. They held to their respective lives. It was only on nights like this one, so far, that they met easily. Fearing no complication they simply leaned into each other with all their weight. The moon was flat and silver, birds were swimming in sleep. The yard light hummed in a pale radiance of moths. The bed upstairs was just right, wide and spare, with a light breeze blowing through the eaves and an owl keeping watch. The scent of the day's sun beat through the boards, old newspaper insulation, cedar. Her own myrrh-dark perfume enveloped her and there was Jack, his hands hardened again by the project he was working on and his voice lower, rougher.

More himself, she had written. *Whatever that means.* Sometimes she still felt hysterical. *No more wretched ambivalence,* she wrote in apprehensive joy, *maturity, a process of loosely containing my own contradictory impulses?* She was frightening herself. *I don't want to be so vulnerable! I have to maintain some distance. What would I do, for instance, if he'd actually died? My core is threatened!* She saw her core as just that, encasing hard, bitter, possibly poisonous seeds that were very precious to her. Even times he made her utterly happy, bringing her to unwelcome tears, she forced herself to notice something unattractive about him—his ears, unevenly set on his head, bent funny on one corner. A bad haircut. Some crude remark that gave her comfort.

Jack stopped the truck in the yard and got out, walked toward Eleanor with a lunging eagerness. He could feel her face in his hands, her delicate bones. All the way up the road he had pictured her unfolding beside him, sweeping the pillow with her hair grown shaggy and dark and streaked. Perhaps it was true they were bound together in a thief's trust. It seemed to Jack that anything this good had to be stolen from other hearts. Perhaps such deep love is always stolen, as there is not enough to go around. When he was with Eleanor, all the bodies and loves and voices and attachments they had passed through to return to each other swirled off into a furious, packed dimension, leaving the present empty but for the two of them. He almost felt he could be faithful to her, but the prospect filled him both with peace and dismay. One more step, one more fall, and he *would* be faithful. Oh no! She would too. She had said so, almost angrily, her teeth gritted. Surprised. He stopped and took a swallowing breath, there, and filled himself with the richness of the night. Across his throat and arms her curious fingers, soon, and her lips, already parted as she rushed down the steps and stepped to him, quickly, barefoot in the tough grass.

A lamp burned in its golden sheath on a low oval wooden table.

Crushed grass and the scent of ironing, a haunting of burnt sugar and beeswax. They crossed a bumpy red and purple rug twisted of worn wool. Shadows slid beside them as they moved to the stairway. Jack looked curiously into Eleanor's face and stroked her hair to the side, hooked it behind her ear like a curtain. He traced her cheekbones, chin, teardrop lobes, curved lips, then put his hands around her waist and pushed her hips tenderly downward until she sat on the bare-board polished steps, straight as a girl. She was wearing a skirt he'd given her, billowing and silky green patterned with delicate vines, almost opaque, not quite, sheer enough so it draped across and fell along her legs in soft pleats when he pushed it to her waist.

She smiled into his eyes.

He knelt several steps below and pressed his hands up along the inner slide of her thighs until his thumbs rested in the small breadth of bare skin. Jack lowered his forehead to her waist and wrapped his arms around her and then breathed on her as though his breath misted glass before he pressed her labia apart and sank his tongue across her clitoris. He began to kiss her with slow poignancy and as he did his thoughts drifted. An old movie where a woman wore a dress like Eleanor's came into his mind, then he wondered what expression was on her face now, and his knees hurt. She tasted slightly tart, warm. *Apple*, he thought, half-recalling his convent search, faintly salty, then she didn't taste like anything and grew distinct in his mouth and he felt powerful and tearful and wanted to be inside of her.

Let me, he almost said, but she was climaxing. He took her back into his mouth quickly. Gray rain, falling cold and quiet, soaking into the ground. Or cool moss and a running stream. If she came that quietly the first time, this would be one of the best nights. Jack would last; he was better now than the first times they had driven out onto the bare roads together and taken off their clothes, wasn't he? She said she could not remember. He cradled her hips in his arms, lowered his head onto her stomach. She bent around him in the skirt and the light folds of cloth flowed over him. Jack made love more the way he built bookshelves and toys than the way he built his subdivision houses, thank god. Eleanor had said that once. He didn't think it was funny. He loved her too much sometimes. He touched her labia tenderly now, closing her with a soft gesture. Then, he suddenly unbuckled his jeans and pushed into her, hard, on his knees, and began to climb like a petitioner, like a man wearing away the stone steps of a cathedral, one step at a time.

"Some of these steps are better," Eleanor breathed, laughing.

"You liked the first one best."

He lifted her slightly. She pulled herself up on the banister, and he began to stroke his penis inside of her, careful, looking down at her. She met his eyes and he shook his head to clear his thoughts, to change his focus, or he'd come. He stopped.

"This one. I like this step."

Sauntering along and then lost. Another step. He went slower and deeper and they stared at each other. He bent and kissed her with his whole heart and they fell into the kiss forgetting everything except the mystery of how they fit. After a while, they went up another step. Then another, faster, crying out. He slipped out of her and lost his balance. He went into her again, eagerly, hurting her. She pushed him away, breathed slowly, then took him in again but he slid down, she too, scraping her shoulder. Jack landed hard on his knee, swore foolishly. He righted her, then tipped her slightly back like a cup, holding her, and closed his eyes and moved and moved. Trust. The scent of oleander. Old wood. *My god*, he stopped, worried and absurd. "You could get a splinter." She held him tight between her legs.

Another step. Now watching each other. Then looking far into the distance between them.

Outside, the spears of grass rustled in their sheaths.

We are conjured voiceless out of nothing and must return to an unknowing state. What happens in between is an uncontrolled dance, and what we ask for in love is no more than a momentary chance to get the steps right, to move in harmony until the music stops.

They reached the top landing and lay in the hall, breathing peacefully. Looking up at a cracked and intimate low ceiling where some child had bounced a ball and left rounded dirt marks, they rested without speaking.

Over them, eight new moon smudges, maybe ten in a random arc.

Through you, in you, with you, as long and often as I can stand you, thought Eleanor, and in reaching for his hand she felt humbled, at least slightly, by her need.

When she touched his hand, Jack flinched closer. At that moment something in him shifted and gave way — sand, aggregate, uncertain ground, and he closed his eyes, slid down to a fiercer level. The depth of what he felt about Eleanor broke in upon Jack with such heat that he shuddered, and then melted right through. Tears slid down his cheeks and he began to weep beside this woman, for the other woman, but so quietly and naturally that he needed no comfort and made no sound. It had not been easy for her, for June, when she froze to death, no. But it was also hard to bear the pain of coming back to life.

§